Make time for Debbie Macomber.

DEBBIE MACOMBER

Not just for Christmas

DEBBIE MACOMBER

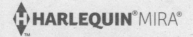

Published in Great Britain 2015
by Harlequin MIRA, an imprint of Harlequin (UK) Limited,
Eton House, 18-24 Paradise Road,
Richmond, Surrey, TW9 1SR

© 2015 Harlequin Books S.A.

ISBN 978-1-848-45411-8

The publisher acknowledges the copyright holder of the individual works as follows:

Buffalo Valley © 2001 Debbie Macomber
Love by Degree © 1987 Debbie Macomber

58-1015

Harlequin (UK) Limited's policy is to use papers that are natural, renewable and recyclable products and made from wood grown in sustainable forests. The logging and manufacturing processes conform to the legal environmental regulations of the country of origin.

Printed and bound by
CPI Group (UK) Ltd, Croydon, CR0 4YY

BUFFALO VALLEY

In memory of my mom and dad, Ted and Connie Adler.
Boy, did I get lucky to have you for my parents!
I will always love you both.

One

So this was North Dakota. Gazing steadily ahead, Vaughn Kyle barreled down the freeway just outside Grand Forks. Within a few miles, the four lanes had narrowed to two. Dreary, dirt-smudged snow lay piled up along both sides of the highway. Fresh snow had begun to fall, pristine and bright, glinting in the late-afternoon sun.

His parents had retired earlier in the year, leaving Denver, where Vaughn had been born and raised, and returning to the state they'd left long ago. They'd moved north, away from the majestic peaks of the Rocky Mountains to the endlessly boring landscape of the Dakotas. *This* was supposed to be beautiful? Maybe in summer, he mused, when the fields of grain rippled with the wind, acre after acre. Now, though, in December, in the dead of winter, the beauty of this place escaped him. All that was visible was a winding stretch of black asphalt cutting through flat, monotonous terrain that stretched for miles in every direction.

After seven years as an Airborne Ranger in the U.S.

Army's Second Battalion based in Fort Lewis, Washington, Vaughn was poised to begin the second stage of his working life. He had his discharge papers and he'd recently been hired by Value-X, a mega-retailer with headquarters in Seattle. Value-X was one of America's most notable success stories. New stores were opening every day all across the United States and Canada.

His course was set for the future, thanks largely to Natalie Nichols. They'd met two years earlier through mutual friends. Natalie was smart, savvy and ambitious; Value-X had recognized her skills and she'd advanced quickly, being promoted to a vice presidency before the age of thirty.

Vaughn had been attracted by her dedication and purpose, and he'd admired her ambition. His own work ethic was strong; as he'd come to realize, that was increasingly rare in this age of quick fixes and no-fault living. Natalie was the one who'd convinced him to leave the army. He was ready. When he'd enlisted after finishing college, he'd done so intending to make the military his career. In the seven years since, he'd learned the advantages and drawbacks of soldiering.

He didn't mind the regimented life, but the career possibilities weren't all he'd hoped they would be. What he lacked, as Natalie had pointed out, was opportunity. He was limited in how far he could rise through the ranks or how quickly, while the private sector was wide-open and looking for promising employees like him. He'd been interviewed by three headhunters who recruited candidates for a variety of corporations and in just a few weeks had six job offers.

At first he'd felt there might be a conflict of interest, taking a position with the same company as Natalie. However, she didn't view it that way; they would be a team, she'd told Vaughn, and with that remarkable persuasive skill of hers had convinced him to come on board. He wouldn't officially start until after the first of the year, but he was already on assignment.

Value-X was buying property in Buffalo Valley, North Dakota. Since Vaughn was going to be in the vicinity, visiting his parents in nearby Grand Forks, Natalie had asked him to pay the town a visit. It wasn't uncommon for a community to put up token resistance to the company's arrival. In most cases, any negative publicity was successfully handled, using a proven strategy that included barraging the local media with stories showing the company's "human face." After a recent public-relations disaster in Montana, Natalie was eager to avoid a repeat. She'd asked Vaughn to do a "climate check" in Buffalo Valley, but it was important, she insisted, that he not let anyone know he was now a Value-X employee, not even his parents. Vaughn had reluctantly agreed.

He'd done this because he trusted Natalie's judgment. And because he was in love with her. They'd talked about marriage, although she seemed hesitant. Her reasons for postponing it were logical, presented in her usual no-nonsense manner. She refused to be "subservient to emotion," as she called it, and Vaughn was impressed by her clear-cut vision of what she wanted and how to achieve it. They'd get married when the time was right for both of them.

He was eager to have her meet his family. Natalie would

be joining him on December twenty-seventh, but he wished she could've rearranged her schedule to travel with him.

On this cold Friday afternoon two weeks before Christmas, Vaughn had decided to drive into Buffalo Valley. Because of Hassie Knight, he didn't need to invent an excuse for his parents. Hassie was the mother of his namesake. She'd lost her only son—his parents' closest friend—in Vietnam three years before Vaughn was born. Every birthday, until he'd reached the age of twenty-one, Hassie had mailed him a letter with a twenty-five-dollar U.S. Savings Bond.

In all that time, he'd never met her. From first grade on, he'd dutifully sent her a thank-you note for every gift. That was the extent of their contact, but he still felt a genuine fondness for her—and gratitude. Hassie had been the one to start him on a savings program. As a young adult Vaughn had cashed in those savings bonds and begun acquiring a portfolio of stocks that over the years had become a hefty nest egg.

An hour after he left Grand Forks, Vaughn slowed his speed, certain that if he blinked he might miss Buffalo Valley entirely. Value-X could put this place on the map. That was one benefit the company offered small towns. He wasn't sure what kind of business community existed in Buffalo Valley. He knew about Knight's Pharmacy of course, because Hassie owned that. Apparently the town was large enough to have its own cemetery, too; Hassie had mailed him a picture of her son's gravesite years earlier.

Buffalo Valley was directly off the road. You didn't take an exit the way you would in most places. You just drove off the highway. He slowed, made a right turn where the road sign indicated. The car pitched as it left the pavement and hit ruts in the frozen dirt road. He'd gone at least a hundred feet before the paved road resumed.

He passed a few scattered houses, and as he turned the corner, he discovered, somewhat to his surprise, a main street with businesses lining both sides. There was even a hotel of sorts, called Buffalo Bob's 3 of a Kind. The bank building, a sprawling brick structure, seemed new and quite extensive. This was amazing. He wasn't sure what he'd expected, but nothing like this. Buffalo Valley was a real town, not a cluster of run-down houses and boarded-up stores, like some of the prairie towns his parents had told him about.

Hassie's store caught his attention next. It was a quaint, old-fashioned pharmacy, with big picture windows and large white lettering. Christmas lights framed the window, flashing alternately red and green. In smaller letters below KNIGHT'S PHARMACY, a soda fountain was advertised. Vaughn hadn't tasted a real soda made with hand-scooped ice cream and flavored syrup since his childhood.

He parked, climbed out of his rental car and stood on the sidewalk, glancing around. This was a decent-size town, decorated for the holidays with festive displays in nearly every window. A city park could be seen in the distance, and the Buffalo Valley Quilting Company appeared to take up a large portion of the block across the street. He remembered an article about it in the file Natalie had given him.

The cold stung his face and snow swirled around him. Rather than stand there risking frostbite, Vaughn walked into the pharmacy. The bell above the door jingled and he was instantly greeted by a blast of heat that chased the chill from his bones.

"Can I help you?" He couldn't see who spoke, but the voice sounded young, so he assumed it wasn't Hassie. The woman or girl, whoever she was, stood behind the raised counter at the back of the store.

"I'm looking for Hassie Knight," Vaughn called, edging his way down the narrow aisle. This pharmacy apparently carried everything: cosmetics, greeting cards, over-the-counter medicine, gourmet chocolate, toothpaste and tissues—just about anything you might require.

"I'm sorry, Hassie's out for the day. Can I be of help?"

He supposed he didn't need to see Hassie, although it would have been nice.

"I'm Carrie Hendrickson." A petite blonde in a white jacket materialized before him, hand extended. "I'm an intern working with Hassie."

"Vaughn Kyle," he said, stretching out his own hand. He liked the way her eyes squarely met his. Her expression held a hint of suspicion, but Vaughn was prepared for that. Natalie had mentioned the North Dakota attitude toward strangers—a wariness that ranged from mild doubt to outright hostility. It was one reason she worried about this proposed building site.

"Hassie and I have never officially met, but she does know me," he added reassuringly. "I was named after her son."

"You're *the* Vaughn Kyle?" she asked, her voice revealing excitement now. "Did Hassie know you were coming and completely forget? I can't imagine her doing that."

"No, no, it was nothing like that. I just happened to be in the area and thought I'd stop by and introduce myself."

Her suspicion evaporated and was replaced with a wide, welcoming smile. "I'm so pleased to meet you. Hassie will be thrilled." She gestured to the counter. "Can I get you anything? Coffee? A soft drink?"

"Actually, I wouldn't mind an old-fashioned soda."

"They're Hassie's specialty, but I'll do my best."

"Don't worry about it." On second thought, he decided something warm might be preferable. "I'll have a coffee."

She led him to the soda fountain and Vaughn sat on a padded stool while Carrie ducked beneath the counter and reappeared on the other side.

"Do you know when Hassie's due back?" he asked.

"Around six," Carrie told him, lifting the glass pot and filling his cup. "You need space for cream?" she asked.

He answered with a quick shake of his head. She didn't cut off the steady stream of weak coffee until it'd reached the very brim of his cup.

The door opened, bells jingling, and a woman dressed in a black leather jacket walked into the store. She had three scarves wrapped around her neck, nearly obscuring her face.

"Hi, Merrily," Carrie called, then scrambled under the fountain barrier. "I'll have Bobby's prescription ready in just a moment." She hurried to the back of the store. "While you're waiting, introduce yourself to Vaughn Kyle."

Merrily glanced toward the counter and waved, and Vaughn raised his mug to her.

"That's *Hassie's* Vaughn Kyle," Carrie said emphatically. "Vaughn was named after her son," she added.

"Well, why didn't you say so?" Merrily walked over to shake his hand. "What are you doing here?" she asked, unwinding the woolen scarves.

Now, that was an interesting question, Vaughn thought. He certainly hadn't anticipated anyone knowing about him.

"He came to meet Hassie," Carrie said as she returned with the prescription. She handed Merrily a small white sack. "How's Bobby feeling?"

"Better, I think. Poor little guy seems prone to ear infections." She turned to Vaughn with a smile. "Nice meeting you," she said. She wrapped the mufflers around her face again before she headed out the door.

"You, too," Vaughn murmered.

Carrie reached across the counter and grabbed a second mug for herself. "Hassie told you about the War Memorial, didn't she? We're all proud of that." Not waiting for a response, she continued, "The town built the Memorial three years ago, and it honors everyone from Buffalo Valley who died in war. The only one most of us actually remember is Hassie's son. But there were others. We lost Harvey Schmidt in the Korean War and five men in World War II, but none of their families live in the area anymore."

"You knew Vaughn Knight?" The blonde seemed far too young to have known Hassie's son.

"Not personally. But from the time I was small, Hassie told my brothers and me about Vaughn. It's been her mission to make sure he isn't forgotten."

Vaughn had heard about Vaughn Knight from his own parents of course, since they'd both been close to Hassie's son.

Carrie sipped her coffee. "Hassie told me it was one of

the greatest honors of her life that your parents chose to remember her son through you."

Vaughn nodded, disappointed that he'd missed meeting the older woman. "What time did you say Hassie would be back?"

"Around six, I guess."

Vaughn checked his watch. He didn't intend to make an entire day of this.

"If Hassie had known you were coming, I don't think *anything* could've kept her away."

"I should have phoned beforehand," he muttered. "But..."

"I hope you'll wait."

Vaughn glanced at his watch again. Three hours was far longer than he wanted to stick around. "Tell her I'll come by some other time."

"*Please* stay. Hassie would feel terrible if she learned you'd left without meeting her." She hesitated, obviously thinking. "Listen," she said, "I'll phone Leta Betts and ask if she can fill in for me for a couple of hours."

Vaughn reconsidered. He might get all the information he needed from Carrie; then he could meet Hassie on strictly social terms. He'd been vaguely uncomfortable about questioning Hassie, anyway.

"Please," she said, "it would mean the world to Hassie, and I'd be delighted to give you a tour of town."

Perfect. He'd learn everything Natalie wanted to know and more. "That's a generous offer. Are you sure you don't mind?"

"I'd consider it a pleasure," she said, and smiled.

With her looking up at him that way , smiling and appreciative, Vaughn couldn't help noticing that Carrie Hendrickson was a very attractive woman. Not that Natalie had anything to worry about, he told himself staunchly.

Working closely with Hassie as an intern pharmacist, Carrie Hendrickson was keenly aware of how eager the older woman was to meet her son's namesake. A few months ago, Hassie had heard that the Kyles had retired in Grand Forks and she'd mailed off a note, inviting them to visit Buffalo Valley. Apparently they planned to do that sometime in the new year. Hassie would be ecstatic about finally meeting their son.

Carrie loved Hassie Knight, who was her mentor and her friend. Following Carrie's divorce, Hassie had given her sympathy—and good, brisk, commonsense advice. She'd guided her through the fog of her pain and encouraged her to look toward the future. Many an afternoon they'd spent talking, reminiscing, sitting quietly together. Hassie had shared the grief of her own losses and helped Carrie deal with Alec's betrayal in ways her own mother never could. Hassie was the person who'd suggested she return to college. Carrie had taken her advice; nearly six years ago she'd enrolled at the University of North Dakota in Grand Forks. Now she was about to finish her internship with Knight's Pharmacy and achieve her Pharm.D and become a Doctor of Pharmacy. The last few years had been bleak financially, but the reward would be worth all the sacrifices.

After her divorce, she'd moved back in with her parents. She felt deeply grateful for their generosity but she *was* twenty-seven years old and longed for more independence and a home of her own. Well, it would happen eventually; she'd just have to wait.

Meanwhile, working side by side with Hassie, Carrie had learned a great deal. When it came time for the older woman to retire, Carrie would be willing and able to assume her role in the pharmacy and in the town. People knew and trusted her. Already they approached her with their troubles and concerns as naturally as they did Hassie. Alec's infidelity had reinforced the importance of trust and honor for Carrie. Those were precepts she lived by. The people of Buffalo Valley knew she would keep their problems to herself.

The town was a success story in an area where there'd been few. The Hendrickson farm, like many others, had fallen victim to low crop prices. Unable to make a living farming the land that had supported them for three generations, her father had leased the acreage to his older sons and moved into town. Together with Carrie's two younger brothers, he'd opened a hardware store.

For as long as she could remember, Knight's Pharmacy had been the very heart of this town. Hassie was getting on in years and probably should've retired long ago. She wouldn't, though, not while the community still needed her, not only to dispense prescriptions and basic medical advice but also to be their counselor and confidante.

Carrie knew she could never replace Hassie, because that would be impossible. But she'd always been good at chemistry and math, and had done well at her pharmaceutical studies. She also cared about the town and had an intense interest in people. Hassie had often told her she was naturally intuitive and sensitive toward others; Carrie was pleased by that, although her intuition had been notably absent during her ex-husband's affair. Hassie said she was exactly the pharmacist Buffalo Valley needed and had given her the faith in herself to believe she could complete the six years of schooling required to obtain her license.

"I'll get my coat and hat and be right back," she told Vaughn after calling Leta. Hassie's friend worked at the pharmacy part-time and was as eager as Carrie to make sure that Hassie met Vaughn.

"You're certain this isn't an imposition?"

"Absolutely certain," she told him.

Leta arrived promptly and after making swift introductions, Carrie removed the white pharmacist's jacket and put on her long wool coat.

"What would you like to see first?" she asked when she rejoined him.

"Whatever you'd like to show me."

"Then let's go to the City Park." Although there were a number of places she wanted to take him, the park seemed the best place to start. As they left the pharmacy, Carrie noticed it had stopped snowing, but she suspected the temperature had dropped several degrees. She led him across the street and then down a block, past the quilt store and several others.

"I know Hassie would want you to see the War Memorial," she said, glancing up at Vaughn. Now that she stood beside him, she was surprised to see how tall he was—possibly six-two. All four of her brothers were six feet, but Carrie took after her mother's side of the family and was small-boned and petite. His dark good looks didn't escape her notice, either.

"First came the park," she explained, walking briskly to ward off the cold. Carrie loved the City Park and every-thing it said about their community. The people of Buffalo Valley had worked together to make this barren plot of land a place of which to be proud. "The land itself was a gift from Lily Quantrill," she said. "Heath Quantrill, her grand-son, is the president of Buffalo Valley Bank." She pointed toward the brick structure at the far end of Main Street.

"Isn't there a branch in Grand Forks?"

"There are branches all across the state," Carrie told him.

"The headquarters is here?"

She nodded. "Heath moved everything to Buffalo Val-ley two years ago. I know it was a hard decision, but this is his home now, and he was tired of commuting to Grand Forks three days a week."

"It's an impressive building."

"Heath's an impressive bank president. I hope you get the chance to meet him and his wife, Rachel."

"I do, too," Vaughn said.

"Heath donated the lumber for the children's play equip-ment," she said as they entered the park and strolled past the jungle gym, slides and swings. "But Brandon Wyatt, along with Jeb McKenna and Gage Sinclair, actually built all these things." She realized the names didn't mean any-thing to Vaughn, but she wanted him to get a sense of what the park stood for in this community. Each family had con-tributed something, from planting the grass to laying the concrete walkway.

"It looks well used."

An outsider like Vaughn couldn't possibly understand

how much the children of Buffalo Valley cherished the park. "My family owns the hardware," she continued, pointing to the opposite side of the park toward the store. "We donated the wood for the picnic tables."

"I notice they aren't secured with chains," Vaughn said.

"We don't have much crime in Buffalo Valley." It distressed her to visit public areas where everything, including picnic tables and garbage cans, was tied down by chains to prevent theft. But no one had ever stolen from the park or any other public place in Buffalo Valley. There'd never been any real vandalism, either.

"No crime?" He sounded as though he didn't believe her.

"Well, some, but it's mostly petty stuff. A few windows soaped at Halloween, that kind of thing. The occasional fight or display of drunkenness. We did have a murder once, about eighty years ago. According to the stories, it was a crime of passion." Quickly changing the subject, she said, "The War Memorial was designed by Kevin Betts. I don't know if you've heard of him, but he was born and raised right here."

"Sorry, I haven't," Vaughn said with a shrug.

"He's Leta's son, and he's an artist who's making a name for himself." Everyone in town was proud of Kevin. "This sculpture—" she gestured as they neared it "—was one of his very first." She watched Vaughn's expression when he saw it and was stirred by the immediate appreciation that showed in his eyes.

Kevin was a gifted artist, not only because he was technically skilled but because his work evoked emotion in people. The bronze sculpture was simple and yet profound. Half-a-dozen rifles were stacked together, upright and leaning against one another, with a helmet balanced on top. Beside the guns a young soldier knelt, his shoulders bowed in grief. No one seeing the piece could fail to be moved, to respond with sorrow and a bittersweet pain.

Vaughn stood before the memorial and didn't say anything right away. Then he squatted down and ran his finger over the name of Vaughn Knight. "My parents still talk about him. He was the one who brought them together," Vaughn said, and slowly straightened. "I'm glad he won't be forgotten."

"He won't be," Carrie assured him. "With this memorial, his name will always be here to remind everyone."

Vaughn thrust his gloved hands into his coat pockets.

"Cold?" Carrie asked.

He shook his head. "I know about the pharmacy and you've mentioned the hardware store. Tell me about the other businesses in town."

They walked toward Main Street and Carrie told him about each one in turn, starting with Joanie Wyatt's video-rental and craft store and ending with her parents' place.

"It was a leap of faith for you to move into town, wasn't it?" Vaughn said.

Carrie nodded pensively. "Yeah, but it's paid off. My two oldest brothers are still farming and the two younger ones work exclusively with Mom and Dad. It's a good arrangement all around."

"Are you hungry?" Vaughn asked unexpectedly.

She laughed. "You offering to feed me?" It was a bit early, but dinner would pass the time until Hassie returned.

"Unless there's a reason for you to hurry home."

"No reason. I'm divorced." Even now, six years later,

the words left a bitter taste on her tongue. She focused her gaze directly in front of her.

"I'm sorry," he said.

"I am, too." She forced a cheerful note into her voice, as if to say she was over it.

"I thought I'd suggest Buffalo Bob's 3 of a Kind. I was intrigued by what you told me about him."

"He's certainly a character," she agreed. "But before we go there, I'd like to show you Maddy's Grocery." Carrie loved the wonderful and witty Christmas display Maddy put up every year. Eight reindeer were suspended from the ceiling, with the front half of Santa's sleigh coming out of the wall.

Vaughn laughed when he saw it. His reaction was one of genuine enjoyment and not the short derisive laugh of someone mocking Maddy's efforts. On their way to 3 of a Kind, they strolled past the Buffalo Valley Quilting Company.

"This is the success story of the decade," Carrie boasted as she motioned to the holiday quilt displayed in the first set of windows. "Sarah Urlacher started the business in her father's house, dyeing the muslin herself from all-natural products. The designs are her own, too."

Vaughn stopped to look at the quilt in the window.

"It all began when Lindsay Sinclair introduced Sarah's quilts to her uncle. He owns an upscale furniture store in Atlanta, and before she knew it, Sarah had trouble keeping up with the demand. Now people all over the country buy her quilts."

"That's great."

"Sarah's business has boosted the economy of Buffalo

Valley to the point that we can now afford things that are commonplace in other towns."

"Such as?"

"The sidewalks got refurbished last summer, and the town could never have paid for that without the tax revenue Sarah's business brings in." Carrie didn't mention the new community well and several other improvements that had taken place over the past few years.

"I'll let Leta know where we are so she can tell Hassie," Carrie said, and made a quick stop at the pharmacy. She was back within moments. Vaughn waited for her outside.

There was no one at the restaurant or in the bar when they arrived. Studying Buffalo Bob with fresh eyes, Carrie could only guess what Vaughn must think. The ex-biker was a burly man. He was an oddity here in a town where most men came off the farm. With his thinning hair drawn back into a ponytail and his muscular arms covered in tattoos, he looked as though he'd be more comfortable with a biker gang than waiting tables.

"How ya doin', Carrie?" he greeted her when she took a seat across the table from Vaughn.

"Good, Bob. Come meet Vaughn Kyle."

"Welcome to Buffalo Valley," Bob said, extending his hand for a hearty shake. "Merrily told me you'd dropped by." Bob gave them each a menu. "Take a look, but the special tonight is Salisbury steak. I don't mind telling you it's excellent." He grinned. "And who would know better than me?"

"I'm convinced," Vaughn told him with an answering smile. "I'll have the special."

"Me, too," Carrie said, returning the menu.

Bob left them, and Carrie tried to relax but found it difficult. She hadn't been alone with a man, other than her brothers, in a very long time. Following her divorce, she'd only dated twice, and both occasions had been awkward. Her schooling, plus her internship, didn't leave much room for a social life, anyway.

Vaughn sat back in his chair. "Tell me about Hassie," he suggested easily.

Carrie felt the tightness leave her shoulders. On the subject of Hassie, she could talk his ear off. "What would you like to know first?"

"Whatever you feel is important."

"She's been my hero for as long as I can remember. I don't know what would've happened to this town without her." Carrie wanted him to realize how deeply Hassie was loved by everyone in Buffalo Valley. "She's older now, and she's slowing down some." Carrie had seen the evidence of that in the months since she'd come to work as an intern. She almost suspected that Hassie had been holding on until she got there.

Vaughn glanced at Buffalo Bob as he brought their salads and nodded his thanks. "Every year, along with my birthday card and a U.S. Savings Bond, she wrote me a short message." His mouth lifted in a half smile. "She called it *words to live by.*"

"Give me an example," Carrie said, curious.

"I don't remember them all, but...okay, she told me about the importance of being on time. Only, she did it by making up this little poem...." He hesitated and a slow grin crossed his face. "She once wrote that if at first I don't succeed, it just means I'm normal."

"That sounds like Hassie."

"She has a wonderful way of putting things." He paused, a reflective look on his face. "When I was sixteen, she told me the grass isn't greener on the other side of the fence, it's greener where it's watered."

"I think it's wonderful that you remembered them."

"How could I not, when she made them so much fun? She was like an extra grandmother."

Hearing that warmed Carrie's heart, because she knew Hassie felt toward him the way she would a grandson.

They were silent as they ate their salads. Buffalo Bob had made even a plain lettuce, cucumber and tomato salad taste delicious with the addition of a tart-sweet cranberry dressing. They were just finishing when Bob reappeared, carrying two plates heaped with food. He placed them in front of Vaughn and Carrie, then stepped back, and said, "Enjoy."

Vaughn stared after him as he returned to the kitchen. "He's not the typical sort of person you find in a place like this, is he?"

"Bob's a sweetheart," she said defensively. "He's hardworking and well-liked and a wonderful father and—"

"Tell me how he happened to land in Buffalo Valley," Vaughn broke in. He reached for his fork, tasting the fluffy mashed potatoes and tender gravy-covered steak.

"He came here when the town was at its lowest point. My uncle Earl owned this hotel and he'd been trying to sell it for years. Seeing that there weren't any buyers and he was losing money every month, my uncle devised an unusual poker game. It cost a thousand dollars to play, but the winner walked away with the hotel, restaurant and bar. Lock, stock and barrel."

Vaughn's brows arched. "And Bob won it with three of a kind."

"Exactly."

Vaughn shook his head. "More power to him."

"A lot has changed since then, all of it for the better. Bob married Merrily, and two and a half years ago, they had little Bobby."

"The one who's prone to ear infections?"

She nodded. "You've never seen better parents. Those two dote on that little boy something fierce. In fact, Bob and Merrily are terrific with all the kids in town." Carrie paused long enough to sample her dinner. "Hey, this is terrific."

Vaughn agreed with her. "In addition to his other talents, Buffalo Bob's a good cook. He wasn't kidding about that."

"I don't know what his life was like before he came to Buffalo Valley, but he's one of us now."

Vaughn was about to ask a question when the door opened and Hassie hurried inside.

Carrie was instantly on her feet. One look told her Hassie was exhausted. Her shoulders were slumped and she seemed close to collapse.

"Hassie," Carrie said, wrapping her arm protectively around the older woman's waist. "This is Vaughn Kyle."

It was almost as if Hassie didn't hear her at first. "Vaughn," she repeated, and then her face brightened visibly. "My goodness, did you let me know you were coming and it slipped my mind?"

Vaughn pulled out a chair for her to sit down. "No, I very rudely showed up without an invitation."

"I wish I'd known."

"It's no problem. Carrie was kind enough to spend the afternoon with me."

"Let me take a good look at you," Hassie said. She cupped his face with both hands and a smile emerged. "You're so handsome," she whispered. "You have such kind eyes."

If her praise embarrassed or flustered him, Vaughn didn't reveal it.

"How long can you stay?" she asked.

"Actually, I should probably think about heading back to Grand Forks soon."

"No," Hassie protested, "That's hardly enough time for me to show you everything."

"Carrie already gave me a tour of town."

"That's good, but I have a number of things I've saved that I'd like you to have—things that were my son's."

Her disappointment was unmistakeable, and Carrie glanced at Vaughn, trying to signal him, hoping he'd change his mind.

"I want to see them."

Carrie could have hugged him right then and there.

"But," he added, "you've had a long, tiring day. Perhaps it would be better if I came back later."

Hassie didn't bother to deny what was obvious. "Would it be too much to ask you to come here on Sunday?" Both her hands gripped his, as if she was afraid to let him go.

Carrie found herself just as eager to hear his response.

"I'll meet you at the store shortly after noon," he said. "I'll look forward to seeing you then."

Carrie felt a surge of relief—and anticipation. She couldn't help smiling, first at Hassie, then at Vaughn.

Happiness shimmered in the old woman's eyes as she placed one hand on Carrie's shoulder and leaned heavily against her.

"That would be perfect," she said quietly. "Thank you, Vaughn."

Two

Hassie felt old and weary, especially after a day like this. But God had rewarded her patience by sending Vaughn Kyle to Buffalo Valley. Seeing him, however briefly, had lifted her spirits. Best of all was his promise to return on Sunday afternoon.

Tired though she was, Hassie brewed herself a cup of tea and sat at her kitchen table, mulling over the events of the day. Ambrose Kohn had been a thorn in her side for many years. His family had lived and worked in town for generations, but with impeccable timing, the Kohns had moved to Devils Lake just before the economy in Buffalo Valley collapsed.

Ambrose owned several pieces of property here and a building or two. The theater belonged to him, and he'd been quick enough to close it down, despite the town council's efforts to convince him otherwise. The old building still had plenty of life in it, but it'd sat abandoned and neglected until the first year Lindsay Snyder came to Buffalo Valley as the high-school teacher. She'd wanted to use it for a Christmas play. If Hassie remembered correctly, Ambrose had demanded she go out with him first before he gave permission. That annoyed Hassie even now, several years later.

Lindsay had attended some social function with Ambrose, and it had nearly ruined her relationship with Gage Sinclair. But she and Gage had resolved their differences. They'd been married for more than five years now and were parents of two beautiful daughters.

Ambrose, despite his underhanded methods, had walked away a winner, as well. After the community had cleaned up that old theater and put on the high-school Christmas program, he'd reopened the movie house and it'd been in operation ever since.

Unfortunately Ambrose hadn't learned anything from that experience. He hadn't learned that people in Buffalo Valley loved their town and that they supported one another. He hadn't figured out that for them, Buffalo Valley was *home,* not just a place to live. Now the middle-aged bachelor held the fate of the community in his hands. Value-X, a huge retailer, wanted to move into town and they wanted to set up shop on land owned by Ambrose. The company had a reputation for sweeping into small towns and then systematically destroying independent and family-owned businesses. Six months earlier, Hassie had watched a television report on the effect the mega-retailer had on communities. At the time she'd never dreamed Buffalo Valley might be targeted. Naturally the company insisted this was progress and a boon to the town's economy. There were already articles in some of the regional papers, touting the company's supposedly civic-minded attitudes. Profit-minded was more like it.

No one needed to tell Hassie what would happen to Buffalo Valley if Value-X decided to follow through with its plans. All the small businesses that had recently started would die a fast and painful death. Her own pharmacy wouldn't be immune.

Ambrose owned twenty acres just outside of town; this was the property Value-X was interested in acquiring, and he wasn't opposed to selling it—no matter how badly it damaged the community.

Nothing Hassie said had the least bit of impact on him. Buffalo Bob, as president of the town council, had tried to reason with him, too, again without success. Heath Quantrill had thrown up his hands in frustration at the man's stubborn refusal to listen.

While Ambrose didn't live in Buffalo Valley, he did have a powerful influence on its future. For that reason alone, he should think carefully about his decision to sell that parcel of land. Progress or not, it wasn't the kind of future she or anyone here saw for Buffalo Valley. Jerry, her husband, might have been able to talk sense into Ambrose, but Jerry had died the year after Vaughn. She'd lost them both so close together.

The TV report on Value-X had made a strong impression on Hassie. What had stayed in her mind most clearly were the interviews with business owners, some with three- and four-generation histories. They'd been forced to close down, unable to compete. Local traditions had been lost, pride broken. Men and women wept openly, in despair and hopelessness. Downtown areas died out.

Hassie couldn't bear to think what would happen to Buffalo Valley if Ambrose sold that land to those outsiders. Why, it would undo all the work the town council had done over the past six years. The outcome was too dismal to consider.

Joanie Wyatt's video-rental and craft store would probably be one of the first to fold. And the Hendricksons— they'd sunk everything they had in this world and more into AceMan Hardware. Value-X would undercut the lowest prices they could charge and ring the store's death knell for sure.

Dennis Urlacher supplied car parts to the community at his filling station. Although that was only a small portion of his business, Dennis had once mentioned that his largest profit margin came from the auto parts and not the fuel. It wouldn't be long before his business was affected, too. Even Rachel Quantrill's new hamburger stand would lose customers. Maddy's Grocery would suffer, too; how long she'd be able to hold on depended on Value-X's plans. It was said that many of the newer stores included groceries.

None of that concerned Ambrose. All he knew was that he'd been offered a fair price for a piece of land that had sat vacant for years. He'd let it be known that he fully intended to sell those acres. If anyone else was interested, he'd entertain other offers. Ambrose had made one thing perfectly clear: the offer had to be substantially higher than the deal Value-X had proposed. No one in town, not even Heath Quantrill, had a thick-enough bankroll to get into a bidding war with the huge retailer.

Hassie sipped her tea and purposely turned her thoughts in a more pleasant direction. What a fine-looking young man Vaughn Kyle was. After all these years, she was grateful to finally meet him. His letters had meant so much to her, and she'd saved each thank-you note from the time he was six years old.

For a short while after her son was buried, Hassie and Barbara, the boy's mother, had been close. They'd stayed in touch, but then a year later the wedding announcement arrived. Barbara, the beautiful young woman her son had loved, was marrying Rick Kyle, who'd been one of Vaughn's best friends.

Hassie didn't begrudge the couple happiness, but she hadn't attended the wedding. Their marriage was a painful reminder that life continues. If circumstances had been different, this might have been her own son's wedding.

Two years later, Rick and Barbara had mailed her the birth announcement. They'd named their first child after Hassie's son. Two years later came another birth announcement, this time for a girl they named Gloria. Sight unseen, Hassie had loved that boy and thought of him as the grandson Vaughn could never give her. Her own daughter, Valerie, had two girls and Hassie adored them, but since Val and her family lived in Hawaii, there was little opportunity to see them. Vaughn Kyle had assumed a special significance for her. Neither his parents nor anyone else knew how deep her feelings ran. With a determined effort, she'd remained on the sidelines of his life, writing occasional letters and sending gifts at the appropriate times.

Now she would have the opportunity to give Vaughn the things she'd set aside for him so many years ago. It'd been her prayer that they meet before she died.

She had to stop herself from being greedy. She would gladly accept whatever time Vaughn Kyle was willing to grant her.

* * *

Carrie found herself smiling as she walked into the family home shortly after six. She paused in the entryway to remove the handknit scarf from around her neck and shrug out of her coat. Softly humming a Christmas tune, she savored the warm feelings left by her visit with Vaughn. She'd enjoyed getting to know him. Even though it'd been years since she'd spent this much time in a man's company, the initial awkwardness between them had dissipated quickly.

Vaughn seemed genuinely interested in learning what he could about Hassie and Buffalo Valley. What she appreciated most was that he hadn't asked any prying questions about her divorce. A lot of people assumed she wanted to tell her side of it, but Carrie found no joy in reliving the most painful, humiliating experience of her life.

Their dinner conversation had flowed smoothly. He was easy to talk to, and Carrie loved telling him about Buffalo Valley. She was proud to recount its history, especially the developments of the past five years. The improvements could be attributed to several factors, but almost all of them went right back to Hassie Knight and her determination and optimism. Hassie refused to let the town fade into nothingness, refused to let it die like countless other communities throughout the Dakotas.

When Carrie walked into the living room, her mother glanced up from her needlework and her two younger brothers hurried in from the kitchen. All three fixed their eyes on her. Everyone seemed to be waiting for her to speak.

"What?" Carrie demanded.

"We're curious about your dinner date," her mother said mildly.

Carrie should've realized her family would hear she'd gone out with Vaughn. *How* they knew she could only speculate, but in a small town word traveled even faster than it did on the Internet.

"How'd it go?" Ken asked, looking as though he'd welcome the opportunity to defend her honor should the occasion arise.

Part of the pain of her divorce came from knowing that she was the first in their family's history to whom it had happened. Long-standing marriages were a tradition she would gladly have continued. But she couldn't stay married to a man who didn't honor his vows, a man whose unfaithfulness undermined her self-respect, as well as their marriage. Her four brothers had hinted that things with Alec would have worked out differently if they'd been around to see to it. Needless to say, the last thing she wanted was her brothers, much as she loved them, playing the role of enforcers.

"He's very nice," she said, carefully weighing her words. She didn't want to give the impression that there was more to their meeting than a simple, friendly dinner.

"He didn't try anything, did he?" Chuck asked.

Carrie nearly laughed out loud. "Of course he didn't. Where's Dad?" she asked, wondering why her father hadn't leaped into the conversation.

Before anyone could respond, her father shuffled into the room, wearing his old slippers, a newspaper tucked under his arm and his reading glasses perched on the end of his nose. He stopped abruptly when he saw her.

"So how was your hot date?" he asked. He stood in front of his easy chair and waited for her to answer.

"It was just dinner," she protested. "The only reason he asked me out was to kill time while he waited for Hassie." It was unlikely they'd be doing this again, which she supposed was just as well. She had to admit she *wanted* to, but from what he'd said, he was only in the area for the Christmas holidays and then he was going home to Seattle. There was no point in starting something you couldn't finish, she thought. Not that she knew if he was even interested in her...or available.

"Will you be seeing him again?" her mother asked, but Carrie wasn't fooled by her nonchalant tone.

"He's coming back Sunday afternoon to—"

"That's great." Her mother smiled, clearly pleased.

"He isn't returning to see *me*." It was important her family understand that she had nothing to do with his decision. The sole reason for his visit was to spend time with Hassie.

"That's a shame." Her father claimed his chair, turning automatically to the sports page.

"Did you invite him to the tree-lighting ceremony?" Ken asked.

Her father lowered the newspaper and her mother paused in the middle of a stitch to await her response.

"No," Carrie admitted reluctantly. She'd thought of mentioning it, but couldn't see the purpose. She glanced around the room, looking at each hopeful face.

What she didn't say was that she would've welcomed the opportunity to know Vaughn Kyle better. The few hours she'd spent with him had helped her realize that her heart was still capable of response, that it hadn't shriveled up inside her like an orange left too long in the fruit bowl.

For that she was grateful.

As Vaughn pulled the rental car into the long driveway that led to his parents' home, he saw that his mother had turned on the back porch light. It wasn't really necessary, since the outside of the entire house was decorated with Christmas lights.

He knew his mother had made tentative plans for a dinner with friends on Sunday afternoon and might not be pleased by his absence. However, Vaughn didn't mind returning to Buffalo Valley. He'd enjoyed meeting Carrie and learning some of the town's recent history. He'd report this information to Natalie; she might find it useful. Carrie Hendrickson was an interesting contrast to the women he'd met and dated in Seattle during the past few years—including Natalie, his sort-of fiancée. Carrie had shied away from talking about herself, which was a refreshing change from what he'd grown accustomed to hearing. A recent dinner date with Natalie had been spent discussing every aspect of her career and the Value-X corporation—as if their work was all they had to talk about. He'd come away with a letdown feeling, feeling, somehow, that he'd missed out on something important…only he didn't know quite what. After all, he *admired* Natalie's drive and ambition and her unemotional approach to life.

His mother was finishing the dinner dishes when he entered the kitchen. "How was your visit?" she asked, rinsing a pan before setting it on the drainboard.

"Wonderful."

"How's Hassie?" she asked, looking expectantly at him as she reached for the towel to dry her hands. "You did give her my love, didn't you?"

"She was exhausted." He explained that the pharmacist had been at a meeting when he arrived and that her assistant had convinced him to wait until she got back. Neither she nor Carrie had mentioned the reason for the meeting, but whatever it was had drained her, emotionally and physically.

His mother's brow furrowed with concern. "She's not ill, is she?"

"I don't think so, but I didn't want to tire her out any more than she already was, so I told her I'd be back on Sunday."

His mother's face clouded and he knew what was coming. The subject of Vaughn Knight always distressed her. Every time his name was brought up, she grew quiet. He suspected she'd postponed a promised visit to Hassie because, for whatever reason, she found it hard to talk about Vaughn. More than once he'd seen tears fill her eyes. His mother wasn't the only one; his father also tended to avoid conversations about Hassie's son. All Vaughn knew was that both his parents thought a great deal of the friend who'd lost his life in a rice paddy thirty-three years earlier. So much that it still caused them pain.

"I'm glad you're doing this," she said. "Over the years I've wanted to talk about Vaughn, but I get choked up whenever time I try."

She grabbed a bottle of hand lotion and occupied herself with that for a few moments, but Vaughn wasn't fooled.

She didn't want him to see that her eyes were brimming with tears.

"Hassie will do a far better job of telling you about Vaughn than your father or I could."

Impulsively Vaughn hugged his mother, then joined his father, who was watching television in the living room.

On Sunday the drive into Buffalo Valley seemed to go faster than it had on Friday. He knew exactly where he needed to go, and the very landscape he'd found monotonous two days earlier now seemed familiar, even welcoming.

When he pulled into town, Buffalo Bob was spreading salt on the sidewalk in front of his own place and the businesses on either side. He waved, and Vaughn returned the gesture, then eased into a parking spot near the pharmacy. Once again he was struck by what an appealing town Buffalo Valley was. It felt as though he'd stepped back in time, to an era when family and a sense of community were priorities, when neighbor helped neighbor and people felt responsible for one another.

A sign on the door stated that the drugstore was open from noon until five on Sundays during December. When he walked inside, Vaughn found Hassie behind the counter. He automatically looked for Carrie and wasn't disappointed when he saw her over by the cash register, checking receipts. She paused in her task as soon as she saw him.

To his surprise, his mind had drifted toward her a number of times since Friday. He was attracted by her charm, which was real and uncontrived. She was genuine and warm, and he liked the pride in her eyes when she talked about her town.

She froze, as if she, too, had been thinking of him. That was a pleasant thought and one that sent a shiver of guilt through him. He was as good as engaged to Natalie, and the last thing he should be doing was flirting with another woman.

"Right on time," Hassie said, sounding much livelier this afternoon than she had two days earlier.

"I'm rarely tardy when I have a date with a beautiful woman," he teased, and watched both Hassie and Carrie smile. He generally didn't have much use for flattery, but occasionally it served a purpose. In this case, his rather silly statement had given everyone, including him, a moment of pleasure.

"You going to be all right here by yourself?" She turned to Carrie.

"Of course. You two go and visit, and don't you worry about a thing."

"I'll just get my coat," Hassie said, and disappeared to retrieve it. While she was gone, he had a few minutes with Carrie.

"I'm glad you're doing this for Hassie," she said. "It means so much to her to be sharing her son's life with you."

"I'm not doing it out of any sense of charity." Vaughn was truly interested in learning what he could about his namesake.

Hassie returned, wearing a long, dark coat, and they walked over to her house, which was one street off Main. Vaughn slowed his gait to match hers, tucking her arm

in the crook of his elbow. Together they strolled leisurely
down the newly shoveled sidewalk.

The house resembled something out of a 1950s movie.
The furniture was large and bulky, covered in thick
navy-blue fabric. Doilies decorated the back of the chair,
and three were strategically placed across the back of
the matching sofa. Even the television set was an old-
fashioned floor model.

"It'll only take me a minute to make tea," Hassie announced heading toward the kitchen. He was given instruc
tions to sit down and to look through the photo albums
she'd already laid out.

Vaughn opened the biggest album. The first photograph
he saw was a black-and-white version of a much younger
Hassie standing with a baby cradled in her arms. A tall,
handsome man stood awkwardly beside her, grinning self-
consciously. His hand was on the shoulder of a little girl
about four or five who stood in front of them, her dark
brown hair in long braids.

Thereafter, photograph after photograph documented the
life of Vaughn Knight. He was in Boy Scouts and active in
his church. His school pictures showed increasing growth
and maturity. When he reached high school, Vaughn had
grown tall and athletic; a series of newspaper articles de-
tailed his success on the basketball court and the football
field. The year he was a senior, Buffalo Valley High School
won the state football championship, with Vaughn Knight
as the star quarterback. Another article named him Most
Valuable Player.

His high-school graduation picture revealed the face of
a young man eager to explore the world.

Hassie rejoined him, carrying a tray with a ceramic pot and two matching cups, as well as a plate of small cookies.

Vaughn stood and took the tray from her, placing it on the coffee table, and waited while she poured. He noticed that her hands were unsteady, but he didn't interrupt or try to assist her.

When she'd finished, she picked up a round, plain hatbox and removed the lid. "The top letter is the first one that mentions your mother."

Vaughn reached for the envelope.

September 30, 1966

Dear Mom and Dad,
I'm in love. Don't laugh when you read this. Rick and I went to a hootenanny last night and there was this terrific girl there. Her name's Barbara Lowell, and guess what? She's from Grand Forks. She's got long blond hair and the most incredible smile you've ever seen. After the hootenanny we drank coffee and talked for hours. I've never felt like this about any other girl. She's smart and funny and so beautiful I had a hard time not staring at her. Even after I left her, I was so wrapped up in meeting her I couldn't sleep. First thing this morning, I called her and we talked for two hours. Rick is thoroughly disgusted with me and I don't blame him, but I've never been in love before.

As soon as I can, I want to bring her home for you to meet. You'll understand why I feel the way I do once you see her for yourselves.

Love,
Vaughn

"The Rick he's writing about is my dad?" Vaughn asked.

Hassie nodded. "Here's another one you might find interesting." She lifted a batch of letters from the box. It was apparent from the way she sorted through the dates that she'd reread each letter countless times.

July 16, 1967

Dear Mom and Dad,

I've made my decision, but I have to tell you it was probably the most difficult I've ever had to make. I love Barb, and both of us want to get married right away. If I were thinking just of me, that's exactly what we'd do before I ship out. But I'm following your example, Dad. You and Mom waited until after the war to marry, and you came back safe and whole. I will, too.

Barb cried when I told her I felt it was best to delay the wedding until after my tour. Although you never advised me one way or the other, I had the feeling you thought it was better this way.

Vaughn stopped reading. "Did you want him to wait before marrying my mother?"

Hassie closed her eyes. "His father and I thought they were both too young. In the years that followed, I lived to regret that. Perhaps if Vaughn had married your mother, there might have been a grandchild. I realize that's terribly selfish, and I hope you'll forgive me."

"There's nothing to forgive."

"I always wondered if Jerry would've lived longer if we'd had grandchildren. Valerie was still in college at the time and wasn't married yet. A few years after that, she moved to Hawaii to take a job and met her husband there, but by then it was too late for Jerry."

"So your husband took the news of Vaughn's death very hard?"

"Once we received word about Vaughn, my husband was never the same. He was close to both children, but the shock of Vaughn's death somehow made him lose his emotional balance. Much as he loved Valerie and me, he couldn't get over the loss of his son. He went into a deep depression and started having heart problems. A year later, he died, too."

"Heart attack?"

"Technically, yes, but Vaughn's death is what really killed him, despite what that death certificate said. He simply gave up caring about anything. I wish..." Her voice trailed off.

"I'm sorry," Vaughn said, and meant it.

"Don't be." She patted his hand. "God knew better. Had your mother and my son married, you would never have been born."

It must have hit her hard that her son's fiancée and closest friend married each other within a year of his death. "Were you upset when my parents got married?" he asked.

"A little in the beginning, but then I realized that was exactly what Vaughn would have wanted. He did love her, and I know in my heart of hearts that she loved him, too."

"She did." Vaughn could say that without hesitation.

Hassie plucked a tissue from the nearby box and dabbed at her eyes. "I'd like you to have this." She reached for a second box and withdrew a heavy felt crest displaying the letters BVHS. It took Vaughn a moment to recognize that it was from a letterman's jacket.

"Vaughn was very proud of this. He earned it in wrestling. He was a natural at most sports. Basketball and football were barely a challenge, but that wasn't the case with wrestling. Many an afternoon he'd walk into the pharmacy and announce to his father and me that he was quitting. By dinnertime he'd change his mind and then he'd go back the next day." She paused, dabbing at her eyes again. "Our children were the very best of Jerry and me. Vaughn was a good son, and losing him changed all of us forever."

"I'd be honored to have this letter," Vaughn said.

"Thank you," Hassie whispered. She smiled faintly through her tears. "You must think me an old fool."

"No," he was quick to tell her. "I'm very glad you showed me all this." For the first time Vaughn Knight was more than a name, someone remembered who'd been lost in a war fought half a world away. He was alive in the words of his letters, in the photographs and in the heart of his mother.

"His letters from Vietnam are in this box," Hassie said. "They'll give you a feel for what it was like. If you're interested…"

Having served in the military, Vaughn was, of course, interested. He sat back and read the first letter. When he'd finally finished them all, it'd grown dark and Hassie was busy in the kitchen.

"What time is it?" he asked.

"It's after six."

"No." He found that hard to believe. "I had no idea I'd

kept you this long. I apologize, Hassie. You should have stopped me."

She shook her head. "I couldn't. Your interest was a pleasure to me. Everything was fine with the store—Carrie's fully capable of handling anything that might come up. Besides, we're closed now."

"He could've been a writer, your son," Vaughn said, setting aside the last letter. For a few hours he'd been completely drawn into Vaughn Knight's descriptions of people and landscapes and events. Although the details were lightly sketched, a vivid picture of the young soldier's life had revealed itself through his words.

"I often thought that myself," Hassie agreed. After a brief silence she said, "I didn't want to interrupt you to ask about dinner. I hope it wasn't overly presumptuous to assume you'd join me."

"I'd like that very much."

Hassie nodded once, slowly, as if she considered his company of great worth.

While she put the finishing touches on the meal, Vaughn phoned his parents to tell them he'd be later than anticipated. "Be sure and give Hassie my love," his mother instructed. "Tell her your father and I plan to visit her soon."

"I will," he promised.

When he ended the phone conversation, he found Hassie setting the table. He insisted on taking over, eager to contribute something to their dinner. His admiration and love for the older woman had grown this afternoon in ways he hadn't thought possible on such short acquaintance. She'd opened his eyes to a couple of important things. First and foremost, he'd learned about the man he'd been named after and discovered he had quite a lot to live up to. Second, he'd come to see his parents in a new light. He understood how their fallen friend had shaped their lives and their marriage. It was no wonder they didn't often speak of Vaughn Knight. The years might have dulled the pain, but the sense of loss was as strong in them as it was in Hassie.

They chatted over dinner, and his mood lightened. Hassie was wise and considerate; she seemed to understand how serious his thoughts had become.

"The community is lighting the Christmas tree this evening," she said casually as Vaughn carried their dishes to the sink.

"Are you going?" he asked.

"I wouldn't miss it for the world," Hassie informed him. "The Christmas tree is set up beside the War Memorial. Nearly everyone in town will be there—" she paused and looked at him "—including Carrie."

"Are you playing matchmaker with me, Hassie Knight?" he asked. He had a feeling she didn't miss much—and that she'd seen the way his gaze had been drawn to Carrie when he'd entered the pharmacy.

Hassie chuckled. "She's smitten, you know."

Smitten. What a wonderful old-fashioned word, Vaughn mused. It would take a better man than him not to feel flattered.

"You could do worse."

"And how do you know I don't already have a girlfriend waiting for me in Seattle?" he asked, and wondered what Hassie would think of Natalie. For some reason he had the impression she wouldn't think much of her sharp-edged sophistication. It'd taken him a while to see past Natalie's polished exterior; once he had, he'd realized she was just like everyone else, trying to be noticed and to make a name for herself.

"You don't," Hassie returned confidently.

He was about to tell her about Natalie, when Hassie said, "Come with me. Come and watch the community tree being lit. There's no better way to learn about Buffalo Valley."

Vaughn's purpose, other than meeting Hassie, was to do exactly that. Still, seeing Carrie again appealed to him, too—more than it should.

"That's just what I need to put me in the Christmas spirit," Vaughn said. "I'd consider it an honor to accompany you."

"Wonderful." Hassie clasped her hands together as though to keep herself from clapping with delight. "I can't tell you how happy this makes me."

He helped her on with her coat, then grabbed his own. Taking her arm again, Vaughn guided her out the door and down the front steps. By the time they rounded the corner to Main Street and the City Park, the town was coming to life. There were groups of people converging on the park and cars stopping here and there. The air was filled with festivity—carols played over a loudspeaker, kids shrieking excitedly, shouts of welcome…and laughter everywhere. Vaughn could practically *feel* the happiness all around him.

"This is about as close as it gets to a traffic jam in Buffalo Valley," Hassie told him.

As soon as they appeared, it seemed everyone in town called a greeting to Hassie. Vaughn had never seen anything to compare with the reverence and love people obviously felt for her.

"You've been holding out on me, Hassie Knight," an older man teased as he approached. "I didn't realize I had competition."

"Cut it out, Joshua McKenna." Hassie grinned. "Meet Vaughn Kyle."

"Mighty pleased to meet you." The man thrust out his hand for Vaughn to shake.

"Nearly everyone in a fifty-mile radius is coming," Joshua said, glancing around him. More and more cars arrived, and the park was actually getting crowded.

"I don't see Calla. She's not going to make it home this year?"

"And miss spoiling her baby brother?" Joshua returned. "You're joking, right?"

Hassie laughed delightedly. "I should have known better."

"Jeb, Maddy and the kids are already here."

The names flew over Vaughn's head, but it was apparent that Hassie loved each family.

"Maddy owns the grocery," Joshua explained as they strolled across the street and entered the park. "She's married to my son. Best thing that ever happened to him."

"Oh, yes—I saw the grocery," Vaughn said. "Maddy. I remember. The fantastic reindeer."

Joshua grinned widely. "Yup, that's our Maddy. Loves any excuse to decorate—and does a great job."

"They have two of the most precious children you'll ever want to see," Hassie added, "with another on the way."

"The first pregnancy and this latest one were real surprises."

"I'll bet Jeb's developed a liking for blizzards," Hassie murmured, and the two older folks burst into laughter.

"You'd have to know the history of that family to understand what's so amusing," Carrie said, joining them.

"Hello again," Vaughn murmured.

"Hi."

Vaughn had trouble looking away.

"How about you and Carrie getting me some hot chocolate?" the older woman asked.

"Bring some for me, too, while you're at it," Joshua said.

"I think we just got our marching orders," Carrie told him, her eyes smiling. "Is that okay?"

"I don't mind if you don't," Vaughn replied.

The cold had brought color to her cheeks, and her long blond hair straggled out from under her wool hat. "It's fine with me. Buffalo Bob and Merrily are serving cocoa and cookies over there," she said a little breathlessly.

"I'll be right back," Vaughn said over his shoulder as he followed Carrie.

"Don't rush," Hassie called after him...and then he thought he saw her wink at him.

Three

The Christmas lights strung around the outside of the old house welcomed Vaughn back to his parents' home. His mother had been born and raised in Grand Forks, but his grandparents had moved to Arizona when he was six. Vaughn had no recollection of visiting the Dakotas, although he was certain they had. His memories centered on the Denver area and his father's family. Not until Rick was accepted for early retirement did they decide to return to the home that had been in the Lowell family for more than a hundred years.

The television blared from the living room as Vaughn let himself into the house, entering through the door off the kitchen after stomping the snow from his shoes on the back porch. He unzipped his jacket and hung it on a peg, along with his muffler.

"Is that you, Vaughn?" his mother called.

"No, it's Santa," he joked.

He watched as his mother, still holding her needlepoint, hurried into the kitchen. "You're not hungry, are you?"

"I filled up on cookies and hot chocolate."

His mother studied him as if to gauge how the meeting with Hassie had gone—the *real* question she wanted to ask, he suspected. "Did you have a...good visit?"

"Yes." He nodded reassuringly. "We talked before dinner, but afterward there was a tree-lighting ceremony in the park."

"You attended that?" His mother sounded pleased.

"Sure, why not?" His response was flippant, as though this was the very thing he'd normally do. In truth, though, Vaughn couldn't recall attending anything like it since he was in grade school. The evening had been quite an experience. The whole town had come alive with music and laughter and people enjoying one another's company. Christmas had never been a big deal to Vaughn—but he'd never seen an entire community join together like this, either. He knew it had made a lasting impression on him, that it left him longing for the same kind of warmth. For a true spirit of celebration, far removed from sophisticated parties and decorator-trimmed trees.

"How is Hassie?" his mother asked.

Vaughn wasn't sure what to say. Hassie was without a doubt one of the most dynamic women he'd ever met. She possessed character and depth and a heart that poured out love for her family and her community. He'd immediately seen how deeply she was loved and respected. After these hours in her company, Vaughn had understood why. "She's an extraordinary woman."

"I know." His mother's voice was soft, a little tentative.

Before Vaughn could say more, she'd retreated into the living room.

Vaughn followed and his father muted the television, obviously waiting for him to enlighten them about his visit.

"Hassie let me read the letters her son wrote from Vietnam."

His mother resumed her needlepoint and lowered her head, as though the stitches demanded her full attention.

"They were riveting. I learned about the war itself, things I could never have learned from a book, and about the man who wrote them." At the time, Hassie's son had been younger than Vaughn was now. In his letters, Vaughn had recognized the other man's sense of humanity, his hatred of war and his desire to make a difference, to share in a struggle for freedom.

"We met at the University of Michigan during our freshman year of college," his father said, and his eyes went blank. He seemed to be back in a different place, a different time. Vaughn knew he hadn't been accepted into the service himself because of poor eyesight. "He was my roommate. Both of us were away from home for the first time and in an environment completely foreign and unfamiliar. I suppose it's only natural that we became close."

His mother added in a low voice, "He was the most generous person I've ever known."

"He got a part-time job tutoring a youngster who had leukemia," his father continued, his gaze focused on the television screen. "He was hired for three hours a week, but Vaughn spent much more time with him than that. He played games with Joey, talked to him, cheered him up, and when Joey died at thirteen, the boy's mother said Vaughn had been his best friend."

"That's the kind of person he was," his mother said.

"Hassie gave me the school letter he earned in wrestling. And then, after I walked her back home, she said there was something else she wanted me to have." His parents looked up when he paused. Even now, Vaughn could hardly believe Hassie would give him such a gift.

"What, son?"

"Her husband's gold pocket watch. It would've been Vaughn's had he lived." Hassie had placed it in his hands with tears filming her eyes, then closed his fingers around it.

"Treasure it, Vaughn," his mother whispered.

"I do." Vaughn's first reaction had been to refuse something that was clearly a valuable family heirloom, something that meant a great deal to the old woman. He'd felt the significance of her gift and was moved by the solemnity of her words and gestures when she'd presented it to him.

He would always keep it safe. And he would pass it down to his oldest son or daughter.

"What else did Hassie tell you?" his father asked.

"She…said how much Vaughn had loved Mom."

"He did."

Vaughn studied his father, looking for any sign of jealousy. If he'd been in his father's shoes—well, he wasn't entirely sure *how* he'd feel.

"We planned to marry," his mother said, "but Hassie probably told you that."

He nodded. "She showed me the letter in which Vaughn

explains why it would be best to wait until he returned from Vietnam."

"Only, he didn't return. And everything worked out in a completely different way." His mother took his father's hand and held it and they gazed at each other for a moment. "But a good way," she said quietly.

"I often wondered what Hassie really thought about the two of us getting married," his father said. He stared at Vaughn as if, after meeting Hassie, he could supply the answer.

Indeed, Vaughn had seen the look that came over her face when she mentioned his parents' marriage. "At first I think she took it hard." This didn't appear to surprise either of his parents.

"Our marriage was a reminder that Vaughn was never coming home," his mother said, "and that no matter how much pain the world brings us, life continues."

"She said as much herself."

"I think...she was disappointed in us both."

"Perhaps in the beginning," Vaughn agreed, "but she changed her mind later. She told me she felt that her son approved."

"I'm sure he did," his mother whispered.

His father reached abruptly for the remote, indicating that the conversation was over. Sound flared back, and Vaughn got up and went to the kitchen to pour himself a cup of coffee before rejoining his parents.

"Oh, dear, I almost forgot to tell you," his mother said "Natalie phoned."

Vaughn's first reaction was that he didn't want to talk to her. Not tonight. Not after such an emotionally overwhelming day. Knowing Natalie, she'd want to discuss business, and that was the last thing on his mind. He needed to think before he returned the call, needed to absorb what he'd learned first—about the town, about Hassie…about himself.

"It isn't too late to call her back," his mother said. "With the time difference, it's barely eight on the West Coast."

"I know," he said absently, his thoughts now on Carrie Hendrickson. Much of the evening had been spent with her. After they'd brought hot chocolate to Hassie and Joshua McKenna, she'd introduced him to her family.

Vaughn had seen the wary look in her brothers' eyes and realized how protective they were of her. He wished he'd had more of a chance to talk to Carrie, but they were constantly interrupted. She was a favorite with her nieces and nephews, who were forever running up to her, involving her in their games and their squabbles. She was a natural peacemaker, he observed, one of those people whose very presence brought out the best impulses in others. Like Hassie. And the people in town valued Carrie in much the same way; that was easy to tell. They came to her for advice and comfort. They were drawn to her just as he was.

"Your father and I are looking forward to meeting Natalie," his mother said, breaking into his musings.

Vaughn started guiltily. He was as good as engaged— although, he supposed, all they'd really done was discuss the possibility of marriage. He hadn't divulged his plans to either of his parents. At Natalie's request, he hadn't even told them about his job. "She's anxious to meet you, too," he said, but without a lot of enthusiasm. The contrast between Natalie and Carrie flashed like a neon sign in his brain. One was warm and personable and focused on the needs of her community, the other sharp, savvy and ambitious. When he'd arrived in North Dakota, he thought he knew what he wanted; all at once, he wasn't sure.

"You've been seeing her for two years now," his mother went on, watching him.

"Barbara, the boy doesn't need you to tell him that."

Vaughn sipped his coffee.This was one conversation he had no wish to continue. "Carrie and I are going Christmas shopping tomorrow," he said, instead.

His mother lowered the needlepoint to her lap and stared at him. "Carrie? Who's Carrie?"

Vaughn didn't realize his mistake until it was too late. "A friend."

His mother raised her eyebrows as if his answer didn't please her. "When did you have time to make friends?"

"She works with Hassie at the pharmacy."

"I see." It appeared his mother did see, because she said nothing more.

Vaughn wished he understood his own feelings. A week ago he would have rushed to return Natalie's call. He wasn't avoiding *her*, he decided, but the subject of Value-X and Buffalo Valley. In a matter of days—one day, really—he'd become oddly protective of the town…and its people. Hassie, of course, but Carrie, too. Natalie was bound to ask him questions he no longer wanted to answer.

One thing was clear; he needed to think the situation through very carefully.

Craving solitude, Vaughn swallowed the last of his coffee, then announced he was heading for bed.

His mother glanced up at the wall clock. "Aren't you calling Natalie?"

He frowned. "Later. Don't worry about it, Mom."

"Vaughn has to rest up for shopping," his father teased.

"Ah, yes, the great shopping expedition. Where will it be, by the way?"

"The mall here in town."

"You're actually going to a mall at this time of year?" His father looked at him as though he'd lost his sanity.

Vaughn gave a nonchalant shrug. He didn't know what had possessed him to suggest he and Carrie meet at Columbia Mall. His excuse had been that Carrie was a wonderful source of information about the town. He'd never had the opportunity to bring up the subject of Value-X, and wanted to get her reactions to it. Or so he told himself.

The truth was, he wanted to know her better.

Hassie sat up in bed, her eyes on the photograph of her son on the bedroom wall. She looked at Jerry's picture next and Valerie's, then turned back to Vaughn's. It was only natural that she'd be thinking about her son tonight.

Time passed with such inexorable swiftness, she reflected. She had startlingly clear memories of Vaughn as a toddler, stumbling toward her, arms outstretched. If she closed her eyes, she could almost hear his laughter. She'd loved to scoop him into her arms and hug him close until he squirmed, wanting to run and play with his older sister. As they grew older, Valerie had listened to his confidences and offered a big sister's sage advice.

How carefree life had been for her and Jerry in the early 1950s. Simple pleasures had meant a great deal back then.

She could think of no greater comfort than sitting with her husband after a day at the pharmacy, a day they'd spent working together. Jerry would slip his arm around her shoulder and she'd press her head against his. He'd loved to whisper the sweetest words in her ear, and oh, she'd enjoyed being in his arms. In those days, it seemed the sun would never stop shining and the world would always be filled with happiness.

Turning out the light, Hassie nestled under the covers and let her memories take her back. Valerie and Vaughn used to come to the pharmacy every afternoon after school. To this day she could still picture the two of them sitting at the soda fountain, waiting to be served an after-school snack. They were a normal sister and brother, constantly bickering. Valerie always teased Vaughn, and when she did, he'd tug her pigtails hard enough to bring tears to her eyes. Then it would be up to Hassie to chastise them both. Softhearted Jerry had left the discipline to her. Hassie hated it, but knew her children needed to understand that their actions had consequences.

The years flew by so fast! Looking back, Hassie wished she'd appreciated each day a little more, treasured each moment with her children while they were young. Before she could account for all the years that had passed, it was 1960, and Vaughn was in high school.

Jerry was especially proud of Vaughn's athletic talent. He, too, had been a sports star in his youth. Vaughn had played team sports throughout his four years in high school, and they'd never missed a game. One or the other, and often both of them, were at his games, even if it meant closing the pharmacy, although they didn't do that often. They always sat in the same section of the stands so Vaughn would know where to find them. When his team came onto the field, it wasn't unusual for him to turn toward the bleachers and survey the crowd until he located his parents. Then he'd smile and briefly raise one hand.

Without even trying, Hassie could hear the crowds and recall the cheerleaders' triumphant leaps, while the school band played in the background.

Watching Vaughn play ball had been hard on Hassie's nerves. Twice that she could remember, her son had been injured. Both times Jerry had to stop her from running onto the field. She stood with the other concerned parents, her hands over her mouth, as the coaches assessed his injuries. On both occasions Vaughn had walked off the playing field unaided, but it'd been pride that had carried him. The first time his arm had been broken, and the second, his nose.

His high-school years had been wonderful. The girls always had eyes for Vaughn. Not only was he a star athlete and academically accomplished, he was tall and good-looking. The phone nearly rang off the hook during his junior and senior years. There'd never been anyone special, though, until he met Barbara Lowell in college. She'd been his first love and his last.

Hassie recalled how handsome he'd looked in his brand-new suit for the junior-senior prom, although he'd been uncomfortable in the starched white dress shirt. The photo from the dance revealed how ill at ease he'd been. His expression, Jerry had said, was that of someone who expected to be hit by a water balloon.

Hassie had suggested he ask Theresa Burkhart to the biggest dance of the year. He'd done so, but he'd never asked her out for a second date. When Hassie asked him why, Vaughn shrugged and had nothing more to say. Every afternoon for a week after the prom, Theresa had stopped at the soda fountain, obviuosly hoping to run into Vaughn. Each afternoon she left, looking disappointed.

Packing Vaughn's suitcase the day before he went off to the University of Michigan was another fond memory. She'd lovingly placed his new clothes in the suitcase that would accompany him on this first trip away from home. Although saddened by his departure, she took comfort in knowing he'd only be gone for a few years This wasn't a new experience, since Valerie had left four years earlier and was attending Oregon State. She was working part-time and seemed in no particular hurry to finish her education. Jerry and Hassie had been reassured by Vaughn's promise to return as a pharmacist himself. He shared their commitment to community and their belief in tradition.

Soon the kitchen table was littered with his letters home. The letter in which he first mentioned meeting Barbara had brought back memories of Hassie's own—like meeting Jerry at college just before the war. The day that letter arrived, she'd sat at the kitchen table with her husband and they'd held hands and reminisced about the early days of their own romance.

Then the unthinkable happened. News of a war in a country she'd barely heard of escalated daily. The papers, television and radio were filled with reports, despite President Johnson's promises to limit the United States' involvement. Then the day came when Vaughn phoned home and announced, like so many young men his age, that he'd been drafted. A numbness had spread from Hassie's hand and traveled up her arm. It didn't stop until it had reached her heart. Vaughn was going to war. Like his father before him, he would carry a rifle and see death.

This wasn't supposed to happen. For a while, men in college were exempt, but with the war's escalation, they were now included. Vaughn took the news well, but not Hassie. He had to do his part, he told her. It was too easy to pass the burden onto someone else. Citizenship came with a price tag.

Suddenly bombs were exploding all around her. Terrified, Hassie hid her head in her hands, certain she was about to die. Bullets whizzed past her and she gasped, her heart cramping with a terrible fear. All at once she was cold, colder than she could ever remember being, and then she was flat on her back with the sure knowledge that she'd been hit. The sky was an intense shade of blue, and she was simultaneously lying there and hovering far above. But when she looked down, it wasn't her face she saw. It was the face of her dying son. His blood drained out of him with unstoppable speed as the frantic medic worked over him.

Her son, the child of her heart, was dying. He saw her and tried to smile, to tell her it was all right, but his eyes closed and he was gone. Her baby was forever gone.

A crushing load of grief weighed on Hassie's heart. She cried out and, groaning, sat upright.

It was then she realized she'd fallen asleep. This had all been a dream. Awash with memories, she'd drifted into a dream so real she could hear the fading echoes of exploding ammunition as she dragged herself out of a past world and back to reality.

As her eyes adjusted to the dark, her gaze darted from one familiar object to another. From the bedroom door where her housecoat hung on a hook to the dresser top with the silver mirror and brush set Jerry had given her on their tenth anniversary.

"Vaughn." His name was a broken whisper, and she realized that she couldn't remember what he looked like. His face, so well loved, refused to come. Strain as she might, she couldn't see him. Panic descended, and she tossed aside the blankets and slid out of bed. It wasn't her son's image that filled her mind, but the face of another young man. Another Vaughn.

Vaughn Kyle.

"Of course," she whispered, clutching the bedpost. Leaning against it, she heaved a deep, quivering sigh and climbed back into bed.

Wrapping the quilt around her, she tucked her arm beneath her pillow and closed her eyes. Yes, it made sense that she'd dream of Vaughn that night. Her Vaughn. It also made sense that it was Vaughn Kyle's face she now saw. After all, she'd spent much of the day with him.

Barbara and Rick had done a good job raising him. Vaughn was a fine man, honest and genuine, sensitive yet forthright. She was grateful she'd had the opportunity to meet him before she died.

Giving him the gold watch had been a spur-of-the-moment decision. It was the one possession of Jerry's she'd held back from Valerie and her two granddaughters. Valerie lived in Hawaii and although they were close, they rarely visited each other. Hassie had flown to the island once, but all those tourists and hordes of people had made her nervous. Not only that, she wasn't comfortable in planes, and the long flight made her nervous. A few years back, after a scare with Hassie's heart, Valerie had flown out to spend time with her, but had soon grown bored and restless.

Hassie didn't think Val's daughters, Alison and Charlotte, would have much interest in their grandfather's watch. But it was precious to her, so she'd kept it.

She knew when she pressed the watch into Vaughn's palm that this was the right thing to do. He looked as if he was about to argue with her, but he didn't and she was glad. Still, his hesitation told her more clearly than any words that he understood the significance of her gift.

Warm once more, Hassie stretched out her legs, enjoying the feel of the sheets against her bare skin. She smiled, remembering the exchange she'd witnessed between Carrie and Vaughn Kyle last night. She hoped something came of it. After her divorce Carrie was understandably wary about relationships, but Hassie felt confident that Vaughn would never intentionally do anything to hurt her.

"Can't something be done?" Carrie asked, pacing in front of Heath Quantrill's polished wood desk. As the president of Buffalo Valley Bank, he just might know of some way to stop Value-X from moving into town. In the past day or so, news of the retailer's plans had spread through town faster than an August brushfire. Carrie had first heard of it that morning. She suspected Hassie knew and had been protecting her; she also suspected there'd been rumors last night, but she'd been too involved with Vaughn to notice.

Heath's frown darkened. It went without saying that he wasn't any happier about this than she was. "I'm sorry, Carrie, but Ambrose Kohn is a difficult man to deal with. The town council has spoken to him several times. Hassie tried and I did, too, but he isn't willing to listen."

"You knew before this morning?" she fired back. "Hassie, too?" That was what she thought—and it explained a great deal. Hassie just hadn't been herself lately, but every inquiry was met with denial.

Heath nodded.

"Doesn't Mr. Kohn realize what he's doing?" Carrie found it hard to believe he could be so callous toward the town.

"He knows all too well."

"People have a right to know that the entire future of our town is at risk." She could only imagine what would happen to her father's store if Value-X set up shop.

Heath obviously agreed with her. "Hassie suggested we keep this under wraps until after Christmas, and the rest of the council decided to go along with her. I don't know how the news leaked." He scowled and rolled his gold pen between flat palms.

Delaying the bad news changed nothing. This morning at breakfast her father had announced what he'd learned. He was already alternating between depression and panic. He'd heard it from Joanie Wyatt at the treelighting ceremony. The Wyatts had sent away for stock information, and Joanie had read over a prospectus; she'd seen that Buffalo Valley was listed as a possible expansion site. She'd immediately phoned Buffalo Bob, who'd reluctantly confirmed it.

"Nothing's been signed yet," Heath said, as though that should make her feel better. It didn't.

She glanced at her watch, wishing she had more time to get all this straight in her mind. Although she was eager to meet Vaughn at the Columbia Mall as promised, she wasn't in the mood for Christmas activities. Not with this Value-X problem hanging over all their heads.

"Have you talked to anyone at the corporate office?" she asked.

Heath nodded.

"They weren't interested in listening, were they?" Heath's disheartened look was answer enough. "It's *progress,* right?"

"Right," Heath muttered. "Listen, I've got a meeting in ten minutes. I'm sorry, Carrie. I know what this will mean for your father's business and Knight's Pharmacy, too. I'm doing the best I can."

"Can't you buy the property yourself?"

"I approached Kohn about that, but…"

"He won't sell it to you?" Carrie asked in an outraged voice.

"Let's say he'd love a bidding war—one I'd be sure to lose." Heath stood and retrieved his overcoat from a closet.

Her gaze pleaded with his. "You've *got* to find a way to keep Value-X out of Buffalo Valley."

"Kohn hasn't heard the last of this," Heath promised as he escorted her out of the bank.

Carrie accompanied him to his four-wheel-drive vehicle.

"Is there anything *I* can do?" she asked, feeling the need to act.

Heath shook his head as he opened his car door. "Don't worry, Carrie, this isn't over yet. Not by a long shot."

All Carrie could do was trust that, somehow or other, he'd convince Ambrose Kohn to be reasonable.

The drive into Grand Forks passed in a fog. Burdened by the news, Carrie was surprised when the two lanes widened to four as she reached the outskirts of the big city.

Vaughn was waiting for her inside the mall at a coffee shop they'd designated as their meeting place. He stood as she approached. She was struck again by what an attractive man he was. Her ex-husband had been attractive, too, but Alec's good looks had belied his selfish, arrogant nature. She'd learned, the hard way, that a handsome face proved nothing about the inner man. No, handsome is as handsome does, her grandma always said. Which made Vaughn Kyle very handsome, indeed.

He'd been so gentle and caring with Hassie. He'd spent time with her, listened to her talk about her son. Carrie marveled at his patience and his good humor and the respect he seemed to genuinely feel for Hassie and for the town. When he'd asked her to meet him in Grand Forks to help him finish his shopping, she'd agreed. It'd been a long, long time since a man had impressed her as much as Vaughn Kyle.

"Thanks for coming," he said now.

Although it was relatively early, the mall was already frantic. With exactly a week left before Christmas, the entire population of Grand Forks had apparently decided to cram itself inside.

"The only person I still need to buy for is my mother,"

he told her, looking around as though he already regretted this.

"What about perfume?" Carrie wasn't feeling too inspired, either.

"She's allergic to a lot of those scents."

"Okay, how about…" Carrie proceeded to rattle off several other suggestions, all of which he categorically dismissed for one reason or another.

"Do you have any more ideas?" he asked, looking desperate.

"Not yet, but we might stumble across something while we're here."

Vaughn sighed. "That doesn't sound promising." He glanced around. "How about if we find a quiet restaurant and discuss it over lunch?"

He didn't need to ask twice. She was as anxious to get away from the crowds as he was. They found an Italian place Joanie and Brandon Wyatt had once recommended and were seated almost immediately. Sitting at their table with its red-and-white-checkered tablecloth, Carrie could see why her friends liked it here. The casual atmosphere was perfect. If the food was half as good as the smells wafting from the kitchen, she was in for a treat.

Carrie quickly made her decision and closed the menu. Lowering her gaze, she pushed thoughts of Value-X from her mind for the umpteenth time. Her worries kept intruding on the pleasant day she was hoping to have.

"You'd better tell me," Vaughn said. His hand reached for hers and he gently squeezed it. "Something's wrong."

Apparently she hadn't done a very good job of hiding

her concerns. Rather than blurt everything out, she stared down at the tablecloth for a long moment.

"We learned this morning that Value-X is considering Buffalo Valley as a possible site," she finally said. "Apparently they've already negotiated for a piece of land. I don't need to tell you what that'll do to our community."

"It might be a good thing," he said slowly. "Try to think positive."

"If this is progress, we don't want anything to do with it," she muttered. Vaughn couldn't *possibly* understand. She was sorry she'd brought up the subject. "We happen to like our town just the way it is."

"It isn't that—"

"We're going to fight it," she said confidently.

"How?" Vaughn asked. "Isn't that a little like David fighting Goliath?"

"Perhaps, but like David, you can bet we aren't going to idly sit by and do nothing." Already plans had started to form in her mind. "Other communities have succeeded. We can, too."

"You're serious about this?"

"Damn straight I am."

"Don't you think you're overlooking the positive aspects of a company like Value-X opening a store in Buffalo Valley? They have a lot to offer."

Carrie glared at him. "You don't get it, do you?"

"I guess not. Help me understand." Vaughn leaned back in his chair, his expression serious.

"Value-X will ruin *everything*. We don't want it, we don't need it." Carrie struggled to keep her voice even.

Vaughn studied her. "I imagine you're a formidable opponent when you put your mind to something."

"It isn't only me," she told him. "The entire town is up in arms. We haven't come this far to let some heartless enterprise wipe out all our efforts."

Vaughn frowned. "Value-X will mean the end of Knight's Pharmacy, won't it?"

That was only the beginning as far as Carrie could tell. "And AceMan Hardware." She ran one finger across the tines of the fork. "The only business I can't see it affecting is the Buffalo Valley Quilting Company." Carrie shot him a look and wondered why she hadn't thought of this earlier. "That's it!"

"What is?"

"A quilt. It's the perfect Christmas gift for your mother."

Vaughn didn't appear convinced. "A quilt?"

"They're special. Hand-sewn, and you could go traditional or innovative."

"How much are they?"

"I don't know the full range of prices," she said, "but if the quilt is more than you want to spend, there're table runners and place mats and lap robes."

"Hmm." The idea seemed to take hold. "That does sound like a gift she'd enjoy."

"I'm sure she would," Carrie said. "I can't believe I didn't think of it earlier."

"So how do I go about this?"

"If you don't want to drive back to Buffalo Valley so soon, I could choose one for you," she offered.

"Perhaps Mom should pick it out herself."

"Great idea—and I know Hassie would love to see her."

"I think it would do my mother a world of good to renew her friendship with Hassie."

The waitress arrived and took their orders. Seafood linguine for her, lasagna for him. And a glass of red wine for each. "Hey, it's Christmas," Vaughn said with a grin.

He took his cell phone from his jacket and flipped it open. Within seconds, he had his mother on the line.

"What about tomorrow?" he asked, looking at Carrie.

"I'm sure that'll be fine."

"Hassie will be there, won't she?"

Carrie nodded. "She's scheduled to work in the morning, but she has the afternoon free. I'll cover for her, if need be."

He relayed the information to his mother, then ended the conversation and slid the phone back inside his jacket. Smiling at her, he said, "Thanks, Carrie."

A warm feeling came over her, and once again she lowered her gaze. Vaughn Kyle—kind to old women and a thoughtful son. He was exciting and he was interesting and he made her heart beat furiously. She could only regret that he was heading back to Seattle so soon after Christmas.

Four

"I suppose you heard," Hassie said when Leta Betts came bustling into the pharmacy late in the afternoon. The word about Value-X had filtered through Buffalo Valley, and the town was rife with speculation. Nearly everyone she knew had stopped by to talk it over with her, as though she had a solution to this perplexing problem.

"I don't like it," Leta muttered, walking behind the counter of the soda fountain and pulling out a well-used teapot. "Want me to make you a cup?"

"Please." Hassie had filled prescriptions all afternoon, between interruptions, and she was ready for a break. She'd known that Leta would come by at some point; fortunately, there was a lull just now, which made it a good time to talk to her dearest friend.

"Where's Carrie?" Leta found two mugs and set them on the counter.

"It's her day off."

"I heard she went to see Heath."

Hassie had heard about that, as well. Carrie had a good heart and cared about this community with the same intensity as Hassie did. Once Carrie received her Pharm.D., Hassie had planned to turn the business over to her. That was before the threat of Value-X, however. If that threat became a reality, Hassie couldn't sell the pharmacy, not in good conscience. In all likelihood the place would be out of business within a year after the big retailer moved in.

"It's a shame, you know," Leta murmured. She dragged a chair closer to the counter and perched on the seat. Leaning forward, she braced her elbows on the edge, sighing deeply. "Who'd have thought something like this would ever happen?"

Hassie shook her head helplessly. She'd worked so hard to save this town. And now, even if oblivion wasn't to be its fate, a corporation like Value-X could make Buffalo Valley unrecognizable, could turn it into something that bore no resemblance to the place it had been. The place it *should* be.

"What are we going to do?" Leta asked.

Hassie sat next to her and assumed the same slouched pose. Leta was her friend and employee, and there wasn't anything Hassie couldn't tell her. But this situation with the conglomerate had her poleaxed. She was at her wit's end. "I don't know," she admitted.

"We'll think of something," Leta insisted, and poured tea into the mugs. She set one in front of Hassie and then added a teaspoon of sugar to her own.

"Not this time," Hassie said as she reached for the mug, letting it warm her hands. She was too old and too tired. A few years back she'd fought for her town with determination and ingenuity, but this new war would have to be waged by someone else. She'd done her part.

"This was how we both felt when we learned Lindsay had decided to return to Atlanta, remember?" Leta prodded.

As though Hassie would ever forget. At the last minute Leta's son, Gage, had realized he'd be making the worst mistake of his life if he let Lindsay leave without telling her how much he loved her. As a result, Lindsay had not only stayed on as a high-school teacher, she'd married Gage. Leta was a grandmother twice over, thanks to the young couple.

"Value-X is too powerful for me." A bit of research had revealed that the retailer was accustomed to exactly this kind of local resistance. They had their battle plans worked out to the smallest detail. Hassie remembered from the television exposé that the company had a legal team, as well as public-relations people, all of them experts at squelching opposition. Hassie knew the town council couldn't afford any high-priced attorneys to plead their case. Even if they banded together, they were no match for the company's corporate attorneys. They were cutthroat, they'd seen it all, done it all. According to the documentary, they'd won in the majority of their cases. Like it or not, Value-X simply overran a community.

"We can't give up," Leta insisted. She glared at Hassie, as though waiting for some of the old fight to surface.

It wouldn't, though. Not anymore. Slowly Hassie lowered her gaze, refusing to meet her friend's eyes. "It's a lost cause," she murmured.

"This doesn't sound like you, Hassie."

"No," she agreed, glancing at her tired reflection in the mirror above the soda fountain, "but it won't matter that much if I lose the pharmacy."

Leta's jaw sagged open. "Wh-what—"

"I should've retired years ago. The only reason I held on as long as I did is the community needs a pharmacy and—"

"What about Carrie?"

Hassie had been so pleased and grateful when Carrie had come to work as an intern. This was what she'd always wanted for the pharmacy. Years ago she'd expected her son to take over, but Vietnam had robbed her of that dream. The hopelessness of the situation settled squarely over her heart.

"I'm sure Value-X will require a pharmacist. Carrie can apply there."

Silent, Leta stared into the distance.

"I'm tired," Hassie said. "Valerie's been after me to retire, move to Hawaii.... Maybe I should."

"You in Hawaii? Never!" Leta shook her head fiercely. "I've always followed your lead—we all have. I don't know what would've become of us if not for you."

"Fiddlesticks." Hassie forced a laugh. "Value-X is coming to town, and that's all there is to it. We might as well accept the inevitable. Not long from now, both of us will be shopping there and wondering how we ever lived without such a store in town."

"You're probably right," Leta returned, but her words rang false.

"Let's just enjoy Christmas," Hassie suggested, gesturing at the garlands strung from the old-fashioned ceiling lights. "What are your plans?"

"Kevin won't be home, but he'll call from Paris on Christmas Eve. Gage and Lindsay invited me to spend Christmas Day with them." Hassie knew that Leta would take delight in spoiling four-year-old Joy and two-year-old Madeline.

"Bob and Merrily invited me over in the morning to open gifts with them and Bobby," Hassie told her friend. They thought of her as Bobby's unofficial grandmother. Early in their marriage, Bob and Merrily had lost a son— although not to death. They'd fostered a child from an abusive environment and had wanted to adopt him, but in the end, the California authorities had seen fit to place the boy with another family. It'd been a difficult time for the couple. Having lost a son herself, Hassie had understood their grief as only someone who'd walked that path could understand it. She'd tried to bring them comfort and the example of her endurance. Bob and Merrily never forgot her kindness, little as it was. Over the past few years, they'd become as close to her as family.

"You finally met Vaughn Kyle," Leta said. "That's definitely a highlight of this Christmas season."

"Yes," Hassie agreed, somewhat cheered. It'd been an unanticipated pleasure, one she'd always remember. In the hours they'd spent with each other, she'd forged a bond with the young man. Meeting Vaughn had left Hassie feeling closer to her own son, although he'd been dead for thirty-three years. Hard to believe so much time had passed since his death….

"That was him with Carrie at the tree-lighting ceremony, wasn't it?"

Hassie felt a small, sudden joy, sending a ray of light

into the gloom she'd experienced earlier. "She's spending the afternoon with him in Grand Forks."

"It's time she put the divorce behind her."

Hassie felt the same way but didn't comment.

"Do you think something might come of it?" Leta asked, her voice slightly raised.

Hassie couldn't answer. Her hours with Vaughn had been taken up with the past, and she hadn't discovered much at all about his future plans. She knew he'd been honorably discharged from the military and had accepted a position with a Seattle-based company, although he'd never said which one. Probably a big software firm, she decided. From what she understood, he'd be starting work after the first of the year. She felt it was a good sign that he'd come to spend two weeks with his parents.

"He's been to town twice already," Leta offered. "That's encouraging, don't you think?"

"I suppose."

A small smile quivered at the edges of Leta's mouth. "I remember when Gage first got interested in Lindsay. That boy drummed up a hundred excuses to drive into town."

"Remember Jeb and Maddy?" Hassie murmured, her eyes flashing with the memory. These were the thoughts she preferred to cling to. Stories with happy resolutions. Good things happening to good people.

Leta's responding grin brightened her face. "I'm not likely to forget. We hadn't seen hide nor hair of him in months."

"Years," Hassie corrected. Following the farming accident that cost Jeb McKenna his leg, the farmer-turned-buffalo-rancher became a recluse. Hassie recalled the days

Joshua had to practically drag his son into town for Christmas dinner. Then Maddy Washburn bought the grocery and started her delivery service. After those two were trapped together in a blizzard, why, there was no counting the number of times Jeb showed up in Buffalo Valley.

"Do you remember the day Margaret Eilers stormed into town and yanked Matt out of Buffalo Bob's?" Leta asked, laughing outright.

"Sure do. She nearly beat him to a pulp." Tears of laughter filled Hassie's eyes. "Can't say I blame her. Those two certainly had their troubles."

Margaret had set her sights on Matt Eilers and wanted him in the worst way, faults and all. That was what she got, too. Not three months after they were married, Margaret found out that Matt had gotten a cocktail waitress pregnant. Granted, it had happened *before* the marriage, but Margaret had still felt angry and betrayed.

"Look at them now," Leta said, sobering. "I don't know any couple more in love." She drank a sip of her tea. "If Margaret and Matt can overcome their problems, why can't Buffalo Valley sort out this thing with Value-X?"

For the first time all week, Hassie felt hopeful. "Maybe you're right, Leta. Maybe you're right."

Carrie sat down at the kitchen table and reached for the cream, adding it to her coffee. Even though she was twenty-seven years old, she found it comforting to watch her mother stir up a batch of gingerbread cookies. The house was redolent with the scent of cinnamon and other spices.

Her morning had been busy. After a lengthy conversation with Lindsay Sinclair, who'd been in contact with the Value-X corporate offices, Carrie had spent an hour on the Internet learning what she could about the big retailer.

"Did you have a good time yesterday afternoon?" Diane Hendrickson asked. She set the mixing bowl in the refrigerator, then joined Carrie at the table.

"I had a *wonderful* time." She was surprised to realize how much she meant that. Lowering her eyes momentarily, she looked back up. "I told Vaughn about Alec."

Her mother held her gaze. Carrie didn't often speak of her failed marriage, especially not to new acquaintances.

"It came up naturally, and for the first time I didn't feel that terrible sense of...of defeat. I don't think I'll ever be the same person again, but after talking to Vaughn, I knew I don't want to be."

Her mother smiled softly. "There was nothing wrong with you, Carrie."

"That's true, Mom, but I was at fault, too. I suspected Alec was involved with someone else. I simply preferred not to *face* it. The evidence was right in front of my eyes months before he told me. I don't ever again want to be the kind of woman who ignores the truth."

"You've never—"

"Oh, Mom," she said, loving her mother all the more for her unwavering loyalty. "It's time to move forward."

"With Vaughn Kyle?"

Carrie had thought of little else in the past three days. "Too soon to tell."

"But you like him?" her mother pressed.

She nodded. "I do." It felt good to admit it. Good to think that her life wouldn't be forever weighed down by

a mistake she'd made when she was too young to understand that her marriage was doomed. Her husband's betrayal had blindsided her. Outwardly she'd picked up the
pieces of her shattered pride and continued her life, but in
her heart, Carrie had never completely recovered. Alec
had shattered her self-esteem. Somehow she'd convinced
herself that there must've been something lacking in *her;*
it'd taken her a long time to realize the lack had been his.

Carrie drank the rest of her coffee and placed the cup
in the sink. "We spoke about Value-X, too, Vaughn and
I. At first he didn't seem to see how a company like that
would hurt Buffalo Valley. In fact, he felt it might even
have a positive effect. If so, I don't see one. But he let me
vent my frustrations and helped me clarify my thinking."

"Will you be seeing him again?" her mother asked innocently enough.

"Most likely. He's bringing his mother into town this
morning. He's buying her one of Sarah's quilts for Christmas and thought she'd like to choose it herself."

"What a thoughtful gift."

Carrie didn't mention that she'd been the one to suggest
it. "They're meeting Hassie later." They hadn't made any
definite plans, but Carrie hoped to meet Vaughn's mother.
She was almost sure he'd stop by, either here or at the store;
in fact, she was counting on it.

The doorbell chimed right then, and fingers crossed,
Carrie decided it had to be Vaughn. Her mother went to
answer the door.

"Carrie," she called from the living room, "you have
a visitor."

"I hope you don't mind me dropping by unexpectedly," he was saying to her mother when Carrie walked in. Vaughn stood awkwardly near the door. He removed his gloves and stuffed them in his pockets.

"Hello, Vaughn." Carrie didn't bother to disguise her pleasure at seeing him again.

"Hi." He looked directly into her eyes. "Would you be free to meet my mother? I left her a few moments ago, drooling over Sarah's quilts."

"I'd like that." Carrie reached into the hall closet for her coat and scarf. "What did you think of the quilts?" she asked, buttoning her coat. She wanted him to appreciate Sarah's talent.

"They're incredible. You're right, it's the perfect gift for Mom."

Carrie supposed she had no business feeling proud; the quilt shop wasn't hers and she had nothing to do with it. But everyone in Buffalo Valley took pride in Sarah's accomplishments. It was more than the fact that Sarah had started the company in her father's living room. People viewed her success as a reflection of what had happened to the town itself—the gradual change from obscurity and scant survival to prosperity and acclaim. Her struggles were their own, and by the same token, her successes were a reason to celebrate.

"I wanted you to know how much I enjoyed our time together yesterday," Vaughn said, matching his steps to hers as they took a shortcut through the park. "I appreciate the suggestion about the quilt. And I learned a lot about you—and Buffalo Valley. You helped me see the town in an entirely different way."

"I was grateful you let me talk out my feelings about Value-X…and everything else."

Vaughn's arm came around her and he briefly squeezed her shoulder. There was no need to refer to the divorce. He understood what she meant.

"I talked to Lindsay Sinclair earlier," Carrie said, changing the subject. "She phoned the corporate office and asked if the rumors are true."

"I thought you said they were negotiating for property."

"That's what I told Lindsay, but she doesn't trust Ambrose Kohn. She said she wouldn't put it past him to let people *think* Value-X was interested in the property so Heath or someone else would leap forward and offer to buy it. He's not exactly the kind of person to generate a lot of trust."

"What did your friend find out when she talked to the corporate people?"

"First they said they didn't want to comment on their plans, but when Lindsay pressed the spokeswoman, she admitted that Buffalo Valley's definitely under consideration." Carrie's shoulders tensed. "Lindsay took the opportunity to let her know they aren't welcome in Buffalo Valley." When she'd heard about that part of the conversation, Carrie had cheered.

"What did the company spokeswoman say then?"

Carrie laughed. "Apparently Value-X's official response is that according to their studies, a growing community such as Buffalo Valley doesn't have enough retail choices."

Vaughn snorted.

"That's what I thought. They're sending a representative after Christmas. This person is supposed to win us over and show us everything Value-X can do for Buffalo Valley." She couldn't keep the sarcasm out of her voice.

"It wouldn't hurt to listen," he said mildly.

Carrie whirled on him. "We'll listen, but having a huge chain store in town is *not* what we want. Joanie Wyatt's already started a petition, so when the company representative arrives, he or she will be met with the signature of every single person in town."

Vaughn said nothing.

"What Value-X doesn't understand is that Buffalo Valley is a small town with small-town values and that's exactly the way we want to keep it. If they move in, they'll ruin everything that makes us who we are."

Vaughn stopped in front of a picnic bench, cleared away the snow with his arm and sat down. "What about jobs? Value-X will offer a lot of opportunity to young people. I've heard repeatedly that farming communities are seeing their young adults move away because of the lack of financial security."

"That's not necessarily true, the part about Value-X bringing jobs. After I talked to Lindsay, I got on the Internet and did some research myself. I learned that most of the positions Value-X brings into a town are part-time and low-paying. They offer few benefits to their employees. The worst aspect is that they destroy more jobs than they create."

Vaughn's frown deepened.

"I apologize," she said. "I didn't mean to get carried away about our problems with Value-X."

Standing, Vaughn still seemed deep in thought. "No, I want to hear this. It bothers me that the company isn't listening to your concerns."

"They don't *want* to listen."

"But you said they're sending a representative."

"Right," she said with a snicker. "To talk to us, not to listen. They're under the mistaken impression that we'll be swayed by a few promises and slick words. They've decided we need to think bigger and bolder and stop acting like a small town."

"But Buffalo Valley *is* a small town."

Carrie gave a sharp nod. "Exactly."

As they approached the Buffalo Valley Quilting Compay, Carrie noticed the middle-aged woman standing inside by the window, looking out into the street. When Vaughn and Carrie appeared, she smiled and waved, then pointed to the quilt on display.

Carrie waved back, silently applauding his mother's choice.

Mrs. Kyle smiled. Her eyes moved to her son and then to Carrie; her expression grew quizzical. Carrie didn't have time to guess what that meant before Mrs. Kyle opened the glass door, stepped out and introduced herself.

Barbara Kyle knew that when she agreed to accompany Vaughn into Buffalo Valley, she'd be seeing Hassie Knight. A meeting was inevitable. They hadn't been together since the day they'd stood in the pouring rain as a military casket was lowered into the ground.

Following the funeral, she'd kept in touch with Vaughn's mother. They'd called each other frequently. But despite the war, despite her grief, Barbara's college courses had continued, and she'd had to immerse herself in a very different kind of reality.

Rick had lost his best friend, and they began to seek solace from each other. Falling in love with him was a surprise. Barbara hadn't expected that, hadn't thought it was possible to love again after losing Vaughn. Rick wasn't a replacement. No one could ever replace the man she'd loved. He understood, because in his own way he'd loved Vaughn, too.

When they announced their engagement, Hassie had pulled away from Barbara. Neither spoke of it, but they both knew that their relationship had fundamentally changed and that their former closeness could no longer exist. Vaughn's parents didn't attend the wedding, although they'd mailed a card and sent a generous check.

Barbara thought now that naming their son after Vaughn Knight had as much to do with Hassie as it did with their feelings for Vaughn. Perhaps she'd hoped to bridge the distance between them....

Until he was twenty-one, Hassie had remembered Vaughn Kyle every year on his birthday, but that was the only time Barbara and Rick heard from her. When Rick accepted early retirement and they'd decided to move back to North Dakota, Barbara recognized that, sooner or later, she'd see Hassie again. A month or so after they'd moved, Hassie had welcomed them with a brief note. It seemed fitting that Barbara's son had been the one to arrange this meeting, to bring them together again.

"Hassie wanted me to bring you to the house, instead of the pharmacy," Vaughn said as they left the quilting store.

"You're coming with us, aren't you?" Barbara asked Carrie. She'd quickly grasped that Vaughn was attracted to this woman, and she could understand why. However, she didn't pretend to know what was happening. Natalie had phoned several times, wanting to speak to Vaughn; she wasn't amused that he'd apparently turned off his cell phone. Barbara didn't feel it was her place to inform the other woman that Vaughn was out with someone else. The situation concerned her, but she couldn't interfere and had to trust that he was treating both women with honesty and fairness.

"I'd love to come to Hassie's with you," Carrie told them, "but I said I'd fill in at the store for her. You two go and have a good visit, and I'll see you later."

As they crossed the street, Carrie headed toward the pharmacy, and Barbara and Vaughn went in the opposite direction.

"Does the pharmacy still have the soda fountain?" Barbara asked her son.

"Sure does. In fact, I thought I'd leave you and Hassie to visit, and I'd steal away to Knight's to let Carrie fix me a soda."

"You're spending a lot of time with her, aren't you?" Barbara couldn't resist asking.

"Am I?"

Barbara didn't answer him. There was probably some perfect maternal response, but darned if she knew what it was.

Hassie's house came into view, and Barbara automatically slowed her pace. It'd been thirty-three years since she'd walked up these steps. Thirty-three years since she'd attended the wake, sat in a corner of the living room with Vaughn's older sister and wept bitter tears. At the end of a day that had been too long for all of them, Vaughn's mother had hugged her close and then instructed a family friend to make sure Barbara got safely home to Grand Forks.

"Mom?" Vaughn studied her and seemed to sense that something was wrong.

"It's all right," she said. Funny how quickly those old emotions resurfaced. Her stomach churned as if it'd been only a few months since she'd last walked this path. But thirty-three years, a lifetime, had passed.

Hassie opened the door before Barbara could ring the bell. They stood there for a moment, gazing into each other's eyes

Hassie smiled then, a welcoming smile that seemed to reach deep inside her with its warmth and generosity. "Barbara," the older woman said, flinging open the screen door.

When she'd entered the house, Hassie hugged her for long minutes, and Barbara felt the tears gather in her eyes.

"I'm so glad you came." Hassie finally released her and embraced Vaughn, who stood quietly behind his mother. "I assume Vaughn told you about our visit?"

"Yes, he did. I can't tell you how honored we all are that you'd give him Mr. Knight's gold watch."

"It seemed right that he have it." She took Barbara's coat and hung it in the hall closet. "I won't take yours," she said to Vaughn, her back to them both. "You're probably planning to sneak over to the shop for a soda."

"How'd you guess?"

"I was young once myself," Hassie said, and shooed him out the door.

"Carrie's a wonderful young woman," Hassie told her as soon as Vaughn had left.

"They certainly seem to have taken a liking to one another," Barbara said noncommittally. She liked what she'd seen of Carrie—but what about Natalie? Well, that was Vaughn's business, she reminded herself again.

Hassie led her into the living room. "I hope you don't mind, but I've already poured the tea."

"Not at all."

The silver service was set up on the coffee table and two delicate china cups were neatly positioned, steam rising from the recently poured tea. A plate of cookies had been placed nearby.

"I don't often get an excuse to use my good tea service and china these days," Hassie murmured.

The two women sat side by side on the dark-blue sofa and sipped their tea. Neither really knew where to start, Barbara reflected. She took a deep breath.

"I've thought of you often," she said. "Especially since you were so generous with our son."

"He must have thought me a silly old woman, writing him little tidbits of advice."

"Hassie," Barbara said, and touched Hassie's forearm. "*No one* could think that." She shook her head. "He saved every birthday card you ever sent him. And he remembered what you wrote. He grew up honorable and generous, and I can't help thinking you played a part in that."

Hassie smiled her appreciation. "Nonsense, but it's very kind of you to say so."

Barbara glanced around the room. "Being here brings back so many memories," she said. The house, this room, was exactly as she remembered. She suspected that even after all these years, Vaughn's bedroom was virtually untouched. She remembered the high-school banner he had pinned to the wall and the bedroom set, old-fashioned even then. Valerie's old room was probably the same as it had been, as well, just like the rest of this house.

Hassie didn't comment, and Barbara sensed that the older woman had hung on to the past as much as she could and found comfort in what was familiar. Hassie's strength was considerable, but her loss had been too great. *Losses,* Barbara recalled. Jerry had died not long afterward, and Valerie had moved to Hawaii.

"Do you like living in Grand Forks?" Hassie asked, turning away from reminders of grief.

"Very much. My parents leased out the house when they moved to Arizona. Rick and I always intended to move here one day, and I'm really happy we did. This will be our first Christmas in North Dakota since Vaughn was five or six."

"With family again."

"Actually, there'll only be Rick, Vaughn and me. All my family has moved away, and Gloria, our daughter, lives in Dallas."

"Have Christmas here with me," Hassie urged, and then as if she regretted the impulse, she shook her head. "No, please forget I asked. I'm sorry to impose. It's just the rambling of an old woman."

"Hassie, if you're serious, we'd love nothing better than to spend the day with you."

Hassie's eyes shone. "You mean you'd actually consider coming?"

"We'd be honored. I know Rick would love to see you again. He wanted to join me today, but he was already committed to something else—some volunteer work he's doing."

"You're sure about Christmas?"

"Very sure," Barbara insisted. "But I can't allow you to do all the cooking."

"Oh," Hassie said, "it's no problem. I'd enjoy preparing my favorite recipes."

"We'll share the meal preparation, then," Barbara compromised, and Hassie aggreed.

"We'll be having Christmas dinner," Barbara murmured, "with a dear, dear friend."

"I can't think of anything I'd enjoy more."

Barbara couldn't, either.

Five

Carrie found Leta tending Knight's Pharmacy when she arrived after saying goodbye to Vaughn and his mother.

"Thanks for filling in for me," she said, hurrying to the back of the store. She stored her coat and purse and pulled on her white jacket.

"I don't mind staying," Leta told her. "In fact, Hassie asked me if I would. She thought you and Vaughn might like a few hours together." Leta wiped down the counter, and Carrie noticed how the other woman's eyes managed to evade hers.

"Aren't you two being just a little obvious?" she teased.

"Perhaps," Leta said, "but we both think it's high time you got into circulation again."

"Like a library book?" Carrie said with a grin. "I've been on the shelf too long?"

"Laugh if you want, but it's true. You've been avoiding a social life. That's not good for a woman of your age."

Carrie was about to explain that, while she appreciated

their efforts, she'd already spent time with Vaughn. Before she could, though, the bell above the door chimed, and Lindsay Sinclair and her two daughters stepped into the warmth of the pharmacy.

"Grandma." Four-year-old Joy ran toward Leta, who scooped the girl up in her arms for an enthusiastic hug.

"I've had the most incredible morning," Lindsay announced.

"Value-X?" Carrie asked.

Lindsay nodded. "The spokeswoman actually phoned me back."

"She called you?" Leta asked, voice incredulous, as she set Joy back on the floor.

"Yes, and for some reason, she seemed to view me as a contact who represented the community. That's fine, since everyone in town shares my opinion." Lindsay removed her hat and shook out her hair. "She wanted me to understand that Value-X intends to be a good neighbor, quote, unquote."

"Yeah, right!" Carrie muttered sarcastically.

"I'll just bet," Leta added. "They assume we're nothing but a bunch of dumb hicks."

"To be fair," Lindsay said, glancing between the other two women, "we don't know *what* they think of us—not that we have any interest in their opinion. But we are fully capable of mounting a campaign to keep them out."

"I was thinking the same thing," Carrie said.

"Organization is the key," Leta put in.

"You'll be at the Cookie Exchange tonight, won't you?" Lindsay asked Carrie. "I know Leta will." She smiled at her mother-in-law. "I thought that would be the best time to get all the women together. We can talk then."

"Good idea. Mom and I will be there for sure." The women's group at the church held the cookie exchange every Christmas. Joyce Dawson, the pastor's wife, had been instrumental in organizing the event, and every woman in town and the surrounding community could be counted on to attend.

"Value-X won't know what hit them," Leta said happily.

The bell chimed a second time, and Vaughn entered the store. For a moment, he seemed startled to see the three women, but then his gaze sought out Carrie's. "Should I come back later?"

"Not at all," Leta said. "There's no need for Carrie to work today. I've got everything covered."

Carrie was grateful for what her friends were trying to do, but she did have responsibilities. Leta seemed to read her thoughts. "If any prescriptions get phoned in, I'll find you," she promised. "I'll leave a message with your mom."

"Ever hear the expression about not looking a gift horse in the mouth?" Lindsay whispered.

"Well, it appears I'm not wanted or needed around here," Carrie said before Leta and Hassie's intentions became any plainer than they already were. She walked past Lindsay, who winked at her. After collecting her coat and purse, Carrie left with Vaughn.

"Where would you like to go?" he asked as soon as they were outside.

She hadn't had lunch yet and suspected Vaughn hadn't, either. "I know we had Italian yesterday, but I love pizza."

"Me, too."

"Buffalo Valley has some of the best homemade pizza you'll ever eat."

He lifted his eyebrows. "Sounds good to me."

They started down the street, their pace relaxed. Snow had just begun to fall, drifting earthward in large, soft flakes. Christmas-card snow, Carrie thought. As they walked, she told him the story about Rachel's pizza, and how it had led to her restaurant and subsequent success.

"You mean she makes the sauce herself?"

Carrie nodded. "I worked for Rachel one summer and I watched her make a batch. She starts with fresh tomatoes straight from her garden. It's amazingly good. I think she could sell her recipe, but of course, she doesn't want to."

A pickup approached and slowed as it came alongside Vaughn and Carrie. Glancing over her shoulder, Carrie saw her two older brothers, Tom and Pete. She tried to ignore them, but that was impossible.

"Hey, Carrie," Tom called, leaning his elbow out the open passenger window.

She acknowledged his greeting with a short wave, hoping he'd simply move on. Not that this was likely. Apparently Chuck and Ken had mentioned Vaughn, and now they, too, were looking for an introduction.

"Don't you want us to meet your friend?"

"Not right now," she called back, and sent Vaughn an apologetic glance. Because she was the only girl, all four of her brothers were protective of her, even more so after her divorce.

"You ashamed of your family?" This came from Pete, who was driving.

Carrie sighed, praying that her brothers wouldn't say

or do anything to further embarrass her. Pete parked the truck and both men climbed out, slamming their doors extra hard. Both wore thick winter coats and wool caps with the earflaps dangling. They were large men and did their best to appear intimidating.

She made the introductions, gesturing weakly toward her brothers. Vaughn stepped forward and shook hands with both of them.

"Nice to finally meet you," Tom said, resting his foot on the truck's bumper. "Now I'd like to know what your intentions are toward my sister."

"Tom!" Furious, Carrie clenched her fists. "This is *none* of your business."

"The day you stop being my sister is the day I stop caring who you date."

"Well…" Vaughn clearly had no idea what to say.

Her brothers putting him on the spot like this was outrageous. Picking up a handful of snow, Carrie immediately formed a ball and threw it at her oldest brother, hitting him square in the chest. Not waiting for his reaction, Carrie grabbed Vaughn's arm and shouted, "Run!"

"You asked for this, Carrie Ann," Tom shouted as Carrie and Vaughn raced across the street. They had just entered the park when Carrie felt her backside pelted by two snowballs.

"This is war," Vaughn yelled when he saw that she'd been hit. He leaned down and packed his own snow, then hurled two balls in quick succession, hitting both Pete and Tom. Her brothers reacted with stunned surprise.

Laughing and dodging around the play equipment with her brothers in hot pursuit, Carrie had trouble keeping pace with Vaughn. He yelled instructions and pointed toward the back of Hamburger Heaven. The stand was closed for the winter and offered ample protection, but a few moments later, her brothers found them and began to bombard them with a flurry of snowballs. Although most of them hit the side of the building, it was obvious that Vaughn and Carrie couldn't stay there long.

"You ready to surrender yet?" Pete demanded.

"Never," Vaughn answered for them.

"This way," Carrie told him. With the community Christmas tree blocking their movements, she led him across the street. Hidden by a loaded hay truck that passed behind them, Carrie steered him toward her parents' store.

"This is what I'd consider enemy territory," Vaughn whispered as they slipped behind the building and out of view.

"But it's the last place they'll look," she assured him.

"Smart thinking." Vaughn beamed her a delighted smile.

She smiled back—and realized she hadn't felt this kind of pure, uninhibited pleasure in...years. Since childhood, probably. When she didn't break eye contact and started to laugh, he said, "What?"

She shook her head, not wanting to put into words the joy she felt.

A sound startled them both, and they froze. Carrie was certain her brothers had found them again, but if it *was* Pete and Tom, they left without searching farther.

Relieved, Carrie sighed and slumped against the wall. "I believe we're safe for the moment. Are you still interested in that pizza?"

Vaughn nodded, but she saw a strange expression in his

eyes as he continued to gaze down at her. Carrie tried to look away and couldn't. She knew he intended to kiss her, and she shut her eyes as he moved closer. She'd been waiting for this moment, anticipating it. Wrapping her arms around his neck, she leaned into him. He drew off his gloves and then her wool hat and dropped them. Weaving his hands into her hair, he kissed her...and deepened the kiss until they were both breathless. Carrie trembled and buried her face in his shoulder. Neither spoke. As he held her tight, it seemed for those few moments that their hearts beat in unison.

He kissed her again, his mouth both firm and soft. When he eased away, Carried noticed that his brow had furrowed, and she thought she read doubt in his eyes. Uncertainty. She touched his face, wondering at the confusion she saw in him. "Is anything wrong?" she asked.

He answered with a quick shake of his head. "Everything is right."

And yet he sounded reluctant. She wanted to ask him more, but he moved away from her and peeked around the back wall. "Do you think it's safe now?" he asked.

"It should be. Pete and Tom were just having fun with us."

"Protective older brothers."

"Exactly."

"I watched over Gloria, too," he said. "She's two years younger than me."

"Just imagine that four times over."

"I don't need to," Vaughn said, ostentatiously brushing evidence of the snow battle from his sleeves.

They didn't see Pete or Tom on their way over, so Carrie assumed they'd gone about their business. As she'd told Vaughn, it'd been all in fun and at least her brothers knew when to admit defeat.

Predictably enough, Vaughn raved about the pizza. In fact, he bought a second one to take home and reheat. When they'd eaten, they returned to Hassie's, where his mother had just finished her visit. All four of them walked to where Vaughn had parked the car outside Sarah's quilt store. When they reached it, Hassie and Barbara Kyle hugged for a long moment.

"Thank you for coming," Hassie said, dabbing at her eyes.

Carrie knew it had been an emotional visit for both women.

"No—thank *you* for...for being Hassie," Barbara said, and they hugged again. "I'll be in touch about Christmas."

Vaughn opened the car door for his mother and helped her inside, an old-fashioned courtesy that reminded Carrie of her father and uncles.

Carrie stood on the sidewalk next to Hassie as Vaughn placed his pizza carefully on the backseat.

"They're coming to spend Christmas with me," Hassie said. "I haven't looked forward to anything so much in years. It'll be like when the children were still home."

Carrie knew Hassie intended to spend Christmas morning with Bob and Merrily and little Bobby, but she'd turned down invitations from almost everyone in town for dinner. Carrie was relieved that Hassie wouldn't spend the afternoon alone—and she envied her Vaughn's company.

He climbed into the car beside his mother and started

the engine. Before he backed out of the parking space, his eyes met Carrie's. She raised her hand and he returned the gesture. She felt as if her heart was reaching out to him…and his to her.

Six

Hassie had been looking forward to this night. The Dawsons had moved to Buffalo Valley four years earlier; at that time the only church in town had been Catholic and was closed after Father McGrath's retirement. Then Reverend John Dawson and his wife had arrived.

What a blessing the couple had turned out to be! Joyce knew instinctively what to say to make people feel welcome. John's sermons were inspiring, and his advice was both sensitive and practical.

Her first Christmas in Buffalo Valley, Joyce had organized the Cookie Exchange, which had become a yearly event.

Hassie had baked oatmeal-cranberry cookies early that morning and set out a plate for her visit with Barbara. Both had gotten so involved in their conversation that they hadn't tasted a single one. Hassie shook her head, smiling. It was as though all those years of not seeing each other had simply vanished after their initial awkwardness had passed. The visit had gone by far too quickly; Barbara had to leave long before Hassie was ready. What amazed Hassie was that she'd found herself saying things she hadn't even realized she felt.

Her daughter's decision to live in Hawaii was one example. She'd never understood what had prompted Valerie's choice. Yes, there'd been a job offer, but Valerie had *pursued* that job. The fact was, she'd wanted to get as far away from North Dakota as she possibly could. Hassie understood this for the very first time.

When Barbara had inquired about Valerie, Hassie explained that her daughter had chosen to remove herself from the pain of losing her only brother and then her father. Never before had Hassie consciously acknowledged that. Yet the moment she said the words, she knew they were true.

Later that evening when Hassie got to the church for the Cookie Exchange, the place was blazing with light. Although she was twenty minutes early, the parking lot was already half-full. The first person she saw once she'd set her platter of cookies on the table was Calla Stern. Sarah's once-rebellious daughter had become a lovely young woman. She was in her junior year of college now, if Hassie recalled correctly, and there was talk of her applying for admission to law school. She attended the University of Chicago and shared an apartment nearby, but at heart Calla remained a small-town girl.

As soon as Calla saw Hassie, she broke off her conversation and hurried across the room, arms outstretched.

"When did you get home?" Hassie asked, hugging her close.

"This afternoon. Oh, Hassie, I just heard about Value-X. What are we going to do?"

"I don't know, Calla, and this might shock you all, but I've decided I'm too old to fight them."

Calla frowned.

"That's what Leta told us."

"We can't stand in the way of progress." *If progress it is.* Change, anyway. Perhaps if Hassie repeated that often enough, she might come to accept it. This wasn't what she wanted, but as she'd learned long ago, the world didn't revolve around what she assumed was best.

"Let's enjoy this evening," Hassie urged, "and put these worries behind us until the new year."

"I'll try," the girl promised.

"Good." Hassie slid her arm through Calla's. "Now tell me, are you still seeing Kevin?" Calla had been dating Leta's boy off and on since her last year of high school.

"Occasionally. He's so busy, and I'm in school most of the time. Anyway, with him in Paris for six months…"

"Calla would make a wonderful daughter-in-law," Leta said, joining them.

"Oh, you!" Calla hugged her tightly, laughing as Hassie seconded Leta's remark.

"Stop it, you two," the girl chided. "I'm dating someone else at the moment and so is Kevin. We're good friends, but that's all. For now, anyway."

"Damn," Leta muttered.

"Give them time," Hassie told her.

"Exactly," Calla said with a soft smile, and after kissing them both, added, "Now excuse me while I go mingle."

Hassie watched her leave. She thought Calla and Kevin

would eventually get married, but probably not for some years. Not until educations were completed and careers launched. Still, they understood each other and shared the experience of having grown up in Buffalo Valley.

No sooner had Calla wandered off than Maddy appeared with four-year-old Julianne. She was heavily pregnant with her third child, but she'd lost none of her composure or contentment.

"Maddy," Hassie said, pleased to see her. "Here, let me help you with all that." Maddy was juggling her coat and purse, plus a huge box of homemade cookies.

"Mommy, can I play with Joy?" Julianne asked, tugging at Maddy's sleeve.

"Yes, sweetheart, and tell Lindsay I'll be right there."

"Where's little Caleb?" Hassie asked.

"With his daddy. After all, this is a *girls'* night out," Maddy said. Hassie knew this third pregnancy was as unexpected as their first. With three babies in five years, Jeb and Maddy were sure to have their hands full for quite a while.

Jeb's mother must be looking down from heaven, mighty pleased with her son, Hassie mused. Thanks to Maddy, he'd gone from curmudgeonly recluse to good husband and proud father.

Hassie and Leta busied themselves arranging platters of cookies on the long tables. Joyce made several trips to the business office to run recipes off on the copier so they'd be available for whoever wanted them.

Margaret Eilers and her daughter, Hailey, were among the last to arrive. Hailey, at three, bore a strong resemblance to her father and to her brother, David. Looking at Margaret and the child, no one would guess she wasn't the girl's birth mother. Hassie had nothing but praise for the way Matt and Margaret had worked out the awkward situation involving their children.

In the beginning Hassie hadn't been keen on Matt Eilers. No one in town held a high opinion of the rancher. But Margaret had fallen hard for Matt; she wanted to marry him and nothing would change her mind. After Bernard died and left her the ranch, Matt started seeing more and more of her. A few months later, there was a wedding. Then, lo and behold, Margaret turned up pregnant—at the same time as that woman in Devils Lake.

The babies were born within a few weeks of each other, Hailey first and then little David. Hailey had been living with the couple for most of her three years. She was a darling little girl, which Hassie attributed primarily to the love and attention Margaret lavished on her.

The room rang with laughter and cheer, and Hassie basked in the sounds that ebbed and flowed around her. Her day had started early and been an emotional one. When she noticed chairs arranged along the wall, she slipped quietly off and sat down. A few minutes later Leta came to sit beside her.

"Just listen," Hassie said, closing her eyes.

"What am I supposed to be listening to?" Leta asked.

"The joy," Hassie told her. "The friendship. These women are the very breath of this community." Hassie was grateful she'd lived long enough to witness the town's reversal of fortunes. It was because of women like Lindsay and Rachel and Maddy and Sarah and Joanie Wyatt.... And maybe she herself had played a small part.

"What I can't get over is all the babies," Leta said. "Future generations for Buffalo Valley."

"Rachel Quantrill is pregnant again," Hassie said, nodding at the young woman on the other side of the room talking with Sarah. Hassie was particularly fond of Rachel. She'd watched the young widow struggle to get by after the death of her first husband. She'd driven a school bus and worked as a part-time bookkeeper for Hassie. Later she'd opened the pizza-delivery service. That was how she'd met Heath. New to the banking business, Heath had rejected her loan application. His grandmother, who'd started the bank, had been furious with him, Hassie recalled. But things had a way of working out for the best. Lily Quantrill had lived to see her grandson and Rachel marry. Rachel had brought a son into the marriage, and later she and Heath had a daughter they'd named after Lily. A third child was expected in early summer.

"I'll have to remember that," Hassie murmured absently.

Leta gave her a puzzled look. "What?"

Hassie wasn't aware she'd spoken aloud. "About things working out for the best." Despite her efforts, her thoughts had returned to Value-X and the potential for disaster. All her hopes for this town and the people she loved so dearly were at stake.

"You feeling all right?" Leta asked in a concerned tone.

"I'm fine," Hassie assured her. "Just tired. It's been a busy day."

Joyce Dawson sat down at the piano, and soon the room was filled with sweetly raised voices. The women and children gathered around, breaking naturally into two-part harmony. To Hassie it sounded as though the very angels from heaven were singing.

"Hassie—" Carrie Hendrickson crouched by her chair "—are you ill?"

Leta answered for her. "She's just tired."

"No wonder," Carrie murmured. "She was up before dawn baking cookies and then there was the visit from Barbara Kyle, plus a big order came in for the pharmacy."

Hassie grinned, amused that they spoke as if she wasn't even there.

"Let me walk you home," Carrie suggested, taking her hand.

"Fiddlesticks. I'm perfectly capable of walking back on my own. No need for you to leave the party."

"I insist," Carrie said. "It'll only take a few minutes and no one will miss me."

Hassie was weary, wearier than she cared to admit, so she agreed. Carrie retrieved their coats and led the way outside, sliding her arm through Hassie's to lend her support. They walked slowly, in companionable silence. The night sky was bright and clear, the stars scattered against it like diamonds. Most of the snow had been swept aside and the sidewalks salted.

As they crossed the street, a truck pulled up to the curb and rolled down the window. "You two need a ride?" Chuck Hendrickson asked.

"We're fine, thanks, anyway," Carrie told her brother.

"Say, that fellow you had dinner with phoned a few minutes ago."

"Must be Vaughn," Hassie said. It did seem that Carrie and Vaughn were seeing a lot of each other, and that pleased her. From now on, Hassie resolved to look only at the positive side of things. She refused to let herself fret over situations she couldn't control.

"I'll call him back once I'm finished over at the church," Carrie told her brother, who drove off.

"You could do worse, Carrie," Hassie said. "He's a fine man."

"I think so, too."

"Not every man is another Alec."

"I know," she said.

Hassie patted Carrie's hand. She would go home and think good thoughts for the young woman and for Buffalo Valley. Happy, positive thoughts.

"It's about time you called," Natalie snapped. There'd been no word of greeting.

Vaughn sat on the bed in his parents' guest room and pressed his cell phone to his ear. He felt guilty about not returning Natalie's repeated calls. He'd delayed it, needing to put his thoughts in order first. He felt guilty about other things, too, but he didn't want to think about Carrie, not when he had to deal with Natalie.

No one in Buffalo Valley knew he'd taken a job with Value-X. Not his parents. Not Hassie. And certainly not Carrie. His visit to North Dakota at a time when the company was considering an outlet in this area had seemed a fortuitous coincidence. Now it felt like the very opposite. He'd agreed to check out the town, but that had been a mistake he regretted heartily. And Natalie was hounding him for information.

"You're right, I should've phoned sooner," he admitted.

"Yes, you should have." Her voice softened. "I've missed hearing from you."

He didn't have an excuse to offer her, and the truth was...well, difficult to explain. Not only did he have serious doubts about working for this company, he'd met Carrie, and the attraction between them was undeniable.

Just a few days ago his future had seemed assured, but now, after meeting Hassie and Carrie, his entire sense of what was right had been challenged. And his assumptions about love and marriage, about Natalie—they'd changed, too.

Natalie's voice was hard when she spoke again. "I was beginning to wonder if I made a mistake recommending you for this position. I put my reputation on the line."

"I assumed I'd been hired on my own merits."

"You were but..." She sighed heavily. "Let's forget all that, shall we? I didn't know what to think when you didn't phone." She gave a stilted laugh. "I realize you're not officially on the payroll until January, but it's so advantageous for you to be near this little town."

"The town has a name."

"I know that," she said, and some of the stiffness returned to her voice. "I'm sorry, Vaughn, but I've had a trying day. Apparently Buffalo Valley is mounting opposition against Value-X."

"I know."

"You do?" She slowly released her breath. "You can't imagine how hectic everything is here, with the holidays and everything else. Now *this*. I spoke with a woman in town. I can't remember her name exactly. Lesley, Lindy..."

"Lindsay Sinclair."

"You know her?"

"I've met her."

"She made the town's position very clear," Natalie continued. "It seems we've got some public-relations work ahead of us. Okay, we can deal with that—we've done it before. We know how to present our case in a positive light. It won't take much to change their attitude, and really, at this point, they really don't have much choice."

Vaughn was sorry to hear that. So it was too late; Value-X had obviously succeeded in buying the property. This was what he'd feared. "Lindsay told me Value-X is sending someone out after Christmas."

"I volunteered for the job myself," she said, excited now. "It was providential, don't you think? I can meet your parents and settle this unfortunate matter with Buffalo Valley at the same time. Combine business with pleasure, in other words." She sounded pleased with herself for having so neatly arranged this trip. "I've got everything in motion for a Value-X campaign."

"I hope you'll be willing to listen to the town's concerns."

"Well, yes, of course I'll listen, but I'm hoping to present our case, too. In fact, I've already authorized a letter to be delivered to every family in Buffalo Valley. It's scheduled to arrive just after the first of the year."

"A letter?"

"Everyone thinks it's a great idea." Her satisfaction was unmistakable. "I wrote it myself for a personal touch. I want the town to understand that they've unfairly prejudged Value-X. I told them not to look at any negatives they might've heard about the company, but at the positives—everything we can do for their community. We plan to be a good neighbor."

Vaughn knew that Natalie's letter would most likely anger the people of Buffalo Valley, not reassure them. "I didn't realize you'd signed the deal on the land," he muttered. Without being completely aware of it, Vaughn had held out hope that the controversy would die a natural death if the land deal fell through. His heart sank. It looked as if he'd have no choice now but to get involved. The question was: on which side would he stand? If he followed his heart, he'd join Hassie and Carrie in their fight, but if he did that, he'd compromise his future with Value-X and Natalie...

Natalie hesitated before she answered. "There've been a few snags with the property deal. Mr. Kohn isn't an easy man to work with."

Vaughn's relief was swift. So there *was* hope. "That's what I hear about Ambrose Kohn."

"Have you met him?"

"No, he lives in Devils Lake. Listen, Natalie, I have to tell you I'm not convinced Buffalo Valley is a good site."

She laughed, but he could tell she wasn't amused. "You haven't even started work yet and you're already telling me my job?"

"*You* chose Buffalo Valley as a development site?"

"I sure did," she said smugly. "We did a study on small towns that have shown substantial growth over the last five years. Buffalo Valley is a perfect target area for retail expansion."

Vaughn's hand tightened around the telephone receiver. "They don't have enough retail choices," he muttered.

"Exactly." Apparently she hadn't noticed the sarcasm in his voice.

Vaughn felt tension creeping across his shoulders. He probably couldn't influence her to change her letter or withdraw it; he was in no position to tell Natalie news she didn't want to hear.

She returned to the subject of Ambrose Kohn. "I'm interested in what you know about him," she said.

"I don't know him, but I have heard about him." Vaughn didn't feel comfortable saying anything more than he already had. As it was, he felt traitor enough.

"He *will* sign, and soon." Natalie's confidence sounded unshakable. "The transaction is as good as done."

Vaughn rotated his neck in order to ease the tension.

"I know what's happened," she said, catching him by surprise. "You've seen this little town and now you have doubts that Value-X is doing the right thing."

It was as though she'd read his mind. He found himself nodding.

"You're confused," Natalie continued. "It happens to a lot of us when we first hire on with the company. Don't worry, it's something we all work through. Trust me, Vaughn, Value-X knows what it's doing."

"Buffalo Valley is afraid of losing its character."

"Every town is in the beginning. They get over it. Sooner or later, each town comes to realize that we know what's best for them. Buffalo Valley will, too."

This was worse than he'd thought. Vaughn rubbed his hand down his face. Still sitting on the edge of his bed, he tilted his head back to stare up at the ceiling. This was *really* bad.

Value-X had no intention of listening to the concerns of Buffalo Valley's citizens. In its arrogance, the retailer had decided on a course of action, one that reflected solely its own interests.

"I'm looking forward to seeing you," Natalie told him, lowering her voice seductively.

It was almost more than Vaughn could do to echo the sentiment.

When he finished the conversation, he returned to the kitchen to find his mother dishing up ice cream.

"You interested?" she asked, holding up the scoop.

"Sure, why not?" he muttered. He took a third bowl from the cupboard and handed it to his mother, who pried open the carton lid.

"Tell me more about Natalie," she said.

Vaughn didn't know what to say. "You'll meet her soon enough."

"She's joining us after Christmas, right?" She studied him hard, and Vaughn knew what she was thinking. He'd spent almost every day of the past week with Carrie. He was with one woman and had another waiting in the wings—that was how it looked. His mother's eyes filled with questions.

"Natalie is coming, then?" she repeated when he didn't answer.

"So it seems." He sighed. She'd show up even if he asked her to stay home. Value-X was paying for the trip.

"You don't sound too happy about it," his mother murmured, her eyes narrowed. "What about Carrie?"

"Mom…"

"I know, I know, but I can't help wondering if you're

really sure of what you want. I saw the look Carrie gave you as we left Buffalo Valley earlier today."

Vaughn frowned.

"She deserves your honesty."

He was in full agreement; he owed Carrie the truth, and not only about his relationship with Natalie. He had to tell her about Value-X.

As soon as his mother left the kitchen, Vaughn reached for the phone. Unfortunately Carrie wasn't home. He recalled now that she'd mentioned something about meeting with the church women's group, but that'd slipped his mind. He left a message with one of her brothers.

After that, he joined his parents in the living room. He settled on the sofa next to his mother and focused his attention on a television show about Christmas traditions around the world.

An hour later the phone pealed and his mother automatically rose to answer it. She returned almost immediately. "It's Carrie for you."

Vaughn went into the kitchen.

"Hi," she said excitedly when he picked up the receiver. "I just got back from the Cookie Exchange and got your message."

"How was it?"

"Great, as usual. There was a lot of talk about this Value-X problem. We're going to take active measures to keep the company out of town."

She'd given him the perfect lead. This was his chance to explain the whole confused mess. But Vaughn didn't. He couldn't, not over the phone. It was something that needed to be said face-to-face, he decided. Okay, so he was a coward.

Carrie seemed to be waiting for a response, so to keep the conversation going, he asked, "What can be done?"

"According to Hassie, nothing. She's afraid we can't win, especially after everything she's heard and read. According to all the news stories, the company practically always comes out on top. Still, there are a few towns that didn't give in, including one in Montana, I think." She paused. "Hassie's real problem is that she's just tired out. But I'm not, and neither are the rest of us."

Vaughn could hear the fighting spirit in her voice.

"I suggest you start with Ambrose Kohn." That was probably more than he should've said, but the words escaped before he could judge their wisdom.

"We're having an organizational meeting as soon as it can be arranged, and I'll recommend that."

"Great," he mumbled, wishing he could tell her he didn't want to hear any of this. It put him in a terrible position. He'd be a traitor to Value-X and Natalie if he withheld these facts, and a traitor to Carrie if he relayed them.

"...tomorrow night."

"I'm sorry," Vaughn said, trapped in his own dilemma. "What did you say?"

"Can you come? It's the high-school play. I know it doesn't sound like much, but we're all proud of it. The play's about the history of Buffalo Valley and the families that settled here. It'll give you a feel for the town."

Vaughn's own great-grandparents on his mother's side had settled in the Dakotas in the late 1800s. He pondered Carrie's words. Knowing more about the town's past might help him decide what to do about his relationship with Value-X—and Natalie. It was a faint hope—and maybe just another delaying tactic—but he had nothing else to cling to.

"Will you come as my guest?" she asked.

"I'll look forward to it."

She gave him the details and Vaughn hung up the phone feeling as vulnerable and unsure as ever.

"How'd it go?" his mother asked when he returned to the living room.

"Fine," he muttered. "Just fine."

Seven

The theater was filled to capacity. People crowded the aisle, chatting and visiting with one another. Carrie had been fortunate to get good seats for herself and Vaughn, thanks to Lindsay Sinclair.

"I didn't know there were this many people in Buffalo Valley," Vaughn said, twisting around to glance over his shoulder.

"There aren't. Folks come from all over. The Cowans drove down from Canada. Her great-grandmother is one of the main characters in the play."

Vaughn looked at his program. "So, Lindsay Sinclair is the producer and director of Dakota Christmas."

Carrie nodded. "Lindsay's the person responsible for all this," she said, gesturing toward her friend. "None of it would've happened without her."

Carrie went on to explain how the play had been created and described everything Lindsay had done to make sure it got performed. At the end of the story she told him that the theater belonged to Ambrose Kohn.

"*The* Ambrose Kohn?" Vaughn's brows arched.

"When Lindsay first arrived, the theater was nothing but cobwebs and dirt. She was a first-year teacher and one of the stipulations when she accepted the job was that the community would pitch in and help."

"In what way?"

"In whatever way she required. She asked the town's older people to talk to the kids. It started with Joshua McKenna. At the time he was president of the town council, plus he knows quite a bit of local history. After that, Lindsay lined up community representatives to come to the school on Friday afternoons. Joshua was the one who gave her the idea of having the kids write the play."

"The high-schoolers wrote the play?"

"The original script was created by the kids Lindsay taught six years ago. Each new group of students refines it a little bit."

"This is the sixth year?" He glanced around with what appeared to be renewed appreciation. "Pretty impressive audience."

"It's a fabulous play. Why else would so many people return year after year?"

"What's your favorite part?"

"I love all of it. There's a scene early on when a tornado hits the town and everything's destroyed. The people lose heart. Entire crops are wiped out and families are left homeless. You can just *feel* their agony." She didn't mean to get carried away, but no matter how often she'd seen it, the scene brought tears to Carrie's eyes.

"What happens then?" Vaughn asked.

"Everyone pulls together. The people whose fields were spared share their crops with the ones who lost everything. With everyone working together, they rebuild the farms destroyed in the tornado and save the town."

Vaughn nodded slowly. "Teamwork," he murmured.

"That was a message that really hit home for all of us. So many of the farmers continue to struggle financially. The play helped remind us that we need to work together. Then and now."

"Are you talking about Value-X?"

Carrie shook her head. "Not only Value-X. We have more problems than just that. As you probably know, farm prices are low and have been for years. Most folks around here feel that no one appreciates the contribution of the small farmer anymore. A lot of people were demoralized by what was happening."

"Is it better now?"

"Yes, but only because farmers in the area have banded together. They still aren't getting decent prices for their crops, but they've found ways around that."

Carrie looked away; she had to swallow the lump in her throat. Her own family had been forced off the farm. The land had produced record yields, and it still wasn't enough to make ends meet. After several years of dismal wheat prices, the family had realized the farm could no longer support them all. That was when her parents and younger brothers had moved into town.

This had happened shortly after she'd filed for divorce. At first it had seemed inevitable that they'd have to sell the land, but then her two older brothers had decided to lease it. Pete and Tom were married by this time, and along with their wives, they'd made the decision to stay.

Buffalo Valley had started to show signs of new life—with the reopening of the hotel and bar, as well as Rachel's pizza restaurant. And Lindsay, of course, had brought fresh hope to the community in so many ways....

Carrie's mother had come into a small inheritance, and her parents chose to invest it in a business. Buffalo Valley was badly in need of an all-purpose hardware store. Carrie's father felt confident that if people could shop locally, they would, so the family had risked everything with this venture. To date, it had been a wise choice, but now with the mega-chain threatening to swallow up smaller businesses, the Hendricksons were in grave danger of losing it all.

"The American farmer refuses to be discounted," Carrie said, clearing her throat. "When was the last time you purchased pasta?"

"Pasta? As in noodles?" Vaughn asked in a puzzled voice. "Not recently. What makes you ask?"

"Ever hear of Velma brand?"

"Can't say I have."

Carrie tucked her arm through his. "It's made with wheat grown right here in Buffalo Valley. Brandon Wyatt and Gage Sinclair are part of the program. A year ago they joined several other local farmers, including my brothers, and some not so local, and cut out the middleman."

"You mean a group of farmers decided to start their own pasta company?"

"That's exactly what I mean."

"Ingenious," Vaughn said. "Incredible. So that's what

you were talking about when you said they'd found ways around the poor prices."

"Yeah. There's often a solution—but sometimes you have to find it yourself."

"Carrie."

Carrie looked up to see Lindsay and Gage Sinclair standing in the aisle near them.

Carrie started to make the introductions, then remembered that Vaughn had met Lindsay in the pharmacy two days before.

"Vaughn, this is my husband, Gage," Lindsay said.

Vaughn stood and held out his hand to Gage. He and Carrie made their way into the aisle.

"I understand you're an Airborne Ranger," Gage said.

"Was," Vaughn corrected.

The two men began a conversation about military life, and Lindsay stepped closer to Carrie.

"Thanks for getting us such great seats," Carrie said. Lindsay was a substitute teacher now but still worked on the play every year.

"No problem." Lindsay glanced pointedly at Vaughn. "How's it going?"

Carrie didn't know how to answer. Her divorce had devastated her, and since then she'd thrown herself into her studies, forging ahead, insulating her heart. She'd been protecting herself from any risk of pain, but at the same time she'd eliminated any hope of finding love. Then Vaughn entered her life. His patience with Hassie had touched her. His willingness to hear her concerns about the changes that seemed to be coming to Buffalo Valley inspired her to fight for what she knew was right.

Carrie looked at Vaughn and sighed. "He gives me hope," she whispered.

"I remember the first time I saw Gage," Lindsay whispered back. "He looked at me and... I know it's a cliché, but it was as if someone had zapped me with an electrical jolt. I didn't even know this man's name and it was as though I'd *connected* with him."

The music started and Gage reached for Lindsay's hand. "We'd better find our seats."

Gage and Lindsay left, and Carrie and Vaughn returned to their own seats. No sooner had they settled in than the curtain went up.

Several times during the evening, Carrie caught Vaughn studying her. She felt his eyes on her, and when she turned to meet his gaze, he took her hand and entwined his fingers with hers. Carrie had the sensation that something was troubling him, but now wasn't the time to ask.

"Kids in high school actually wrote the play themselves?" Vaughn asked Carrie for the second time. He found it difficult to believe that a group of teenagers could have created and put on such a high-quality production. The acting was a bit amateurish, true, but the emotion and heart that went into each scene stirred him more than he would've thought possible.

After seeing the play, Vaughn realized he could no longer evade a decision regarding Value-X. Not after these vivid depictions of the struggles Buffalo Valley had faced. Through the years, bad weather and bouts of pestilence had plagued the land. The tales of the "dust bowl" years had given him a small taste of the hopelessness the farmers endured. The play ended with a farm family standing in the middle of a wheat field, their heads held high, their arms linked. Just thinking about that scene raised goose bumps on his arms.

"High-school kids," he repeated before Carrie could respond.

"It was as good as I said it was, don't you agree?"

Words fell short of describing the powerful sensation he'd experienced throughout the play.

"Would you like to come over to Buffalo Bob's for hot cider? A lot of folks do," Carrie said. "But I should warn you, Pete and Tom will be there."

Vaughn would enjoy going another round with Carrie's brothers, but unfortunately he had a long drive back to Grand Forks. "Another time," he told her. He wasn't in the mood to socialize.

As they stepped from the warmth of the theater into the cold night air, his breath became visible in foggy wisps. The cold seemed to press against him with an intensity he hadn't expected.

"Let me get you home," Vaughn said, placing his arm around her. He wasn't accustomed to cold so severe it made his lungs ache just to draw a breath.

Carrie wrapped her scarf more securely about her neck and pulled on her wool hat. Normally they would have walked the short distance, but not when the cold was so bitter, the wind so vicious.

Vaughn helped her into his rental car, then hurried around the front and climbed into the driver's seat.

Neither spoke as he drove the few short blocks to her family's home. Vaughn wondered if Carrie had realized no one would be there. The house was dark. Had he asked, she would've invited him inside, but he preferred talking to her there, in the dark.

"Carrie, listen, there's something I have to tell you." He stared straight ahead, unable to look at her.

"I know what you're going to say."

He jerked his gaze to hers. Her blue eyes were barely visible in the moonlight, but he saw enough to be aware that she only *thought* she knew.

"We've known each other a very short time," she said. "You'll be leaving soon."

"It doesn't have anything to do with you and me."

"Oh." He could hear her surprise and embarrassment. "I'm sorry. I didn't mean to speak out of turn."

"At the same time, it has *everything* to do with us," he said, and slid his arm around her neck and drew her to him. He breathed in her scent—clean and light and floral; he felt her body against him, softly yielding. After a moment of debating the wisdom of what he was about to do, he exhaled harshly.

"Vaughn, what is it?"

He didn't know where he'd find the courage to tell her. She raised her head to look at him, her eyes full of warmth and concern. Kissing her was wrong; he knew it even as he lowered his mouth to hers. He didn't care, he *had* to kiss her one last time before he was forced to watch the transformation that would come over her when she learned the truth. In a few seconds he was going to hurt and disillusion her.

His mouth was on hers with excitement, with need. The kiss was intense. Real. It seemed to him that the woman in his arms had flung open her life for him, and that thought left his senses reeling.

The guilt he felt was nearly overwhelming.

Her hat had fallen off, and Vaughn slipped his fingers into her hair. He held her close, refusing to release her. From the way she clung to him, she didn't want him to let her go.

"Tell me?" she pleaded.

"Carrie…" He shut his eyes and held his breath for a moment. "I came to Buffalo Valley for more reasons than you know."

"Hassie?"

"For Hassie, yes, but…I'd also been asked to check on something for a friend."

"Check on what?"

"The only way to say this is straight out. I work for Value-X."

Carrie froze. *"What?"* she asked, her voice confused. Uncomprehending.

"Value-X's corporate headquarters are in Seattle."

"I thought you were just discharged from the army."

"I was."

She pulled away from him and scraped the hair back from her face as though to see him more clearly. "I don't understand."

"I don't expect you to. I took a job with Value-X after my discharge."

"They sent you here?" Her back was stiff now, and she leaned away from him. A moment earlier she couldn't get close enough, and now she was as far from him as the confines of the vehicle would allow. "Are your parents involved in this?"

"No! They don't even know."

She shook her head over and over, raising both hands to her face. "I need to think," she said.

"I don't officially start with the company until January."

"You're a *spy*?"

"No. The vice president of new development asked me to check out the town. I was going to be in the area, anyway. It made perfect sense, and..."

"And so you did."

He couldn't very well deny it. "You have every right to be furious."

"You're damn straight I do," she said, grabbing the door handle.

Vaughn stopped her by reaching for her hand. "I can't do it."

She glared at him. "Can't do what?"

"Work for Value-X. I'm faxing in my resignation first thing tomorrow morning." No one would be in the office to read it until after Christmas, but that couldn't be helped.

Carrie still appeared stunned. "I don't know what to say," she muttered. "I need time to think."

"All right. I know this is a shock. I won't blame you if you decide you want nothing more to do with me. That decision is yours." He sincerely hoped his honesty would prove his sincerity.

She climbed out of the car and without another word, ran toward the house. Vaughn waited at the curb until she was safely inside and then, with a heavy heart, he drove back to Grand Forks.

His parents were still up, playing a game of Scrabble at the kitchen table, when he walked in.

His mother looked up and smiled. "How was the play?"

"Excellent," he answered.

His father picked up four new alphabet squares. "I heard it was put on by a bunch of kids."

"That's true, but they did an incredible job." Vaughn turned a chair around and straddled it.

"How's Carrie?" his mother asked innocently enough.

Vaughn's response was so long in coming that Barbara frowned. She seemed about to repeat her question when he spoke, intending to forestall her.

"If no one minds," he said quickly, "I think I'll go to bed."

"Sure," his father said, concentrating on the game.

"You don't want a cup of tea first?" his mother asked, still frowning.

"I'm sure," he said.

Inside the guest room, Vaughn threw himself on the bed. The guilt and remorse that had haunted him on the sixty-minute drive from Buffalo Valley hadn't dissipated.

He folded his hands beneath his head and gazed up at the ceiling, his thoughts twisting and turning as he attempted to reason everything out. Now that Carrie knew the truth, he should feel better, but he didn't.

Resigning from Value-X was only a small part of what he had to do. He wouldn't be this attracted to Carrie if he truly loved Natalie. He closed his eyes and could only imagine what Natalie would say once she discovered what he'd done. Avoiding a confrontation with her would be impossible. She was coming to Buffalo Valley, and what was that old adage? *Hell hath no fury like a woman scorned.* He could feel the flames licking at his feet even now. Oh, yes, this was only the beginning.

He trusted that Carrie would eventually forgive him for his deception concerning Value-X and his role with the company. He'd been as candid with her as he could.

Unfortunately Value-X wasn't the only issue. He didn't have the courage to tell Carrie about Natalie. Not yet. He didn't want to force her to accept more than one disappointment at a time. Once she'd dealt with the fact that he was connected with Value-X, he'd explain his relationship to Natalie. By then, that relationship would be over.

Sitting up, Vaughn swung his legs over the side of the bed and sat there for several minutes. His mind wasn't going to let him sleep, so it was a waste of time to even try.

The kitchen light was off when he stepped into the hallway. He assumed his parents had finished their game and retired for the night. Perhaps if he had something to eat, it might help him relax. To his surprise, he found his father sitting in the darkened living room, watching the late-night news. The Christmas tree in the corner twinkled with festive lights that illuminated the gifts piled beneath.

"I thought you'd gone to bed," his father said.

"I thought I had, too," Vaughn answered, joining him. They both stared at the screen, although there was nothing on except a too-familiar commercial. Yet anyone might have thought they were viewing it for the first time.

His father suddenly roused himself and turned off the TV. "Something on your mind?" he asked after an uncomfortable moment of silence.

Vaughn hesitated, wondering if he should share his burden.

His father yawned loudly. "You'd better start talking soon if you're inclined to do so, because I'm about to hit the sack."

Vaughn laughed despite himself. "Go to bed. This is something I've got to settle myself."

"All right," Rick Kyle told him. "If you're sure..."

"'Night, Dad," Vaughn said, grateful for having been raised by two loving parents.

"You coming to bed or not?" Gage Sinclair called to his wife. Lindsay had been fussing ever since they'd driven back to the farm. After they'd put the girls down for the night, she'd decided to sort laundry. Then it was something in the kitchen. He had no idea what she was up to now.

"Lindsay," he shouted a second time, already in bed himself.

"I'll be there in a minute." Her voice came from the living room.

"That's what you said fifteen minutes ago."

Tossing aside the comforter, he got out of bed and reached for his robe before walking into the other room. Sure enough, he found her sitting on the sofa, knitting. This particular project looked like it was going to be a sweater for Joy. "Tell me what's bothering you," he said, sinking down in his recliner.

"Things," she returned a moment later.

"You're not upset with me, are you?"

She lowered her knitting and stared at him. "Has there

ever been a time I was afraid to tell you exactly what I thought, Gage Sinclair?"

Gage didn't have to consider that for very long. "No," he said decisively.

"Exactly."

"Then what is it?" he pressed. All at once he knew. The answer should have been obvious. "Value-X?"

His wife nodded. "My mind's been buzzing ever since I talked to the company. That woman was so arrogant. I don't doubt for a moment that Value-X will be as ruthless as they need to be."

"Sweetheart, there isn't anything we can do about it now."

"I know, but I can't stop thinking. We've got to get organized."

"I agree."

"It's just that with Christmas only a few days away, everyone's so busy we can't find even a couple of hours."

"That's what happens this time of year."

"But the future of the entire *town* is at risk."

"Don't you think other towns have tried to keep them out?" He didn't mean to be a pessimist, but truth was truth. No matter what kind of slant they put on it, nothing was going to change.

"What worries me most is Hassie's attitude," Lindsay admitted. "I've never known her to give up without one hell of a fight."

"Sweetheart, she's single-handedly slayed dragons for this town. It's someone else's turn."

"I know." This was said with a sadness that tugged at his heart. Gage knew his wife had a special relationship with Hassie. He also knew that without Hassie Knight, he might never have married Lindsay. Now it was impossible to imagine his life without her and their daughters. It wasn't anything he even wanted to contemplate.

"I saw you talking to Maddy," Gage said. The two women had been friends nearly all their lives, and they still relied on each other when either had a problem. This problem, though, was shared by the whole town. Predictably, Lindsay had taken on Buffalo Valley's latest dilemma—taken on Hassie's role, too, he thought.

That was what he loved about her, and at the same time dreaded. His wife didn't know the meaning of the word *no.* She simply refused to give up. When she'd first moved to Buffalo Valley, they'd been constantly at odds; he was crazy about her, yet couldn't say a word to her without an argument erupting.

They'd met one hot summer afternoon at Hassie's. Lindsay had left town but she'd stayed in his mind. For weeks afterward she filled his thoughts, and if that wasn't bad enough, she invaded his dreams. When he learned she'd accepted the teaching position at the high school, he managed to convince himself that this Southern belle wouldn't last longer than the first snowflake. His behavior toward her had been scornful, even combative—an attempt to keep from making a fool of himself. It hadn't worked, since he'd done a mighty fine job of looking like a dolt.

Then there was the matter of finding their aunt, the illegitimate child of her grandmother and his grandfather. Gage had wanted no part of that. He'd violently disagreed with her decision to intrude on this unknown woman's life.

He'd been wrong about that, and during the past few

years, Angela Kirkpatrick had become an important figure in their lives.

It didn't stop there. Lindsay had known what was best for Kevin, too. His much younger brother was never meant to be a farmer. Kevin hated what Gage loved most. But Kevin's talent meant that he would one day be named among the country's major artists. Lindsay had recognized his brother's gift when Gage had turned a blind eye to it.

Having seen the error of his ways—repeatedly—Gage had come to trust his wife's judgment and intuition. "What do you suggest we do?" he asked, getting up and sitting next to her on the sofa.

"I just don't know, and neither does Maddy," Lindsay told him, shrugging helplessly. She put aside her knitting, muttering that she couldn't concentrate anymore. Not *his* fault, she assured him. It was just this Value-X thing.

He clasped her hand and she gripped his hard. She scrambled into his lap, pressing her head against his shoulder. Gathering her close, Gage savored the feel of his wife in his arms.

"I tried to talk to Hassie about it, but she said I should turn my thinking around and try to look at the positive side of the situation."

"Have you?" Gage asked, dropping a kiss on her forehead.

"No. I can't get past what'll happen to Buffalo Valley once Value-X arrives."

The prospects for the future weren't bright in view of what had become of other communities the retailer had entered.

Neither spoke for several moments, then Gage changed the subject. "I enjoyed meeting Vaughn Kyle."

"You two certainly seemed to hit it off."

"We got to talking about army life."

"Wouldn't it be wonderful if he moved to Buffalo Valley and he and Carrie got married?" his wife said. Sometimes he forgot what a romantic she could be. And yet…time and again, her instincts about people proved to be correct. She was the one who'd claimed Maddy and Jeb were falling in love, although Gage would've sworn on a stack of Bibles that it wasn't happening.

"Carrie and Vaughn?" he repeated.

"Mark my words, Gage."

Lindsay wasn't going to get an argument out of him. "You ready for bed now?"

"Ready," she told him, kissing his jaw and sending shivers down his back.

"Me, too," he whispered.

Eight

"I've got a meeting in town this morning," Margaret Eilers announced at the breakfast table Saturday morning, three days before Christmas.

This came as news to Matt. His wife hadn't mentioned anything about going into Buffalo Valley. Something was in the air, though. The phone had been ringing off the hook for the better part of a week. He knew the women around here were up in arms about the Value-X problem, although Matt didn't see what could be done. Neither did any of the other men in town.

"Can you watch the kids for me, Sadie?" His wife smiled at the housekeeper, who'd been with the family since Margaret's childhood.

Sadie brought a stack of pancakes to the table and wiped her hands on her apron. "Not this morning," she said in that brusque way of hers.

Anyone who didn't know Sadie might assume she was put out by the request. She wasn't. This was simply her manner, and they were all used to it. Matt had learned more than one lesson from the highly capable housekeeper. She'd become an ally and friend shortly after he married Margaret, and he was forever grateful for all she'd done to see him through his troubles.

"I'm leaving at noon, remember?" Sadie reminded them.

"That's right," Margaret muttered, glancing at Matt.

"What's going on in town?" he asked. Margaret wasn't one to make unnecessary trips, nor was she the type of woman to find an excuse to shop.

"I'm meeting with the other women. We're going to discuss ideas on how to deal with the threat from Value-X," she told him.

"Sweetheart, that's already been discussed to death. The town council has tried, Hassie's—"

"Everyone's been talking to Ambrose Kohn individually. We've got to mount a defense as a community."

"And do what? Sign petitions?" He didn't mean to sound negative, but he sincerely doubted that Value-X cared what the community thought. They'd already set the wheels in motion. Matt suspected many a town such as theirs had tried to mount a defense, but it had been hopeless from the start. Value-X knew how to win.

"We can't sit by and do nothing," Margaret insisted.

"But it's almost Christmas."

"Exactly, and Value-X is counting on the community to delay a response until after the holidays. By then it could be too late. That's what the meeting's about. I'm willing to fight now, and so are the other women in town."

"What about the men?"

"You're welcome to join us, but…"

"But the women are spearheading this."

"That's because none of you men believe it can be done." Her smile belied the sharpness of her words. "You can still come if you want."

"No, thanks," Matt said, waving a hand in dismissal. "I've got the kids to look after."

Margaret smiled and reached over to spear a hotcake with her fork. They'd been married three years, and Matt fell more in love with her every day. Times had been hard in the beginning, but it seemed that once they'd survived that rough period, they'd grown closer than ever. Of one thing Matt was certain—his wife brought out the very best in him. He loved her with an intensity that gave him strength.

"So I can leave Hailey and David with you?"

"I did have plans this morning, but they can wait." He'd hoped to finish the gift he was working on for Margaret. The antique rocker had belonged to her father. Matt had stumbled upon it in the loft up in the barn, and Sadie had told him its history. Joshua McKenna had repaired it earlier, and Matt had sanded and varnished the wood. Sadie had sewed new cushions for the seat and back. Matt had hoped to add a final coat of varnish that morning so it would be ready for Margaret on Christmas morning. Well…he'd have to find time tonight.

"I don't know what you women think you're going to accomplish," he said, "but if you sincerely believe it'll make a difference, then I'll do my part—and I'll wish you well."

Margaret thanked him with a brilliant smile, rose from the table and kissed him. The kiss was deep and full of promise. She was letting him know he'd be rewarded a hundred times over at a more appropriate hour.

Soon afterward Margaret headed into town. Once the kids were up, dressed and fed, Matt decided he wanted to know exactly what the women intended. Reaching for the phone, he called Jeb McKenna, his closest neighbor.

"Is Maddy gone, too?" he asked. Matt heard children crying in the background.

"I've got my hands full."

"Me, too," Matt confessed.

"Do you know what they're planning?" Jeb asked.

"I don't have a clue, but I'm sorry now that I didn't go with her. They have great intentions, but what can they do that hasn't already been tried?"

"You signed the petition?"

"Along with everyone else in town," Matt told him.

"Buffalo Bob contacted the governor and asked for help."

"Did he hear back?" Now, that was promising.

"Not yet."

Matt sighed impatiently. "I feel like we should be there."

"I do, too."

"Daddy." Hailey tugged at his jeans. "Can we go to town and have a soda?"

Matt grinned at his daughter. "Just a minute, honey." What an inspiration. "I'll meet you at the soda fountain," Matt suggested. "That way we can keep the kids occupied and we can talk ourselves."

"Good idea," Jeb said.

Matt pushed a tape into the truck's console and sang Christmas songs with his children as he drove into town.

When he parked outside Hassie's, he noticed several other vehicles there, too. The two youngsters followed him excitedly into the drugstore.

The soda fountain appeared to be the most popular place in town; Gage Sinclair was there with his two daughters, and Jeb McKenna had arrived ahead of him. So had Brandon Wyatt and six-year-old Jason. Every stool at the fountain was occupied.

Matt acknowledged his friends with a quick nod.

"Hey, Matt," Jeb said in a jocular tone, "seeing that you called us together, I'm hoping you've come up with a few ideas to share."

"Me?" Matt glanced at Jeb, who shifted his weight. "I called a couple of the other guys, too. I think we made a mistake by taking such a negative attitude. Now the women are stuck trying to cope with the problem all by themselves."

The door opened and Dennis Urlacher walked in with his three-year-old son. Little Josh might be named after Sarah's father, but he was the spitting image of his own.

"I'm not late, am I?" Dennis asked, taken aback by the sight of all the children.

Leta was doing her best to keep up with orders, but she was obviously overwhelmed. As soon as she delivered one soda, she got an order for two more. Apparently Hassie was at the meeting over at Sarah's shop, as well. The men stood in a small circle while the children sat at the counter. Their joyous laughter made all the fathers smile, none more than Matt.

"So, does anyone have any ideas?" Dennis asked.

"Did you get anywhere with the governor's office?" Jeb asked Bob.

Bob shook his head. "I got the runaround. Reading between the lines, I could tell the politicians don't want to get involved in this fight. Buffalo Valley is on its own."

"Okay," Matt said, "maybe the politicians don't want to take sides in this issue, but there are plenty of other influential people who aren't afraid of challenging Value-X."

"Who?"

A flurry of names followed—writers and filmmakers and media personalities—along with a volunteer to contact each one immediately after the holidays. This was exactly the kind of pressure necessary to get the company's attention.

Soon the men were talking excitedly, their voices blending with those of their children. Various ideas were considered, discarded, put aside for research or further thought. The women were right—they had to become a united front.

"Do you seriously believe anyone at the corporate level will listen?" Gage asked. "They've dealt with organized opposition before."

Matt shrugged, although he suspected that if Margaret was the one doing the talking, those muck-a-mucks would soon learn she refused to be ignored. A smile formed on his face as he imagined Margaret standing before the conglomerate's board of directors. They'd listen, all right.

"What's so funny?" Brandon Wyatt asked.

"Nothing." Matt shook his head, dispelling the image.

"Joanie's been real upset about all this."

"Maddy, too," Jeb said. "I don't think the grocery will

be too badly affected, but that's not the point. She's worried about how everyone else will fare."

"Value-X would ruin Joanie's and my business," Brandon said. "But I don't think a bunch of suits in some fancy office in Seattle really care what'll happen to a small video store in Buffalo Valley."

The other men agreed.

"We could hold a rally," Gage suggested.

"The women have already thought of that," Leta inserted, speaking from behind the counter. "They figured it wouldn't have enough impact unless we got major media coverage."

Several of the men nodded; others seemed prepared to argue.

"Hassie's probably got a few ideas," Gage said next. "When she comes back from the meeting, we'll—"

Leta broke in. "Hassie's not with the others," she informed them as she set a chocolate soda on the polished mahogany counter.

"She's not?" The question came from two or three men simultaneously, including Matt.

"Nope. She's at home this morning."

This was news to them all.

"Hassie's not with the other women?" Dennis repeated, frowning. "But…"

"How many of them are over at Sarah's, anyway?" Matt wanted to know.

"They're not at Sarah's," Dennis told them.

"Then where are they?" Matt had assumed that was where the women had met. Sarah had the most space for such a gathering.

"I think they're over at the church with Joyce Dawson," Brandon Wyatt said. "I'm not sure, but something Joanie said..."

Matt figured it wasn't all that important where the women had congregated. The community was coming together, bringing forth ideas. Value-X might be a powerful corporation, but the men and women of Buffalo Valley weren't going to submit humbly to this invasion.

Sleep had eluded Vaughn Kyle all night. The message of the Christmas play had stayed with him. A community standing together, enduring through hard times, its unique character created by that history of struggle and victory. Not *a* community, *this* community. Buffalo Valley.

His confession to Carrie after the performance had played no small part in his inability to sleep. Unfortunately Carrie wasn't the only woman he needed to talk to, and the conversation with Natalie would probably be even harder.

He waited until eight, Seattle time, before calling her. His decision to resign and the reasons for it would infuriate her. And his plan to end their relationship—he didn't even want to think about her reaction to that. He wasn't convinced that she truly loved him, but the humiliation of being rejected would be difficult for her to accept. He sighed; he'd betrayed Carrie twice over and now he was doing the same to Natalie.

The house was still quiet when Vaughn brought the portable phone into his room. Sitting on the bed, he dialed Natalie's home number and waited four long rings before she picked up.

"Hello." Her voice was groggy with sleep. Normally

she'd be awake by now. He'd already started off on the wrong foot, and he had yet to say a word.

"I got you up, didn't I," he said.

"Vaughn," she said sleepily, then yawned. "Hello, darling."

Vaughn tried to ignore the guilt that rushed forward. Mere hours ago, he'd been holding and kissing Carrie.

"This is a surprise," Natalie cooed. "You must really be missing me."

"I need to talk to you about Value-X," Vaughn said, getting directly to the point. There was no easy way to do this.

"Now?" she protested. "You're always telling me all I think about is work. I didn't get home until after eleven last night, and work is the last thing I want to think about now. You know we're under a lot of pressure just before the holidays. There's so much I have to get done, especially since I'll be leaving on this trip."

"I do know, and I apologize." He honestly felt bad about this. "I'll be sending in a fax this morning."

She sighed as if to say she was already bored. "Why?"

He hesitated, bracing himself for her angry outburst. "I've resigned."

"What?" Her shriek was loud enough to actually startle him. "If this is a joke, Vaughn, I am *not* amused."

In some ways he wished it was. He doubted this was one of those situations he'd look back on years from now and find amusing. "You asked me to check out Buffalo Valley."

"So?" she asked. "You mentioned an aunt or someone you knew who lived there. What's the big deal?"

"The big deal is that the town isn't interested in Value-X setting up shop."

Natalie didn't so much as pause. "Honey, listen, we've already been through this. Few communities fully appreciate everything we can do for them. Invariably there's a handful of discontented, ill-informed people who take it upon themselves to make a fuss. For the most part it's a token protest. Rarely is it ever a threat."

"If that's the case, why did you ask me to report back to you on Buffalo Valley?" She'd been worried, Vaughn knew; otherwise she'd never have suggested he check the place out.

"After the bad publicity in that Montana town, I overreacted. That was a mistake," she said quickly. "I see that now. A big mistake! I can't allow you to throw away the opportunity of a lifetime because I sent you into battle unprepared."

"Battle?"

"You know what I mean," she said irritably. "I wasn't thinking clearly. You were going to be in the area and it seemed like such a little thing. I should've known…"

"I'm grateful you asked me to do this," Vaughn countered. "I've learned a whole lot."

"No! No…this is all wrong." Natalie sounded desperate now.

"Buffalo Valley is a nice town. The people here are worried about what'll happen if Value-X moves in."

"But they don't understand that we—"

"They want someone to listen, and it's clear the company isn't going to do that." The purpose of Natalie's visit was to convince the people of Buffalo Valley that they needed Value-X.

"Of course the town wants us to listen, they all do, but what would happen to our jobs if we actually did?"

Natalie made her point without contradiction by Vaughn, although he doubted she recognized the real import of her words.

"Don't do anything stupid," Natalie pleaded. "At least wait until I get there and we can talk this out."

Her arrival was an entirely separate issue. "That brings up another...problem."

"Now what?" she snapped. "I suppose you're going to tell me you've met someone else and you want to dump me."

Vaughn rubbed his hand along his thigh and said nothing.

"This has *got* to be a joke." She gave a short, humorless laugh. "Talk about the Grinch stealing Christmas!"

"I realize my timing is bad—"

"Bad! You don't know the half of it."

"Natalie, listen, I'm genuinely sorry."

"You asked me to be your wife."

Technically, that wasn't true. They'd talked about marriage, but Natalie had shown no great enthusiasm. Now, however, didn't seem to be the time to argue the point. "If you'll recall, you were pretty lukewarm about the idea. That has to tell you something about your feelings for me."

"I was playing it cool," she insisted, sounding close to tears.

Vaughn had never known Natalie to cry, and he experienced deep pangs of regret. "I didn't mean to hurt you, but I had to say something before you showed up here."

He hoped she'd cancel the trip, although he figured that was unlikely.

"I wanted you to be thrilled when I finally agreed to marry you. Now you're saying you don't love me."

"Not exactly..." He did hold tender feelings for her, but he knew with certainty that they were never meant to be together.

"You love me—but you love someone else more?"

Vaughn wasn't sure how to respond. He hadn't declared his feelings for Carrie, but the promise he felt with her outweighed his feelings for Natalie.

"I suppose she's one of the crusaders against Value-X. That would make sense, now that I think about it."

Vaughn didn't answer.

"I'm not giving up on us," Natalie insisted, "not until we've had a chance to speak face-to-face."

He'd already guessed she wouldn't make this easy. "I'd rather you just accepted my decision."

A painful pause followed. "Just what do you plan to do with your life if you resign from Value-X?" she demanded.

"I don't know." His future was as much a mystery to him as it was to her. All Vaughn could say was that he had no intention of remaining with the company.

"You're not thinking clearly," Natalie said.

"Actually, I'm thinking about settling here." He wasn't sure where the words had come from, but until he said them aloud the possibility hadn't even occurred to him.

"In North Dakota," she blurted out, as though he was suffering from temporary insanity. "Now I *know* this is all a bad joke. Who in their right mind would live there?

You know the demographics as well as I do. *No one* lives in a place like that on purpose."

"I would."

"This is ridiculous! I wouldn't believe it if I wasn't hearing it with my own ears. You can't be serious."

Although he knew it was probably a waste of breath, Vaughn felt obliged to tell her about Buffalo Valley. He wanted her to know the people he'd met. She couldn't begin to grasp what he felt unless she understood who and what they were.

"This farming community is small-town America at its best," he said, and wondered if she was even listening. "They have a history of banding together in hard times— and there've been plenty of hard times." He wanted to make her understand the depth of his respect for them, so he relayed to her the plot of the Christmas play.

"That's all very interesting," Natalie told him, her tone bored, "but that was then and this is now. Value-X will come into Buffalo Valley with or without you. With or without me. It doesn't matter how many times you sit and watch a group of teenagers act out the town's history, nothing is going to change."

"It will," Vaughn said.

"I'm not letting you quit. One day you'll thank me."

"Natalie, what are you doing?"

"First I'm going into corporate headquarters to make sure no one reads your resignation letter. Then I'm flying out on the twenty-seventh, just the way I planned, so we can talk this out."

"I wish you wouldn't. Let it go, Natalie."

Her returning laugh sounded like a threat. "I don't think

so. You didn't really believe I'd allow you to cut me loose with a simple phone call, did you?"

He didn't bother to respond. What was the point?

"You see yourself as this hero, this knight in shining armor, and while that's fine and good, it isn't going to work."

Vaughn could see the storm clouds gathering on the horizon.

Sunday morning while his parents attended church, Vaughn drove into Buffalo Valley. He'd made the trek so often in the past week that it seemed almost second nature to head in that direction.

Everything about the town appealed to him. It'd started when he'd first met Hassie and accepted the gold watch that had belonged to her husband. With the watch came an implied trust. He refused to be part of anything that would betray their relationship.

He hadn't heard from Carrie, but he would once she was ready. He didn't think it would take her long to come to terms with his confession. Because of her ex-husband's betrayal, it was vital that he be as open and honest with her as possible. However...he still hadn't explained Natalie's role in his life. Poor Carrie was about to be hit with a second shock, but there wasn't a damn thing he could do to prevent it.

He parked just outside town, at the twenty-acre site for the proposed Value-X. With the wind howling, he climbed out of the car and walked onto the property. Either he was becoming accustomed to the bone-chilling weather or it'd warmed up in the past twenty-four hours. He discovered he could breathe now without feeling as though he was inhaling ice particles.

He'd been there for several minutes when he saw a truck pull up and park next to his vehicle. Two men climbed out and started toward him. He instantly recognized them as Carrie's younger brothers.

"Chuck and Ken, right?" he said as they approached.

Chuck, the older of the two, touched his hat. "Vaughn Kyle?"

Vaughn nodded.

"Did you have a falling-out with Carrie after the play?" Chuck asked. The man was nothing if not direct. His brow had furrowed and the teasing friendliness was gone. "You hurt her and you have me to answer to."

"I have no intention of hurting her."

"Good." He nodded once as if to suggest the subject was closed.

"What are you doing out here?" Ken muttered.

Vaughn wasn't sure what to tell him. He hadn't asked Carrie to keep the fact that he was employed by Value-X a secret, but it was apparent that she had. If either Chuck or Ken knew the truth, they'd have him tarred and feathered and run out of town.

"Just looking," Vaughn told him.

"Looking at what? Empty land?"

"If you had this twenty acres or any portion of it, how would you develop it?" Vaughn asked the pair.

"That's easy," Ken said. "This town needs a feed store— been needing one for years. Most everyone has to drive to Devils Lake for their feed."

A feed store. Now that was interesting. "Why don't you do it?" he suggested.

"No time. The hardware store keeps us busy. Dad needs us there, but if someone were to come along with enough investment capital and a head for business, they'd be guaranteed success."

"Dad carries some of the more common feed, but he doesn't have room for much."

"We got to talking about a feed store just the other day," Ken said, glancing at his brother. "Wondering who might be able to open one."

This morning, Vaughn had casually told Natalie that he might settle in Buffalo Valley. A few days earlier his future was set, and now all at once he was cast adrift. His carefully ordered life was in shambles, and Vaughn didn't like the uncomfortable feeling that gave him.

"It'd take someone with ready cash," Ken told him, his expression pensive, "and that's in short supply around here." He kicked at the snow with the toe of his boot. "People in these parts invest everything in their land."

"You interested?" Chuck asked him bluntly.

Vaughn looked in the direction of town, suddenly aware that this venture piqued his interest. He wanted to be part of Buffalo Valley, part of its future. It'd be a risk, but he'd never backed down from a challenge before and he wasn't planning to start now.

"I don't know a damn thing about running a feed store," he said, meeting the other men's eyes.

Chuck and Ken studied him for a long moment.

"You serious about this?" Chuck finally asked.

Vaughn nodded.

"Between Dad, me and my brothers, we could show you everything you need to know."

"You'd do that?" Vaughn found it hard to believe that these men, who were little more than strangers, would willingly offer him their expertise.

"I saw a light in my sister's eyes that hasn't been there since her divorce," Ken told him. "That made me decide you might be worth taking a chance on." He stared down at the ground, then raised his head. "Now, I realize you moving into town and opening a feed store might have absolutely nothing to do with Carrie. Personally, I hope it does, but I want you to know that whatever happens between you and my sister is your business."

"That's the way it would have to be."

Her two brothers shared a glance and seemed to reach the same conclusion. "You're right about that." Chuck spoke for the pair. "This has nothing to do with Carrie."

"There are a lot of *if*s in all this," Vaughn reminded them. He could see that they were getting excited, but then so was he. Naturally, all of this depended on a dozen different factors. Right now it was little more than the glimmer of an idea. Little more than a possibility. But it gave him a glimpse of what he might do....

"At the moment the future doesn't look all that promising for Buffalo Valley," Ken said, surveying the bare land around them. It went without saying that if Value-X came to town, that would be the end of any talk about a feed store.

On the verge of leaving, Vaughn returned to the subject of their sister. "Have either of you seen Carrie?"

"She's gone for the day," Ken told him.

"All day?"

Chuck shrugged. "She's over with our brother Tom and his family. Did you two have plans?"

"No." How could he expect her to be at his beck and call? "I'll talk to her later," he said with reluctance. Their conversation had to take place soon. He'd rather this business with Natalie was over, but it now seemed that would require a protracted…discussion, for lack of a better word.

"She was upset when you dropped her off at the house after the play." Ken frowned at him in an accusatory way, suggesting Vaughn had some explaining to do. "What happened? What did you do?"

"That's Carrie's and my business. Remember?"

Chuck agreed. "She'd have our heads if she knew we were talking to you about her. We'll stay out of it, but like I said, you hurt her and you'll have me to answer to."

Vaughn nodded and resisted the urge to laugh. Melodramatic though they sounded, her brothers were serious.

"I heard you and your parents are spending Christmas Day with Hassie," Ken said.

News sure traveled fast in a small town. "We're coming for dinner."

"Then I think we might be able to arrange something." The two brothers exchanged another look.

"Arrange what?" Vaughn asked.

"Nothing much, just an opportunity for you to have some time alone with our sister." Chuck and Ken left then, both of them grinning broadly.

Nine

Hassie spent Christmas morning with Buffalo Bob, Merrily and little Bobby, upstairs at the 3 of a Kind. Sitting around the Christmas tree with the family reminded her of what it'd been like years ago, when Valerie and Vaughn were young. The good feelings started right then, and she suspected this would be her best Christmas in a very long while.

Bobby's eyes got round as quarters when his father rolled out a shiny new miniature bicycle with training wheels. It amazed her that a three-year-old could actually ride a bicycle. In another three or four months, the park would be crowded with kids on bikes, enjoying the Dakota sunshine. When Hassie closed her eyes, she could almost hear the sound of their laughter. That would happen, she comforted herself, with or without Value-X.

She exchanged gifts with the family—magazine subscriptions for Bob and Merrily, a book of nursery rhymes for Bobby. Their gift to her was a new pair of lined leather gloves. After coffee and croissants—and hugs and kisses—she left.

Home again, Hassie set the dining-room table with her finest china. Not much reason to use it these days. Yet twice this week she'd had cause to bring it out of the old mahogany cabinet. The first time was her visit with Barbara and now Christmas dinner.

Already the kitchen counter was crowded with a variety of food. Carrie and her mother had thoughtfully dropped off a platter of decorated sugar cookies. Those cookies, plus the ones she'd collected the night of the exchange, added up to enough for the entire town.

Sarah Urlacher and Calla had given her a plate of homemade fudge. Maddy, Lindsay and several of the other women had stopped by with offerings, too—preserves and homemade bread and mincemeat tarts. It was far more than Hassie could eat in two or three Christmases.

Then word had leaked out about Vaughn Kyle and his parents coming for dinner. Before Hassie could stop them, her friends and neighbors had dropped off a plethora of side dishes. Joanie Wyatt sent over baked yams. Rachel Quantrill delivered a green-bean-and-cauliflower casserole. Soon all that was required of Hassie was the bird and dressing. The tantalizing aroma of baking turkey, sage and onions drifted through the house.

Living alone, Hassie didn't bother much with meals. At night, after she closed the pharmacy, her dinner consisted of whatever was quick and easy. When Jerry had been alive and the children still lived at home, she'd been an accomplished cook. Now she considered cooking for one a nuisance. Many a night she dined on soup or a microwave entrée.

The doorbell chimed at exactly one o'clock, and Hassie, who'd been occupying herself with last-minute touches, was ready to receive her company.

"Merry Christmas," Barbara Kyle sang out, hugging Hassie as soon as she opened the front door.

"Merry Christmas. Merry Christmas." Hassie hugged them all.

For the next few minutes the men made trips back and forth between the car and the house. They hauled in festively wrapped presents, plus various contributions to the meal, including three beautiful pies.

"How in heaven's name are the four of us going to eat all these pies?" Hassie asked, giggling like a schoolgirl over such an embarrassment of riches. Pies, cookies, candies. Oh, my, she'd be on a diet till next June if she tasted everything in her kitchen.

"Pecan pie is Rick's favorite," Barbara explained.

"Pumpkin is mine," Vaughn said.

"And fresh apple mixed with cranberry is mine," Barbara said, setting down the third pie. She had to rearrange other dishes on the crowded counter to find room for it.

"Apple mixed with cranberry," Hassie mused aloud. "That sounds delicious."

"I'm willing to share," Barbara said with a laugh.

The meal was even better than Hassie had dared hope. The turkey was moist and succulent, and the sage dressing was her finest ever, if she did say so herself. The four of them sat around the table and passed the serving dishes to one another. They talked and laughed as if each was part of Hassie's family. Anyone seeing them would never have guessed there'd been a thirty-three-year lapse in their relationship.

This was the way Christmas was meant to be, Hassie thought, immersing herself in the good feelings. Barbara had always been a talker, and she effortlessly kept the conversation going. The years had changed Rick Kyle considerably, Hassie noted, smiling over at him. She doubted she would've recognized him now.

The last time Hassie had seen Rick, he'd had shoulder-length brown hair, a bushy mustache and narrow-rimmed glasses. A wooden peace sign had dangled from his neck. As she recalled, he'd worn the craziest color combinations with tie-dyed bell-bottom jeans and sandals.

His hair was mostly gone now, but Barbara claimed bald men could be exceedingly sexy. Hassie wouldn't know about that, but it did her good to see that they were happy and obviously still in love.

Perhaps it was selfish of her, but she liked to believe that if her son had lived, Vaughn would've found the same happiness with Barbara.

"If I eat another bite, I swear someone might mistake me for a stuffed sausage," Barbara declared, pushing back her chair.

"Me, too." Rick wrapped his arms around his belly and groaned.

Hassie looked at Vaughn, who winked and said, "Could someone pass me the mashed potatoes and gravy?"

Laughing, Barbara hurled a roll at him from across the table. Vaughn deftly caught it. "Hey, I'm a growing boy."

When they'd finished, the men cleared off the table and

Hassie brewed a pot of coffee. They gathered in the living room around the small Christmas tree, where Hassie had tucked three small gifts, one for each of her guests. Shopping in Buffalo Valley was limited and there hadn't been much time, so Hassie had found items with special meaning to share with her friends. Three little gifts she knew each would treasure.

For Barbara, it was a pearl pin Jerry had given her after Vaughn's birth. For Rick it was a fountain pen—an antique. Choosing a gift for Vaughn had been difficult. In the end she'd parted with one of the medals the army had awarded her son for bravery. Since Vaughn had recently been in the military himself, she felt he'd appreciate what this medal represented.

They seemed truly touched by her gifts. Barbara's eyes brimmed with tears and she pinned the pearl to her silk blouse. Rick, who didn't appear to be the demonstrative sort, hugged her. And Vaughn seemed at a loss for words.

"I have something to tell you," Vaughn said after several minutes of silence.

"This sounds serious." Hassie saw the look Barbara and Rick exchanged and wondered at its meaning.

Vaughn leaned forward and took Hassie's hands in both his own. "I told Mom and Dad earlier, and they urged me to be honest with you, as well. First, I want you to know I'd never deliberately do anything to hurt you."

"I know that. Honest about what?"

"Value-X. When I left Seattle, I'd accepted a job with them."

Hassie gasped, and her hand flew to her mouth. This

was almost more than she could take in. Vaughn an employee of Value-X?

"I knew the company was planning to expand into Buffalo Valley, but I didn't understand the threat they represented to the community."

"He isn't working for them any longer," Barbara quickly inserted.

"Since I wasn't going to be officially an employee until after the first of the year, one of the vice presidents suggested I not mention my association with the company," Vaughn explained. "It was never my intention to deceive you or anyone in Buffalo Valley." He took a deep breath. "I faxed in my resignation and made it effective immediately."

Hassie felt a little dizzy. It was hard enough to grasp what he was saying, and she could only imagine what Carrie must think, so she asked, "Does Carrie know?"

Vaughn nodded. "I told her the night of the play. I didn't want to wait until after the holidays."

"What did she say?" Hassie asked. She feared that the news might mean the end for this budding relationship, which would be a dreadful shame.

"I haven't had a chance to speak to her since."

Barbara moved forward to the edge of the sofa. "There's more."

Vaughn cast his mother a look that suggested he'd rather she hadn't said anything.

"Tell me." As far as Hassie was concerned, it was too late for secrets now.

Vaughn glanced at his mother again. "I don't want to get anyone's hopes up, because it's much too soon."

"Yes, yes, we know that," Barbara interjected, then waited for him to continue.

Vaughn's reluctance was evident. At last he said, "I'm investigating the possibility of opening a feed store here in town."

For the second time in as many moments, Hassie gasped. Only this time, the shock was one of excitement and pleasure. "Oh, Vaughn, that's an excellent idea. The town could use a feed store."

Rick wrapped his arm around his wife's shoulders, and both of them smiled broadly.

"Vaughn spoke with two of the Hendrickson brothers about it yesterday morning," Barbara said. "They actually suggested it."

Hassie's heart surged with hope. Vaughn was right of course; there was no reason to get carried away. But she couldn't help it. The thought of having Vaughn right here in Buffalo Valley—she was almost afraid to believe it could happen.

"I've got an appointment with Heath Quantrill first thing Wednesday morning," Vaughn explained. "I'll need to put together a business plan and look into financing. The Hendricksons recommended I start there."

"Yes—Heath will give you good advice." Some of the excitement left her as reality came rushing back. "Everything hinges on what happens with Value-X, doesn't it?"

"True." Vaughn gave her a lopsided smile. "But I have a good feeling about this." As Hassie fought the emotion that threatened to overwhelm her, he added, "I want to invest in Buffalo Valley."

Keeping the tears at bay was impossible now. "Why

would you do such a thing?" she asked between sniffles. Reaching into her pocket, she withdrew a linen handkerchief and blew her nose. She must be getting old, because normally she wasn't a woman prone to tears.

"I arrived in North Dakota thinking I knew exactly what I wanted and where I was headed," Vaughn said, "but everything changed. I probably shouldn't have said anything about my idea." He frowned at his mother. "But now that it's out, I'm glad you know."

"God bless you," Hassie whispered, stretching her arms toward Vaughn for a hug. Their embrace was warm. "If God had seen fit to give me a grandson, I would have wanted him to be just like you."

"That's a high compliment," Vaughn said, sitting down again.

"I meant it to be," Hassie told him. She rubbed her wet cheek with the back of her hand. "Look what you did," she said. "It isn't just anyone who can make this old lady weep."

"Shame on you, son," Rick teased, and they all smiled. It took Hassie a few moments to compose herself.

"Look," Barbara said, pointing outside, "it's snowing."

Sure enough, the flakes were falling thick and soft, creating a perfect Christmas scene. "This is the way I always dreamed Christmas would be," Hassie whispered. "Surrounded by family—" she used the word purposely "—on a beautiful winter day."

This was the best Christmas she'd had in many years, and all because of the Kyles—people who'd been brought into Hassie's life by her son. Somehow she could picture Vaughn smiling down, wishing them a Merry Christmas.

* * *

Hassie had invited Carrie to join Vaughn and his parents for dessert on Christmas Day, and Carrie had yet to decide if she'd go. Vaughn's confession about working for Value-X had shocked her. The fact that he'd come into town, gained her confidence and that of everyone else—so he could collect information for the company—had been a betrayal of trust and goodwill. He'd withheld the truth from her and she should be outraged. She *was* outraged.

All week Vaughn had listened to everyone's objections to Value-X and said nothing. As she thought back on their numerous conversations, she realized how often he'd defended the company. At the time she'd assumed he was playing devil's advocate. Now she knew otherwise. Carrie wasn't sure what had happened to make him resign. Whatever it was, she was grateful. Still...

Trust was a basic issue with Carrie. Vaughn had betrayed her, Hassie and the entire town, and she couldn't conveniently look the other way. *Forgive and forget* might work for others, but not for her.

She didn't think Vaughn had told anyone else. Carrie hadn't determined whether that was a good thing or not. She did know she had to hide this from Hassie, who would be heartbroken if she found out. If she didn't show up at Hassie's and then claimed she'd forgotten, Hassie would immediately conclude that something was wrong. Then she'd start asking questions. Questions Carrie didn't want to answer. She could invent plausible excuses, but the problem was that Carrie *did* want to see Vaughn again, despite what he'd told her.

She needed to talk to him, needed to vent her feelings.

The shock of his confession had robbed her of that chance. But finding a private time to speak with him today might prove difficult, if not impossible. In any event, she hadn't given verbal shape to her emotions yet. Talking to him should probably wait, she rationalized.

"Where you going?" Ken asked, following her into the hallway as she gathered her coat, gloves and scarf.

"I bet she's going off to see that new friend of hers," Chuck teased.

"I'm going over to Hassie's," she informed her two younger brothers smugly.

"I suppose *he's* there."

How Pete knew that, Carrie could only guess. She shoved her arms into the silk-lined sleeves of her coat.

"He's there, all right," Tom said, leaning against the door jamb. "His car's parked outside Hassie's."

Carrie ignored him and went to get her purse. She and Hassie had exchanged their gifts on Christmas Eve, but Carrie had borrowed a book on traditional remedies that she needed to return. She retrieved it from the bookcase.

"Will you guys leave me alone?" she cried. All four of her brothers were trailing her from room to room. "Don't you have anything better to do?"

Her brothers glanced at each other and shrugged, then Pete announced, "Not really."

"Do you want to hear what we think of your new boy-friend?" Ken asked.

If they could be this obstinate, so could she. "No."

Carrie headed for the front door. If her four guardian angels wanted to follow her into the cold and snow, that was their choice.

"I like him, Carrie," Ken called after her.

"Me, too." Tom crowded beside him in the doorway.

"He's all right," Pete concurred.

Chuck simply winked and gave her a thumbs-up. This had to be a record. Never before had she dated a man all four of her brothers approved of. Little did they know. She wondered what they'd say if they knew that, until recently, he'd been a Value-X employee. The answer didn't bear considering. She couldn't disillusion them any more than she could Hassie. Against her will, she'd been pulled into his subterfuge, and she hated it.

The snow was falling hard by the time Carrie reached Hassie's house; she barely noticed.

Vaughn answered the door and surprised her by closing it after him as he stepped onto the porch. "Merry Christmas," he said, his eyes never leaving hers.

As much as possible, she avoided looking at him.

"We need to talk, Carrie."

"Here? Now?" She faked a short laugh. "I don't think so, Vaughn."

"Later, then?"

She nodded.

He sighed with unmistakable relief. "Thank you."

She didn't *want* to feel anything. She longed to ignore him, make a token visit and then be on her way. But it was too late for that. Her emotions were painfully confused; she wanted to kiss him and at the same time, she wanted to scream and rage and throw his betrayal in his face.

He pressed his hand to her cheek. "I'm glad you're here."

She'd intended to slap his hand away, but instead, her fingers curled around his, and she closed her eyes and leaned toward him. Then she was angry with herself for being weak and jerked back.

"Come in out of the cold," Hassie called just as Vaughn opened the door and Carrie stepped inside. She took off her coat and tossed it onto the stair railing.

"Have you met my dad?" Vaughn asked, taking Carrie by the elbow and escorting her into the living room. He made the introductions.

"Pleased to meet you," she said, hoping none of the stiffness she felt came through in her voice.

Hassie was on her way to the kitchen. "You're just in time for pie."

"I'll help dish up," Barbara said, following Hassie.

"Me, too," Carrie offered, eager to escape Vaughn.

Barbara Kyle shook her head. "Well take care of it."

The two older women disappeared, which meant that Carrie was left alone with Vaughn and his father. She would've preferred the women's company and felt awkward alone with the two men. Vaughn was obviously eager to talk to her, and she was just as eager to avoid any conversation with him. Yes, there were things she needed to say; she wasn't ready, though—not nearly ready. She glanced in his direction and he mouthed something, but she looked away.

"Hassie and Barb are trying to keep you and Vaughn together," Rick confided to her frankly. Vaughn scowled fiercely. "So you may as well play along," he advised. "Here, sit down, Carrie, and make yourself comfortable."

She sat on the sofa and Vaughn joined her, sitting so close that their thighs brushed. In an effort to ignore him, she stared out the picture window.

"Isn't it a lovely day?" she asked, making conversation

with his father. "The snow—" A flash of color outside caught her attention. It was her younger brothers. Gasping, she leaped to her feet.

"What?" Vaughn asked, getting up, too.

"It's Chuck and Ken," she said, and pointed at the window. Sure enough, they were outside—in an old-fashioned sleigh pulled by two draft horses.

"That's my great-great-grandfather's sleigh," Carrie explained. "He used it to deliver the mail. Dad and Mr. McKenna have been fixing it up. It's been in the barn for the last hundred years."

"That sleigh looks like something straight out of a Christmas movie," Vaughn's father remarked, standing by the window. "Whose horses are they?"

"I think they belong to a friend of Pete's," Carrie said.

Despite her mood, she giggled. Her brothers must have planned this all along. How they'd managed to keep it a secret she could only guess.

The doorbell chimed, and when Hassie answered it, she found Chuck grinning down at her.

"Anyone here interested in a sleigh ride?" he asked, looking around Hassie to where Carrie and Vaughn stood. "There's room for five."

"I'm game," Rick said. "Come on, Barb."

"Hassie?" Vaughn turned to their hostess.

She seemed about to refuse, then smiled broadly and said, "Don't mind if I do."

Vaughn helped Hassie on with her coat and made sure her boots were tightly laced before they ventured outside. Carrie tried not to be affected by the tenderness he displayed toward Hassie, especially when he bent down on one knee to lace her boots. There was nothing condescending in his action, only affection and concern. Meanwhile, Rick held Carrie's coat for her and then Barbara's. By the time they left the house, the old sleigh, pulled by twin chestnut geldings, had attracted quite a bit of attention from the neighborhood.The horses were festively decked out in harnesses decorated with jangling bells.

Barbara, Rick and Hassie sat in the backseat, which fortunately was nicely padded. Once they were settled, Ken handed them a blanket to place over their laps. Carrie and Vaughn took the front seat, which was narrower and made of wood, forcing them close together.

Chuck and Ken walked in front of the horses, leading them down the unfamiliar street.

"Where are you taking us?" Carrie shouted as her brothers climbed onto the sleigh.

"The park," Ken called back.

"Shouldn't we be singing Christmas songs?" Barbara asked.

"Go right ahead," Rick answered, and taking him at his word, Vaughn's mother started with "Jingle Bells." What could be more fitting? Even if it was a "two-horse open sleigh."

Moments later Hassie's rough voice joined Barbara's soft soprano.

Carrie began to sing, too, and soon Vaughn's rich baritone blended with the women's voices. He and Carrie looked at each other. Perhaps it was the magic of the season or the fact that they were in a sleigh singing while they dashed through the snow, their song accompanied by the muffled clopping of hooves and the jingling of harness bells. Whatever the reason, Carrie realized her anger had completely dissipated. Vaughn seemed to genuinely regret what he'd done. He wasn't involved in a plot to destroy Buffalo Valley. To his credit, as soon as he'd recognized the threat Value-X represented to the town, he'd resigned from the company. It couldn't have been easy to walk away from a high-paying job like that.

Vaughn noticed the transformation in her immediately. He stopped singing and leaned close enough to ask, "Am I forgiven?"

Carrie nodded.

His eyes brightened and he slid an arm around her shoulders. Carrie was convinced that if their circumstances had been different, he would've kissed her.

When they reached the middle of the park, they found Carrie's entire family waiting there, applauding their arrival.

Effortlessly they segued from one Christmas carol to another. Everyone seemed to have a favorite. Amid the singing and the laughter, Carrie's mother served hot chocolate from large thermoses.

Vaughn and Carrie left their places in order to give others an opportunity to try out the sleigh. After several trips around the park, Chuck and Ken drove Hassie and Vaughn's parents back to Hassie's. Carrie and Vaughn remained with her family.

With pride, Carrie took Vaughn around and introduced him to everyone he had yet to meet.

"What were Chuck and Ken talking about earlier?" Tom asked, standing next to his wife, Becky.

Vaughn glanced at Carrie. "We discussed a few ideas, nothing more."

"That's not what I understood," Tom said. "Chuck said you'd made an appointment to talk to Heath Quantrill."

"You've got an appointment to see Heath?" Carrie asked. "About what?" She'd suspected earlier that something was up involving her two younger brothers. Sunday night they'd sat with their father at the kitchen table, talking excitedly in low voices. Carrie couldn't figure out what they were doing, and when she asked, their replies had been vague.

Rather than answer her directly, Vaughn looked away.

"More secrets?" she asked him under her breath.

"Vaughn's thinking about opening up a feed store in town," Tom supplied.

"Is this true?" she asked. If so, it was the best kind of secret.

"Nothing's certain yet," he told her, and she could see that he wasn't pleased with her older brother for sharing the news. "Everything's just in the planning stages. The *early* planning stages."

"You'd actually consider moving to Buffalo Valley?"

Vaughn nodded and smiled down on her, but then his gaze clouded. "I still need to talk to you."

"Of course."

"Privately," he insisted.

The park was crowded with her family. Carrie knew that the instant they broke away, one of her brothers or nieces and nephews would seek her out. "We can try," she promised.

"It's important."

Her heart was in her eyes, but Carrie didn't care if he saw that or not. "I'm so excited you might move here."

"I'm excited, too."

He didn't sound it. If anything, he seemed anxious. "What is it?" she asked. She wanted to hear what he needed to say, and she wanted to hear it *now*, even if they couldn't escape her family.

"Someone from Value-X is coming to Buffalo Valley," he murmured.

"You mean the representative Lindsay mentioned?" Carrie was well aware that the company intended to wage a public-relations campaign to win over the community; that was part of their strategy. She suspected the corporate heads at Value-X had only the slightest idea how unwelcome the retailer was in Buffalo Valley. Whatever they were planning simply wouldn't work.

"Yes. Her name's Natalie Nichols and—"

"It doesn't matter," she told him.

"Yes, it does," he countered.

Carrie lowered her voice, wanting him to know he could trust her. "I didn't tell anyone—no one knows."

"Hassie does. I told her myself."

She didn't understand what had prompted that confession, but wasn't sure it had been the wisest thing.

"She deserves honesty, the same way you do." Vaughn's brow creased with concern. "I would've come to meet her, with or without Value-X."

"I know."

"It isn't going to be pretty, Carrie, when Natalie Nichols arrives. Value-X has proved that it's capable of bulldozing its way into a town. They've done it before."

"Not here, not in Buffalo Valley. We won't let it happen." When he shook his head, she whispered, "It's going to be all right, Vaughn." Because her fears about him had been laid to rest, she leaned forward and kissed him.

Vaughn wrapped his arms around her and held her close.

"Hey, what's this?" Pete shouted.

Carrie laughed. "Leave us be," she replied. "Go on! Shoo!" She wasn't about to let her brothers ruin the most romantic moment of her life.

"Never," Tom hollered.

"There's something else," Vaughn said, ignoring her brothers.

"I have a feeling it's going to have to wait," she said, and ducked just in time to miss a flying snowball. Vaughn, however, wasn't quick enough. Snow exploded across his shoulder and he whirled around to face four large Hendrickson males.

"You shouldn't have done that," he said mildly.

"You gonna make me sorry?"

"Oh, yeah." Vaughn's chuckle was full of threat. "Prepare to die, Hendrickson."

Three hours later a cold and exhausted Vaughn made his way back to Hassie's. The snowball fight had eventually involved everyone in Carrie's large family, from two-year-old Eli to his grandfather. They'd stopped only long enough to build snow forts before the battle had resumed with peals of laughter and more hilarity than Vaughn could remember in years.

He'd sincerely meant to tell Carrie about his relationship with Natalie, but the opportunity never arose again.

It became easy to let it ride once they were caught up in the family fun. Come morning, he was driving back to town to meet with Heath; he'd stop by the pharmacy and tell her then.

It was dark when he returned to Hassie's, and his parents were ready to head home to Grand Forks. When they got there, he discovered that Natalie had left five messages on his parents' machine. He was stunned to learn that she'd already arived in North Dakota.

The first message, from the Seattle airport, had been soft and coaxing, claiming she needed to speak to him at his earliest convenience. By the final one, her tone had become hard and demanding. The last part of the message, telling him she'd call early the next morning, had sounded more than a little annoyed.

"Trouble?" his father asked, standing next to the phone as the message finished playing.

Vaughn shook his head. "Nothing I can't handle."

"Good."

"This has been the most wonderful Christmas," his mother said as she turned off the lights. They all went to bed, wishing each other good-night and a final Merry Christmas.

The following morning Vaughn woke early. He showered, shaved and dressed for his meeting with Heath. Sooner or later, he'd have to talk to Natalie, but he wanted as much information as he could gather before the inevitable confrontation. He gulped down a cup of coffee, eager to be on his way, to begin this new phase of his life. His mother hugged him before he left. "What do you want me to say if Natalie shows up?"

"No need to tell her anything," he advised. He'd deal with her when he had to, but not before. The letter she'd mentioned would be in the community post office soon and with that, the campaign would officially start. Vaughn was prepared to do whatever was necessary to keep the retailer out of Buffalo Valley. He had a stake in the town's future now.

He parked near the bank, then hurried inside; to his surprise, Heath's glass-enclosed office looked empty.

"I have an appointment with Mr. Quantrill," Vaughn told the receptionist.

"You're Mr. Kyle?"

Vaughn nodded.

"Mr. Quantrill left a message. He had some last-minute business to attend to and said I should reschedule the appointment. He sent his apologies and asked me to tell you that the Kohn property has sold."

It wasn't until he was standing outside that Vaughn understood the significance of the message. The Kohn property was the land Value-X wanted. So the battle lines had been drawn. No wonder Quantrill was out of the office. There was no longer any reason for Vaughn to meet with him; Quantrill and the community had far more important issues to worry about.

Vaughn walked over to the pharmacy, his steps slow. No doubt Hassie and everyone else in town had heard the news. He knew how discouraged they'd be.

When he entered the pharmacy, Carrie was behind the prescription counter. As the bells over the door cheerfully announced his arrival, she glanced up, and from her disheartened expression, it was clear she'd heard. Her eyes seemed dull and lifeless. For a long moment she stared at him, almost as though he was a stranger.

"I guess you know?" he asked, stepping toward her.

"Oh, yes," she said with such sadness it nearly broke his heart.

"I'll help, Carrie," he told her. "We can beat Value-X if we stand together." He tried to sound positive, but truth was, he didn't know if they could.

"That's not the news I'm talking about," she said, moving out from behind the counter. "I wonder if you've ever heard the old saying, *Fool me once, shame on you, fool me twice, shame on me.*"

Vaughn frowned, not understanding. "What are you talking about?"

"You mentioned the name Natalie Nichols yesterday."

"Yes, she works for Value-X. She—"

"I met her this morning."

"Natalie's here?" Foolishly he'd assumed she'd spent the night in Grand Forks.

"She stayed at the 3 of a Kind last night. She's been trying to reach you—and here you are, right under her nose."

"I don't know what she told you, but—"

"She told me she was your fiancée."

It was all starting to make sense to Vaughn, a sick kind of sense. Natalie's declaration certainly explained that "shame me twice" stuff. "She spoke to your mother this morning," Carrie went on. "Your mother said if you weren't over at the bank to check here with Hassie. Only it was me she found."

"I can explain," he began.

"I'm sure you can, but frankly I'm not interested in

listening." With that, she returned to the pharmaceutical counter and resumed her work as if he was no longer there.

Vaughn waited uncertainly for a moment, but she didn't look anywhere except at her task, at the pills she was counting out.

It was too late for explanations. Too late to regain her trust. Too late for him.

Ten

Vaughn didn't think anything could happen to make this day any worse, but he was wrong.

As soon as he pulled into the driveway at his parents' home, he saw the unfamiliar car. Even before he'd climbed out of his own vehicle, he knew who'd come to visit.

Natalie.

Sure enough, the instant he walked into the house, his father cast him a sympathetic glance.

"You're back," his mother said, her voice strained and unnaturally high.

"Hello, Vaughn," Natalie said from the living room. She held a cup of coffee balanced on her knee. She looked out of place—and decidedly irritated.

He nodded in her direction.

"I think we'll leave the two of you to talk," his mother announced, and exited the room with the speed of someone who's relieved to escape. His father was directly behind her.

With a silent groan, Vaughn turned toward Natalie.

"You didn't answer my phone messages." She set aside

her coffee, glaring at him. "When I couldn't find you, I drove straight to Buffalo Valley, where I spent the night at some hole-in-the-wall. Merry Christmas, Natalie," she said bitterly.

She didn't appear to expect a comment, so he sat down across from her and waited. When she didn't immediately continue, he figured he'd better take his stand.

"I'm finished with Value-X." Nothing she could say or offer him would influence his decision. "You aren't going to change my mind."

"I'll say you're finished. I'll be fortunate to have a job myself after this."

Vaughn doubted that. Natalie was the type who'd always land on her feet. Yes, she'd recommended Vaughn to the company, but they couldn't hold that against her.

"You intend to go through with this...this craziness, don't you?"

No use hedging. "Yes, I do. I've resigned, and since I hadn't officially started work yet, I didn't bother to give any notice."

She sighed and stared down at her coffee. "I wonder if I ever knew you."

Vaughn said nothing. He'd let her say what she wanted, denounce him, threaten him, whatever. She had cause; he wasn't exactly blameless in all this.

"You think I don't know what this is about?" she challenged. She stood, crossing her arms. "It all has to do with you and me."

Vaughn didn't know a kind way to tell her there *wasn't* any "you and me." There'd probably never been a "you and me." Not with Natalie. Looking at her, Vaughn wondered how he could ever have believed he was in love with her. The very traits that had once attracted him now repulsed him. Her ambition blinded her to everything that was unique and special about Buffalo Valley.

"Say something!" she shrilled.

"I'm sorry."

"That's a good start." Her stance relaxed somewhat.

"It doesn't change anything, though." He wasn't being purposely cruel, only frank. "I'm going to do everything I can to keep Value-X out of Buffalo Valley."

"You're mad at me," she insisted. "All this craziness about moving to some backwoods town is a form of punishment. You're trying to make me regret what I said. Vaughn, you simply don't understand how important Value-X is to me and to our future."

"Natalie—"

She ignored him and started pacing. "We've always been good together, Vaughn, you know that."

"Have we, Natalie?" he asked, hoping she was capable of admitting the truth.

"I can't let you do this," she said, clenching her fists.

He shook his head. "It's done."

"But you're destroying your career!"

"I don't want to work for a company like Value-X. Not now and not in the future."

"What are you going to do, then?"

"I don't know," he told her, and it was true. He'd fight the big retailer for as long as his money held out, but after that…he didn't have any answers.

"I can help you," she said. "You're this rough-and-ready Airborne Ranger, trying to be a hero. But you've got to face reality. No one goes against Value-X and walks away a winner. This will cost you more than you can afford to lose."

He ignored her threat. "Thanks but no thanks," he muttered.

She looked crestfallen.

Vaughn had a few questions of his own. "Why did you tell Carrie we're engaged?"

"Because we are!" she cried. "Did we or did we not discuss marriage?"

He didn't respond. She already had her answer.

"Oh, I get it," Natalie raged, her eyes spitting fire. "You found yourself a little side dish while you were away visiting Mom and Dad. You forgot all about me. Is *that* it?"

"We aren't engaged and we aren't getting married." She couldn't seriously believe he intended to continue this relationship when it was obviously a dead end for both of them.

"But we *did* discuss marriage on more than one occasion, and I never said I *wouldn't* marry you. We both understood we'd get married someday."

"I didn't see it that way. Yes, we talked about marriage, but there was no commitment—and very little interest on your part."

"Now you're lying, too."

He bristled, but bit his tongue before he said something he'd regret.

"Well…it's sort of a lie." Natalie lowered her head. "I made a mistake, but not once did I say anything about breaking off our relationship."

"It's over." He didn't know how much plainer he could be.

"I know." She sighed. "Well, if you insist on this lunacy, you're on your own."

He nodded.

"We could've been very good together," she whispered.

"I'm sorry."

"I know, and you'll be a whole lot sorrier once Value-X is through with this town." She rallied then, jerking her head up, chin tilted. "If you want to freeze your butt off in this horrible place, then go right ahead." She reached for her coat and yanked it toward her.

The sound of several car doors closing distracted Vaughn. He glanced out the window to see all four of Carrie's brothers standing in the driveway. He could only surmise that they'd come en masse to finish him off.

"Who's here?" Natalie asked.

"The firing squad," Vaughn answered.

"Terrific. Can I fire the first shot?"

Vaughn didn't respond to her sarcasm. He headed toward the front door, opening it for the four men who marched, single file, into the house. Soon Carrie's brothers stood in the middle of the room, looking from Vaughn to Natalie and then back.

"What happened?" Chuck demanded. "You left town without saying a word."

"I didn't meet with Heath," Vaughn started to explain, but wasn't given the opportunity before another question was hurled at him.

"Aren't you going to introduce us to your sister?"

"I'm Natalie Nichols." She introduced herself, stepping forward and offering each of the Hendrickson brothers her hand. "And I'm not Vaughn's sister."

"Then who are you?" Ken asked, frowning.

"His fiancée. Or I was," she said, "until recently, but now Vaughn's met someone else. He just told me that he no longer wishes to marry me." She appeared to be making a brave effort to hold her chin high and keep her lower lip from trembling. He'd never realized what a good actress Natalie was.

Vaughn resisted rolling his eyes. He remained silent, preferring not to get drawn into a theatrical scene in which *he* was identified as the villain.

"Someone will need to give me directions back to my hotel." She pulled a tissue from her pocket and dabbed at her eyes, being careful not to smear her mascara.

"I can get you there." Ken stepped forward. "I'll be happy to help."

Tom's gaze narrowed on Vaughn. "Did she have something to do with the fact that you didn't see Heath?"

Vaughn shook his head, surprised the Hendrickson brothers hadn't already heard. "The land sold."

"What the hell?"

All four brothers started speaking at once. As luck would have it, Vaughn's parents chose that precise moment to reappear.

"I thought I heard voices," his mother said as she came into the living room.

Tom motioned with his head toward Natalie. "You'd better have a good explanation," he muttered. "You'd better not be engaged to her and seeing Carrie."

"Yeah," Pete agreed. "This is all some kind of misunderstanding, isn't it? Didn't I tell you I'd make you pay if you hurt my sister?"

"He was never actually engaged," his mother said, hurrying to defend Vaughn. "What he told us is—"

That was when his father stepped into the fray. "Barbara, let Vaughn answer for himself, would you?"

This was impossible. Everyone talked at once. Part of the conversation had to do with the land; everyone was clearly upset about that. Then Pete and his mother got involved in a debate about whether Vaughn should be dating Carrie. In the meantime, Ken and Natalie had apparently struck up a friendly conversation. They sat next to each other on the sofa, so close that their knees touched. Vaughn could only guess what she was saying, but frankly, he couldn't care less.

Before everything blew up in his face, Vaughn walked through the kitchen, grabbed his coat and stepped out the back door. He got into his car, which fortunately hadn't been blocked by the other vehicles. Glancing toward the house, he saw everyone gathered in front of the big window in the living room, staring at him. They must have been dumbfounded, because no one seemed to be speaking.

When he reached the end of the long driveway, Vaughn had to make a decision. He could go searching for solitude, a quiet place to recover his dignity. Or he could drive back to Buffalo Valley.

He chose Buffalo Valley. When he'd finished breaking Hassie's heart, he'd do what he could to mend Carrie's.

He'd never meant to hurt Carrie, but that didn't discount the fact that he'd misled her. This wasn't exactly his finest hour.

When they'd first met, he'd found her charming. Later, when he got to know her, he'd been enchanted by her warmth, delighted by her love of family and home. Those were qualities that had come to mean a great deal to him. Carrie was *genuine,* and she was authentic in her relationships. Unlike him...

Vaughn wanted to kick himself for not being honest with her from the start. He didn't have a single excuse. All he could do now was pray that she'd be willing to accept him— and that she'd give him an opportunity to prove himself.

The hour's drive into town passed in a blur, and practically before he knew it he'd pulled off the highway and turned onto what were now familiar roads. Buffalo Valley stretched before him, but he viewed it with new eyes. He recalled his first visit, recalled how stark and bare the town had seemed, almost as if it were devoid of personality. He'd soon recognized how wrong he was.

While the buildings might be outdated and the lampposts antiques, the town itself represented the very heart of the country. The heart of America's heartland. It was where he wanted to be, how he wanted to live.

His mind was clear now. Easing the car into a parking space on Main Street, Vaughn forced himself to consider what he'd say to Hassie. It wasn't a task he relished.

All his talk of opening a feed store had done nothing but build up her hopes. Now he was about to disillusion an old woman who'd invested her whole life in a town that couldn't be saved. Whatever happened, though, he was staying in Buffalo Valley; he'd be part of its struggle and part of its future.

He dared not put this off any longer, and drawing a deep breath, he walked into the pharmacy.

The instant she saw him, Hassie cried out his name. "Vaughn, oh, Vaughn." Tears streaked her weathered cheeks as she hurried across the store, her arms stretched out toward him.

Apparently someone had already brought her the news. Holding open his own arms as she came to him, he hugged her, the sound of her sobs echoing in his ears.

"I'm so sorry," Vaughn whispered, wondering what he could say that would comfort her.

"Sorry?" Hassie eased back, gazing at him through watery eyes. "In the name of heaven, why would you be *sorry?* This is what we've hoped for all along."

Vaughn stared at her, not knowing what to think. "The land sold, Hassie."

"Yes, I know." She clapped her hands, eyes sparkling with delight. "This is better than anything I could've imagined."

"I'm...confused."

"I know." She patted his back and led him to the soda fountain. "Sit down," she ordered. "If there was ever a time for one of my chocolate sodas, this is it."

"What about Value-X?"

"They lost the land. The women of Buffalo Valley got to Ambrose before he signed the deal with Value-X and they bought it out from under the company. The ladies convinced Ambrose he'd be making a mistake."

Vaughn knew that several of the women in town owned businesses; he knew they had a big stake in the community. It floored him that they'd managed to do what no one else had deemed possible.

"But how...when?"

"Do you recall when the women got together?" Hassie asked, leaning over the refrigeration unit, scooping up the ice cream.

"I remember a cookie exchange." Carrie had mentioned something along those lines earlier in the week.

"The meeting took place after that," Hassie said. "Then a committee of six paid Ambrose a visit. I don't know everything they said, but apparently they convinced him to sell *them* those twenty acres. I hear they twisted his arm by appealing to his vanity—promising to name the school after him. He liked that. He also liked the fact that he could sell his land at the same price Value-X offered."

"Is Value-X seeking out any other property?"

Hassie grinned. "They can try, but there isn't a single person in this area who'd sell to them—not at any price."

Vaughn nodded, still feeling a little numb. "What do the women intend to do with the property?" he asked.

Hassie's grin widened. "You mean you don't know?"

He didn't. Since they were all capable, business-minded individuals, Vaughn suspected they already had plans.

Hassie chuckled softly. "You'll have to ask them, but my guess is they'd be willing to sell you a portion of it—that is, if you're still inclined to settle in Buffalo Valley."

Vaughn could barely take it in. "You mean that?"

"Talk to Sarah Urlacher and she'll give you all the details."

"I need to see Carrie first."

Hassie set the glass on the counter. "Ah, yes, Carrie." She made a tsking sound and plunked a paper straw into the thick chocolate soda. "You've got your work cut out there."

Vaughn wrapped his hand around the glass, feeling the cold against his palm. "I assume she's upset."

"That's one way of putting it."

Vaughn slid off the stool. He didn't want to offend Hassie by not drinking the soda, but he'd feel worlds better once he resolved the situation with Carrie. "She at home?"

"Doubt it." Hassie reached for the soda herself and took a long sip before she continued. "My guess is she's sitting on the swings over in the park. I found she likes to go there when something's troubling her. Look there first and if you can't find her, then check the house."

Vaughn thanked her and left immediately. He jogged across the street to the park. The snow forts he'd helped build on Christmas Day—was that only yesterday?—were still standing, a little the worse for wear. Following the freshly shoveled walk, Vaughn made his way toward the play equipment.

Hassie had, as always, given him the right advice. Carrie sat in the middle swing. Her face was red from the cold, and he wondered how long she'd been there.

Vaughn ached to tell her how sorry he was, but he feared that if he said or did the wrong thing now, he might lose her forever.

As he approached, Carrie glanced up, but she didn't acknowledge him. Vaughn, needing to gather his thoughts, didn't say anything, either. Instead, he settled into the swing beside her and waited for the words to come.

"I hurt you, didn't I?" he asked after an awkward moment.

"Were you engaged to her when you came to town?"

This was the difficult part. "No. No, I wasn't."

"She seemed to think so."

He gripped the chain and shifted sideways to see Carrie more clearly. "Before I left Seattle, Natalie and I talked about marriage."

The words seemed to hit her hard.

"She wasn't interested."

"Apparently she's changed her mind."

Vaughn saw that Carrie was staring straight ahead, as though mesmerized by whatever she was watching. "So have I."

Carrie turned toward him, but when their eyes met, she turned away again. "Why?"

"I met someone else."

"You must be a very fickle man, Vaughn Kyle, to ask one woman to marry you and then, while she's making up her mind, start seeing another."

"I realize how bad it sounds."

"Sounds, nothing! Underhanded and unfair is more like it."

"You're right," he said simply. "I have no excuse."

"You must've really enjoyed hearing me spill out my heart." She covered her cheeks with both hands and closed her eyes, as if remembering the things she'd said. They seemed to embarrass her now.

"Carrie, no! It wasn't like that." He thought about the afternoon she'd told him about her ex-husband. He didn't know how to put into words what her trust had done for him. How her straightforward devotion had wiped out the cynicism he'd felt after Natalie's opportunistic approach to love and marriage.

"You're certainly not the kind of man I'd want in my life."

"I need you, Carrie...."

"For what, comic relief?"

"We've only known each other a short while. Who can say where this relationship will take us? Maybe you're right. After you get to know me better, you could very well decide you don't want any more to do with me. If that's the case, I'll accept it. All I'm asking for is a chance."

"To break my heart?"

"No, to give you mine."

She didn't answer him for the longest time. Finally her mouth twisted wryly and she said, "You're afraid of what my brothers will do to you once they learn about...Natalie, aren't you?"

"No man in his right mind would voluntarily tangle with your brothers," he replied, deciding this was not the moment to tell her they'd already met the woman in question. "However, I figure I can take them on if it comes to that. What I'm telling you now has nothing to do with your brothers. It's how I feel about you."

"Don't!" she cried with such passion that Vaughn jumped. "Don't say things you don't mean."

"I am completely sincere." He slid off the swing and crouched down in front of her. He wanted her to see how vulnerable he was to her. Taking her right hand in his, he removed her glove and kissed the inside of her palm.

She pulled back her hand.

"I plan to stay in Buffalo Valley," he continued, undaunted.

Her eyes widened, but she bit her lower lip as if to suppress her reaction.

"I'm going to invest in the community, become part of it, make a contribution."

Carrie's gaze darted away and then returned. "Don't tell me things like that just because you think it's what I want to hear."

"It's true, Carrie."

She closed her eyes and lowered her chin. "I want so badly to believe you."

"Believe me," he whispered, then nuzzled her throat. He didn't kiss her, although the temptation was strong. "All I'm asking for is another chance," he said again.

"Oh, Vaughn." She pressed her hands against his shoulders—to bring him closer or push him away?

Vaughn helped make the decision for her. Crouched down as he was, his face level with her own, he leaned toward her and grazed her lips with his. Her mouth was cold, yet moist and welcoming. She moaned softly and he rubbed his warm lips over hers, seducing her into deepening the kiss.

One moment he was crouched in front of Carrie and she

was leaning forward, giving herself to the kiss. The next he was losing his balance and tumbling backward.

Carrie let out a small cry of alarm as she went with him. Vaughn did what he could to protect her. He threw his arms around her waist and took the brunt of the impact as she landed on top of him in the snow.

"You've knocked me off balance from the moment we met," he said.

Carrie smiled then, for the first time since he'd joined her. "You've done the same thing to me."

"Good."

"No promises, Vaughn."

"I disagree." He brushed the hair from her face, barely aware of the snow and the cold.

She frowned. "What do you mean?"

"There's promise every time I look at you, Carrie Hendrickson. Promise each time I kiss you." Then, because he couldn't keep himself from doing so, he showed her exactly what he meant.

As soon as their lips met, Carrie whimpered and he wrapped his arms more firmly around her.

"This is only the beginning for us," he whispered.

Carrie placed her head on his shoulder and gave a shuddering sigh.

"I was never really worried about your brothers," Vaughn confessed. "*You* were always the one who terrified me." He laughed and rolled, reversing their positions in the snow. Her eyes were smiling as he gazed down on her.

"So you want to give me your heart?" she said, looking up at him. She flattened her hand against his coat.

"Don't you know?" he asked her.

"Know what?"

"You already have it." And then he went about proving it.

Mr. and Mrs. William Hendrickson

and

Mr. and Mrs. Richard Kyle

Request the honor of your presence at a reception

to celebrate

the marriage of their children

Carrie Ann Hendrickson

and

Vaughn Richard Kyle

When: December 15th

Where: Buffalo Bob's 3 of a Kind

Main Street,

Buffalo Valley, North Dakota

RSVP

* * * * *

LOVE BY DEGREE

To all my friends at the Vero Beach Book Center—
Chad, Cynthia, Sheila, Debbie, Jamie and Rose Marie.
Thank you for all you do to support my books.

One

The melodious sounds of a love ballad drifted through the huge three-storey house in Seattle's Capitol Hill. Ellen Cunningham hummed along as she rubbed her wet curls with a thick towel. These late-afternoon hours before her housemates returned were the only time she had the place to herself, so she'd taken advantage of the peaceful interlude to wash her hair. Privacy was at a premium with three men in the house, and she couldn't always count on the upstairs bathroom being available later in the evening.

Twisting the fire-engine-red towel around her head, turban style, Ellen walked barefoot across the hallway toward her bedroom to retrieve her blouse. Halfway there, she heard the faint ding of the oven timer, signalling that her apple pie was ready to come out.

She altered her course and bounded down the wide stairway. Her classes that day had gone exceptionally well. She couldn't remember ever being happier, even though she still missed Yakima, the small apple-growing community in central Washington, where she'd been raised. But she was adjusting well to life in the big city. She'd waited impatiently for the right time—and enough money—to complete her education, and she'd been gratified by the way everything had fallen into place during the past summer. Her older sister had married, and her "baby" brother had entered the military. For a while, Ellen was worried that her widowed mother might suffer from empty nest syndrome, so she'd decided to delay her education another year. But her worries had been groundless, as it turned out. James Simonson, a widower friend of her mother's, had started dropping by the house often enough for Ellen to recognize a romance brewing between them. The time had finally come for Ellen to make the break, and she did it without guilt or self-reproach.

Clutching a pot holder in one hand, she opened the oven door and lifted out the steaming pie. The fragrance of spicy apples spread through the kitchen, mingling with the savory aroma of the stew that simmered on top of the stove. Carefully, Ellen set the pie on a wire rack. Her housemates appreciated her culinary efforts and she enjoyed doing little things to please them. As the oldest, Ellen fit easily into this household of young men; in fact, she felt that the arrangement was ideal. In exchange for cooking, a little mothering on the side and a share of the cleaning, Ellen paid only a nominal rent.

The unexpected sound of the back door opening made her swivel around.

"What's going on?" Standing in the doorway was a man with the most piercing green eyes Ellen had ever seen. She noticed immediately that the rest of his features were strongly defined and perfectly balanced. His cheekbones were high and wide, yet his face was lean and appealing. He frowned, and his mouth twisted in an unspoken question.

In one clenched hand he held a small leather suitcase, which he slowly lowered to the kitchen floor. "Who are you?" He spoke sharply, but it wasn't anger or disdain that edged his voice; it was genuine bewilderment.

Ellen was too shocked to move. When she'd whirled around, the towel had slipped from her head and covered one eye, blocking her vision. But even a one-eyed view of this stranger was enough to intimidate her. She had to admit that his impeccable business suit didn't look very threatening—but then she glanced at his glowering face again.

With as much poise as possible, she raised a hand to straighten the turban and realized that she was standing in the kitchen wearing washed-out jeans and a white bra. Grabbing the towel from her head, she clasped it to her chest for protection. "Who are *you?*" she snapped back.

She must have made a laughable sight, holding a red bath towel in front of her like a matador before a charging bull. This man reminded her of a bull. He was tall, muscular and solidly built. And she somehow knew that when he moved, it would be with effortless power and sudden speed. Not exactly the type of man she'd want to meet in a dark alley. Or a deserted house, for that matter. Already Ellen could see the headlines: Small-Town Girl Assaulted in Capitol Hill Kitchen.

"What are you doing here?" she asked in her sternest voice.

"This is my home!" The words vibrated against the walls like claps of thunder.

"Your home?" Ellen choked out. "But…I live here."

"Not anymore, you don't."

"Who are you?" she demanded a second time.

"Reed Morgan."

Ellen relaxed. "Derek's brother?"

"Half-brother."

No wonder they didn't look anything alike. Derek was a lanky, easy-going nineteen-year-old, with dark hair and equally dark eyes. Ellen would certainly never have expected Derek to have a brother—even a half-brother—like this.

"I—I didn't know you were coming," she hedged, feeling utterly foolish.

"Apparently." He cocked one eyebrow ever so slightly as he stared at her bare shoulders. He shoved his bag out of the doorway, then sighed deeply and ran his hands through his hair. Ellen couldn't help making the irrelevant observation that it was a dark auburn, thick and lustrous with health.

He looked tired and irritable, and he obviously wasn't in the best frame of mind for any explanation as to why she was running around his kitchen half-naked. "Would you like a cup of coffee?" she offered congenially, hoping to ease the shock of her presence.

"What I'd like is for you to put some clothes on."

"Yes, of course." Forcing a smile, Ellen turned abruptly and left the kitchen, feeling humiliated that she could stand there discussing coffee with a stranger when she was practically naked. Running up the stairs, she entered her room and removed her shirt from the end of the bed. Her fingers were trembling as she fastened the buttons.

Her thoughts spun in confusion. If this house was indeed Reed Morgan's, then he had every right to ask her to leave. She sincerely hoped he'd made some mistake. Or that she'd misunderstood. It would be difficult to find another place to share this far into the school term. And her meager savings would be quickly wiped out if she had to live somewhere on her own. Ellen's brow wrinkled with worry as she dragged a brush through her short, bouncy curls, still slightly damp. Being forced to move wouldn't be a tragedy, but definitely a problem, and she was understandably apprehensive. The role of housemother came naturally to Ellen. The boys could hardly boil water without her. She'd only recently broken them in to using the vacuum cleaner and the washing machine without her assistance.

When she returned to the kitchen, she found Reed leaning against the counter, holding a mug of coffee.

"How long has this cozy set-up with you and Derek been going on?"

"About two months now," she answered, pouring herself a cup of coffee. Although she rarely drank it she felt she needed something to occupy her hands. "But it's not what you're implying. Derek and I are nothing more than friends."

"I'll just bet."

Ellen could deal with almost anything except sarcasm. Gritting her teeth until her jaws ached, she replied in an even, controlled voice. "I'm not going to stand here and argue with you. Derek advertised for a housemate and I answered the ad. I came to live here with him and the others and—"

"The *others?*" Reed choked on his mouthful of coffee. "You mean there's more of you around?"

Expelling her breath slowly, Ellen met his scowl. "There's Derek, Pat and—"

"Is Pat male or female?" The sheer strength of his personality seemed to fill the kitchen. But Ellen refused to be intimidated.

"Pat is a male friend who attends classes at the university with Derek and me."

"So you're all students?"

"Yes."

"All freshmen?"

"Yes."

He eyed her curiously. "Aren't you a bit old for that?"

"I'm twenty-five." She wasn't about to explain her circumstances to this man.

The sound of the front door opening and closing drew their attention to the opposite end of the house. Carrying an armload of books, Derek Morgan sauntered into the kitchen and stopped cold when he caught sight of his older brother.

"Hi, Reed." Uncertain eyes flew to Ellen as if seeking reassurance. A worried look pinched the boyishly handsome face. Slowly, he placed his books on the counter.

"Derek."

"I see you've met Ellen." Derek's welcoming smile was decidedly forced.

"We more or less stumbled into each other." Derek's

stiff shoulders relaxed as Reed straightened and set the mug aside.

"I didn't expect you back so soon."

Momentarily, Reed's gaze slid to Ellen. "That much is obvious. Do you want to tell me what's going on here, little brother?"

"It's not as bad is it looks."

"Right now it doesn't look particularly good."

"I can explain everything."

"I hope so."

Nervously swinging her arms, Ellen stepped forward. "If you two will excuse me, I'll be up in my room." The last thing she wanted was to find herself stuck between the two brothers while they settled their differences.

"No, don't go," Derek said quickly. His dark eyes pleaded with her to stay.

Almost involuntarily Ellen glanced at Reed for guidance.

"By all means, stay." But his expression wasn't encouraging.

A growing sense of resentment made her arch her back and thrust out her chin defiantly. Who was this...this *man* to burst into their tranquil lives and raise havoc? The four of them lived congenially together, all doing their parts in the smooth running of the household.

"Are you charging rent?" Reed asked.

Briefly Derek's eyes met Ellen's. "It makes sense, doesn't it? This big old house has practically as many bedrooms as a dorm. I didn't think it would hurt." He swallowed. "I mean, with you being in the Middle East and all. The house was...so empty."

"How much are you paying?" Reed directed the question at Ellen. That sarcastic look was back and Ellen hesitated.

"How much?" Reed repeated.

Ellen knew from the way Derek's eyes widened that they were entering into dangerous territory.

"It's different with Ellen," Derek hurried to explain. "She does all the shopping and the cooking, so the rest of us—"

"Are you sure that's all she provides?" Reed interrupted harshly.

Ellen's gaze didn't waver. "I pay thirty dollars a week, but believe me, I earn my keep." The second the words slipped out, Ellen wanted to take them back.

"I'm sure you do."

Ellen was too furious and outraged to speak. How dared he barge into this house and immediately assume the worst? All right, she'd been walking around half-naked, but she hadn't exactly been expecting company.

Angrily Derek stepped forward. "It's not like that, Reed."

"I discovered her prancing around the kitchen in her bra. What else am I supposed to think?"

Derek groaned and cast an accusing look at Ellen. "I just ran down to get the pie out of the oven," she said in her own defence.

"Let me assure you," Derek said, his voice quavering with righteousness. "You've got this all wrong." He glared indignantly at his older brother. "Ellen isn't that kind of woman. I resent the implication. You owe us both an apology."

From the stunned look on Reed's face, Ellen surmised

that this could well be the first time Derek had stood up to his domineering brother. Her impulse was to clap her hands and shout: "Attaboy!" With immense effort she restrained herself.

Reed wiped a hand over his face and pinched the bridge of his nose. "Perhaps I do."

The front door opened and closed again. "Anyone here?" Monte's eager voice rang from the living room. The slam of his books hitting the stairs echoed through the hallway that led to the kitchen. "Something smells good." Skidding to an abrupt halt just inside the room, the tall student looked around at the somber faces. "What's up? You three look like you're about to attend a funeral."

"Are you Pat?" Reed asked.

"No, Monte."

Reed closed his eyes and wearily rubbed the back of his neck. "Just how many bedrooms have you rented out?"

Derek lowered his gaze to his hands. "Three."

"My room?" Reed asked.

"Yes, well, Ellen needed a place and it seemed logical to give her that one. You were supposed to be gone for a year. What happened?"

"I came home early."

Stepping forward, her fingers nervously laced together, Ellen broke into the tense interchange. "I'll move up a floor. I don't mind." No one was using the third floor of the house, which had at one time been reserved for the servants. The rooms were small and airless, but sleeping there was preferable to suffering the wrath of Derek's brother. Or worse, having to find somewhere else to live.

Reed responded with a dismissive gesture of his hand.

"Don't worry about it. Until things are straightened out, I'll sleep up there. Once I've taken a long, hot shower and gotten some rest I might be able to make sense out of this mess."

"No, please," Ellen persisted. "If I'm in your room, then I should move."

"No," Reed grumbled on his way out the door, waving aside her offer. "It's only my house. I'll sleep in the servants' quarters."

Before Ellen could argue further, Reed was out of the kitchen and halfway up the stairs.

"Is there a problem?" Monte asked, opening the refrigerator. He didn't seem very concerned, but then he rarely worried about anything unless it directly affected his stomach. Ellen didn't know how any one person could eat so much. He never seemed to gain weight, but if it were up to him he'd feed himself exclusively on pizza and french fries.

"Do you want to tell me what's going on?" Ellen pressed Derek, feeling guilty but not quite knowing why. "I assumed your family owned the house."

"Well…sort of." He sank slowly into one of the kitchen chairs.

"It's the *sort of* that worries me." She pulled out the chair across from Derek and looked at him sternly.

"Reed *is* family."

"But he didn't know you were renting out the bedrooms?"

"He told me this job would last nine months to a year. I couldn't see any harm in it. Everywhere I looked there were ads for students wanting rooms to rent. It didn't seem right to live alone in this house with all these bedrooms."

"Maybe I should try to find someplace else to live," Ellen said reluctantly. The more she thought about it, the harder it was to see any other solution now that Reed had returned.

"Not before dinner," Monte protested, bringing a loaf of bread and assorted sandwich makings to the table.

"There's no need for anyone to leave," Derek said with defiant bravado. "Reed will probably only be around for a couple of weeks before he goes away on another assignment."

"Assignment?" Ellen asked, her curiosity piqued.

"Yeah. He travels all over the place—we hardly ever see him. And from what I hear, I don't think Danielle likes him being gone so much, either."

"Danielle?"

"They've been practically engaged for ages and… I don't know the whole story, but apparently Reed's put off tying the knot because he does so much traveling."

"Danielle must really love him if she's willing to wait." Ellen watched as Monte spread several layers of smoked ham over the inch-thick slice of Swiss cheese. She knew better than to warn her housemate that he'd ruin his dinner. After his triple-decker sandwich, Monte could sit down to a five-course meal—and then ask about dessert.

"I guess," Derek answered nonchalantly. "Reed's perfect for her. You'd have to meet Danielle to understand." Reaching into the teddy-bear-shaped cookie jar and helping himself to a handful, Derek continued. "Reed didn't mean to snap at everyone. Usually, he's a great brother. And Danielle's all right," he added without enthusiasm.

"It takes a special kind of woman to stick by a man that long without a commitment."

Derek shrugged. "I suppose. Danielle's got her own reasons, if you know what I mean."

Ellen didn't, but she let it go. "What does Reed do?"

"He's an aeronautical engineer for Boeing. He travels around the world working on different projects. This last one was somewhere in Saudi Arabia."

"What about the house?"

"Well, that's his, an inheritance from his mother's family, but he's gone so much of the time that he asked me if I'd live here and look after the place."

"What about us?" Monte asked. "Will big brother want us to move out?"

"I don't think so. Tomorrow morning I'll ask him. I can't see me all alone in this huge old place. It's not like I'm trying to make a fortune by collecting a lot of rent."

"If Reed wants us to leave, I'm sure something can be arranged." Already Ellen was considering different options. She didn't want her fate to be determined by a whim of Derek's brother.

"Let's not do anything drastic. I doubt he'll mind once he has a chance to think it through," Derek murmured with a thoughtful frown. "At least, I hope he won't."

Later that night as Ellen slipped between the crisply laundered sheets, she wondered about the man whose bed she occupied. Tucking the thick quilt around her shoulders, she fought back a wave of anxiety. Everything had worked out so perfectly that she should've expected *something* to go wrong. If anyone voiced objections to her being in Reed's house, it would probably be his almost-fiancée.

Ellen sighed apprehensively. She had to admit that if the positions were reversed, she wouldn't want the man she loved sharing his house with another woman. Tomorrow she'd check around to see if she could find a new place to live.

Ellen was scrambling eggs the next morning when Reed appeared, coming down the narrow stairs that led from the third floor to the kitchen. He'd shaved, which emphasized the chiseled look of his jaw. His handsome face was weathered and everything about him spoke of health and vitality. Ellen paused, her fork suspended with raw egg dripping from the tines. She wouldn't call Reed Morgan handsome so much as striking. He had an unmistakable masculine appeal. Apparently the duties of an aeronautical engineer were more physically demanding than she'd suspected. Strength showed in the wide muscular shoulders and lean, hard build. He looked even more formidable this morning.

"Good morning," she greeted him cheerfully, as she continued to beat the eggs. "I hope you slept well."

Reed poured coffee into the same mug he'd used the day before. A creature of habit, Ellen mused. "Morning," he responded somewhat gruffly.

"Can I fix you some eggs?"

"Derek and I have already talked. You can all stay."

"Is that a yes or a no to the eggs?"

"I'm trying to tell you that you don't need to worry about impressing me with your cooking."

With a grunt of impatience, Ellen set the bowl aside and leaned forward, slapping her open palms on the countertop. "I'm scrambling eggs here. Whether you want some or not is entirely up to you. Believe me, if I was concerned about impressing you, I wouldn't do it with eggs."

For the first time, Ellen saw a hint of amusement touch those brilliant green eyes. "No, I don't suppose you would."

"Now that we've got that settled, would you like breakfast or not?"

"All right."

His eyes boldly searched hers and for an instant Ellen found herself regretting that there was a Danielle. With an effort, she turned away and brought her concentration back to preparing breakfast.

"Do you do all the cooking?" Just the way he asked made it sound as though he was already criticizing their household arrangements. Ellen bit back a sarcastic reply and busied herself melting butter and putting bread in the toaster. She'd bide her time. If Derek was right, his brother would soon be away on another assignment.

"Most of it," Ellen answered, pouring the eggs into the hot skillet.

"Who pays for the groceries?"

Ellen shrugged, hoping to give the appearance of nonchalance. "We all chip in." She did the shopping and most of the cooking. In return, the boys did their share of the housework—now that she'd taught them how.

The bread popped up from the toaster and Ellen reached for the butter knife, doing her best to ignore the overpowering presence of Reed Morgan.

"What about the shopping?"

"I enjoy it," she said simply, putting two more slices of bread in the toaster.

"I thought women all over America were fighting to get out of the kitchen."

"When a replacement is found, I'll be happy to step aside." She wasn't comfortable with the direction this conversation seemed to be taking. Reed was looking at her as though she was some kind of 1950s throwback.

Ellen liked to cook and as it turned out, the boys needed someone who knew her way around a kitchen, and she needed an inexpensive place to live. Everything had worked out perfectly....

She spooned the cooked eggs onto one plate and piled the toast on another, then carried it to the table, which gave her enough time to control her indignation. She was temporarily playing the role of surrogate mother to a bunch of college-age boys. All right, maybe that made her a little unusual these days, but she enjoyed living with Derek and the others. It helped her feel at home, and for now she needed that.

"Aren't you going to eat?" Reed stopped her on her way out of the kitchen.

"I'll have something later. The only time I can count on the bathroom being free in the mornings is when the boys are having breakfast. That is, unless you were planning to use it?"

Reed's eyes narrowed fractionally. "No."

"What's the matter? You've got that look on your face again."

"What look?"

"The one where you pinch your lips together as if you aren't pleased about something and you're wondering just how much you should say."

His tight expression relaxed into a slow, sensual grin. "Do you always read people this well?"

Ellen shook her head. "Not always. I just want to know what I've done this time."

"Aren't you concerned about living with three men?"

"No. Should I be?" She crossed her arms and leaned against the doorjamb, almost enjoying their conversation. The earlier antagonism had disappeared. She'd agree that her living arrangements were a bit unconventional, but they suited her. The situation was advantageous for her *and* the boys.

"Any one of them could fall in love with you."

With difficulty, Ellen restrained her laughter. "That's unlikely. They see me as their mother."

The corners of his mouth formed deep grooves as he tried—and failed—to suppress a grin. Raising one brow, he did a thorough inspection of her curves.

Hot color flooded her pale cheeks. "All right—a sister. I'm too old for them."

Monte sauntered into the kitchen, followed closely by Pat who muttered, "I thought I smelled breakfast."

"I was just about to call you," she told them and hurried from the room, wanting to avoid a head-on collision with Reed. And that was where this conversation was going.

Fifteen minutes later, Ellen returned to the kitchen. She was dressed in cords and an Irish cable-knit sweater; soft dark curls framed her small oval face. Ellen had no illusions about her looks. Men on the street weren't going to stop and stare, but she knew she was reasonably attractive. With her short, dark hair and deep brown eyes, she considered herself average. Ordinary. Far too ordinary for a man like Reed Morgan. One look at Ellen, and Danielle would feel completely reassured. Angry at the self-pitying thought, she grabbed a pen and tore out a sheet of notebook paper.

Intent on making the shopping list, Ellen was halfway into the kitchen before she noticed Reed standing at the sink, wiping the frying pan dry. The table had been cleared and the dishes were stacked on the counter, ready for the dishwasher.

"Oh," she said, a little startled. "I would've done that."

"While I'm here, I'll do my share." He said it without looking at her, his eyes avoiding hers.

"But this is your home. I certainly don't mind—"

"I wouldn't be comfortable otherwise. Haven't you got a class this morning?" He sounded anxious to be rid of her.

"Not until eleven."

"What's your major?" He'd turned around, leaning against the sink and crossing his arms. He was the picture of nonchalance, but Ellen wasn't fooled. She knew very well that he wasn't pleased about her living in his home, and she felt he'd given his permission reluctantly. She suspected he was even looking for ways to dislike her. Ellen understood that. Reed was bound to face some awkward questions once Danielle discovered there was a woman living in his house. Especially a woman who slept in his bed and took charge of his kitchen. But that would change this afternoon—at least the sleeping in his bed part.

"I'm majoring in education."

"That's the mother in you coming out again."

Ellen hadn't thought of it that way. Reed simply felt more comfortable seeing her in that light—as a maternal, even matronly figure—she decided. She'd let him, if it meant he'd be willing to accept her arrangement with Derek and the others.

"I suppose you're right," she murmured as she began opening and closing cupboard doors, checking the contents on each shelf, and scribbling down several items she'd need the following week.

"What are you doing now?"

Mentally, Ellen counted to ten before answering. She resented his overbearing tone, and despite her earlier resolve to humor him, she snapped, "I'm making a grocery list. Do you have a problem with that?"

"No," he answered gruffly.

"I'll be out of here in just a minute," she said, trying hard to maintain her patience.

"You aren't in my way."

"And while we're on the subject of being in someone's way, I want you to know I plan to move my things out of your room this afternoon."

"Don't. I won't be here long enough to make it worth your while."

Two

So Reed was leaving. Ellen felt guilty and relieved at the same time. Derek had told her Reed would probably be sent on another job soon, but she hadn't expected it to be quite *this* soon.

"There's a project Boeing is sending me on. California this time—the Monterey area."

Resuming her task, Ellen added several more items to the grocery list. "I've heard that's a lovely part of the state."

"It is beautiful." But his voice held no enthusiasm.

Ellen couldn't help feeling a twinge of disappointment for Reed. One look convinced her that he didn't want to leave again. After all, he'd just returned from several months in the Middle East and already he had another assignment in California. If he was dreading this latest job, Ellen could well imagine how Danielle must feel.

"Nonetheless, I think it's important to give you back your room. I'll move my things this afternoon." She'd ask the boys to help and it wouldn't take long.

With his arms crossed, Reed lounged against the door-jamb, watching her.

"And if you feel that my being here is a problem," she went on, thinking of Danielle, "I'll look for another place. The only thing I ask is that you give me a couple of weeks to find something."

He hesitated as though he was considering the offer, then shook his head, grinning slightly. "I don't think that'll be necessary."

"I don't mind telling you I'm relieved to hear it, but I'm prepared to move if necessary."

His left brow rose a fraction of an inch as the grin spread across his face. "Having you here does have certain advantages."

"Such as?"

"You're an excellent cook, the house hasn't been this clean in months and Derek's mother says you're a good influence on these boys."

Ellen had briefly met Mary Morgan, Derek's mother, a few weeks before. "Thank you."

He sauntered over to the coffeepot and poured himself a cup. "And for that matter, Derek's right. This house is too big to sit empty. I'm often out of town, but there's no reason others shouldn't use it. Especially with someone as...domestically inclined as you around to keep things running smoothly."

So he viewed her as little more than a live-in housekeeper and cook! Ellen felt a flush of anger. Before she could say something she'd regret, she turned quickly and fled out the back door on her way to the local grocery store. Actually, Reed Morgan had interpreted the situation correctly, but it somehow bothered her that he saw her in such an unflattering light.

Ellen didn't see Reed again until late that night. Friday evenings were lazy ones for her. She'd dated Charlie Hanson, a fellow student, a couple of times but usually preferred the company of a good book. With her heavy class schedule, most of Ellen's free time was devoted to her studies. Particularly algebra. This one class was getting her down. It didn't matter how hard she hit the books, she couldn't seem to grasp the theory.

Dressed in her housecoat and a pair of bright purple knee socks, she sat at the kitchen table, her legs propped on the chair across from her. Holding a paperback novel open with one hand, she dipped chocolate-chip cookies in a tall glass of milk with the other. At the unexpected sound of the back door opening, she looked curiously up from her book.

Reed seemed surprised to see her. He frowned as his eyes darted past her to the clock above the stove. "You're up late."

"On weekends my mommy doesn't make me go to bed until midnight," she said sarcastically, doing her best to ignore him. Reed managed to look fantastic without even trying. He didn't need her gawking at him to tell him that. If his expensive sports jacket was anything to judge by, he'd spent the evening with Danielle.

"You've got that look," he grumbled.

"What look?"

"The same one you said I have—wanting to say something and unsure if you should."

"Oh." She couldn't very well deny it.

"And what did you want to tell me?"

"Only that you look good." She paused, wondering how much she should say. "You even smell expensive."

His gaze slid over her. "From the way you're dressed, you look to me as though you'd smell of cotton candy."

"Thank you, but actually it's chocolate chip." She pushed the package of cookies in his direction. "Here. Save me from myself."

"No, thanks," Reed murmured and headed toward the living room.

"Don't go in there," Ellen cried, swinging her legs off the chair and coming abruptly to her feet.

Reed's hand was on the kitchen door, ready to open it. "Don't go into the living room?"

"Derek's got a girl in there."

Reed continued to stare at her blankly. "So?"

"So. He's with Michelle Tanner. *The* Michelle Tanner. The girl he's been crazy about for the last six weeks. She finally agreed to a date with him. They rented a movie."

"That doesn't explain why I can't go in there."

"Yes, it does," Ellen whispered. "The last time I peeked, Derek was getting ready to make his move. You'll ruin everything if you barge in there now."

"His move?" Reed didn't seem to like the sound of this. "What do you mean, 'his move'? The kid's barely nineteen."

Ellen smiled. "Honestly, Reed, you must've been young once. Don't you remember what it's like to have a crush on a girl? All Derek's doing is plotting that first kiss."

Reed dropped his hand as he stared at Ellen. He seemed

to focus on her mouth. Then the glittering green eyes skimmed hers, and Ellen's breath caught somewhere between her throat and her lungs as she struggled to pull her gaze away from his. Reed had no business giving her that kind of look. Not when he'd so recently left Danielle's arms. And not when Ellen reacted so profoundly to a mere glance.

"I haven't forgotten," he said. "And as for that remark about being young *once,* I'm not exactly over the hill."

This was ridiculous! With a sigh of annoyance, Ellen sat down again, swinging her feet onto the opposite chair. She picked up her book and forced her eyes—if not her attention— back to the page in front of her. "I'm glad to hear that." If she could get a grip on herself for the next few days everything would be fine. Reed would leave and her life with the boys would settle back into its routine.

She heard the refrigerator opening and watched Reed pour himself a glass of milk, then reach for a handful of chocolate-chip cookies. When he pulled out the chair across from her, Ellen reluctantly lowered her legs.

"What are you reading?"

Feeling irritable and angry for allowing him to affect her, she deliberately waited until she'd finished the page before answering. "A book," she muttered.

"My, my, you're a regular Mary Sunshine. What's wrong—did your boyfriend stand you up tonight?"

With exaggerated patience she slowly lowered the paperback to the table and marked her place. "Listen. I'm twenty-five years old and well beyond the age of *boyfriends.*"

Reed shrugged. "All right. Your lover."

She hadn't meant to imply that at all! And Reed knew it. He'd wanted to fluster her and he'd succeeded.

"Women these days have this habit of letting their mouths hang open," he said pointedly. "I suppose they think it looks sexy, but actually, they resemble beached trout." With that, he deposited his empty glass in the sink and marched briskly up the back stairs.

Ellen closed her eyes and groaned in embarrassment. He must think she was an idiot, and with good reason. She'd done a remarkable job of imitating one. She groaned again, infuriated by the fact that she found Reed Morgan so attractive.

Ellen didn't climb the stairs to her new bedroom on the third floor for another hour. And then it was only after Derek had paid her a quick visit in the kitchen and given her a thumbs-up. At least his night had gone well.

Twenty minutes after she'd turned off her reading light, Ellen lay staring into the silent, shadow-filled room. She wasn't sleepy, and the mystery novel no longer held her interest. Her thoughts were troubled by that brief incident in the kitchen with Reed. Burying her head in her pillow, Ellen yawned and closed her eyes. But sleep still wouldn't come. A half-hour later, she threw back the covers and grabbed her housecoat from the end of the bed. Perhaps another glass of milk would help.

Not bothering to turn on any lights, she took a clean glass from the dishwasher and pulled the carton of milk from the refrigerator. Drink in hand, she stood at the kitchen window, looking out at the huge oak tree in the backyard. Its bare limbs stretched upward like skeletal hands, silhouetted against the full moon.

"I've heard that a woman's work is never done, but this is ridiculous."

She nearly spilled her milk at the sudden sound of Reed's voice behind her. She whirled around and glared at him. "I see there's a full moon tonight. I wonder if it's safe to be alone with you. And wouldn't you know it, I left my silver bullet upstairs."

"No woman's ever accused me of being a werewolf. A number of other things," he murmured, "but never that."

"Maybe that's because you hadn't frightened them half out of their wits."

"I couldn't resist. Sorry," he said, reaching for the milk carton.

"You know, if we'd stop snapping at each other, it might make life a lot easier around here."

"Perhaps," he agreed. "I will admit it's a whole lot easier to talk to you when you're dressed."

Ellen slammed down her empty glass. "I'm getting a little tired of hearing about that."

But Reed went on, clearly unperturbed. "Unfortunately, ever since that first time when I found you in your bra, you've insisted on overdressing. From one extreme to another—too few clothes to too many." He paused. "Do you always wear socks to bed?"

"Usually."

"I pity the man you sleep with."

"Well, you needn't worry—" She expelled a lungful of oxygen. "We're doing it again."

"So, you're suggesting we stop trading insults for the sake of the children."

"I hadn't thought of it that way," she said with an involuntary smile, "but you're right. No one's going to be comfortable if the two of us are constantly sniping at each other. I'm willing to try if you are. Okay?"

"Okay." A smile softened Reed's features, angular and shadowed in the moonlight.

"And I'm not a threat to your relationship with Danielle, am I? In fact, if you'd rather, she need never even know I'm here," Ellen said casually.

"Maybe that would've been best," he conceded, setting aside his empty glass. "But I doubt it. Besides, she already knows. I told her tonight." He muttered something else she didn't catch.

"And?"

"And," he went on, "she says she doesn't mind, but she'd like to meet you."

This was one encounter Ellen wasn't going to enjoy.

The next morning, Ellen brought down her laundry and was using the washing machine and the dryer before Reed and the others were even awake.

She sighed as she tested the iron with the wet tip of her index finger and found that it still wasn't hot, although she'd turned it on at least five minutes earlier. This house was owned by a wealthy engineer, so why were there only two electrical outlets in the kitchen? It meant that she couldn't use the washer, the dryer and the iron at the same time without causing a blow-out.

"Darn it," she groaned, setting the iron upright on the padded board.

"What's the matter?" Reed asked from the doorway leading into the kitchen. He got himself a cup of coffee.

"This iron."

"Hey, Ellen, if you're doing some ironing, would you press a few things for me?" Monte asked, walking barefoot into the kitchen. He peered into the refrigerator and took out a slice of cold pizza.

"I was afraid this would happen," she grumbled, still upset by the house's electrical problems.

"Ellen's not your personal maid," Reed said sharply. "If you've got something you want pressed, do it yourself."

A hand on her hip, Ellen turned to Reed, defiantly meeting his glare. "If you don't mind, I can answer for myself."

"Fine," he snorted and took a sip of his coffee.

She directed her next words to Monte, who stood looking at her expectantly. "I am not your personal maid. If you want something pressed, do it yourself."

Monte glanced from Reed to Ellen and back to Reed again. "Sorry I asked," he mumbled on his way out of the kitchen. The door was left swinging in his wake.

"You said that well," Reed commented with a soft chuckle.

"Believe me, I was conned into enough schemes by my sister and brother to know how to handle Monte and the others."

Reed's gaze was admiring. "If your brother's anything like mine, I don't doubt it."

"All brothers are alike," she said. Unable to hold back a grin, Ellen tested the iron a second time and noticed that it was only slightly warmer. "Have you ever thought about putting another outlet in this kitchen?"

Reed looked at her in surprise. "No. Do you need one?"

"Need one?" she echoed. "There are only two in here. It's ridiculous."

Reed scanned the kitchen. "I hadn't thought about it." Setting his coffee mug aside, he shook his head. "Your mood's not much better today than it was last night." With that remark, he hurried out of the room, following in Monte's footsteps.

Frustrated, Ellen tightened her grip on the iron. Reed was right. She was being unreasonable and she really didn't understand why. But she was honest enough to admit, at least to herself, that she was attracted to this man whose house she occupied. She realized she'd have to erect a wall of reserve between them to protect them both from embarrassment.

"Morning, Ellen," Derek said as he entered the kitchen and threw himself into a chair. As he emptied a box of cornflakes into a huge bowl, he said, "I've got some shirts that need pressing."

"If you want anything pressed, do it yourself," she almost shouted.

Stunned, Derek blinked. "Okay."

Setting the iron upright again, Ellen released a lengthy sigh. "I didn't mean to scream at you."

"That's all right."

Turning off the iron, she joined Derek at the table and reached for the cornflakes.

"Are you still worried about that math paper you're supposed to do?" he asked.

"I'm working my way to an early grave over it."

"I would've thought you'd do well in math."

Ellen snickered. "Hardly."

"Have you come up with a topic?"

"Not yet. I'm going to the library later, where I pray some form of inspiration will strike me."

"Have you asked the other people in your class what they're writing about?" Derek asked as he refilled his bowl, this time with rice puffs.

Ellen nodded. "That's what worries me most. The brain who sits beside me is doing hers on the probability of solving Goldbach's conjecture in our lifetime."

Derek's eyes widened. "That's a tough act to follow."

"Let me tell you about the guy who sits behind me. He's doing his paper on mathematics during World War II."

"You're in the big leagues now," Derek said with a sympathetic shake of his head.

"I know," Ellen lamented. She was taking this course only because it was compulsory; all she wanted out of it was a passing grade. The quadratic formula certainly wasn't going to have any lasting influence on *her* life.

"Good luck," Derek said.

"Thanks. I'm going to need it."

After straightening up the kitchen, Ellen changed into old jeans and a faded sweatshirt. The jeans had been washed so many times they were nearly white. They fit her hips so snugly she could hardly slide her fingers into the pockets, but she hated the idea of throwing them out.

She tied an old red scarf around her hair and headed for the garage. While rooting around for a ladder a few days earlier, she'd discovered some pruning shears. She'd noticed several overgrown bushes in the backyard and decided to tackle those first, before cleaning the drainpipes.

After an hour, she had a pile of underbrush large enough

to be worth a haul to the dump. She'd have one of the boys do that later. For now, the drainpipes demanded her attention.

"Derek!" she called as she pushed open the back door. She knew her face was flushed and damp from exertion.

"Yeah?" His voice drifted toward her from the living room.

Ellen wandered in to discover him on the phone. "I'm ready for you now."

"Now?" His eyes pleaded with her as his palm covered the mouthpiece. "It's Michelle."

"All right, I'll ask Monte."

"Thanks." He gave her a smile of appreciation.

But Monte was nowhere to be found, and Pat was at the Y shooting baskets with some friends. When she stuck her head into the living room again, she saw Derek still draped over the sofa, deep in conversation. Unwilling to interfere with the course of young love, she decided she could probably manage to climb onto the roof unaided.

Dragging the aluminum ladder from the garage, she thought she might not need Derek's help anyway. She'd mentioned her plan earlier in the week, and he hadn't looked particularly enthusiastic.

With the extension ladder braced against the side of the house, she climbed onto the roof of the back porch. Very carefully, she reached for the ladder and extended it to the very top of the house.

She maneuvered herself back onto the ladder and climbed slowly and cautiously up.

Once she'd managed to position herself on the slanting roof, she was fine. She even took a moment to enjoy the spectacular view. She could see Lake Washington, with its deep-green water, and the spacious grounds of the university campus.

Using the brush she'd tucked—with some struggle—into her back pocket, Ellen began clearing away the leaves and other debris that clogged the gutters and drainpipes.

She was about half finished when she heard raised voices below. Pausing, she sat down, drawing her knees against her chest, and watched the scene unfolding on the front lawn. Reed and his brother were embroiled in a heated discussion—with Reed doing most of the talking. Derek was raking leaves and didn't seem at all pleased about devoting his Saturday morning to chores. Ellen guessed that Reed had summarily interrupted the telephone conversation between Derek and Michelle.

With a lackadaisical swish of the rake, Derek flung the multicolored leaves skyward. Ellen restrained a laugh. Reed had obviously pulled rank and felt no hesitation about giving him orders.

To her further amusement, Reed then motioned toward his black Porsche, apparently suggesting that his brother wash the car when he'd finished with the leaves. Still chuckling, Ellen grabbed for the brush, but she missed and accidentally sent it tumbling down the side of the roof. It hit the green shingles over the front porch with a loud thump before flying onto the grass only a few feet from where Derek and Reed were standing.

Two pairs of astonished eyes turned swiftly in her direction. "Hi," she called down and waved. "I don't suppose I could talk one of you into bringing that up to me?" She braced her feet and pulled herself into a standing position as she waited for a reply.

Reed pointed his finger at her and yelled, "What do you think you're doing up there?"

"Playing tiddlywinks," she shouted back. "What do *you* think I'm doing?"

"I don't know, but I want you down."

"In a minute."

"Now."

"Yes, *sir*." She gave him a mocking salute and would have bowed if she hadn't been afraid she might lose her footing.

Derek burst out laughing but was quickly silenced by a scathing glance from his older brother.

"Tell Derek to bring me the broom," Ellen called, moving closer to the edge.

Ellen couldn't decipher Reed's response, but from the way he stormed around the back of the house, she figured it was best to come down before he had a heart attack. She had the ladder lowered to the back-porch roof before she saw him.

"You idiot!" he shouted. He was standing in the driveway, hands on his hips, glaring at her in fury. "I can't believe anyone would do anything so stupid."

"What do you mean?" The calmness of her words belied the way the blood pulsed through her veins. Alarm rang in his voice and that surprised her. She certainly hadn't expected Reed, of all people, to be concerned about her safety. He held the ladder steady until she'd climbed down and was standing squarely in front of him. Then he started pacing. For a minute Ellen didn't know what to think.

"What's wrong?" she asked. "You look as pale as a sheet."

"What's wrong?" he sputtered. "You were on the *roof* and—"

"I wasn't in any danger."

He shook his head, clearly upset. "There are people who specialize in that sort of thing. I don't want you up there again. Understand?"

"Yes, but—"

"No buts. You do anything that stupid again and you're out of here. Have you got that?"

"Yes," she said with forced calm. "I understand."

"Good."

Before she could think of anything else to say, Reed was gone.

"You all right?" Derek asked a minute later. Shocked by Reed's outburst, Ellen hadn't moved. Rarely had anyone been that angry with her. Heavens, she'd cleaned out drainpipes lots of times. Her father had died when Ellen was fourteen, and over the years she'd assumed most of the maintenance duties around the house. She'd learned that, with the help of a good book and a well-stocked hardware store, there wasn't anything she couldn't fix. She'd repaired the plumbing, built bookshelves and done a multitude of household projects. It was just part of her life. Reed had acted as though she'd done something hazardous, as though she'd taken some extraordinary risk, and that seemed totally ridiculous to her. She knew what she was doing. Besides, heights didn't frighten her; they never had.

"Ellen?" Derek prompted.

"I'm fine."

"I've never seen Reed act like that. He didn't mean anything."

"I know," she whispered, brushing the dirt from her knees. Derek drifted off, leaving her to return the ladder to the garage single-handed.

Reed found her an hour later folding laundry in her bedroom. He knocked on the open door.

"Yes?" She looked up expectantly.

"I owe you an apology."

She continued folding towels at the foot of her bed. "Oh?"

"I didn't mean to come at you like Attila the Hun."

Hugging a University of Washington T-shirt to her stomach, she lowered her gaze to the bedspread and nodded. "Apology accepted and I'll offer one of my own. I didn't mean to come back at you like a spoiled brat."

"Accepted." They smiled at each other and she caught her breath as those incredible green eyes gazed into hers. It was a repeat of the scene in the kitchen the night before. For a long, silent moment they did nothing but stare, and she realized that a welter of conflicting emotions must have registered on her face. A similar turmoil raged on his.

"If it'll make you feel any better, I won't go up on the roof again," she said at last.

"I'd appreciate it." His lips barely moved. The words were more of a sigh than a sentence.

She managed a slight nod in response.

At the sound of footsteps, they guiltily looked away.

"Say, Ellen." Pat stopped in the doorway, a basketball under his left arm. "Got time to shoot a few baskets with me?"

"Sure," she whispered, stepping around Reed. At that moment, she would've agreed to just about anything to escape his company. There was something happening between them and she felt frightened and confused and excited, all at the same time.

The basketball hoop was positioned above the garage door at the end of the long driveway. Pat was attending the University of Washington with the express hope of making the Husky basketball team. His whole life revolved around the game. He was rarely seen without a ball tucked under his arm and sometimes Ellen wondered if he showered with it. She was well aware that the invitation to practice a few free throws with him was not meant to be taken literally. The only slam dunk Ellen had ever accomplished was with a doughnut in her hot chocolate. Her main job was to stand on the sidelines and be awed by Pat's talent.

They hadn't been in the driveway fifteen minutes when the back door opened and Derek strolled out. "Say, Ellen, have you got a minute?" he asked, frowning.

"What's the problem?"

"It's Michelle."

Sitting on the concrete porch step, Derek looked at Ellen with those wide pleading eyes of his.

Ellen sat beside him and wrapped her arms around her bent knees. "What's wrong with Michelle?"

"Nothing. She's beautiful and I think she might even fall in love with me, given the chance." He paused to sigh expressively. "I asked her out to dinner tonight."

"She agreed. Right?" If Michelle was anywhere near as taken with Derek as he was with her, she wasn't likely to refuse.

The boyishly thin shoulders heaved in a gesture of despair. "She can't."

"Why not?" Ellen watched as Pat bounced the basketball across the driveway, pivoted, jumped high in the air and sent the ball through the net.

"Michelle promised her older sister that she'd baby-sit tonight."

"That's too bad." Ellen gave him a sympathetic look.

"The thing is, she'd probably go out with me if there was someone who could watch her niece and nephew for her."

"Uh-huh." Pat made another skillful play and Ellen applauded vigorously. He rewarded her with a triumphant smile.

"Then you will?"

Ellen switched her attention from Pat's antics at the basketball hoop back to Derek. "Will I what?"

"Babysit Michelle's niece and nephew?"

"What?" she exploded. "Not me. I've got to do research for a term paper."

"Ellen, please, please, please."

"No. No. No." She sliced the air forcefully with her hand and got to her feet.

Derek rose with her. "I sense some resistance to this idea."

"The boy's a genius," she mumbled under her breath as she hurried into the kitchen. "I've got to write my term paper. You know that."

Derek followed her inside. "Ellen, please? I promise I'll never ask anything of you again."

"I've heard that before." She tried to ignore him as he

trailed her to the refrigerator and watched her take out sandwich makings for lunch.

"It's a matter of the utmost importance," Derek pleaded anew.

"What is?" Reed spoke from behind the paper he was reading at the kitchen table.

"My date with Michelle. Listen, Ellen, I bet Reed would help you. You're not doing anything tonight, are you?"

Reed lowered the newspaper. "Help Ellen with what?"

"Babysitting."

Reed glanced from the intent expression on his younger brother's face to the stubborn look on Ellen's. "You two leave me out of this."

"Ellen. Dear, *sweet* Ellen, you've got to understand that it could be weeks—weeks," he repeated dramatically, "before Michelle will be able to go out with me again."

Ellen put down an armload of cheese, ham and assorted jars of mustard and pickles. "*No!* Can I make it any plainer than that? I'm sorry, Derek, honest. But I can't."

"Reed," Derek pleaded with his brother. "Say something that'll convince her."

"Like I said, I'm out of this one."

He raised the paper again, but Ellen could sense a smile hidden behind it. Still, she doubted that Reed would be foolish enough to involve himself in this situation.

"Ellen, puleease."

"No." Ellen realized that if she wanted any peace, she'd have to forget about lunch and make an immediate escape. She whirled around and headed out of the kitchen, the door swinging in her wake.

"I think she's weakening," she heard Derek say as he followed her.

She was on her way up the stairs when she caught sight of Derek in the dining room, coming toward her on his knees, hands folded in supplication. "Won't you please reconsider?"

Ellen groaned. "What do I need to say to convince you? I've got to get to the library. That paper is due Monday morning."

"I'll write it for you."

"No, thanks."

At just that moment Reed came through the door. "It shouldn't be too difficult to find a reliable sitter. There are a few families with teenagers in the neighbourhood, as I recall."

"I...don't know," Derek hedged.

"If we can't find anyone, then Danielle and I'll manage. It'll be good practice for us. Besides, just how much trouble can two kids be?"

When she heard that, Ellen had to swallow a burst of laughter. Reed obviously hadn't spent much time around children, she thought with a mischievous grin.

"How old did you say these kids are?" She couldn't resist asking.

"Nine and four." Derek's dark eyes brightened as he leaped to his feet and gave his brother a grateful smile. "So I can tell Michelle everything's taken care of?"

"I suppose." Reed turned to Ellen. "I was young once myself," he said pointedly, reminding her of the comment she'd made the night before.

"I really appreciate this, Reed," Derek was saying. "I'll

be your slave for life. I'd even lend you money if I had some. By the way, can I borrow your car tonight?"

"Don't press your luck."

"Right." Derek chuckled, bounding up the stairs. He paused for a moment. "Oh, I forgot to tell you. Michelle's bringing the kids over here, okay?"

He didn't wait for a response.

The doorbell chimed close to six o'clock, just as Ellen was gathering up her books and preparing to leave for the library.

"That'll be Michelle," Derek called excitedly. "Can you get it, Ellen?"

"No problem."

Coloring books and crayons were arranged on the coffee table, along with some building blocks Reed must have purchased that afternoon. From bits and pieces of information she'd picked up, she concluded that Reed had discovered it wasn't quite as easy to find a baby-sitter as he'd assumed. And with no other recourse, he and Danielle were apparently taking over the task. Ellen wished him luck, but she really did need to concentrate on this stupid term paper. Reed hadn't suggested that Ellen wait around to meet Danielle. But she had to admit she'd been wondering about the woman from the time Derek had first mentioned her.

"Hello, Ellen." Blonde Michelle greeted Ellen with a warm, eager smile. They'd met briefly the other night, when she'd come over to watch the movie. "This sure is great of Derek's brother and his girlfriend, isn't it?"

"It sure is."

The four-year-old boy was clinging to Michelle's trouser leg so that her gait was stiff-kneed as she limped into the house with the child attached.

"Jimmy, this is Ellen. You'll be staying in her house tonight while Auntie Michelle goes out to dinner with Derek."

"I want my mommy."

"He won't be a problem," Michelle told Ellen confidently.

"I thought there were two children."

"Yeah, the baby's in the car. I'll be right back."

"Baby?" Ellen swallowed down a laugh. "What baby?"

"Jenny's nine months."

"Nine *months?*" A small uncontrollable giggle slid from her throat. This would be marvelous. Reed with a nine-month-old was almost too good to miss.

"Jimmy, you stay here." Somehow Michelle was able to pry the four-year-old's fingers from her leg and pass the struggling child to Ellen.

Kicking and thrashing, Jimmy broke into loud sobs as Ellen carried him into the living room. "Here's a coloring book. Do you like to color, Jimmy?"

But he refused to talk to Ellen or even look at her as he buried his face in the sofa cushions. "I want my mommy," he wailed again.

By the time Michelle had returned with a baby carrier and a fussing nine-month-old, Derek sauntered out from the kitchen. "Hey, Michelle, you're lookin' good."

Reed, who was following closely behind, came to a shocked standstill when he saw the baby. "I thought you said they were nine and four."

"I did," Derek explained patiently, his eyes devouring the blonde at his side.

"They won't be any trouble," Michelle cooed as Derek placed an arm around her shoulders and led her toward the open door.

"Derek, we need to talk," Reed insisted.

"Haven't got time now. Our reservations are for seven." His hand slid from Michelle's shoulders to her waist. "I'm taking my lady out for a night on the town."

"Derek," Reed demanded.

"Oh." Michelle tore her gaze from Derek's. "The diaper bag is in the entry. Jenny should be dry, but you might want to check her later. She'll probably cry for a few minutes once she sees I'm gone, but that'll stop almost immediately."

Reed's face was grim as he cast a speculative glance at Jimmy, who was still howling for his mother. The happily gurgling Jenny stared up at the unfamiliar dark-haired man and noticed for the first time that she was at the mercy of a stranger. She immediately burst into heart-wrenching tears.

"I want my mommy," Jimmy wailed yet again.

"I can see you've got everything under control," Ellen said, reaching for her coat. "I'm sure Danielle will be here any minute."

"Ellen..."

"Don't expect me back soon. I've got hours of research ahead of me."

"You aren't really going to leave, are you?" Reed gave her a horrified look.

"I wish I could stay," she lied breezily. "Another time." With that, she was out the door, smiling as she bounded down the steps.

Three

An uneasy feeling struck Ellen as she stood waiting at the bus stop. But she resolutely hardened herself against the impulse to rush back to Reed and his disconsolate charges. Danielle would show up any minute and Ellen really was obliged to do the research for her yet-to-be-determined math paper. Besides, she reminded herself, Reed had volunteered to babysit and she wasn't responsible for rescuing him. But his eyes had pleaded with her so earnestly. Ellen felt herself beginning to weaken. *No!* she mumbled under her breath. Reed had Danielle, and as far as Ellen was concerned, they were on their own.

However, by the time she arrived at the undergraduate library, Ellen discovered that she couldn't get Reed's pleading look out of her mind. From everything she'd heard about Danielle, Ellen figured the woman probably didn't know the first thing about babies. As for the term paper, she supposed she could put it off until Sunday. After all, she'd found excuses all day to avoid working on it. She'd done the laundry, trimmed the shrubs, cleaned the drain-pipes and washed the upstairs walls in an effort to escape that paper. One more night wasn't going to make much difference.

Hurriedly, she signed out some books and journals that looked as though they might be helpful and headed for the bus stop. Ellen had to admit that she was curious enough to want to meet Danielle. Reed's girlfriend had to be some-one very special to put up with his frequent absences—or else a schemer, as Derek had implied. But Ellen couldn't see Reed being duped by a woman, no matter how clever or sophisticated she might be.

Her speculations came to an end as the bus arrived, and she quickly jumped on for the short ride home.

Reed was kneeling on the carpet changing the still-tear-ful Jenny's diaper when Ellen walked in the front door. He seemed to have aged ten years in the past hour. The long sleeves of his wool shirt were rolled up to the elbows as he struggled with the tape on Jenny's disposable diaper.

Reed shook his head and sagged with relief. "Good thing you're here. She hasn't stopped crying from the minute you left."

"You look like you're doing a good job without me. Where's Danielle?" She glanced around, smiling at Jimmy; the little boy hadn't moved from the sofa, his face still hidden in the cushions.

Reed muttered a few words under his breath. "She couldn't stay." He finally finished with the diaper. "That wasn't so difficult after all," he said, glancing proudly at Ellen as he stood Jenny up on the floor, holding the baby upright by her small arms.

Ellen swallowed a laugh. The diaper hung crookedly, bunched up in front. She was trying to think of a tactful way of pointing it out to Reed when the whole thing began to slide down Jenny's pudgy legs, settling at her ankles.

"Maybe you should try," Reed conceded, handing her the baby. Within minutes, Ellen had successfully secured the diaper. Unfortunately, she didn't manage to soothe the baby any more than Reed had.

Cradling Jenny in her arms, Ellen paced the area in front of the fireplace, at a loss to comfort the sobbing child. "I doubt I'll do any better. It's been a long while since my brother was this size."

"Women are always better at this kind of stuff," Reed argued, rubbing a hand over his face. "Most women," he amended, with such a look of frustration that Ellen smiled.

"I'll bet Jimmy knows what to do," she suggested next, pleased with her inspiration. The little boy might actually come up with something helpful, and involving him in their attempts to comfort Jenny might distract him from his own unhappiness. Or so Ellen hoped. "Jimmy's a good big brother. Isn't that right, honey?"

The child lifted his face from the cushion. "I want my mommy."

"Let's pretend Ellen is your mommy," Reed coaxed.

"No! She's like that other lady who said bad words."

Meanwhile, Jenny wailed all the louder. Digging around in the bag, Reed found a stuffed teddy bear and pressed it into her arms. But Jenny angrily tossed the toy aside, the tears flowing unabated down her face.

"Come on, Jimmy," Reed said desperately. "We need a little help here. Your sister's crying."

Holding his hands over his eyes, Jimmy straightened and peeked through two fingers. The distraught Jenny continued to cry at full volume in spite of Ellen's best efforts.

"Mommy bounces her."

Ellen had been gently doing that from the beginning. "What else?" she asked.

"She likes her boo-loo."

"What's that?"

"Her teddy bear."

"I've already tried that," Reed said. "What else does your mommy do when she cries like this?"

Jimmy was thoughtful for a moment. "Oh." The four-year-old's eyes sparkled. "Mommy nurses her."

Reed and Ellen glanced at each other and dissolved into giggles. The laughter faded from his eyes and was replaced with a roguish grin. "That could be interesting."

Hiding a smile, Ellen decided to ignore Reed's comment. "Sorry, Jenny," she said softly to the baby girl.

"But maybe he's got an idea," Reed suggested. "Could she be hungry?"

"It's worth a try. At this point, anything is."

Jenny's bellowing had finally dwindled into a few hiccuping sobs. And for some reason, Jimmy suddenly straightened and stared at Reed's craggy face, at his deep auburn hair and brilliant green eyes. Then he pointed to the plaid wool shirt, its long sleeves rolled up to the elbow. "Are you a lumberjack?"

"A lumberjack?" Reed repeated, looking puzzled. He broke into a full laugh. "No, but I imagine I must look like one to you."

Rummaging through the diaper bag, Ellen found a plastic bottle filled with what was presumably formula. Jenny eyed it skeptically, but no sooner had Ellen removed the cap than Jenny grabbed it from her hands and began sucking eagerly at the nipple.

Sighing, Ellen sank into the rocking chair and swayed back and forth with the baby tucked in her arms. "I guess that settles that."

The silence was so blissful that she wanted to wrap it around herself. She felt the tension drain from her muscles as she relaxed in the rocking chair. From what Jimmy had dropped, she surmised that Danielle hadn't been much help. Everything she'd learned about the other woman told Ellen that Danielle would probably find young children frustrating—and apparently she had.

Jimmy had crawled into Reed's lap with a book and demanded the lumberjack read to him. Together the two leafed through the storybook. Several times during the peaceful interlude, Ellen's eyes met Reed's across the room and they exchanged a contented smile.

Jenny sucked tranquilly at the bottle, and her eyes slowly drooped shut. At peace with her world, the baby was satisfied to be held and rocked to sleep. Ellen gazed down at the angelic face and brushed fine wisps of hair from the untroubled forehead. Releasing her breath in a slow, drawnout sigh, she glanced up to discover Reed watching her, the little boy still sitting quietly on his lap.

"Ellen?" Reed spoke in a low voice. "Did you finish your math paper?"

"Finish it?" She groaned. "Are you kidding? I haven't even started it."

"What's a math paper?" Jimmy asked.

Rocking the baby, Ellen looked solemnly over at the boy. "Well, it's something I have to write for a math class. And if I don't write a paper, I haven't got a hope of passing the course." She didn't think he'd understand any algebraic terms. For that matter, neither did she.

"What's math?"

"Numbers," Reed told the boy.

"And, in this case, sometimes letters—like x and y."

"I like numbers," Jimmy declared. "I like three and nine and seven."

"Well, Jimmy, my boy, how would you like to write my paper for me?"

"Can I?"

Ellen grinned at him. "You bet."

Reed got out pencil and paper and set the four-year-old to work.

Glancing up, she gave Reed a smile. "See how easy this is? You're good with kids." Reed smiled in answer as he carefully drew numbers for Jimmy to copy.

After several minutes of this activity, Jimmy decided it was time to put on his pajamas. Seeing him yawn, Reed brought down a pillow and blanket and tucked him into a hastily made bed on the sofa. Then he read a bedtime story until the four-year-old again yawned loudly and fell almost instantly asleep.

Ellen still hadn't moved, fearing that the slightest jolt would rouse the baby.

"Why don't we set her down in the baby seat?" Reed said.

"I'm afraid she'll wake up."

"If she does, you can rock her again."

His suggestion made sense and besides, her arms were beginning to ache. "Okay." He moved to her side and took the sleeping child. Ellen held her breath momentarily when Jenny stirred. But the little girl simply rolled her head against the cushion and returned to sleep.

Ellen rose to her feet and turned the lamp down to its dimmest setting, surrounding them with a warm circle of light.

"I couldn't have done it without you," Reed whispered, coming to stand beside her. He rested his hand at the back of her neck.

An unfamiliar warmth seeped through Ellen, and she began to talk quickly, hoping to conceal her sudden nervousness. "Sure you could have. It looked to me as if you had everything under control."

Reed snorted. "I was ten minutes away from calling the crisis clinic. Thanks for coming to the rescue." He casually withdrew his hand, and Ellen felt both relieved and disappointed.

"You're welcome." She was dying to know what had happened with Danielle, but she didn't want to ask. Apparently, the other woman hadn't stayed around for long.

"Have you eaten?"

Ellen had been so busy that she'd forgotten about dinner, but once Reed mentioned it, she realized how hungry she was. "No, and I'm starved."

"Do you like Chinese food?"

"Love it."

"Good. There's enough for an army out in the kitchen. I ordered it earlier."

Ellen didn't need to be told that he'd made dinner plans

with Danielle in mind. He'd expected to share an intimate evening with her. "Listen," she began awkwardly, clasping her hands. "I really have to get going on this term paper. Why don't you call Danielle and invite her back? Now that the kids are asleep, I'm sure everything will be better. I—"

"Children make Danielle nervous. She warned me about it, but I refused to listen. She's home now and has probably taken some aspirin and gone to sleep. I can't see letting good food go to waste. Besides, this gives me an opportunity to thank you."

"Oh." It was the longest speech that Reed had made. "All right," she agreed with a slight nod.

While Reed warmed the food in the microwave, Ellen set out plates and forks and prepared a large pot of green tea, placing it in the middle of the table. The swinging door that connected the kitchen with the living room was left open in case either child woke.

"What do we need plates for?" Reed asked with a questioning arch of his brow.

"Plates are the customary eating device."

"Not tonight."

"Not tonight?" Something amusing glinted in Reed's eyes as he set out several white boxes and brandished two pairs of chopsticks. "Since it's only the two of us, we can eat right out of the boxes."

"I'm not very adept with chopsticks." The smell drifting from the open boxes was tangy and enticing.

"You'll learn if you're hungry."

"I'm famished."

"Good." Deftly he took the first pair of chopsticks and

showed her how to work them with her thumb and index finger.

Imitating his movements Ellen discovered that her fingers weren't nearly as agile as his. Two or three tries at picking up small pieces of spicy diced chicken succeeded only in frustrating her.

"Here." Reed fed her a bite from the end of his chopsticks. "Be a little more patient with yourself."

"That's easy for you to say while you're eating your fill and I'm starving to death."

"It'll come."

Ellen grumbled under her breath, but a few tries later she managed to deliver a portion of the hot food to her eager mouth.

"See, I told you you'd pick this up fast enough."

"Do you always tell someone 'I told you so'?" she asked with pretended annoyance. The mood was too congenial for any real discontent. Ellen felt that they'd shared a special time together looking after the two small children. More than special—astonishing. They hadn't clashed once or found a single thing to squabble over.

"I enjoy teasing you. Your eyes have an irresistible way of lighting up when you're angry."

"If you continue to insist that I eat with these absurd pieces of wood, you'll see my eyes brighten the entire room."

"I'm looking forward to that," he murmured with a laugh. "No forks. You can't properly enjoy Chinese food unless you use chopsticks."

"I can't properly *taste* it without a fork."

"Here, I'll feed you." Again he brought a spicy morsel to her mouth.

A drop of the sauce fell onto her chin and Ellen wiped it off. "You aren't any better at this than me." She dipped the chopsticks into the chicken mixture and attempted to transport a tidbit to Reed's mouth. It balanced precariously on the end of her chopsticks, and Reed lowered his mouth to catch it before it could land in his lap.

"You're improving," he told her, his voice low and slightly husky.

Their eyes met. Unable to face the caressing look in his warm gaze, Ellen bent her head and pretended to be engrossed in her dinner. But her appetite was instantly gone—vanished.

A tense silence filled the room. The air between them was so charged that she felt breathless and weak, as though she'd lost the energy to move or speak. Ellen didn't dare raise her eyes for fear of what she'd see in his.

"Ellen."

She took a deep breath and scrambled to her feet. "I think I hear Jimmy," she whispered.

"Maybe it was Jenny," Reed added hurriedly.

Ellen paused in the doorway between the two rooms. They were both overwhelmingly aware that neither child had made a sound. "I guess they're still asleep."

"That's good." The scraping sound of his chair against the floor told her that Reed, too, had risen from the table. When she turned, she found him depositing the leftovers in the refrigerator. His preoccupation with the task gave her a moment to reflect on what had just happened. There were too many problems involved in pursuing this attraction; the best thing was to ignore it and hope the craziness passed. They were mature adults, not adolescents, and besides, this would complicate her life, which was something she didn't need right now. Neither, she was sure, did he. Especially with Danielle in the picture.

"If you don't mind, I'm going to head upstairs," she began awkwardly, taking a step in retreat.

"Okay, then. And thanks. I appreciated the help."

"I appreciated the dinner," she returned.

"See you in the morning."

"Right." Neither seemed eager to bring the evening to an end.

"Good night, Ellen."

"Night, Reed. Call if you need me."

"I will."

Turning decisively, she took the stairs and was panting by the time she'd climbed up the second narrow flight. Since the third floor had originally been built to accommodate servants, the five bedrooms were small and opened onto a large central room, which was where Ellen had placed her bed. She'd chosen the largest of the bedrooms as her study.

She sat resolutely down at her desk and leafed through several books, hoping to come across an idea she could use for her term paper. But her thoughts were dominated by the man two floors below. Clutching a study on the origins of algebra to her chest, she sighed deeply and wondered whether Danielle truly valued Reed. She must, Ellen decided, or she wouldn't be so willing to sit at home waiting, while her fiancé traipsed around the world directing a variety of projects.

Reed had been so patient and good-natured with Jimmy and Jenny. When the little boy had climbed into his lap, Reed had read to him and held him with a tenderness that stirred her heart. And Reed was generous to a fault. Another man might have told Pat, Monte and Ellen to pack their bags. This was his home, after all, and Derek had been wrong to rent out the rooms without Reed's knowledge. But Reed had let them stay.

Disgruntled with the trend her thoughts were taking, Ellen forced her mind back to the books in front of her. But it wasn't long before her concentration started to drift again. Reed had Danielle, and she had…Charlie Hanson. First thing in the morning, she'd call dependable old Charlie and suggest they get together; he'd probably be as surprised as he was pleased to hear from her. Feeling relieved and a little light-headed, Ellen turned off the light and went to bed.

"What are you doing?" Reed arrived in the kitchen early the next afternoon, looking as though he'd just finished eighteen holes of golf or a vigorous game of tennis. He'd already left by the time she'd wandered down to the kitchen that morning.

"Ellen?" he repeated impatiently.

She'd taken the wall plates off the electrical outlets and pulled the receptacle out of its box, from which two thin colored wires now protruded. "I'm trying to figure out why this outlet won't heat the iron," she answered without looking in his direction.

"You're what!" he bellowed.

She wiped her face to remove a layer of dust before she straightened. "Don't yell at me."

"Good grief, woman. You run around on the roof like a trapeze artist, cook like a dream and do electrical work on the side. Is there anything you *can't* do?"

"Algebra," she muttered.

Reed closed the instruction manual Ellen had propped against the sugar bowl in the middle of the table. He took her by the shoulders and pushed her gently aside, then re-attached the electrical wires and fastened the whole thing back in place.

As he finished securing the wall plate, Ellen burst out, "What did you do that for? I've almost got the problem traced."

"No doubt, but if you don't mind, I'd rather have a real electrician look at this."

"What can I say? It's your house."

"Right. Now sit down." He nudged her into a chair. "How much longer are you going to delay writing that term paper?"

"It's written," she snapped. She wasn't particularly pleased with it, but at least the assignment was done. Her subject matter might impress four-year-old Jimmy, but she wasn't too confident that her professor would feel the same way.

"Do you want me to look it over?"

The offer surprised her. "No, thanks." She stuck the screwdriver in the pocket of her gray-striped coveralls.

"Well, that wasn't so hard, was it?"

"I just don't think I've got a snowball's chance of getting a decent grade on it. Anyway, I have to go and iron a dress. I've got a date."

A dark brow lifted over inscrutable green eyes and he seemed about to say something.

"Reed." Unexpectedly, the kitchen door swung open and a soft, feminine voice purred his name. "What's taking you so long?"

"Danielle, I'd like you to meet Ellen."

"Hello." Ellen resisted the urge to kick Reed. If he was going to introduce her to his friend, the least he could have done was waited until she looked a little more presentable. Just as she'd figured, Danielle was beautiful. No, the word was *gorgeous*. She wore a cute pale blue tennis outfit with a short, pleated skirt. A dark blue silk scarf held back the curly cascade of long blond hair—Ellen should have known the other woman would be blonde. Naturally, Danielle possessed a trim waist, perfect legs and blue eyes to match the heavens. She'd apparently just finished playing golf or tennis with Reed, but she still looked cool and elegant.

"I feel as though I already know you," Danielle was saying with a pleasant smile. "Reed told me how much help you were with the children."

"It was nothing, really." Embarrassed by her ridiculous outfit, Ellen tried to conceal as much of it as possible by grabbing the electrical repair book and clasping it to her stomach.

"Not according to Reed." Danielle slipped her arm around his and smiled adoringly up at him. "Unfortunately, I came down with a terrible headache."

"Danielle doesn't have your knack with young children," Reed said.

"If we decide to have our own, things will be different," Danielle continued sweetly. "But I'm not convinced I'm the maternal type."

Ellen sent the couple a wan smile. "If you'll excuse me, I've got to go change my clothes."

"Of course. It was nice meeting you, Elaine."

"Ellen," Reed and Ellen corrected simultaneously.

"You, too." Gallantly, Ellen stifled the childish impulse to call the other woman Diane. As she turned and hurried up the stairs leading from the kitchen, she heard Danielle whisper that she didn't mind at all if Ellen lived in Reed's home. Of course not, Ellen muttered to herself. How could Danielle possibly be jealous?

Winded by the time she'd marched up both flights, Ellen walked into the tiny bedroom where she stored her clothes. She threw down the electrical manual and slammed the door shut. Then she sighed with despair as she saw her reflection in the full-length mirror on the back of the door; it revealed baggy coveralls, a faded white T-shirt and smudges of dirt across her cheekbone. She struck a seductive pose with her hand on her hip and vampishly puffed up her hair. "Of course, I don't mind if sweet little Elaine lives here, darling," she mimicked in a high-pitched falsely sweet voice.

Dropping her coveralls to the ground, Ellen gruffly kicked them aside. Hands on her hips, she glared at her reflection. Her figure was no less attractive than Danielle's, and her face was pretty enough—even if she did say so herself. But Danielle had barely looked at Ellen and certainly hadn't seen her as a potential rival.

As she brushed her hair away from her face, Ellen's

shoulders suddenly dropped. She was losing her mind! She liked living with the boys. Their arrangement was ideal, yet here she was, complaining bitterly because her presence hadn't been challenged.

Carefully choosing a light pink blouse and denim skirt, Ellen told herself that Charlie, at least, would appreciate her. And for now, Ellen needed that. Her self-confidence had been shaken by Danielle's casual acceptance of her role in Reed's house. She didn't like Danielle. But then, she hadn't expected to.

"Ellen." Her name was followed by a loud pounding on the bedroom door. "Wake up! There's a phone call for you."

"Okay," she mumbled into her pillow, still caught in the dregs of sleep. It felt so warm and cozy under the blankets that she didn't want to stir. Charlie had taken her to dinner and a movie and they'd returned a little after ten. The boys had stayed in that evening, but Reed was out and Ellen didn't need to ask with whom. She hadn't heard him come home.

"Ellen!"

"I'm awake, I'm awake," she grumbled, slipping one leg free of the covers and dangling it over the edge of the bed. The sudden cold that assailed her bare foot made her eyes flutter open in momentary shock.

"It's long distance."

Her eyes did open then. She knew only one person who could be calling. Her mother!

Hurriedly tossing the covers aside, she grabbed her

housecoat and scurried out of the room. "Why didn't you tell me it was long distance?"

"I tried," Pat said. "But you were more interested in sleeping."

A glance at her clock radio told her it was barely seven.

Taking a deep, calming breath, Ellen walked quickly down one flight of stairs and picked up the phone at the end of the hallway.

"Good morning, Mom."

"How'd you know it was me?"

Although they emailed each other regularly, this was the first time her mother had actually phoned since she'd left home. "Lucky guess."

"Who was that young man who answered the phone?"

"Patrick."

"The basketball kid."

Her mother had read every word of her emails. "That's him."

"Has Monte eaten you out of house and home yet?"

"Just about."

"And has this Derek kid finally summoned up enough nerve to ask out...what was her name again?"

"Michelle."

"Right. That's the one."

"They saw each other twice this weekend," Ellen told her, feeling a sharp pang of homesickness.

"And what about you, Ellen? Are you dating?" It wasn't an idle question. Through the years, Ellen's mother had often fretted that her oldest child was giving up her youth in order to care for the family. Ellen didn't deny that she'd made sacrifices, but they'd been willing ones.

Her emails had been chatty, but she hadn't mentioned Charlie, and Ellen wasn't sure she wanted her mother to know about him. Her relationship with him was based on friendship and nothing more, although Ellen suspected that Charlie would've liked it to develop into something romantic.

"Mom, you didn't phone me long distance on a Monday morning to discuss my social life."

"You're right. I called to discuss mine."

"And?" Ellen's heart hammered against her ribs. She already knew what was coming. She'd known it months ago, even before she'd moved to Seattle. Her mother was going to remarry. After ten years of widowhood, Barbara Cunningham had found another man to love.

"And—" her mother faltered "—James has asked me to be his wife."

"And?" It seemed to Ellen that her vocabulary had suddenly been reduced to one word.

"And I've said yes."

Ellen closed her eyes, expecting to feel a rush of bittersweet nostalgia for the father she remembered so well and had loved so much. Instead, she felt only gladness that her mother had discovered this new happiness.

"Congratulations, Mom."

"Do you mean that?"

"With all my heart. When's the wedding?"

"Well, actually..." Her mother hedged again. "Honey, don't be angry."

"Angry?"

"We're already married. I'm calling from Reno."

"Oh."

"Are you mad?"

"Of course not."

"James has a winter home in Arizona and we're going to stay there until April."

"April," Ellen repeated, feeling a little dazed.

"If you object, honey, I'll come back to Yakima for Christmas."

"No…I don't object. It's just kind of sudden."

"Dad's been gone ten years."

"I know, Mom. Don't worry, okay?"

"I'll email you soon."

"Do that. And much happiness, Mom. You and James deserve it."

"Thank you, love."

They spoke for a few more minutes before saying good-bye. Ellen walked down the stairs in a state of stunned disbelief, absentmindedly tightening the belt of her house-coat. In a matter of months, her entire family had disin-tegrated. Her sister and mother had married and Bud had joined the military.

"Good morning," she cautiously greeted Reed, who was sitting at the kitchen table dressed and reading the paper.

"Morning," he responded dryly, as he lowered his paper.

Her hands trembling, Ellen reached for a mug, but it slipped out of her fingers and hit the counter, luckily with-out breaking.

Reed carefully folded the newspaper and studied her face. "What's wrong? You look like you've just seen a ghost."

"My mom's married," she murmured in a subdued voice. Tears burned in her eyes. She was no longer sure just what she was feeling. Happiness for her mother, yes, but also sadness as she remembered her father and his untimely death.

"Remarried?" he asked.

"Yes." She sat down across from him, holding the mug in both hands and staring into its depths. "It's not like this is sudden. Dad's been gone a lot of years. What surprises me is all the emotion I'm feeling."

"That's only natural. I remember how I felt when my dad remarried. I'd known about Mary and Dad for months. But the day of the wedding I couldn't help feeling, somehow, that my father had betrayed my mother's memory. Those were heavy thoughts for a ten-year-old boy." His hand reached for hers. "As I recall, that was the last time I cried."

Ellen nodded. It was the only way she could thank him, because speaking was impossible just then. She knew instinctively that Reed didn't often share the hurts of his youth.

Just when her throat had relaxed and she felt she could speak, Derek threw open the back door and dashed in, tossing his older brother a set of keys.

"I had them add a quart of oil," Derek said. "Are you sure you can't stay longer?"

The sip of coffee sank to the pit of Ellen's stomach and sat there. "You're leaving?" It seemed as though someone had jerked her chair out from under her.

He released her hand and gave it a gentle pat. "You'll be fine."

Ellen forced her concentration back to her coffee. For

days she'd been telling herself that she'd be relieved and
delighted when Reed left. Now she dreaded it. More than
anything, she wanted him to stay.

Four

"Ellen," Derek shouted as he burst in the front door, his hands full of mail. "Can I invite Michelle to dinner on Friday night?"

Casually, Ellen looked up from the textbook she was studying. By mutual agreement, they all went their separate ways on Friday evenings and Ellen didn't cook. If one of the boys happened to be in the house, he heated up soup or put together a sandwich or made do with leftovers. In Monte's case, he did all three.

"What are you planning to fix?" Ellen responded cagily.

"Cook? Me?" Derek slapped his hand against his chest and looked utterly shocked. "I can't cook. You know that."

"But you're inviting company."

His gaze dropped and he restlessly shuffled his feet. "I was hoping that maybe this one Friday you could..." He paused and his head jerked up. "You don't have a date, do you?" He sounded as if that was the worst possible thing that could happen.

"Not this Friday."

"Oh, good. For a minute there, I thought we might have a problem."

"We?" She rolled her eyes. "I don't have a problem, but it sounds like you do." She wasn't going to let him con her into his schemes quite so easily.

"But you'll be here."

"I was planning on soaking in the tub, giving my hair a hot-oil treatment and hibernating with a good book."

"But you could still make dinner, couldn't you? Something simple like seafood jambalaya with shrimp, stuffed eggplant and pecan pie for dessert."

"Are you planning to rob a bank, as well?" At his blank stare, she elaborated. "Honestly, Derek, have you checked out the price of seafood lately?"

"No, but you cooked that Cajun meal not long ago and—"

"Shrimp was on sale," she broke in.

He continued undaunted. "And it was probably the most delicious meal I've ever tasted in my whole life. I was kicking myself because Reed wasn't here and he would have loved it as much as everyone else."

At the mention of Reed's name, Ellen's lashes fell, hiding the confusion and longing in her eyes. The house had been full of college boys, yet it had seemed astonishingly empty without Reed. He'd been with them barely a week and Ellen couldn't believe how much his presence had affected her. The morning he'd left, she'd walked him out to his truck, trying to think of a way to say goodbye and to thank him for understanding the emotions that raged through her at the news of her mother's remarriage. But nothing had turned out quite as she'd expected. Reed had seemed just as reluctant to say goodbye as she was, and before climbing into the truck, he'd leaned forward and lightly brushed his lips over hers. The kiss had been so spontaneous that Ellen wasn't sure if he'd really meant to do it. But intentional or not, he *had,* and the memory of that kiss stayed with her. Now hardly a day passed that he didn't enter her thoughts.

A couple of times when she was on the second floor she'd wandered into her old bedroom, forgetting that it now belonged to Reed. Both times, she'd lingered there, enjoying the sensation of remembering Reed and their verbal battles.

Repeatedly Ellen told herself that it was because Derek's brother was over twenty-one and she could therefore carry on an adult conversation with him. Although she was genuinely fond of the boys, she'd discovered that a constant diet of their antics and their adolescent preoccupations—Pat's basketball, Monte's appetite and Derek's Michelle—didn't exactly make for stimulating conversation.

"You really are a fantastic cook," Derek went on. "Even better than my mother. You know, only the other day Monte was saying—"

"Don't you think you're putting it on a little thick, Derek?"

He blinked. "I just wanted to tell you how much I'd appreciate it if you decided to do me this tiny favor."

"You'll buy the ingredients yourself?"

"The grocery budget couldn't manage it?"

"Not unless everyone else is willing to eat oatmeal three times a week for the remainder of the month."

"I don't suppose they would be," he muttered. "All right, make me a list and I'll buy what you need."

Ellen was half hoping that once he saw the price of fresh shrimp, he'd realize it might be cheaper to take Michelle to a seafood restaurant.

"Oh, by the way," Derek said, examining one of the envelopes in his hand. "You got a letter. Looks like it's from Reed."

"Reed?" Her lungs slowly contracted as she said his name, and it was all she could do not to snatch the envelope out of Derek's hand. The instant he gave it to her, she tore it open.

"What does he say?" Derek asked, sorting through the rest of the mail. "He didn't write me."

Ellen quickly scanned the contents. "He's asking if the electrician has showed up yet. That's all."

"Oh? Then why didn't he just call? Or send an email?"

She didn't respond, but made a show of putting the letter back inside the envelope. "I'll go into the kitchen and make that grocery list before I forget."

"I'm really grateful, Ellen, honest."

"Sure," she grumbled.

As soon as the kitchen door swung shut, Ellen took out Reed's letter again, intent on savoring every word.

Dear Ellen,

I realized I don't have your email address, so I thought I'd do this the old-fashioned way—by mail. There's something so leisurely and personal about writing a letter, isn't there?

You're right, the Monterey area is beautiful. I wish

I could say that everything else is as peaceful as the scenery here. Unfortunately it's not. Things have been hectic. But if all goes well, I should be back at the house by Saturday, which is earlier than I expected.

Have you become accustomed to the idea that your mother's remarried? I know it was a shock. Like I said, I remember how I felt, and that was many years ago. I've been thinking about it all—and wondering about you. If I'd known what was happening, I might have been able to postpone this trip. You looked like you needed someone. And knowing you, it isn't often that you're willing to lean on anyone. Not the independent, self-sufficient woman I discovered walking around my kitchen half-naked. I can almost see your face getting red when you read that. I shouldn't tease you, but I can't help it.

By the way, I contacted a friend of mine who owns an electrical business and told him about the problem with the kitchen outlet. He said he'd try to stop by soon. He'll call first.

I wanted you to know that I was thinking about you—and the boys, but mostly you. Actually, I'm pleased you're there to keep those kids in line.

Take care and I'll see you late Saturday.

Say hi to the boys for me. I'm trusting that they aren't giving you any problems.

Reed

Ellen folded the letter and slipped it into her pocket. She crossed her arms, smiling to herself, feeling incredibly good. So Reed had been thinking about her. And she sensed that it was more than the troublesome kitchen outlet that had prompted his letter. Although she knew it would be dangerous for her to read too much into Reed's message, Ellen couldn't help feeling encouraged.

She propped open her cookbook, compiling the list of items Derek would need for his fancy dinner with Michelle. A few minutes later, her spirits soared still higher when the electrical contractor phoned and arranged a date and a time to check the faulty outlet. Somehow, that seemed like a good omen to her—a kind of proof that she really was in Reed's thoughts.

"Was the phone for me?" Derek called from halfway down the stairs.

Ellen finished writing the information on the pad by the phone before answering. "It was the electrician."

"Oh. I'm expecting a call from Michelle."

"Speaking of your true love, here's your grocery list."

Derek took it and slowly ran his finger down the items she'd need for his dinner with Michelle. "Is this going to cost more than twenty-five dollars?" He glanced up, his face doubtful.

"The pecans alone will be that much," she exaggerated.

With only a hint of disappointment, Derek shook his head. "I think maybe Michelle and I should find a nice, cozy, *inexpensive* restaurant."

Satisfied that her plan had worked so well, Ellen hid a smile. "Good idea. By the way," she added, "Reed says he'll be home Saturday."

"So soon? He's just been gone two weeks."

"Apparently it's a short job."

"Apparently," Derek grumbled. "I don't have to be here, do I? Michelle wanted me to help her and her sister paint."

"Derek," Ellen said. "I didn't even know you could wield a brush. The upstairs hallway—"

"Forget it," he told her sharply. "I'm only doing this to help Michelle."

"Right, but I'm sure Michelle would be willing to help you in exchange."

"Hey, we're students, not slaves."

The following afternoon, the electrician arrived and was in and out of the house within thirty minutes. Ellen felt proud that she'd correctly traced the problem. She could probably have fixed it if Reed hadn't become so frantic at the thought of her fumbling around with the wiring. Still, recalling his reaction made her smile.

That evening, Ellen had finished loading the dishwasher and had just settled down at the kitchen table to study when the phone rang. Pat, who happened to be walking past it, answered.

"It's Reed," he told Ellen. "He wants to talk to you."

With reflexes that surprised even her, Ellen bounded out of her chair.

"Reed," she said into the receiver, holding it tightly against her ear. "Hello, how are you?"

"Fine. Did the electrician come?"

"He was here this afternoon."

"Any problems?"

"No," she breathed. He sounded wonderfully close, his voice warm and vibrant. "In fact, I was on the right track. I probably could've handled it myself."

"I don't want you to even think about fixing anything like that. You could end up killing yourself or someone else. I absolutely forbid it."

"Aye, aye, sir." His words had the immediate effect of igniting her temper, sending the hot blood roaring through her veins. She hadn't been able to stop thinking about Reed since he'd left, but two minutes after picking up the phone, she was ready to argue with him again.

There was a long, awkward silence. Reed was the first to speak, expelling his breath sharply. "I didn't mean to snap your head off," he said. "I'm sorry."

"Thank you," she responded, instantly soothed.

"How's everything else going?"

"Fine."

"Have the boys talked you into any more of their schemes?"

"They keep trying."

"They wouldn't be college kids if they didn't."

"I know." It piqued her a little that Reed assumed she could be manipulated by three teenagers. "Don't worry about me. I can hold my own with these guys."

His low sensuous chuckle did funny things to her pulse. "It's not you I'm concerned about."

"Just what are you implying?" she asked with mock seriousness.

"I'm going to play this one smart and leave that last comment open-ended."

"Clever of you, my friend, very clever."

"I thought as much."

After a short pause, Ellen quickly asked, "How's everything with you?" She knew there really wasn't anything more to say, but she didn't want the conversation to end. Talking to Reed was almost as good as having him there.

"Much better, thanks. I shouldn't have any problem getting home by Saturday."

"Good."

Another short silence followed.

"Well, I guess that's all I've got to say. If I'm going to be any later than Saturday, I'll give you a call."

"Drive carefully."

"I will. Bye, Ellen."

"Goodbye, Reed." Smiling, she replaced the receiver. When she glanced up, all three boys were staring at her, their arms crossed dramatically over their chests.

"I think something's going on here." Pat spoke first. "I answered the phone and Reed asked for Ellen. He didn't even ask for Derek—his own brother."

"Right." Derek nodded vigorously.

"I'm wondering," Monte said, rubbing his chin. "Could we have the makings of a romance on our hands?"

"I think we do," Pat concurred.

"Stop it." Ellen did her best to join in the banter, although she felt the color flooding her cheeks. "It makes sense that Reed would want to talk to me. I'm the oldest."

"But I'm his brother," Derek countered.

"I refuse to listen to any of this," she said with a small laugh and turned back to the kitchen. "You three are being ridiculous. Reed's dating Danielle."

All three followed her. "He could have married Danielle months ago if he was really interested," Derek informed the small gathering.

"Be still, my beating heart," Monte joked, melodramatically folding both hands over his chest and pretending to swoon.

Not to be outdone, Pat rested the back of his hand against his forehead and rolled his eyes. "Ah, love."

"I'm out of here." Before anyone could argue, Ellen ran up the back stairs to her room, laughing as she went. She had to admit she'd found the boys' little performances quite funny. But if they pulled any of their pranks around Reed, it would be extremely embarrassing. Ellen resolved to say something to them when the time seemed appropriate.

Friday afternoon, Ellen walked into the kitchen, her book bag clutched tightly to her chest.

"What's the matter? You're as pale as a ghost," Monte remarked, cramming a chocolate-chip cookie in his mouth.

Derek and Pat turned toward her, their faces revealing concern.

"I got my algebra paper back today."

"And?" Derek prompted.

"I don't know. I haven't looked."

"Why not?"

"Because I know how tough Engstrom was on the others. The girl who wrote about solving that oddball conjecture got a C-minus and the guy who was so enthusiastic about Mathematics in World War II got a D. With impressive subjects like that getting low grades, I'm doomed."

"But you worked hard on that paper." Loyally, Derek defended her and placed a consoling arm around her shoulders. "You found out a whole bunch of interesting facts about the number nine."

"You did your paper on that?" Pat asked, his smooth brow wrinkling with amusement.

"Don't laugh." She already felt enough of a fool.

"It isn't going to do any good to worry," Monte insisted, pulling the folded assignment from between her fingers.

Ellen watched his expression intently as he looked at the paper, then handed it to Derek who raised his brows and gave it to Pat.

"Well?"

"You got a B-minus," Pat said in obvious surprise. "I don't believe it."

"Me neither." Ellen reveled in the delicious feeling of relief. She sank luxuriously into a chair. "I'm calling Charlie." Almost immediately she jumped up again and dashed to the phone. "This is too exciting! I'm celebrating."

The other three had drifted into the living room and two minutes later, she joined them there. "Charlie's out, but his roommate said he'd give him the message." Too happy to contain her excitement, she added, "But I'm not sitting home alone. How about if we go out for pizza tonight? My treat."

"Sorry, Ellen." Derek looked up with a frown. "I've already made plans with Michelle."

"I'm getting together with a bunch of guys at the gym," Pat informed her. "Throw a few baskets."

"And I told my mom I'd be home for dinner."

Some of the excitement drained from her, but she put on a brave front. "No problem. We'll do it another night."

"I'll go."

The small group whirled around, shocked to discover Reed standing there, framed in the living-room doorway.

Five

"Reed," Ellen burst out, astonished. "When did you get here?" The instant she'd finished speaking, she realized how stupid the question was. He'd just walked in the back door.

With a grin, he checked his wristwatch. "About fifteen seconds ago."

"How was the trip?" Derek asked.

"Did you drive straight through?" Pat asked, then said, "I don't suppose you had a chance to see the Lakers play, did you?"

"You must be exhausted," Ellen murmured, noting how tired his eyes looked.

As his smiling gaze met hers, the fine laugh lines that fanned out from his eyes became more pronounced. "I'm hungry *and* tired. Didn't I just hear you offer to buy me pizza?"

"Ellen got a B-minus on her crazy algebra paper," Monte said with pride.

Rolling her eyes playfully toward the ceiling, Ellen laughed. "Who would have guessed it—I'm a mathematical genius!"

"So that's the reason for this dinner. I thought you might have won the lottery."

He was more deeply tanned than Ellen remembered. Handsome. Vital. And incredibly male. He seemed glad to be home, she thought. Not a hint of hostility showed in the eyes that smiled back at her.

"No such luck."

Derek made a show of glancing at his watch. "I gotta go or I'll be late picking up Michelle. It's good to see you, Reed."

"Yeah, welcome home," Pat said, reaching for his basketball. "I'll see you later."

Reed raised his right hand in salute and picked up his suitcase, then headed up the wide stairs. "Give me fifteen minutes to shower and I'll meet you down here."

The minute Reed's back was turned, Monte placed his hand over his heart and batted his lashes wildly as he mouthed something about love, true love. Ellen practically threw him out of the house, slamming the door after him.

At the top of the stairs, Reed turned and glanced down at her. "What was that all about?"

Ellen leaned against the closed door, one hand covering her mouth to smother her giggles. But the laughter drained from her as she looked at his puzzled face, and she slowly straightened. She cleared her throat. "Nothing. Did you want me to order pizza? Or do you want to go out?"

"Whatever you prefer."

"If you leave it up to me, my choice would be to get away from these four walls."

"I'll be ready in a few minutes."

Ellen suppressed a shudder at the thought of what would've happened had Reed caught a glimpse of Monte's antics. She herself handled the boys' teasing with good-natured indulgence, but she was fairly sure that Reed would take offense at their nonsense. And heaven forbid that Danielle should ever catch a hint of what was going on—not that anything *was* going on.

With her thoughts becoming more muddled every minute, Ellen made her way to the third floor to change into a pair of gray tailored pants and a frilly pale blue silk blouse. One glance in the mirror and she sadly shook her head. They were only going out for pizza—there was no need to wear anything so elaborate. Hurriedly, she changed into dark brown cords and a turtleneck sweater the color of summer wheat. Then she ran a brush through her short curls and freshened her lipstick.

When Ellen returned to the living room, Reed was already waiting for her. "You're sure you don't mind going out?" she asked again.

"Are you dodging your pizza offer?"

He was so serious that Ellen couldn't help laughing. "Not at all."

"Good. I hope you like spicy sausage with lots of olives."

"Love it."

His hand rested on her shoulder. "And a cold beer."

"This is sounding better all the time." Ellen would have guessed that Reed was the type of man who drank martinis or expensive cocktails. In some ways, he was completely down-to-earth and in others, surprisingly complex. Perceptive, unpretentious and unpredictable—she knew that much about him, but she didn't expect to understand him anytime soon.

Reed helped her into his pickup, which was parked in the driveway. The evening sky was already dark and Ellen regretted not having brought her coat.

"Cold?" Reed asked her when they stopped at a red light.

"Only a little."

He adjusted the switches for the heater and soon a rush of warm air filled the cab. Reed chatted easily, telling her about his project in California and explaining why his work demanded so much travel. "That's changing now."

"Oh?" She couldn't restrain a little shiver of gladness at his announcement. "Will you be coming home more often?"

"Not for another three or four months. I'm up for promotion and then I'll be able to pick and choose my assignments more carefully. Over the past four years, I've traveled enough to last me a lifetime."

"Then it's true that there's no place like home."

"Be it ever so humble," he added with a chuckle.

"I don't exactly consider a three-storey, twenty-room turn-of-the-century mansion all that humble."

"Throw in four college students and you'll quickly discover how unassuming it can become."

"Oh?"

"You like that word, don't you?"

"Yes," she agreed, her mouth curving into a lazy smile. "It's amazing how much you can say with that one little sound."

Reed exited the freeway close to the Seattle Center and continued north. At her questioning glance, he explained, "The best pizza in Seattle is made at a small place near the Center. You don't mind coming this far, do you?"

"Of course not. I'll travel a whole lot farther than this for a good pizza." Suddenly slouching forward, she dropped her forehead into her hand. "Oh, no. It's happening."

"What is?"

"I'm beginning to sound like Monte."

They both laughed. It felt so good to be sitting there with Reed, sharing an easy, relaxed companionship, that Ellen could almost forget about Danielle. Almost, but not quite.

Although Ellen had said she'd pay for the pizza, Reed insisted on picking up the tab. They sat across from each other at a narrow booth in the corner of the semidarkened room. A lighted red candle in a glass bowl flickered on the table between them and Ellen decided this was the perfect atmosphere. The old-fashioned jukebox blared out the latest country hits, drowning out the possibility of any audible conversation, but that seemed just as well since she was feeling strangely tongue-tied.

When their number was called, Reed slid from the booth and returned a minute later with two frothy beers in ice-cold mugs and a huge steaming pizza.

"I hope you don't expect us to eat all this?" Ellen said, shouting above the music. The pizza certainly smelled enticing, but Ellen doubted she'd manage to eat more than two or three pieces.

"We'll put a dent in it, anyway," Reed said, resuming his seat. "I bought the largest, figuring the boys would enjoy the leftovers."

"You're a terrific older brother."

The song on the jukebox was fading into silence at last.

"There are times I'd like to shake some sense into Derek, though," Reed said.

Ellen looked down at the spicy pizza and put a small slice on her plate. Strings of melted cheese still linked the piece to the rest of the pie. She pulled them loose and licked her fingers. "I can imagine how you felt when you discovered that Derek had accidentally-on-purpose forgotten to tell you about renting out rooms."

Reed shrugged noncommittally. "I was thinking more about the time he let you climb on top of the roof," he muttered.

"He didn't *let* me, I went all by myself."

"But you won't do it again. Right?"

"Right." Ellen nodded reluctantly. Behind Reed's slow smiles and easy banter, she recognized his unrelenting male pride. "You still haven't forgiven me for that, have you?"

"Not you. Derek."

"I think this is one of those subjects on which we should agree to disagree."

"Have you heard from your mother?" Reed asked, apparently just as willing to change the subject.

"Yes. She's emailed me several times. She seems very happy and after a day or two, I discovered I couldn't be more pleased for her. She deserves a lot of contentment."

"I knew you'd realize that." Warmth briefly showed in his green eyes.

"I felt a lot better after talking to you. I was surprised when Mom announced her marriage, but I shouldn't have been. The signs were there all along. I suppose once the three of us kids were gone, she felt free to remarry. And I suppose she thought that presenting it to the family as a fait accompli would make it easier for all of us."

There was a comfortable silence as they finished eating. The pizza was thick with sausage and cheese, and Ellen placed her hands on her stomach after leisurely eating two narrow pieces. "I'm stuffed," she declared, leaning back. "But you're right, this has got to be the best pizza in town."

"I thought you'd like it."

Reed brought over a carry-out box and Ellen carefully put the leftovers inside.

"How about a movie?" he asked once they were in the car park.

Astounded, Ellen darted him a sideways glance, but his features were unreadable. "You're kidding, aren't you?"

"I wouldn't have asked you if I was."

"But you must be exhausted." Ellen guessed he'd probably spent most of the day driving.

"A little," he admitted.

Her frown deepened. Suddenly, it no longer seemed right for them to be together—because of Danielle. The problem was that Ellen had been so pleased to see him that she hadn't stopped to think about the consequences of their going out together. "Thanks anyway, but it's been a long week. I think I'll call it a night."

When they reached the house, Reed parked on the street rather than the driveway. The light from the stars and the silvery moon penetrated the branches that hung overhead and created shadows on his face. Neither of them seemed eager to leave the warm cab of the pickup truck. The mood was intimate and Ellen didn't want to disturb this moment of tranquillity. Lowering her gaze, she admitted to herself how attracted she was to Reed and how much she liked him. She admitted, too, that it was wrong for her to feel this way about him.

"You're quiet all of a sudden."

Ellen's smile was decidedly forced. She turned toward him to apologise for putting a damper on their evening, but the words never left her lips. Instead, her eyes met his. Paralyzed, she stared at Reed, fighting to disguise the intense attraction she felt for him. It seemed the most natural thing in the world to lean toward him and brush her lips against his. She could smell the woodsy scent of his aftershave and could almost taste his mouth on hers. With determination, she pulled her gaze away and reached for the door, like a drowning person grasping a life preserver.

She was on the front porch by the time Reed joined her. Her fingers shook as she inserted the key in the lock.

"Ellen." He spoke her name softly and placed his hand on her shoulder.

"I don't know why we went out tonight." Her voice was high and strained as she drew free of his touch. "We shouldn't have been together."

In response, Reed mockingly lifted one eyebrow. "I believe it was you who asked me."

"Be serious, will you," she snapped irritably and shoved open the door.

Reed slammed it shut behind him and followed her into the kitchen. He set the pizza on the counter, then turned to face her. "What the hell do you mean? I *was* being serious."

"You shouldn't have been with me tonight."

"Why not?"

"Where's Danielle? I'm not the one who's been patiently waiting around for you. *She* is. You had no business taking me out to dinner and then suggesting a movie. You're my landlord, not my boyfriend."

"Let's get two things straight here. First, what's between Danielle and me is none of *your* business. And second, you invited *me* out. Remember?"

"But...it wasn't like that and you know it."

"Besides, I thought you said you were far too old for *boyfriends.*" She detected an undertone of amusement in his voice.

Confused, Ellen marched into the living room and immediately busied herself straightening magazines. Reed charged in after her, leaving the kitchen door swinging in his wake. Clutching a sofa pillow, she searched for some witty retort. Naturally, whenever she needed a clever comeback, her mind was a total blank.

"You're making a joke out of everything," she told him, angry that her voice was shaking. "And I don't like that. If you want to play games, do it with someone other than me."

"Ellen, listen—"

The phone rang and she jerked her attention to the hallway.

"I didn't mean—" Reed paused and raked his fingers through his hair. The phone pealed a second time. "Go ahead and answer that."

She hurried away, relieved to interrupt this disturbing conversation. "Hello." Her voice sounded breathless, as though she'd raced down the stairs.

"Ellen? This is Charlie. I got a message that you phoned."

For one crazy instant, Ellen forgot why she'd wanted to talk to Charlie. "I phoned? Oh, right. Remember that algebra paper I was struggling with? Well, I got it back today."

"How'd you do?"

A little of the surprised pleasure returned. "I still can't believe it. I got a B-minus. My simple paper about the wonders of the number nine received one of the highest marks in the class. I'm still in shock."

Charlie's delighted chuckle came over the wire. "This calls for a celebration. How about if we go out tomorrow night? Dinner, drinks, the works."

Ellen almost regretted the impulse to contact Charlie. She sincerely liked him, and she hated the thought of stringing him along or taking advantage of his attraction to her. "Nothing so elaborate. Chinese food and a movie would be great."

"You let me worry about that. Just be ready by seven."

"Charlie"

"No arguing. I'll see you at seven."

By the time Ellen got off the phone, Reed was nowhere to be seen. Nor was he around the following afternoon. The boys didn't comment and she couldn't very well ask about him without arousing their suspicions. As it was, the less she mentioned Reed around them, the better. The boys had obviously read more into the letter, phone call and dinner than Reed had intended. But she couldn't blame them; she'd read enough into it herself to be frightened by what was happening between them. He'd almost kissed her when he'd parked in front of the house. And she'd wanted him to—that was what disturbed her most. But if she allowed her emotions to get involved, she knew that someone would probably end up being hurt. And the most likely *someone* was Ellen herself.

Besides, if Reed was attracted to Danielle's sleek elegance, then he would hardly be interested in her own more homespun qualities.

A few minutes before seven, Ellen was ready for her evening with Charlie. She stood before the downstairs hallway mirror to put the finishing touches on her appearance, fastening her gold earrings and straightening the single chain necklace.

"Where's Reed been today?" Pat inquired of no one in particular.

"His sports car is gone," Monte said, munching on a chocolate bar. "I noticed it wasn't in the garage when I took out the garbage."

Slowly Ellen sauntered into the living room. She didn't want to appear too curious, but at the same time, she was definitely interested in the conversation.

She had flopped into a chair and picked up a two-month-old magazine before she noticed all three boys staring at her.

"What are you looking at me for?"

"We thought you might know something."

"About what?" she asked, playing dumb.

"Reed," all three said simultaneously.

"Why should I know anything?" Her gaze flittered from them to the magazine and back again.

"You went out with him last night."

"We didn't *go out* the way you're implying."

Pat pointed an accusing finger at her. "The two of you

were alone together, and both of you have been acting weird ever since."

"And I say the three of you have overactive imaginations."

"All I know is that Reed was like a wounded bear this morning," Derek volunteered.

"Everyone's entitled to an off day." Hoping to give a casual impression, she leafed through the magazine, idly fanning the pages with her thumb.

"That might explain Reed. But what about you?"

"Me?"

"For the first time since you moved in, you weren't downstairs until after ten."

"I slept in. Is that a crime?"

"It just might be. You and Reed are both acting really strange. It's like the two of you are avoiding each other and we want to know why."

"It's your imagination. Believe me, if there was anything to tell you, I would."

"Sure, you would," Derek mocked.

From the corner of her eye, Ellen saw Charlie's car pull up in front of the house. Releasing a sigh of relief, she quickly stood and gave the boys a falsely bright smile. "If you'll excuse me, my date has arrived."

"Should we tell Reed you're out with Charlie if he wants to know where you are?" Monte looked uncomfortable asking the question.

"Of course. Besides, he probably already knows. He's free to see anyone he wants and so am I. For that matter, so are you." She whirled around and made her way to the front door, pulling it open before Charlie even got a chance to ring the doorbell.

The evening didn't go well. Charlie took her out for a steak dinner and spent more money than Ellen knew he could afford. She regretted having phoned him. Charlie had obviously interpreted her call as a sign that she was interested in becoming romantically involved. She wasn't, and didn't know how to make it clear without offending him.

"Did you have a good time?" he asked as they drove back toward Capitol Hill.

"Lovely, thank you, Charlie."

His hand reached for hers and squeezed it reassuringly. "We don't go out enough."

"Neither of us can afford it too often."

"We don't need to go to a fancy restaurant to be together," he said lightly. "Just being with you is a joy."

"Thank you." If only Charlie weren't so nice. She hated the idea of hurting him. But she couldn't allow him to go on hoping that she would ever return his feelings. As much as she dreaded it, she knew she had to disillusion him. Anything else would be cruel and dishonest.

"I don't think I've made a secret of how I feel about you, Ellen. You're wonderful."

"Come on, Charlie, I'm not that different from a thousand other girls on campus." She tried to swallow the tightness in her throat. "In fact, I saw the way that girl in our sociology class—what's her name—Lisa, has been looking at you lately."

"I hadn't noticed."

"I believe you've got yourself an admirer."

"But I'm only interested in you."

"Charlie, listen. I think you're a very special person. I—"

"Shh," he demanded softly as he parked in front of Ellen's house and turned off the engine. He slid his arm along the back of the seat and caressed her shoulder. "I don't want you to say anything."

"But I feel I may have—"

"Ellen," he whispered seductively. "Be quiet and just let me kiss you."

Before she could utter another word, Charlie claimed her mouth in a short but surprisingly ardent kiss. Charlie had kissed her on several occasions, but that was as far as things had ever gone.

When his arms tightened around her, Ellen resisted.

"Invite me in for coffee," he whispered urgently in her ear.

She pressed her forehead against his shirt collar. "Not tonight."

He tensed. "Can I see you again soon?"

"I don't know. We see each other every day. Why don't we just meet after class for coffee one day next week?"

"But I want more than that," he protested.

"I know," she answered, dropping her eyes. She felt confused and miserable.

Ellen could tell he was disappointed from the way he climbed out of the car and trudged around to her side. There was tense silence between them as he walked her up to the front door and kissed her a second time. Again, Ellen had to break away from him by pushing her hands against his chest.

"Thank you for everything," she whispered.

"Right. Thanks, but no thanks."

"Oh, Charlie, don't start that. Not now."

Eyes downcast, he wearily rubbed a hand along the side of his face. "I guess I'll see you Monday," he said with a sigh.

"Thanks for the lovely evening." She didn't let herself inside until Charlie had climbed into his car and driven away.

Releasing a jagged breath, Ellen had just started to unbutton her coat when she glanced up to find Reed standing in the living room, glowering at her.

"Is something wrong?" The undisguised anger that twisted his mouth and hardened his gaze was a shock.

"Do you always linger outside with your boyfriends?"

"We didn't linger."

"Right." He dragged one hand roughly through his hair and marched a few paces toward her, only to do an abrupt about-face. "I saw the two of you necking."

"Necking?" Ellen was so startled by his unreasonable anger that she didn't know whether to laugh or argue. "Be serious, will you? Two chaste kisses hardly constitute necking."

"What kind of influence are you on Derek and the others?" He couldn't seem to stand still and paced back and forth in agitation.

He was obviously furious, but Ellen didn't understand why. He couldn't possibly believe these absurd insinuations. Perhaps he was upset about something else and merely taking it out on her. "Reed, what's wrong?" she finally asked.

"I saw you out there."

"You were spying on me?"

"I wasn't spying," he snapped.

"Charlie and I were in his car. You must've been staring out the window to have seen us."

He didn't answer her, but instead hurled another accusation in her direction. "You're corrupting the boys."

"I'm *what?*" She couldn't believe what she was hearing. "What year do you think this is?" She shook her head, bewildered. "They're nineteen. Trust me, they've kissed girls before."

"You can kiss anyone you like. Just don't do it in front of the boys."

From the way this conversation was going, Ellen could see that Reed was in no mood to listen to reason. "I think we should discuss this some other time," she said quietly.

"We'll talk about it right now."

Ignoring his domineering tone as much as possible, Ellen forced a smile. "Good night, Reed. I'll see you in the morning."

She was halfway to the stairs when he called her, his voice calm. "Ellen."

She turned around, holding herself tense, watching him stride quickly across the short distance that separated them. With his thumb and forefinger, he caught her chin, tilting it slightly so he could study her face. He rubbed his thumb across her lips. "Funny, you don't look kissed."

In one breath he was accusing her of necking and in the next, claiming she was unkissed. Not knowing how to respond, Ellen didn't. She merely gazed at him, her eyes wide and questioning.

"If you're going to engage in that sort of activity, the

least you can do—" He paused. With each word his mouth drew closer and closer to hers until his lips hovered over her own and their breath mingled. "The least you can do is look kissed." His hand located the vein pounding wildly in her throat as his mouth settled over hers.

Slowly, patiently, his mouth moved over hers with an exquisite tenderness that left her quivering with anticipation and delight. Timidly, her hands crept across his chest to link behind his neck. Again his lips descended on hers, more hungrily now, as he groaned and pulled her even closer.

Ellen felt her face grow hot as she surrendered to the sensations that stole through her. Yet all the while, her mind was telling her she had no right to feel this contentment, this warmth. Reed belonged to another woman. Not to her…to someone else.

Color seeped into her face. When she'd understood that he intended to kiss her, her first thought had been to resist. But once she'd felt his mouth on hers, all her resolve had drained away. Embarrassed now, she realized she'd pliantly wrapped her arms around his neck. And worse, she'd responded with enough enthusiasm for him to know exactly what she was feeling.

He pressed his mouth to her forehead as though he couldn't bear to release her.

Ellen struggled to breathe normally. She let her arms slip from his neck to his chest and through the palm of her hand she could feel the rapid beating of his heart. She closed her eyes, knowing that her own pulse was pounding no less wildly.

She could feel his mouth move against her temple. "I've

been wanting to do that for days." The grudging admission came in a voice that was low and taut.

The words to tell him that she'd wanted it just as much were quickly silenced by the sound of someone walking into the room.

Guiltily Reed and Ellen jerked apart. Her face turned a deep shade of red as Derek stopped in his tracks, staring at them.

"Hi."

"Hi," Reed and Ellen said together.

"Hey, I'm not interrupting anything, am I? If you like, I could turn around and pretend I didn't see a thing."

"Do it," Reed ordered.

"No," Ellen said in the same moment.

Derek's eyes sparkled with boyish delight. "You know," he said, "I had a feeling about the two of you." While he spoke, he was taking small steps backward until he stood pressed against the polished kitchen door. He gave his brother a thumbs-up as he nudged open the door with one foot and hurriedly backed out of the room.

"Now look what you've done," Ellen wailed.

"Me? As I recall you were just as eager for this as I was."

"It was a mistake," she blurted out. A ridiculous, illogical mistake. He'd accused her of being a bad influence on the boys and then proceeded to kiss her senseless.

"You're telling me." A distinct coolness entered his eyes. "It's probably a good thing I'm leaving."

There was no hiding her stricken look. "Again? So soon?"

"After what's just happened, I'd say it wasn't soon enough."

"But…where to this time?"

"Denver. I'll be back before Thanksgiving."

Mentally, Ellen calculated that he'd be away another two weeks.

When he spoke again, his voice was gentle. "It's just as well, don't you think?"

Six

"Looks like rain." Pat stood in front of the window above the kitchen sink and frowned at the thick black clouds that darkened the late afternoon sky. "Why does it have to rain?"

Ellen glanced up at him. "Are you seeking a scientific response or will a simple 'I don't know' suffice?"

The kitchen door swung open and Derek sauntered in. "Has anyone seen Reed?"

Instantly, Ellen's gaze dropped to her textbook. Reed had returned to Seattle two days earlier and so far, they'd done an admirable job of avoiding each other. Both mornings, he'd left for his office before she was up. Each evening, he'd come home, showered, changed and then gone off again. It didn't require much detective work to figure out that he was with Danielle. Ellen had attempted—unsuccessfully—not to think of Reed at all. And especially not of him and Danielle together.

She secretly wished she'd had the nerve to arrange an

opportunity to talk to Reed. So much remained unclear in her mind. Reed had kissed her and it had been wonderful, yet that was something neither seemed willing to admit. It was as if they'd tacitly agreed that the kiss had been a terrible mistake and should be forgotten. The problem was, Ellen *couldn't* forget it.

"Reed hasn't been around the house much," Pat answered.

"I know." Derek sounded slightly disgruntled and cast an accusing look in Ellen's direction. "It's almost like he doesn't live here anymore."

"He doesn't. Not really." Pat stepped away from the window and gently set his basketball on a chair. "It's sort of like he's a guest who stops in now and then."

Ellen preferred not to be drawn into this conversation. She hastily closed her book and stood up to leave.

"Hey, Ellen." Pat stopped her.

She sighed and met his questioning gaze with a nervous smile. "Yes?"

"I'll be leaving in a few minutes. Have a nice Thanksgiving."

Relieved that the subject of Reed had been dropped, she threw him a brilliant smile. "You, too."

"Where are you having dinner tomorrow?" Derek asked, as if the thought had unexpectedly occurred to him.

Her mother was still in Arizona, her sister had gone to visit her in-laws and Bud couldn't get leave, so Ellen had decided to stay in Seattle. "Here."

"In this house?" Derek's eyes widened with concern. "But why? Shouldn't you be with your family?"

"My family is going in different directions this year.

It's no problem. In fact, I'm looking forward to having the whole house to myself."

"There's no reason to spend the day alone," Derek argued. "My parents wouldn't mind putting out an extra plate. There's always plenty of food."

Her heart was touched by the sincerity of his invitation. "Thank you, but honestly, I prefer it this way."

"It's because of Reed, isn't it?" Both boys studied her with inquisitive eyes.

"Nonsense."

"But, Ellen, he isn't going to be there."

"Reed isn't the reason," she assured him. Undoubtedly, Reed would be spending the holiday with Danielle. She made an effort to ignore the flash of pain that accompanied the thought; she knew she had no right to feel hurt if Reed chose to spend Thanksgiving with his "almost" fiancée.

"You're sure?" Derek didn't look convinced.

"You could come and spend the day with my family," Pat offered next.

"Will you two quit acting like it's such a terrible tragedy? I'm going to *enjoy* an entire day alone. Look at these nails." She fanned her fingers and held them up for their inspection. "For once, I'll have an uninterrupted block of time to do all the things I've delayed for weeks."

"All right, but if you change your mind, give me a call."

"I asked her first," Derek argued. "You'll call me. Right?"

"Right to you both."

Thanksgiving morning, Ellen woke to a torrential downpour. Rain pelted against the window and the day seemed destined to be a melancholy one. She lounged in her room and read, enjoying the luxury of not having to rush around, preparing breakfast for the whole household.

She wandered down to the kitchen, where she was greeted by a heavy silence. The house was definitely empty. Apparently, Reed, too, had started his day early. Ellen couldn't decide whether she was pleased or annoyed that she had seen so little of him since his return from Denver. He'd been the one to avoid her, and she'd concluded that two could play his silly game. So she'd purposely stayed out of his way. She smiled sadly as she reflected on the past few days. She and Reed had been acting like a couple of adolescents.

She ate a bowl of cornflakes and spent the next hour wiping down the cupboards, with the radio tuned to the soft-rock music station. Whenever a particularly romantic ballad aired, she danced around the kitchen with an imaginary partner. Not so imaginary, really. In her mind, she was in Reed's arms.

The silence became more oppressive during the afternoon, while Ellen busied herself fussing over her nails. When the final layer of polish had dried, she decided to turn on the television to drown out the quiet. An hour into the football game, Ellen noticed that it was nearly dinnertime, and she suddenly felt hungry.

She made popcorn in the microwave and splurged by dripping melted butter over the top. She carried the bowl into the living room and got back on the sofa, tucking her legs beneath her. She'd just found a comfortable position when she heard a noise in the kitchen.

Frowning, she twisted around, wondering who it could be.

The door into the living room swung open and Ellen's heart rate soared into double time.

"Reed?" She blinked to make sure he wasn't an apparition.

"Hello."

He didn't vanish. Instead he took several steps in her direction. "That popcorn smells great."

Without considering the wisdom of her offer, she held out the bowl to him. "Help yourself."

"Thanks." He took off his jacket and tossed it over the back of a chair before joining her on the sofa. He leaned forward, studying the TV. "Who's winning?"

Ellen was momentarily confused, until she realized he was asking about the football game. "I don't know. I haven't paid that much attention."

Reed reached for another handful of popcorn and Ellen set the bowl on the coffee table. Her emotions were muddled. She couldn't imagine what Reed was doing here when he was supposed to be at Danielle's. Although the question burned in her mind, she couldn't bring herself to ask. She glanced at him covertly, but Reed was staring at the TV as though he was alone in the room.

"I'll get us something to drink," she volunteered.

"Great."

Even while she was speaking, Reed hadn't looked in her direction. Slightly piqued by his attitude, she stalked into the kitchen and took two Pepsis out of the refrigerator.

When she returned with the soft drinks and two glasses filled with ice, Reed took one set from her. "Thanks," he murmured, popping open the can. He carefully poured his soda over the ice and set the can aside before taking a sip.

"You're welcome." She flopped down again, pretending to watch television. But her mind was spinning in a hundred different directions. When she couldn't tolerate it any longer, she blurted out the question that dominated her thoughts.

"Reed, what are you doing here?"

He took a long swallow before answering her. "I happen to live here."

"You know what I mean. You should be with Danielle."

"I was earlier, but I decided I preferred your company."

"I don't need your sympathy," she snapped, then swallowed painfully and averted her gaze. Her fingers tightened around the cold glass until the chill extended up her arm. "I'm perfectly content to spend the day alone. I just wish everyone would quit saving me from myself."

His low chuckle was unexpected. "That wasn't my intention."

"Then why are you here?"

"I already told you."

"I can't accept that," she said shakily. He was toying with her emotions, and the thought made her all the more furious.

"All right." Determinedly, he set down his drink and turned toward her. "I felt this was the perfect opportunity for us to talk."

"You haven't said more than ten words to me in three days. What makes this one day so special?"

"We're alone, aren't we, and that's more than we can usually say." His voice was strained. He hesitated a moment, his lips pressed together in a thin, hard line. "I don't know what's happening with us."

"Nothing's happening," she said wildly. "You kissed me, and we both admitted it was a mistake. Can't we leave it at that?"

"No," he answered dryly. "I don't believe it was such a major tragedy, and neither do you."

If it had really been a mistake, Ellen wouldn't have remembered it with such vivid clarity. Nor would she yearn for the taste of him again and again, or hurt so much when she knew he was with Danielle.

Swiftly she turned her eyes away from the disturbing intensity of his, unwilling to reveal the depth of her feelings.

"It wasn't a mistake, was it, Ellen?" he prompted in a husky voice.

She squeezed her eyes shut and shook her head. "No," she whispered, but the word was barely audible.

He gathered her close and she felt his deep shudder of satisfaction as he buried his face in her hair. Long moments passed before he spoke. "Nothing that felt so right could have been a mistake."

Tenderly he kissed her, his lips touching hers with a gentleness she hadn't expected. As if he feared she was somehow fragile; as if he found her highly precious. Without conscious decision, she slipped her arms around him.

"The whole time Danielle and I were together this afternoon, I was wishing it was you. Today, of all days, it seemed important to be with you."

Ellen gazed up into his eyes and saw not only his gentleness, but his confusion. Her fingers slid into the thick hair around his lean, rugged face. "Danielle couldn't have been pleased when you left."

"She wasn't. I didn't even know how to explain it to her. I don't know how to explain it to myself."

Ellen swallowed the dryness that constricted her throat. "Do you want me to move out of the house?"

"No," he said forcefully, then added more quietly, "I think I'd go crazy if you did. Are you a witch who's cast some spell over me?"

She tried unsuccessfully to answer him, but no words of denial came. The knowledge that he was experiencing these strange whirling emotions was enough to overwhelm her.

"If so, the spell is working," he murmured, although he didn't sound particularly happy about the idea.

"I'm confused, too," she admitted and leaned her forehead against his chest. She could feel his heart pounding beneath her open hand.

His long fingers stroked her hair. "I know." He leaned down and kissed the top of her head. "The night you went out with Charlie, I was completely unreasonable. I need to apologize for the things I said. To put it simply, I was jealous. I've acknowledged that, these last weeks in Denver." Some of the tightness left his voice, as though the events of that night had weighed heavily on his mind. "I didn't like the idea of another man holding you, and when I saw the two of you kissing, I think I went a little berserk."

"I...we don't date often."

"I won't ask you not to see him again," he said reluctantly. "I can't ask anything of you."

"Nor can I ask anything of you."

His grip around her tightened. "Let's give this time."

"It's the only thing we can do."

Reed straightened and draped his arm around Ellen's shoulders, drawing her close to his side. Her head nestled against his chest. "I'd like us to start going out together," he said, his chin resting on the crown of her head. "Will that cause a problem for you?"

"Cause a problem?" she repeated uncertainly.

"I'm thinking about the boys."

Remembering their earlier buffoonery and the way they'd taken such delight in teasing her, Ellen shrugged. If those three had any evidence of a romance between her and Reed, they could make everyone's lives miserable. "I don't know."

"Then let's play it cool for a while. We'll move into this gradually until they become accustomed to seeing us together. That way it won't be any big deal."

"I think you might be right." She didn't like pretence or deceit, but she'd be the one subjected to their heckling. They wouldn't dare try it with Reed.

"Can I take you to dinner tomorrow night?"

"I'd like that."

"Not as much as I will. But how are we going to do this? It'll be obvious that we're going out," he mused aloud.

"Not if we leave the house at different times," she said. She could feel his frown. "Is that really necessary?"

"I'm afraid so…."

Ellen and Reed spent the rest of the evening doing nothing more exciting than watching television. His arm remained securely around her shoulders and she felt a sense of deep contentment that was new to her. It was a peaceful interlude during a time that had become increasingly wrought with stress.

Derek got back to the house close to nine-thirty. They both heard him lope in through the kitchen and Reed gave Ellen a quick kiss before withdrawing his arm.

"Hi." Derek entered the room and stood beside the sofa, shuffling his feet. "Dad wondered where you were." His gaze flitted from Ellen to his brother.

"I told them I wouldn't be there for dinner."

"I know. But Danielle called looking for you."

"She knew where I was."

"Apparently not." Reed's younger brother gestured with one hand. "Are you two friends again?"

Reed's eyes found Ellen's and he smiled. "You could say that."

"Good. You haven't been the easiest people to be around lately." Without giving them a chance to respond, he whirled around and marched upstairs.

Ellen placed a hand over her mouth to smother her giggles. "Well, he certainly told us."

Amusement flared in Reed's eyes, and he chuckled softly. "I guess he did, at that." His arm slid around Ellen's shoulders once again. "Have you been difficult lately?"

"I'm never difficult," she said.

"Me neither."

They exchanged smiles and went back to watching their movie.

As much as Ellen tried to concentrate on the television, her mind unwillingly returned to Derek's announcement. "Do you think you should call Danielle?" She cast her eyes down, disguising her discomfort. Spending these past few hours with Reed had been like an unexpected Christmas gift, granted early. But she felt guilty that it had been at the other woman's expense.

Impatience tightened Reed's mouth. "Maybe I'd better. I didn't mean to offend her or her family by leaving early." He paused a moment, then added, "Danielle's kind of high-strung."

Ellen had noticed that, but she had no intention of mentioning it. And she had no intention of listening in on their conversation, either. "While you're doing that, I'll wash up the popcorn dishes, then go to bed."

Reed's eyes widened slightly in a mock reprimand. "It's a little early, isn't it?"

"Perhaps," she said, faking a yawn, "but I've got this hot date tomorrow night and I want to be well rested for it."

The front door opened and Pat sauntered in, carrying his duffle bag. "Hi." He stopped and studied them curiously. "Hi," he repeated.

"I thought you were staying at your parents' for the weekend." Ellen remembered that he'd said something about being gone for the entire four-day holiday.

"Mom gave my bedroom to one of my aunts. I can't see any reason to sleep on the floor when I've got a bed here."

"Makes sense," Reed said with a grin.

"Are you two getting along again?"

"We never fought."

"Yeah, sure," Pat mumbled sarcastically. "And a basket isn't worth two points."

Ellen had been unaware how much her disagreement with Reed had affected the boys. Apparently, Reed's reaction was the same as hers; their eyes met briefly in silent communication.

"I'll go up with you," she told Pat. "See you in the morning, Reed."

"Sure thing."

She left Pat on the second floor to trudge up to the third.

It shouldn't have been a surprise that she slept so well. Her mind was at ease and she awoke feeling contented and hopeful. Neither she nor Reed had made any commitments yet. They didn't know if what they felt would last a day or a lifetime. They were explorers, discovering the uncharted territory of a new relationship.

She hurried down the stairs early the next morning. Reed was already up, sitting at the kitchen table drinking coffee and reading the paper.

"Morning," she said, pouring water into the tea kettle and setting it on the burner.

"Morning." His eyes didn't leave the paper.

Ellen got a mug from the cupboard and walked past Reed on her way to get the canister of tea. His hand reached out and clasped her around the waist, pulling her down into his lap.

Before she could protest, his mouth firmly covered hers. When the kiss was over, Ellen straightened, resting her hands on his shoulders. "What was that for?" she asked to disguise how flustered he made her feel.

"Just to say good morning," he said in a warm, husky voice. "I don't imagine I'll have too many opportunities to do it in such a pleasant manner."

"No," she said and cleared her throat. "Probably not."

Ellen was sitting at the table, with a section of the paper

propped up in front of her, when the boys came into the kitchen.

"Morning," Monte murmured vaguely as he opened the refrigerator. He was barefoot, his hair was uncombed and his shirt was still unbuttoned. "What's for breakfast?"

"Whatever your little heart desires," she told him, neatly folding over a page of the paper.

"Does this mean you're not cooking?"

"That's right."

"But—"

Reed lowered the sports page and glared openly at Monte.

"Cold cereal will be fine," Monte grumbled and took down a large serving bowl, emptying half the contents of a box of rice crisps inside.

"Hey, save some for me," Pat hollered from the doorway. "That's my favorite."

"I was here first."

Derek strolled into the kitchen. "Does everyone have to argue?"

"Everyone?" Reed cocked a brow in his brother's direction.

"First it was you and Ellen, and now it's Pat and Monte."

"Hey, that's right," Monte cried. "You two aren't fighting. That's great." He set his serving bowl of rice crisps on the table. "Does this mean…you're…you know."

Lowering the paper, Ellen eyed him sardonically. "No, I don't know."

"Are you…seeing each other?" A deep flush darkened Monte's face.

"We see each other every day."

"That's not what I'm asking."

"But that's all I'm answering." From the corner of her eye, she caught sight of Pat pantomiming a fiddler, and she groaned inwardly. The boys were going to make it difficult to maintain any kind of romantic relationship with Reed. She cast him a speculative glance. But if Reed had noticed the activity around him, he wasn't letting on, and Ellen was grateful.

"I've got a practice game tonight," Pat told Ellen as he buttered a piece of toast. "Do you want to come?"

Flustered, she automatically sought out Reed. "Sorry... I'd like to come, but I've got a date."

"Bring him along."

"I...don't know if he likes basketball."

"Yeah, he does," Derek supplied. "Charlie and I were talking about it recently and he said it's one of his favorite games."

She didn't want to tell an outright lie. But she would save herself a lot of aggravation if she simply let Derek and the others assume it was Charlie she'd be seeing.

"What about you, Reed?" Derek asked.

His gaze didn't flicker from the paper and Ellen marveled at his ability to appear so dispassionate. "Not tonight. Thanks anyway."

"Have you got a date, too?" Derek pressed.

It seemed as though everyone in the kitchen was watching Reed, waiting for his response. "I generally go out on Friday nights."

"Well," Ellen said, coming to her feet. "I think I'll get moving. I want to take advantage of the holiday to do some errands. Does anybody need anything picked up at the cleaners?"

"I do," Monte said, raising his hand. "If you'll wait a minute, I'll get the slip."

"Sure."

By some miracle, Ellen was able to avoid any more questions for the remainder of the day. She went about her errands and didn't see Reed until late in the afternoon, when their paths happened to cross in the kitchen. He quickly whispered a time and meeting place and explained that he'd leave first. Ellen didn't have a chance to do more than agree before the boys were upon them.

At precisely seven, Ellen met Reed at the grocery store parking lot two blocks from the house. He'd left ten minutes earlier to wait for her there. As soon as he spotted her, he leaned across the cab of the pickup and opened the door on her side. Ellen found it slightly amusing that when he was with her he drove the pickup, and when he was with Danielle he took the sports car. She wondered whether or not this was a conscious decision. In any event, it told her quite a bit about the way Reed viewed the two women in his life.

"Did you get away unscathed?" he asked, chuckling softly.

She slid into the seat beside him in the cab and shook her head. "Not entirely. All three of them were curious about why Charlie wasn't coming to the house to pick me up. I didn't want to lie, so I told them they'd have to ask him."

"Will they?"

"I certainly hope not."

Reed's hand reached for hers and his eyes grew serious. "I'm not convinced that keeping this a secret is the right thing to do."

"I don't like it, either, but it's better than their constant teasing."

"I'll put a stop to that." His voice dropped ominously and Ellen didn't doubt that he'd quickly handle the situation.

"But, Reed, they don't mean any harm. I was hoping we could lead them gradually into accepting us as a couple. Let them get used to seeing us together before we spring it on them that we're...dating."

"Ellen, I don't know."

"Trust me on this," she pleaded, her eyes imploring him. This arrangement, with its furtiveness and deception, was far from ideal, but for now it seemed necessary. She hoped the secrecy could end soon.

His kiss was brief and ardent. "I don't think I could deny you anything." But he didn't sound happy about it.

The restaurant he took her to was located in the south end of Seattle, thirty minutes from Capitol Hill. At first, Ellen was surprised that he'd chosen one so far from home but the food was fantastic and the view from the Des Moines Marina alone would have been worth the drive.

Reed ordered a bottle of an award-winning wine, a sauvignon blanc from a local winery. It was satisfyingly clear and crisp.

"I spoke to Danielle," Reed began.

"Reed." She stopped him, placing her hand over his. "What goes on between you and Danielle has nothing to do with me. We've made no promises and no commitments." In fact, of course, she was dying to know about the other woman Reed had dated for so long. She hoped that if she pretended no interest in his relationship with Danielle, she'd seem more mature and sophisticated than she really was. She didn't want Reid to think she was threatened by Danielle or that she expected anything from him. Hoped, yes. Expected, no.

He looked a little stunned. "But—"

Swiftly she lowered her gaze. "I don't want to know." Naturally, she was longing to hear every detail. As it was, she felt guilty about the other woman. Danielle might have had her faults, but she loved Reed. She must love him to be so patient with his traveling all these months. And when Derek had first mentioned her, he'd spoken as though Reed and Danielle's relationship was a permanent one.

Danielle and Ellen couldn't have been more different. Ellen was practical and down-to-earth. She'd had to be. After her father's death, she'd become the cornerstone that held the family together.

Danielle, on the other hand, had obviously been pampered and indulged all her life. Ellen guessed that she'd been destined from birth to be a wealthy socialite, someone who might, in time, turn to charitable works to occupy herself. They were obviously women with completely dissimilar backgrounds, she and Danielle.

"I'll be in Atlanta the latter part of next week," Reed was saying.

"You're full of good news, aren't you?"

"It's my work, Ellen."

"I wasn't complaining. It just seems that five minutes after you get home, you're off again."

"I won't be long this time. A couple of days. I'll fly in for the meeting and be back soon afterward."

"You'll be here for Christmas?" Her thoughts flew to her family and how much she wished they could meet Reed. Bud, especially. He'd be in Yakima over the holidays and Ellen was planning to take the bus home to spend some time with him. But first she had to get through her exams.

"I'll be here."

"Good." But it was too soon to ask Reed to join her for the trip. He might misinterpret her invitation, see something that wasn't there. She had no desire to pressure him into the sort of commitment that meeting her family might imply.

After their meal, they walked along the pier, holding hands. The evening air was chilly and when Ellen shivered, Reed wrapped his arm around her shoulders.

"I enjoyed tonight," he murmured.

"I did, too." She bent her arm so that her fingers linked with his.

"Tomorrow night—"

"No." She stopped him, turning so that her arm slid around his middle. Tilting her head back, she stared into the troubled green eyes. "Let's not talk about tomorrow. For right now, let's take one day at a time."

His mouth met hers before she could finish speaking. A gentle brushing of lips. Then he deepened the kiss, and his arms tightened around her, and her whole body hummed with joy.

Ellen was lost, irretrievably lost, in the taste and scent of this man. She felt frightened by her response to him— it would be so easy to fall in love with Reed. *Completely* in love. But she couldn't allow that to happen. Not yet. It was too soon.

* * *

Her words about taking each day as it came were forcefully brought to Ellen's mind the following evening. She'd gone to the store and noticed Reed's Porsche parked in the driveway. When she returned, both Reed and the sports car had disappeared.

He was with Danielle.

Seven

"Why couldn't I see that?" Ellen moaned, looking over the algebraic equation Reed had worked out. "If I can fix a stopped-up sink, tune a car engine and manage a budget, why can't I understand something this simple?" She was quickly losing a grip on the more advanced theories they were now studying.

"Here, let me show it to you again."

Her hand lifted the curls off her forehead. "Do you think it'll do any good?"

"Yes, I do." Reed obviously had more faith in her powers of comprehension than she did. Step by step, he led her through another problem. When he explained the textbook examples, the whole process seemed so logical. Yet when she set out to solve a similar equation on her own, nothing went right.

"I give up." Throwing her hands over her head, she leaned back in the kitchen chair and groaned. "I should've realized that algebra would be too much for me. I had difficulty memorizing the multiplication tables, for heaven's sake."

"What you need is a break."

"I couldn't agree more. Twenty years?" She stood up and brought the cookie jar to the table. "Here, this will help ease the suffering." She offered him a chocolate-chip cookie and took one herself.

"Be more patient with yourself," Reed urged.

"There's only two weeks left in this term—and then exams. I need to understand this stuff and I need to understand it now."

He laid his hands on her shoulders, massaging gently. "No, you don't. Come on, I'm taking you to a movie."

"I've got to study," she protested, but not too strenuously. Escaping for an hour or two sounded infinitely more appealing than struggling with these impossible equations.

"There's a wonderful foreign film showing at the Moore Egyptian Theatre and we're going. We can worry about that assignment once we get back."

"But, Reed—"

"No buts. We're going." He took her firmly by the hand and led her into the front hall. Derek and Monte were watching TV and the staccato sounds of machine guns firing could be heard in the background. Neither boy noticed them until Reed opened the hall closet.

"Where are you two headed?" Derek asked, peering around the living-room door as Reed handed Ellen her jacket.

"A movie."

Instantly Derek muted the television. "The two of you alone? Together?"

"I imagine there'll be one or two others at the cinema," Reed responded dryly.

"Can I come?" Monte had joined Derek in the doorway.

Instantly Derek's elbow shoved the other boy in the ribs. "On second thought, just bring me back some pop corn, okay?"

"Sure."

Ellen pulled a knit cap over her ears. "Do either of you want anything else? I'd buy out the concession stand if one of you felt inclined to do my algebra assignment."

"No way."

"Bribing them won't help," Reed commented.

"I know, but I was hoping…."

It was a cold, blustery night. An icy north wind whipped against them as they hurried to Reed's truck. He opened the door for her before running around to the driver's side.

"Brr." Ellen shoved her hands inside her pockets. "If I doubted it was winter before, now I know."

"Come here and I'll warm you." He patted the seat beside him, indicating that she should slide closer.

Willingly she complied, until she sat so near him that her thigh pressed against his. Neither of them moved. It had been several days since they'd been completely alone together and longer still since he'd held or kissed her without interruption. The past week had been filled with frustration. Often she'd noticed Reed's gaze on her, studying her face and her movements, but it seemed that every time he touched her one of the boys would unexpectedly appear.

Reed turned to her. Their thoughts seemed to echo each other's; their eyes locked hungrily. Ellen required no invitation. She'd been longing for his touch. With a tiny cry she reached for him just as his arms came out to encircle her, drawing her even closer.

"This is crazy," he whispered fervently into her hair.

"I know."

As though he couldn't deny himself any longer, he cradled her face with both hands and he slowly lowered his mouth to hers.

Their lips clung and Reed's hand went around her ribs as he held her tight. The kiss was long and thoroughly satisfying.

Panting, he tore his mouth from hers and buried his face in her neck. "We'd better get to that movie."

It was all Ellen could do to nod her head in agreement.

They moved apart and fastened their seat belts, both of them silent.

When Reed started the truck, she saw that his hand was trembling. She was shaking too, but no longer from the cold. Reed had promised to warm her and he had, but not quite in the way she'd expected.

They were silent as Reed pulled onto the street. After days of carefully avoiding any kind of touch, any lingering glances, they'd sat in the driveway kissing in direct view of curious eyes. She realized the boys could easily have been watching them.

Ellen felt caught up in a tide that tossed her closer and closer to a long stretch of rocky beach. Powerless to alter the course of her emotions, she feared for her heart, afraid of being caught in the undertow.

"The engineering department is having a Christmas party this weekend at the Space Needle," Reed murmured.

Ellen nodded. Twice in the past week he'd left the house

wearing formal evening clothes. He hadn't told her where he was going, but she knew. He'd driven the Porsche and he'd come back smelling of expensive perfume. For a Christmas party with his peers, Reed would escort Danielle. She understood that and tried to accept it.

"I want you to come with me."

"Reed," she breathed, uncertain. "Are you sure?"

"Yes." His hand reached for hers. "I want you with me."

"The boys—"

"Forget the boys. I'm tired of playing games with them."

Her smile came from her heart. "I am, too," she whispered.

"I'm going to have a talk with them."

"Don't," she pleaded. "It's not necessary to say anything."

"They'll start in with their teasing," he warned. "I thought you hated that."

"I don't care as much anymore. And if they do, we can say something then."

He frowned briefly. "All right."

The Moore Egyptian was located in the heart of downtown Seattle, so parking was limited. They finally found a spot on the street three blocks away. They left the truck and hurried through the cold, arm in arm, not talking. The French film was a popular one; by the time they got to the cinema, a long line had already formed outside.

A blast of wind sliced through Ellen's jacket and she buried her hands in her pockets. Reed leaned close to ask her something, then paused, slowly straightening.

"Morgan." A tall, brusque-looking man approached Reed.

"Dailey," Reed said, quickly stepping away from Ellen.

"I wouldn't have expected to see you out on a night like this," the man Reed had called Dailey was saying.

"I'm surprised to see you, too."

"This film is supposed to be good," Dailey said.

"Yeah. It's got great reviews."

Dailey's eyes returned to the line and rested on Ellen, seeking an introduction. Reed didn't give him one. Reed was obviously pretending he wasn't with Ellen.

She offered the man a feeble smile, wondering why Reed would move away from her, why he wouldn't introduce her to his acquaintance. The line moved slowly toward the ticket booth and Ellen went with it, leaving Reed talking to Dailey on the pavement. She felt a flare of resentment when he rejoined her a few minutes later.

"That was a friend of a friend."

Ellen didn't respond. Somehow she didn't believe him. And she resented the fact that he'd ignored the most basic of courtesies and left her standing on the sidewalk alone, while he spoke with a friend. The way he'd acted, anyone would assume Reed didn't want the man to know Ellen was with him. That hurt. Fifteen minutes earlier she'd been soaring with happiness at his unexpected invitation to the Christmas party, and now she was consumed with doubt and bitterness. Perhaps this Dailey was a friend of Danielle's and Reed didn't want the other woman to know he was out with Ellen. But that didn't really sound like Reed.

Once inside the cinema, Reed bought a huge bucket of buttered popcorn. They located good seats, despite the crowd, and sat down, neither of them speaking. As the lights went down, Reed placed his hand on the back of her neck.

Ellen stiffened. "Are you sure you want to do that?"

"What?"

"Touch me. Someone you know might recognize you."

"Ellen, listen…"

The credits started to roll on the huge screen and she shook her head, not wanting to hear any of his excuses.

But maintaining her bad mood was impossible with the comedy that played out before them. Unable to stop herself, Ellen laughed until tears formed in her eyes; she was clutching her stomach because it hurt from laughing. Reed seemed just as amused as she was, and a couple of times during the film, their smiling gazes met. Before she knew it, Reed was holding her hand and she didn't resist when he draped his arm over her shoulders.

Afterward, as they strolled outside, he tucked her hand in the crook of his elbow. "I told you a movie would make you feel better."

It had and it hadn't. Yes, she'd needed the break, but Reed's behavior outside the cinema earlier had revived the insecurities she was trying so hard to suppress. She knew she wasn't nearly as beautiful or sophisticated as Danielle.

"You *do* feel better?" His finger lifted her chin to study her eyes.

There was no denying that the film had been wonderful. "I haven't laughed so hard in ages," she told him, smiling.

"Good."

Friday night, Ellen wore her most elaborate outfit—slim black velvet pants and a silver lamé top. She'd spent hours debating whether an evening gown would have been more appropriate, but had finally decided on the pants. Examining herself from every direction in the full-length mirror that hung from her closet door, Ellen released a pent-up breath and closed her eyes. This one night, she wanted everything to be perfect. Her heels felt a little uncomfortable, but she'd get used to them. She rarely had any reason to wear heels. She'd chosen them now because Reed had said there'd be dancing and she wanted to adjust her height to his.

By the time she reached the foot of the stairs, Reed was waiting for her. His eyes softened as he looked at her. "You're lovely."

"Oh, Reed, are you sure? I don't mind changing if you'd rather I wear something else."

His eyes held hers for a long moment. "I don't want you to change a thing."

"Hey, Ellen." Derek burst out of the kitchen, and stopped abruptly. "Wow." For an instant he looked as though he'd lost his breath. "Hey, guys," he called eagerly. "Come and see Ellen."

The other two joined Derek. "You look like a movie star," Pat breathed.

Monte closed his mouth and opened it again. "You're *pretty.*"

"Don't sound so shocked."

"It's just that we've never seen you dressed...like this," Pat mumbled.

"Are you going out with Charlie?"

Ellen glanced at Reed, suddenly unsure. She hadn't dated Charlie in weeks. She hadn't wanted to.

"She's going out with me," Reed explained in an even voice that didn't invite comment.

"With you? Where?" Derek's eyes got that mischievous twinkle Ellen recognized immediately.

"A party."

"What about—" He stopped suddenly, swallowing several times.

"You had a comment?" Reed lifted his eyebrows.

"I thought I was going to say something," Derek muttered, clearly embarrassed, "but then I realized I wasn't."

Hiding a smile, Reed held Ellen's coat for her.

She slipped her arms into the satin-lined sleeves and reached for her beaded bag. "Good night, guys, and don't wait up."

"Right." Monte raised his index finger. "We won't wait up."

Derek took a step forward. "Should I say anything to someone...anyone in case either of you gets a phone call?"

"Try *hello*," Reed answered, shaking his head.

"Right." Derek stuck his hand in his jeans pocket. "Have a good time."

"We intend to."

Ellen managed to hold back her laughter until they were on the front porch. But when the door clicked shut the giggles escaped and she pressed a hand to her mouth. "Derek *thought* he was going to say something."

"Then he realized he wasn't," Reed finished for her, chuckling. His hand at her elbow guided her down the steps. "They're right about one thing. You do look gorgeous."

"Thank you, but I hadn't expected it to be such a shock."

"The problem is, the boys are used to seeing you as a

substitute mother. It's suddenly dawned on them what an attractive woman you are."

"And how was it *you* noticed?"

"The day I arrived and found you in my kitchen wearing only a bra, I knew."

"I was wearing more than that," she argued.

"Maybe, but at the time that was all I saw." He stroked her cheek with the tip of his finger, then tucked her arm in his.

Ellen felt a warm contentment as Reed led her to the sports car. This was the first time she'd been inside, and the significance of that seemed unmistakable. She sensed that somewhere in the past two weeks Reed had made an unconscious decision about their relationship. Maybe she was being silly in judging the strength of their bond by what car he chose to drive. And maybe not. Reed was escorting her to this party in his Porsche because he viewed her in a new light. He saw her now as a beautiful, alluring woman—no longer as the college student who seemed capable of mastering everything but algebra.

The Space Needle came into view as Reed pulled onto Denny Street. The world-famous Needle, which had been built for the 1962 World's Fair, rose 605 feet above the Seattle skyline. Ellen had taken the trip up to the observation deck only once and she'd been thrilled at the unobstructed view of the Olympic and Cascade mountain ranges. Looking out at the unspoiled beauty of Puget Sound, she'd understood immediately why Seattle was described as one of the world's most livable cities.

For this evening, Reed explained, his office had booked the convention rooms on the hundred-foot level of the Needle. The banquet facilities had been an addition, and Ellen wondered what sort of view would be available.

As Reed stopped in front of the Needle, a valet appeared, opening Ellen's door and offering her his gloved hand. She climbed as gracefully as she could from the low-built vehicle. Her smile felt a little strained, and she took a deep breath to dispel the gathering tension. She wanted everything about the evening to be perfect; she longed for Reed to be proud of her, to feel that she belonged in his life—and in his world.

Her curiosity about the view was answered as soon as they stepped from the elevator into the large room. She glanced at the darkened sky that resembled folds of black velvet, sprinkled with glittering gems. When she had a chance she'd walk over toward the windows. For now, she was more concerned with fitting into Reed's circle and being accepted by his friends and colleagues.

Bracing herself for the inevitable round of introductions, she scanned the crowd for the man she'd seen outside the cinema. He didn't seem to be at the party and Ellen breathed easier. If Dailey was there, he would surely make a comment about seeing her with Reed that night, and she wouldn't know how to respond.

As they made their way through the large room, several people called out to Reed. When he introduced Ellen, two or three of them appeared to have trouble concealing their surprise that he wasn't with Danielle. But no one mentioned Danielle and they all seemed to accept Ellen freely, although a couple of people gave her curious looks. Eventually, Ellen relaxed and smiled up at Reed.

"That wasn't so bad, was it?" he asked, his voice tender.

"Not at all."

"Would you like something to drink?"

"Please."

"Wine okay?"

"Of course."

"I'll be right back."

Ellen watched Reed cross the room toward the bar. She was absurdly proud of him and made no attempt to disguise her feelings when he returned to her, carrying two glasses of white wine.

"You shouldn't look at me like that," he murmured, handing her a glass.

"Why?" she teased, her eyes sparkling. "Does it embarrass you?"

"No. It makes me wish I could ignore everyone in this room and kiss you right this minute." A slow, almost boyish grin spread across his features.

"That would certainly cause quite a commotion."

"But not half the commotion it would cause if they knew what else I was thinking."

"Oh?" She hid a smile by taking another sip of wine.

"Are we back to that word again?"

"Just what do you have in mind?"

He dipped his head so that he appeared to be whispering something in her ear, although actually his lips brushed her face. "I'll show you later."

"I'll be waiting."

They stood together, listening to the music and the laughter. Ellen found it curious that he'd introduced her to so few people and then only to those who'd approached him. But she dismissed her qualms as petty and, worse, paranoid. After all, she told herself, she was here to be with Reed, not to make small talk with his friends.

He finished his drink and suggested another. While he returned to the bar for refills, Ellen wandered through the crowd, walking over to the windows for a glimpse of the magnificent view. But as she moved, she kept her gaze trained on Reed.

A group of men stopped him before he could reach the bar. His head was inclined toward them, and he seemed to be giving them his rapt attention. Yet periodically his eyes would flicker through the crowd, searching for her. When he located her by the huge floor-to-ceiling windows, he smiled as though he felt relieved. With an abruptness that bordered on rudeness, he excused himself from the group and strolled in her direction.

"I didn't see where you'd gone."

"I wasn't about to leave you," she told him. Turning, she faced the window, watching the lights of the ferry boats gliding across the dark green waters of Puget Sound.

His hands rested on her shoulders and Ellen leaned back against him, warmed by his nearness. "It's lovely from up here."

"Exquisite," he agreed, his mouth close to her ear. "But I'm not talking about the view." His hands slid lazily down her arms. "Dance with me," he said, taking her hand and leading her to the dance floor.

Ellen walked obediently into his arms, loving the feel of being close to Reed. She pressed her cheek against the smooth fabric of his jacket as they swayed gently to the slow, dreamy music.

"I don't normally do a lot of dancing," he whispered.

Ellen wouldn't have guessed that. He moved with confident grace, and she assumed he'd escorted Danielle around a dance floor more than once. At the thought of the other woman, Ellen grew uneasy, but she forced her tense body to relax. Reed had chosen to bring *her,* and not Danielle, to this party. That had to mean something—something exciting.

"Dancing was just an excuse to hold you."

"You don't need an excuse," she whispered.

"In a room full of people, I do."

"Shall we wish them away?" She closed her eyes, savoring the feel of his hard, lithe body against her own.

He maneuvered them into the darkest corner of the dance floor and immediately claimed her mouth in a kiss that sent her world spinning into orbit.

Mindless of where they were, Ellen arched upward, Reed responded by sliding his hands down her back, down to her hips, drawing her even closer.

He dragged his mouth across her cheek. "I'm sorry we came."

"Why?"

"I don't want to waste time with all these people around. We're hardly ever alone. I want you, Ellen."

His honest, straightforward statement sent the fire roaring through her veins. "I know. I want you, too." Her voice was unsteady. "But it's a good thing we aren't alone very often." At the rate things were progressing between them, Ellen felt relieved that the boys were at the house. Otherwise—

"Hey, Reed." A friendly voice boomed out a few feet away. "Aren't you going to introduce me to your friend?"

Reed stiffened and for a moment Ellen wondered if

he was going to pretend he hadn't heard. He looked at her through half-closed eyes, and she grinned up at him, mutely telling him she didn't mind. Their private world couldn't last forever. She knew that. They were at a party, an office party, and Reed was expected to mingle with his colleagues.

"Hello, Ralph." Reed's arm slid around Ellen's waist, keeping her close.

"Hello there." But Ralph wasn't watching Reed. "Well, aren't you going to introduce me?"

"Ellen Cunningham, Ralph Forester."

Ralph extended his hand and held Ellen's in both of his for a long moment. His eyes were frankly admiring.

"I don't suppose you'd let me steal this beauty away for a dance, would you?" Although the question was directed at Reed, Ralph didn't take his eyes from Ellen. "Leave it to you to be with the most beautiful woman here," the other man teased. "You sure do attract them."

Reed's hand tightened around Ellen. "Ellen?" He left the choice to her.

"I don't mind." She glanced at Reed and noted that his expression was carefully blank. But she knew him too well to be fooled. She could see that his jaw was rigid with tension and that his eyes showed annoyance at the other man's intrusion. Gradually he lowered his arm, releasing her.

Ralph stepped forward and claimed Ellen's hand, leading her onto the dance floor.

She swallowed as she placed her left hand on his shoulder and her right hand in his. Wordlessly they moved to the soft music. But when Ralph tried to bring her closer, Ellen resisted.

"Have you known Reed long?" Ralph asked, his hand trailing sensuously up and down her back.

She tensed. "Several months now." Despite her efforts to keep her voice even and controlled, she sounded slightly breathless.

"How'd you meet?"

"Through his brother." The less said about their living arrangements, the better. Ellen could just guess what Ralph would say if he knew they were living in the same house. "Do you two work together?"

"For the last six years."

They whirled around, and Ellen caught a glimpse of Reed standing against the opposite wall, studying them like a hawk zeroing in on its prey. Ralph apparently noticed him, as well.

"I don't think Reed was all that anxious to have you dance with me."

Ellen merely shrugged.

Ralph chortled gleefully, obviously enjoying Reed's reaction. "Not if the looks he's giving me are any indication. I can't believe it. Reed Morgan is jealous," he said with another chuckle, leading her out of Reed's sight and into the dimly lit center of the floor.

"I'm sure you're mistaken."

"Well, look at him."

All Ellen could see was Reed peering suspiciously at them across the crowded dance floor.

"This is too good to be true," Ralph murmured.

"What do you mean?"

"There isn't a woman in our department who wouldn't give her eyeteeth to go out with Reed."

Ellen was shocked, yet somehow unsurprised. "Oh?"

"Half the women are in love with him and he ignores them. He's friendly, don't get me wrong. But it's all business. Every time a single woman gets transferred into our area it takes her a week, maybe two, to fall for Reed. The rest of us guys just stand back and shake our heads. But with Reed otherwise occupied, we might have a chance."

"He *is* wonderful," Ellen admitted, managing to keep a courteous smile on her face. What Ralph was describing sounded so much like her own feelings that she couldn't doubt the truth of what he said.

Ralph arched his brows and studied her. "You too?"

"I'm afraid so."

"What's this guy got?" He sighed expressively, shaking his head. "Can we bottle it?"

"Unfortunately, I don't think so," Ellen responded lightly, liking Ralph more. His approach might have been a bit overpowering at first, but he was honest and compelling in his own right. "I don't imagine you have much trouble attracting women."

"As long as I don't bring them around Reed, I'm fine." A smile swept his face. "The best thing that could happen would be if he got married. I don't suppose that's in the offing between you two?"

He was so blithely serious that Ellen laughed. "Sorry."

"You're sure?"

Ralph was probably thinking of some rumor he'd heard about Danielle. "There's another woman he's seeing. They've known each other for a long time and apparently, they're quite serious," she explained, keeping her voice calmly detached.

"I don't believe it," Ralph countered, frowning. "Reed wouldn't be tossing daggers at my back if he was involved with someone else. One thing I suspect about this guy, he's a one-woman man."

Ellen closed her eyes, trying to shut out the pain. She didn't know what to believe about Reed anymore. All she could do was hold on to the moment. Wasn't that what she'd told him earlier—that they'd have to take things day by day? She was the one who hadn't wanted to talk about Danielle. In any case, she didn't want to read too much into his actions. She couldn't. She was on the brink of falling in love with him...if she hadn't already. To allow herself to think he might feel the same way was asking for trouble. For heartbreak.

The music ended and Ralph gently let her go. "I'd better return you to Reed or he's likely to come after me."

"Thank you for...everything."

"You're welcome, Ellen." With one hand at her waist, he steered her toward Reed.

They were within a few feet of him when Danielle suddenly appeared. She seemed to have come out of nowhere. "Reed!" She was laughing delightedly, flinging herself into his arms and kissing him intimately. "Oh, darling, you're so right. Being together is more important than any ski trip. I'm so sorry. Will you forgive me?"

Eight

"Ellen," Ralph asked. "Are you all right?"

"I'm fine," she lied.

"Sure you are," he mocked, sliding his arm around her waist and guiding her back to the dance floor. "I take it the blonde is Woman Number One?"

"You got it." The anger was beginning to build inside her. "Beautiful, too, you'll notice."

"Well, you aren't exactly chopped liver."

She gave a small, mirthless laugh. "Nice of you to say so, but by comparison, I come in a poor second."

"I wouldn't say that."

"Then why can't you take your eyes off Danielle?"

"Danielle. Hmm." He looked away from the other woman and stared blankly into Ellen's face. "Sorry." For her part, Ellen instinctively turned her back on Reed, unable to bear the sight of him holding and kissing another woman.

"Someone must have got their wires crossed."

"Like me," Ellen muttered. She'd been an idiot to assume that Reed had meant anything by his invitation. He'd just needed someone to take to this party, and his first choice hadn't been available. She was a substitute, and a second-rate one at that.

"What do you want to do?"

Ellen frowned, her thoughts fragmented. "I don't know yet. Give me a minute to think."

"You two could always fight for him."

"The stronger woman takes the spoils? No, thanks." Despite herself she laughed. It certainly would've created a diversion at this formal, rather staid party.

Craning his neck, Ralph peered over at the other couple. "Reed doesn't seem too pleased to see her."

"I can imagine. The situation's put him in a bit of a bind."

"I admit it's unpleasant for you, but, otherwise, I'm enjoying this immensely."

Who wouldn't? The scene was just short of comical. "I thought you said Reed was a one-woman man."

"I guess I stand corrected."

Ellen was making a few corrections herself, revising some cherished ideas about Reed Morgan.

"I don't suppose you'd consider staying with me for the rest of the evening?" Ralph suggested hopefully.

"Consider it? I'd say it's the best offer I've had in weeks." She might feel like a fool, but she didn't plan to hang around looking like one.

Ralph nudged her and bent his head to whisper in her ear. "Reed's staring at us. And like I said, he doesn't seem pleased."

With a determination born of anger and pride, she forced a smile to her lips and gazed adoringly up at Ralph. "How am I doing?" she asked, batting her lashes at him.

"Wonderful, wonderful." He swung her energetically around to the beat of the music. "Uh-oh, here he comes."

Reed weaved his way through the dancing couples and tapped Ralph on the shoulder. "I'm cutting in."

Ellen tightened her grip on Reed's colleague, silently pleading with him to stay. "Sorry, buddy, but Ellen's with me now that your lady friend has arrived."

"Ellen?" Reed's eyes narrowed as he stared at her intently. The other couples were dancing around them and curiously watching the party of three that had formed in the center of the room.

She couldn't remember ever seeing anyone look more furious than Reed did at this moment. "Maybe I'd better leave," she said in a low, faltering voice.

"I'll take you home," Ralph offered, dropping his hand to her waist.

"You came with me. You'll leave with me." Reed grasped her hand, pulling her toward him.

"Obviously you were making provisions," Ellen said, "on the off-chance Danielle showed up. How else did she get in here?"

"How am I supposed to know? She probably told the manager she was with me."

"And apparently she is," Ellen hissed.

"Maybe Reed and I should wrestle to decide the winner," Ralph suggested, glancing at Ellen and sharing a comical grin.

"Maybe."

Obviously, Reed saw no humor in the situation. Anger darkened his handsome face, and a muscle twitched in his jaw as the tight rein on his patience slipped.

Ralph withdrew his hand. "Go ahead and dance. It's obvious you two have a lot to talk about."

Reed took Ellen in his arms. "I suppose you're furious," he muttered.

"Have I got anything to be angry about?" she asked calmly. Now that the initial shock had worn off, she felt somewhat distanced from the whole predicament.

"Of course you do. But I want a chance to explain."

"Don't bother. I've got the picture."

"I'm sure you don't."

Ellen stubbornly refused to look up at him, resisting for as long as she could, but eventually she gave in. "It doesn't matter. Ralph said he'd take me home and—"

"I've already made my feelings on that subject quite clear."

"Listen, Reed. Your Porsche seats two. Is Danielle supposed to sit on my lap?"

"She came uninvited. Let her find her own way home."

"You don't mean that."

"I certainly do."

"You can't humiliate Danielle like that." Ellen didn't mention how *she* felt. What was the point? "Don't—"

"She deserves it," he broke in.

"Reed, no." Her hold on his forearm tightened. "This is unpleasant enough for all of us. Don't compound it."

The song ended and the music faded from the room. Reed fastened his hand on Ellen's elbow, guiding her across the floor to where Danielle was standing with Ralph. The two of them were sipping champagne.

"Hello again," Ellen began amicably, doing her utmost to appear friendly, trying to smooth over an already awkward situation.

"Hello." Danielle stared at Ellen curiously, apparently not recognizing her.

"You remember Ellen Cunningham, don't you?" Reed said.

"Not that college girl your brother's renting a room to—" Danielle stopped abruptly, shock etched on her perfect features. "*You're* Ellen Cunningham?"

"In the flesh." Still trying to keep things light, she cocked her head toward Ralph and spoke stagily out of the side of her mouth, turning the remark into a farcical aside. "I wasn't at my best when we met the first time."

"You were fiddling around with that electrical outlet and Reed was horrified," Danielle inserted, her voice completely humorless, her eyes narrowed assessingly. "You didn't even look like a girl."

"She does now." Ralph beamed her a brilliant smile.

"Yes." Danielle swallowed, her face puckered with concern. "She looks very...nice."

"Thank you." Ellen bowed her head.

"I've made a terrible mess of things," Danielle continued, casually handing her half-empty glass to a passing waiter. "Reed mentioned the party weeks ago, and Mom and I had this ski party planned. I told him I couldn't attend and then I felt guilty because Reed's been so sweet, escorting me to all the charity balls."

Ellen didn't hear a word of explanation beyond the fact

that Reed had originally asked Danielle to the party. The other woman had just confirmed Ellen's suspicions, and the hurt went through her like a thousand needles. He'd invited her only because Danielle couldn't attend.

"There's no problem," Ellen said in a bland voice. "I understand how these things happen. He asked you first, so you stay and I'll leave."

"I couldn't do that," Danielle murmured.

Reed's eyes were saying the same thing. Ellen ignored him, and she ignored Danielle. Slipping her hand around Ralph's arm, she looked up at him and smiled, silently thanking him for being her friend. "As I said, it's not a problem. Ralph's already offered to take me home."

Reed's expression was impassive, almost aloof, as she turned toward him. "I'm sure you won't mind."

"How understanding of you," Danielle simpered, locking her arm around Reed's.

"It's better than hand-to-hand combat. I don't really care for fighting."

Danielle looked puzzled, while Ralph choked on a swallow of his drink, his face turning several shades of red as he struggled to hide his amusement. The only one who revealed no sense of humor was Reed, whose face grew more and more shadowed.

The band struck up a lively song and the dance floor quickly filled. "Come on, Reed," Danielle said, her blue eyes eager. "Let's dance." She tugged at Reed's hand and gave a little wriggle of her hips. "You know how much I love to dance."

So Reed *had* done his share of dancing with Danielle— probably at all those charity balls she'd mentioned. Ellen had guessed as much and yet he'd tried to give her the impression that he rarely danced.

But noticing the stiff way Reed held himself now, Ellen could almost believe him.

Ralph placed a gentle hand on her shoulder. "I don't know about you, but I'm ready to get out of here."

Watching Reed with Danielle in his arms was absurdly painful; her throat muscles constricted in an effort to hold back tears and she simply nodded.

"Since we'll be skipping the banquet, shall we go have dinner somewhere?"

Ellen blinked. Dinner. "I'm not really hungry," she said.

"Sure you're hungry," Ralph insisted. "We'll stop at a nice restaurant before I drive you home. I know where Reed's place is, so I know where you live. Don't look so shocked. I figured it out from what you and Danielle were saying. But don't worry, I understand—impoverished students sharing a house and all that. So, what do you say? We'll have a leisurely dinner and get home two hours after Reed. That should set him thinking."

Ellen didn't feel in any mood to play games at Reed's expense. "I'd rather not."

Ralph's jovial expression sobered. "You've got it bad."

"I'll be fine."

He smiled. "I know you will. Come on, let's go."

The night that had begun with such promise had evaporated so quickly, leaving a residue of uncertainty and suspicion. As they neared the house, her composure gradually crumbled until she was nervously twisting the delicate strap of her evening bag over and over between her fingers. To his credit, Ralph attempted to carry the conversation, but her responses became less and less animated. She just wanted to get home and bury her head in her pillow.

By the time Ralph pulled up in front of the Capitol Hill house, they were both silent.

"Would you like to come in for coffee?" she asked. The illusion she'd created earlier of flippant humor was gone now. She hurt, and every time she blinked, a picture of Danielle dancing with Reed came to mind. How easy it was to visualize the other woman's arms around his neck, her voluptuous body pressed against his. The image tormented Ellen with every breath she took.

"No, I think I'll make it an early night."

"Thank you," she said affectionately. "I couldn't have handled this without you."

"I was happy to help. And, Ellen, if you want a shoulder to cry on, I'm available."

She dropped her gaze to the tightly coiled strap of her bag. "I'm fine. Really."

He patted her hand. "Somehow I don't quite believe that." Opening the car door, he came around to her side and handed her out.

On the top step of the porch, Ellen kissed his cheek. "Thanks again."

"Good night, Ellen."

"Night." She took out her keys and unlocked the front door. Pushing it open, she discovered that the house was oddly dark and oddly deserted. It was still relatively early and she would've expected the boys to be around. But not having to make excuses to them was a blessing she wasn't about to question.

As she removed her coat and headed for the stairs, she

noticed the shadows bouncing around the darkened living room. She walked over to investigate and, two steps into the room, heard soft violin music.

Ellen stood there paralyzed, taking in the romantic scene before her. A bottle of wine and two glasses were set out on the coffee table. A fire blazed in the brick fireplace. And the music seemed to assault her from all sides.

"Derek," she called out.

Silence.

"All right, Pat and Monte. I know you're here somewhere."

Silence.

"I'd suggest the three of you get rid of this…stuff before Reed comes home. He's with Danielle." With that, she marched up the stairs, uncaring if they heard her.

"With Danielle?" she heard a male voice shout after her.

"What happened?"

Ellen pretended not to hear.

The morning sun sneaked into her window, splashing the pillow where Ellen lay awake staring sightlessly at the ceiling. Sooner or later she'd have to get out of bed, but she couldn't see any reason to rush the process. Besides, the longer she stayed up here, the greater her chances of missing Reed. The unpleasantness of facing him wasn't going to vanish, but she might be able to postpone it for a morning. Although she had to wonder whether Reed was any more keen on seeing her than she was on seeing him. She could always kill time by dragging out her algebra books and studying for the exam—but that was almost as distasteful as facing Reed.

No, she decided suddenly, she'd stay in her room until she was weak with hunger. Checking her wristwatch, she figured that would be about another five minutes.

Someone knocked on her bedroom door. Sitting up, Ellen pulled the sheet to her neck. "Who is it?" she shouted, not particularly eager to talk to anyone.

Reed threw open the door and stalked inside. He stood in the middle of the room with his hands on his hips. "Are you planning to stay up here for the rest of your life?"

"The idea has distinct possibilities." She glared back at him, her eyes flashing with outrage and ill humor. "By the way, you'll note that I asked who was at the door. I didn't say, 'come in.'" Her voice rose to a mockingly high pitch. "You might have walked in on me when I was dressing."

A smile crossed his mouth. "Is that an invitation?"

"Absolutely not." She rose to a kneeling position, taking the sheets and blankets with her, and pointed a finger in the direction of the door. "Would you kindly leave? I'd like to get dressed."

"Don't let me stop you."

"Reed, please," she said irritably. "I'm not in any mood to talk to you."

"I'm not leaving until we do."

"Unfair. I haven't had my cup of tea and my mouth feels like the bottom of Puget Sound."

"All right," he agreed reluctantly. "I'll give you ten minutes."

"How generous of you."

"Considering my frame of mind since you walked out on me last night, I consider it pretty generous."

"Walked out on you!" She flew off the bed. "That's a bit much!"

"Ten minutes," he repeated, his voice low.

The whole time Ellen was dressing, she fumed. Reed had some nerve accusing her of walking out on him. He obviously didn't have any idea what it had cost her to leave him at that party with Danielle. He was thinking only of his own feelings, showing no regard for hers. He hadn't even acknowledged that she'd swallowed her pride to save them all from an extremely embarrassing situation.

Four male faces met hers when she appeared in the kitchen "Good morning," she said with false enthusiasm.

The three boys looked sheepishly away. "Morning," they droned. Each found something at the table to occupy his hands. Pat, who was holding his basketball, carefully examined its grooves. Monte read the back of the cereal box and Derek folded the front page of the paper, pretending to read it.

"Ellen and I would like a few minutes of privacy," Reed announced, frowning at the three boys.

Derek, Monte and Pat stood up simultaneously.

"I don't think there's anything we have to say that the boys can't hear," she said.

The three boys reclaimed their chairs, looking with interest first at Reed and then at Ellen.

Reed's scowl deepened. "Can't you see that Ellen and I need to talk?"

"There's nothing to discuss," Ellen insisted, pouring boiling water into her mug and dipping a tea bag in the water.

"Yes, there is," Reed countered.

"Maybe it would be best if we did leave," Derek hedged, noticeably uneasy with his brother's anger and Ellen's feigned composure.

"You walk out of this room and there will be no packed lunches next week," Ellen said, leaning against the counter. She threw out the bag and began sipping her tea.

"I'm staying." Monte crossed his arms over his chest as though preparing for a long standoff.

Ellen knew she could count on Monte; his stomach would always take precedence. Childishly, she flashed Reed a saucy grin. He wasn't going to bulldoze her into any confrontation.

"Either you're out of here *now*, or you won't have a place to *live* next week," Reed flared back. At Derek's smug expression, Reed added, "And that includes you, little brother."

The boys exchanged shocked glances. "Sorry, Ellen," Derek mumbled on his way out of the kitchen. "I told Michelle I'd be over in a few minutes anyway." Without another moment's hesitation, Reed's brother was out the door.

"Well?" Reed stared at Monte and Pat.

"Yeah, well…I guess I should probably…" Pat looked to Ellen for guidance, his resolve wavering.

"Go ahead." She dismissed them both with a wave of her hand.

"Are you sure you want us to go?" Monte asked anxiously.

Ellen smiled her appreciation at this small display of mettle. "Thanks, but I'll be okay."

The sound of the door swinging back and forth echoed through the kitchen. Ellen drew a deep, calming breath and turned to Reed, who didn't look all that pleased to have her alone, although he'd gone to some lengths to arrange it. His face was pinched, and fine lines fanned out from his eyes and mouth. Either he'd had a late night or he hadn't slept at all. Ellen decided it must have been the former.

"Well, I'm here within ten minutes, just as you decreed. If you've got something to say, then say it."

"Don't rush me," he snapped.

Ellen released an exaggerated sigh. "First you want to talk to me— and then you're not sure. This sounds like someone who asked me to a party once. First he wanted me with him —and then he didn't."

"I wanted you there last night."

"Oh, was I talking about you?" she asked in fake innocence.

"You're not making this easy." He ploughed his fingers through his hair, the abrupt movement at odds with the self-control he usually exhibited.

"Listen," she breathed, casting her eyes down. "You don't need to explain anything. I have a fairly accurate picture of what happened."

"I doubt that." But he didn't elaborate.

"I can understand why you'd prefer Danielle's company."

"I didn't. That had to be one of the most awkward moments of my life. I wanted you—not Danielle."

Sure, she mused sarcastically. That was why he'd introduced her to so few people. She'd had plenty of time in the past twelve hours to think. If she hadn't been so blinded by the stars in her eyes, she would have figured it out sooner. Reed had taken her to his company party and kept her shielded from the other guests; he hadn't wanted her talking to his friends and colleagues. At the time, she'd assumed he wanted her all to himself. Now she understood the reason. The others knew he'd invited Danielle; they knew that Danielle usually accompanied him to these functions. The other woman had an official status in Reed's life. Ellen didn't.

"It wasn't your fault," she told him. "Unfortunately, under the circumstances, this was unavoidable."

"I'd rather Danielle had left instead of you." He walked to her side, deliberately taking the mug of tea from her hand and setting it on the counter. Slowly his arms came around her.

Ellen lacked the will to resist. She closed her eyes as her arms reached around him, almost of their own accord. He felt so warm and vital.

"I want us to spend the day together."

Her earlier intention of studying for her algebra exam went out the window. Despite all her hesitations, all her doubts and fears, she couldn't refuse this chance to be with him. Alone, the two of them. "All right," she answered softly.

"Ellen." His breath stirred her hair. "There's something you should know."

"Hmm?"

"I'm flying out tomorrow morning for two days."

Her eyes flew open. "How long?"

"Two days, but after that, I won't be leaving again until the Christmas holidays are over."

She nodded. Traveling was part of his job, and any woman in his life would have to accept that. She was touched that he felt so concerned for her. "That's fine," she whispered. "I understand."

Ellen couldn't fault Reed's behavior for the remainder of the weekend. Saturday afternoon, they went Christmas shopping at the Tacoma Mall. His choice of shopping area surprised her, since there were several in the immediate area, much closer than Tacoma, which was a forty-five-minute drive away. But they had a good time, wandering from store to store. Before she knew it, Christmas would be upon them and this was the first opportunity she'd had to do any real shopping. With Reed's help, she picked out gifts for the boys and her brother.

"You'll like Bud," she told him, licking a chocolate ice cream cone. They found a place to sit, with their packages gathered around them, and took a fifteen-minute break.

"I imagine I will." A flash of amusement lit his eyes, then he abruptly looked away.

Ellen lowered her ice-cream cone. "What's so funny? Have I got chocolate on my nose?"

"No."

"What, then?"

"You must have forgiven me for what happened at the party."

"What do you mean?"

"The way you looked into the future and said I'd like your brother, as though you and I are going to have a long relationship."

The ice cream suddenly became very important and Ellen licked away at it with an all-consuming energy. "I told you before that I feel things have to be one day at a time with us. There are too many variables in our...relationship." She waved the ice cream in his direction. "And I use that term loosely."

"There *is* a future for us."

"You seem sure of yourself."

"I'm more sure of you." He said it so smoothly that Ellen wondered if she heard him right. She would have challenged his arrogant assumption, but just then, he glanced at his wristwatch and suggested a movie.

By the time they returned to the house it was close to midnight. He kissed her with a tenderness that somehow reminded her of an early-summer dawn, but his touch was as potent as a sultry August afternoon.

"Ellen?" he murmured into her hair.

"Hmm?"

"I think you'd better go upstairs now."

The warmth of his touch had melted away the last traces of icy reserve. She didn't want to leave him. "Why?"

His hands gripped her shoulders, pushing her away from him, putting an arm's length between them. "Because if you don't leave now, I may climb those stairs with you."

At his straightforward, honest statement, Ellen swallowed hard. "I enjoyed today. Thank you, Reed." He dropped his arms and she placed a trembling hand on the railing. "Have a safe trip."

"I will." He took a step toward her. "I wish I didn't have to go." His hand cupped her chin and he drew her face toward his, kissing her with a hunger that shook Ellen to the core. She needed all her strength not to throw her arms around him again.

Monday afternoon, when Ellen walked into the house after her classes, the three boys were waiting for her. They looked up at her with peculiar expressions on their faces, as though they'd never seen her before and they couldn't understand how she'd wandered into their kitchen.

"All right, what's up?"

"Up?" Derek asked.

"You've got that guilty look."

"*We're* not the guilty party," Pat said.

She sighed. "You'd better let me know what's going on so I can deal with it before Reed gets back."

Monte swung open the kitchen door so that the dining-room table came into view. In the center of the table stood the largest bouquet of red roses Ellen had ever seen.

A shocked gasp slid from the back of her throat. "Who... who sent those?"

"We thought you'd ask so we took the liberty of reading the card."

Their prying barely registered in her numbed brain as she walked slowly into the room and removed the small card pinned to the bright red ribbon. It could have been Bud—but he didn't have the kind of money to buy roses. And if he did, Ellen suspected he wouldn't get them for his sister.

"Reed did it," Pat inserted eagerly.

"Reed?"

"We were as surprised as you."

Her gaze fell to the tiny envelope. She removed the card, biting her lip when she read the message. *I miss you. Reed.*

"He said he misses you," Derek added.

"I see that."

"Good grief, he'll be back tomorrow. How can he possibly miss you in such a short time?"

"I don't know." Her finger lovingly caressed the petals

of a dewy rosebud. They were so beautiful, but their message was even more so.

"I'll bet this is his way of telling you he's sorry about the party," Derek murmured.

"Not that any of us actually knows what happened. We'd like to, but it'd be considered bad manners to ask," Pat explained. "That is, unless you'd like to tell us why he'd take you to the party and then come back alone."

"He didn't get in until three that morning," Monte said accusingly. "You aren't going to let him off so easy are you, Ellen?"

Bowing her head to smell the sweet fragrance, she closed her eyes. "Roses cover a multitude of sins."

"Reed's feeling guilty, I think," Derek said with authority. "But he cares, or else he wouldn't have gone to this much trouble."

"Maybe he just wants to keep the peace," Monte suggested. "My dad bought my mom flowers once for no reason."

"We all live together. Reed's probably figured out that he had to do something if he wanted to maintain the status quo."

"Right," Ellen agreed tartly, scooping up the flowers to take to her room. Maybe it was selfish to deprive the boys of their beauty, but she didn't care. They'd been meant for her, as a private message from Reed, and she wanted them close.

The following day, Ellen cut her last morning class, knowing that Reed's flight was getting in around noon. She could ill afford to skip algebra, but it wouldn't have done her any good to stay. She would've spent the entire time thinking about Reed—so it made more sense to hurry home.

She stepped off the bus a block from the house and even from that distance she could see his truck parked in the driveway. It was the first—and only—thing she noticed. She sprinted toward the house and dashed up the front steps.

Flinging open the door, she called breathlessly, "Anyone here?"

Both Reed and Derek came out of the kitchen.

Her eyes met Reed's from across the room. "Hi," she said in a low, husky voice. "Welcome home."

He advanced toward her, his gaze holding hers.

Neither spoke as Ellen threw her bag of books on the sofa and moved just as quickly toward him.

He caught her around the waist as though he'd been away for months instead of days, hugging her fiercely.

Ellen savored the warmth of his embrace, closing her eyes to the overwhelming emotion she suddenly felt. Reed was becoming far too important in her life. But she no longer had the power to resist him. If she ever had...

"His plane was right on time," Derek was saying. "And the airport was hardly busy. And—"

Irritably, Reed tossed a look over his shoulder. "Little brother, get lost."

Nine

"I've got a game today," Pat said, his fork cutting into the syrup-laden pancakes. "Can you come?"

Ellen's eyes met Reed's in mute communication. No longer did they bother to hide their attraction to each other from the boys. They couldn't. "What time?"

"Six."

"I can be there."

"What about you, Reed?"

Reed wiped the corners of his mouth with the paper napkin. "Sorry, I've got a meeting. But I should be home in time for the victory celebration."

Ellen thrilled at the way the boys automatically linked her name and Reed's. It had been like that from the time he'd returned from his most recent trip. But then, they'd given the boys plenty of reason to think of her and Reed as a couple. He and Ellen were with each other every free moment; the time they spent together was exclusively theirs. And Ellen loved it. She loved Reed, she loved being with him…and she loved every single thing about him. Almost. His reticence on the subject of Danielle had her a little worried, but she pushed it to the back of her mind. She couldn't bring herself to question him, especially after her own insistence that they not discuss Danielle. She no longer felt that way—she wanted reassurance—but she'd decided she'd just assume that the relationship was over. As far as she knew, Reed hadn't spoken to Danielle since the night of the Christmas party. Even stronger evidence was the fact that he drove his truck every day. The Porsche sat in the garage, gathering dust.

Reed stood up and delivered his breakfast plate to the sink. "Ellen, walk me to the door?"

"Sure."

"For Pete's sake, the door's only two feet away," Derek scoffed. "You travel all over the world and all of a sudden you need someone to show you where the back door is?"

Ellen didn't see the look the two brothers exchanged, but Derek's mouth curved upward in a knowing grin. "Oh, I get it. Hey, guys, they want to be alone."

"Just a minute." Monte wolfed down the last of his breakfast, still chewing as he carried his plate to the counter.

Ellen was mildly surprised that Reed didn't comment on Derek's needling, but she supposed they were both accustomed to it.

One by one, the boys left the kitchen. Silently, Reed stood by the back door, waiting. When the last one had departed, he slipped his arms around Ellen.

"You're getting mighty brave," she whispered, smiling into his intense green eyes. Lately, Reed almost seemed to invite the boys' comments. And when they responded, the teasing rolled off his back like rain off a well-waxed car.

"It's torture being around you every day and not touching you," he said just before his mouth descended on hers in an excruciatingly slow kiss that seemed to melt Ellen's very bones.

Reality seemed light-years away as she clung to him, and she struggled to recover her equilibrium. "Reed," she whispered, "you have to get to work."

"Right." But he didn't stop kissing her.

"And I've got classes." If he didn't end this soon, they'd both reach the point of no return. Each time he held and kissed her, it became more difficult to break away.

"I know. I know." His voice echoed through the fog that held her captive. "Now isn't the time or place."

Her arms tightened around his middle as she burrowed her face into his chest. One second, she was telling Reed they had to stop and in the next, she refused to let him go.

"I'll be late tonight," he murmured into her hair.

She remembered that he'd told Pat something about a meeting. "Me, too," she said. "I'm going to the basketball game."

"Right. Want to go out to dinner afterward?" His breath fanned her temple. "Just the two of us. I love being alone with you."

Ellen wanted to cry with frustration. "I can't. I promised the boys dinner. Plus exams start next week and I've got to study."

"Need any help?"

"Only with one subject." She looked up at him and sadly shook her head. "I don't suppose you can guess which one."

"Aren't you glad you've got me?"

"Eternally grateful." Ellen would never have believed that algebra could be both her downfall and her greatest ally. If it weren't for that one subject, she wouldn't have had the excuse to sit down with Reed every night to work through her assignments. But then, she didn't really need an excuse anymore....

"We'll see how grateful you are when grades come out."

"I hate to disappoint you, but it's going to take a lot more than your excellent tutoring to rescue me from my fate this time." The exam was crucial. If she didn't do well, she'd probably end up repeating the class. The thought filled her with dread. It would be a waste of her time and, even worse, a waste of precious funds.

Reed kissed her lightly before releasing her. "Have a good day."

"You, too." She stood at the door until he'd climbed inside the pickup and waved when he backed out of the driveway.

Ellen loaded the dirty dishes into the dishwasher and cleaned off the counter, humming a Christmas carol as she worked.

One of the boys knocked on the door. "Is it safe to come in yet?"

"Sure. Come on in."

All three innocently strolled into the kitchen. "You and Reed are getting kind of friendly, aren't you?"

Running hot tap water into the sink, Ellen nodded. "I suppose."

"Reed hasn't seen Danielle in a while."

Ellen didn't comment, but she did feel encouraged that Derek's conclusion was the same as hers.

"You know what I think?" he asked, hopping onto the counter so she was forced to look at him.

"I can only guess."

"I think Reed's getting serious about you."

"That's nice."

"*Nice*—is that all you can say?" He gave her a look of disgust. "That's my brother you're talking about. He could have any woman he wanted."

"I know." She poured soap into the dishwasher, then closed the door and turned the dial. The sound of rushing water drowned out Derek's next comment.

"Sorry, I have to get to class. I'll talk to you later." She sauntered past Pat and Monte, offering them a cheerful smile.

"She's got it bad." Ellen heard Monte comment. That was the same thing Ralph had said the night of the party. "She hardly even bakes anymore. Remember how she used to make cookies every week?"

"I didn't know love did that to a person," Pat grumbled.

"I'm not sure I like Ellen in love," Monte flung after her as she stepped out the door.

"I just hope she doesn't get hurt."

The boy's remarks echoed in her mind as the day wore on. Ellen didn't need to hear their doubts; she had more than enough of her own. Qualms assailed her when she least expected it—like during the morning's algebra class, or during the long afternoon that followed.

But one look at Reed that evening and all her anxieties evaporated. As soon as she entered the house, she walked straight into the living room, hoping to find him there, and she did.

He put some papers back in a file when she walked in. "How was the game?"

"Pat scored seventeen points and is a hero. Unfortunately, the Huskies lost." Sometimes, that was just the way life went—winning small victories yet losing the war.

She hurried into the kitchen to begin dinner preparations.

"Something smells good." Monte bounded in half an hour later, sniffing appreciatively.

"There's a roast in the oven and an apple pie on the counter," she answered him. She'd bought the pie in hopes of celebrating the Huskies' victory. Now it would soothe their loss. "I imagine everyone's starved."

"I am," Monte announced.

"That goes without saying," Reed called from the living room.

Gradually, the other boys trailed in, and it was time to eat.

After dinner, the evening was spent at the kitchen table, poring over her textbooks. Reed came in twice to make her a fresh cup of tea. Standing behind her chair, he glanced over her shoulder at the psychology book.

"Do you want me to get you anything?" she asked. She was studying in the kitchen, rather than in her room, just to be close to Reed. Admittedly, her room offered more seclusion, but she preferred being around people—one person, actually.

"I don't need a thing." He kissed the top of her head. "And if I did, I'd get it myself. You study."

"Thanks."

"When's the first exam?"

"Monday."

He nodded. "You'll do fine."

"I don't want fine," she countered nervously. "I want fantastic."

"Then you'll do fantastic."

"Where are the boys?" The house was uncommonly silent for a weekday evening.

"Studying. I'm pleased to see they're taking exams as seriously as you are."

"We have to," she mumbled, her gaze dropping to her notebook.

"All right. I get the message. I'll quit pestering you."

"You're not pestering me."

"Right." He bent to kiss the side of her neck as his fingers stroked her arms.

Shivers raced down her spine and Ellen closed her eyes, unconsciously swaying toward him. "Now…now you're pestering me."

He chuckled, leaving her alone at the kitchen table when she would much rather have had him with her every minute of every day.

The next morning, Ellen stood by the door, watching Reed pull out of the driveway.

"Why do you do that?" Pat asked, giving her a glance that said she looked foolish standing there.

"Do what?" She decided the best reaction was to pretend she didn't have any idea what he was talking about.

"Watch Reed leave every morning. He's not likely to have an accident pulling out of the driveway."

Ellen didn't have the courage to confess that she watched so she could see whether Reed drove the pickup or the Porsche. It would sound ridiculous to admit that she gauged their relationship by which vehicle he chose to drive that day.

"She watches because she can't bear to see him go," Derek answered when she didn't. "From what I hear, Michelle does the same thing. What can I say? The woman's crazy about me."

"Oh, yeah?" Monte snickered. "And that's the reason she was with Rick Bloomfield the other day?"

"She was?" Derek sounded completely shocked. "There's an explanation for that. Michelle and I have an understanding."

"Sure you do," Monte teased. "She can date whoever she wants and you can date whoever you want. Some *understanding*."

To prove to the boys that she wasn't as infatuated as they assumed—and maybe to prove the same thing to herself—Ellen didn't watch Reed leave for work the next two mornings. It was pointless, anyway. So what if he drove his Porsche? He had the car, and she could see no reason for him to not drive it. Except for her unspoken insecurities. And there seemed to be plenty of those. As Derek had said earlier in the week, Reed could have any woman he wanted.

She was the first one home that afternoon. Derek was

probably sorting things out with Michelle, Pat had basketball practice and no doubt Monte was in someone's kitchen.

Gathering the ingredients for spaghetti sauce, she arranged them neatly on the counter. She was busy reading over her recipe when the phone rang.

"Hello," she said absently.

"This is Capitol Hill Cleaners. Mr. Morgan's evening suit is ready."

"Pardon?" Reed hadn't told her he was having anything cleaned. Ellen usually picked up his dry cleaning because it was no inconvenience to stop there on her way home from school. And she hadn't minded at all. As silly as it seemed, she'd felt very wifely doing that for him.

"Is it for Reed or Derek?" It was just like Derek to forget something like that.

"The slip says it's for Mr. Reed Morgan."

"Oh?"

"Is there a problem with picking it up? He brought it in yesterday and told us he had to have it this evening."

This evening? Reed was going out tonight?

"From what he said, this is for some special event."

Well, he wouldn't wear a suit to a barbecue. "I'll let him know."

"Thank you. Oh, and be sure to mention that we close at six tonight."

"Yes, I will."

A strange numbness overpowered Ellen as she hung up. Something was wrong. Something was very, very wrong. Without even realizing it, she moved rapidly through the kitchen and then outside.

Reed had often told her the importance of reading a

problem in algebra. Read it carefully, he always said, and don't make any quick assumptions. It seemed crazy to remember that now. But he was right. She couldn't jump to conclusions just because he was going out for the evening. He had every right to do so. She was suddenly furious with herself. All those times he'd offered information about Danielle and she'd refused to listen, trying to play it so cool, trying to appear so unconcerned when on the inside she was dying to know.

By the time she reached the garage she was trembling, but it wasn't from the cold December air. She knew without looking that Reed had driven his sports car to work. The door creaked as she pushed it open to discover the pickup, sitting there in all its glory.

"Okay, he drove his Porsche. That doesn't have to mean anything. He isn't necessarily seeing Danielle. There's a logical explanation for this." Even if he *was* seeing Danielle, she had no right to say anything. They'd made no promises to each other.

Rubbing the chill from her arms, Ellen returned to the house. But the kitchen's warmth did little to chase away the bitter cold that cut her to the heart. Ellen moved numbly toward the phone and ran her finger down the long list of numbers that hung on the wall beside it. When she located the one for Reed's office, she punched out the seven numbers, then waited, her mind in turmoil.

"Mr. Morgan's office," came the efficient voice.

"Hello…this is Ellen Cunningham. I live, that is, I'm a friend of Mr. Morgan's."

"Yes, I remember seeing you the night of the Christmas party," the voice responded warmly. "We didn't have a chance to meet. Would you like me to put you through to Mr. Morgan?"

"No," she said hastily. "Could you give him a message?" Not waiting for a reply, she continued, "Tell him his suit is ready at the cleaners for that...party tonight."

"Oh, good, he wanted me to call. Thanks for saving me the trouble. Was there anything else?"

Tears welled in Ellen's eyes. "No, that's it."

Being reminded by Reed's assistant that they hadn't met the night of the Christmas party forcefully brought to Ellen's attention how few of his friends she did know. None, really. He'd gone out of his way *not* to introduce her to people.

"Just a minute," Ellen cried, her hand clenching the receiver. "There *is* something else you can tell Mr. Morgan. Tell him goodbye." With that, she severed the connection.

A tear rolled down her cheek, searing a path as it made its way to her chin. She'd been a fool not to have seen the situation more clearly. Reed had a good thing going, with her living at the house. She was close to falling in love with him. In fact, she was already there and anyone looking at her could tell. It certainly wasn't any secret from the boys. She cooked his meals, ran his errands, vacuumed his rugs. How convenient she'd become. How useful she'd been to the smooth running of his household.

But Reed had never said a word about his feelings. Sure, they'd gone out, but always to places where no one was likely to recognize him. And the one time Reed did see someone he knew, he'd pretended he wasn't with her. When he *had* included her in a social event, he'd only introduced her to a handful of people, as though...as though he didn't really want others to know her. As it turned out, that evening had been a disaster, and this time he'd apparently decided to take Danielle. The other woman was far more familiar with the social graces.

Fine. She'd let Reed escort Danielle tonight. But she was going to quit making life so pleasant for him. How appropriate that she now used the old servants' quarters, she thought bitterly. Because that was all she was to him—a servant. Well, no more. She would never be content to live a backstairs life. If Reed didn't want to be seen with her, or include her in his life, that was his decision. But she couldn't...she *wouldn't* continue to live this way.

Without analyzing her actions, Ellen punched out a second set of numbers.

"Charlie, it's Ellen," she said quickly, trying to swallow back tears.

"Ellen? It doesn't sound like you."

"I know." The tightness in her chest extended all the way to her throat, choking off her breath until it escaped in a sob.

"Ellen, are you all right?"

"Yes...no." The fact that she'd called Charlie was a sign of her desperation. He was so sweet and she didn't want to do anything to hurt him. "Charlie, I hate to ask, but I need a friend."

"I'm here."

He said it without the least hesitation, and his unquestioning loyalty made her weep all the louder. "Oh, Charlie, I've got to find a new place to live and I need to do it today."

"My sister's got a friend looking for a roommate. Do you want me to call her?"

"Please." Straightening, she wiped the tears from her face. Charlie might have had his faults, but he'd recognized the panic in her voice and immediately assumed control. Just now, that was what she needed—a friend to temporarily take charge of things. "How soon can you talk to her?"

"Now. I'll call her and get right back to you. On second thought, I'll come directly to your place. If you can't move in with Patty's friend, my parents will put you up."

"Oh, Charlie, how can I ever thank you?"

The sound of his chuckle was like a clean, fresh breeze. "I'll come up with a way later." His voice softened. "You know how I feel about you, Ellen. If you only want me for a friend, I understand. But I'm determined to be a good friend."

The back door closed with a bang. "Anyone home?"

Guiltily, Ellen turned around, coming face to face with Monte. She replaced the receiver, took a deep breath and squared her shoulders. She'd hoped to get away without having to talk to anyone.

"Ellen?" Concern clouded his face. "What's wrong? You look like you've been crying." He narrowed his eyes. "You *have* been crying. What happened?"

"Nothing." She took a minute to wipe her eyes with a tissue. "Listen, I'll be up in my room, but I'd appreciate some time alone, so don't get me unless it's important."

"Sure. Anything you say. Are you sick? Should I call Reed?"

"No!" she almost shouted at him, then instantly regretted reacting so harshly. "Please don't contact him…. He's busy tonight anyway." She rubbed a hand over her face. "And listen, about dinner—"

"Hey, don't worry. I can cook."

"You?" This wasn't the time to get into an argument. How messy he made the kitchen was no longer her problem. "There's a recipe on the counter if you want to tackle spaghetti sauce."

"Sure. I can do that. How long am I supposed to boil the noodles?"

One of her lesser concerns at the moment was boiling noodles. "Just read the back of the package."

Already he was rolling up his sleeves. "I'll take care of everything. You go lie down and do whatever women do when they're crying and pretending they're not."

"Thanks," she returned evenly. "I'll do that." Only in this case, she wasn't going to lie on her bed, hiding her face in her pillow. She was going to pack up everything she owned and cart it away before Reed even had a hint that she was leaving.

Sniffling as she worked, Ellen dumped the contents of her drawers into open suitcases. A couple of times she stopped to blow her nose. She detested tears. At the age of fifteen, she'd broken her leg and gritted her teeth against the agony. But she hadn't shed a tear. Now she wept as though it were the end of the world. Why, oh why, did her emotions have to be so unpredictable?

Carrying her suitcases down the first flight of stairs, she paused on the boys' floor to shift the weight. Because she was concentrating on her task and not watching where she was going, she walked headlong into Derek. "Sorry," she muttered.

"Ellen." He glanced at her suitcases and said her name as though he'd unexpectedly stumbled into the Queen of Sheba. "What…what are you doing?"

"Moving."

"Moving? But…why?"

"It's a long story."

"You're crying." He sounded even more shocked by her tears than by the fact that she was moving out of the house.

"It's Reed, isn't it? What did he do?"

"He didn't do a thing. Stay out of it, Derek. I mean that."

He looked stunned. "Sure." He stepped aside and stuck his hand in his pocket. "Anything you say."

She made a second trip downstairs, this time bringing a couple of tote bags and the clothes from her closet, which she draped over the top of the two suitcases. There wasn't room in her luggage for everything. She realized she'd have to put the rest of her belongings in boxes.

Assuming she'd find a few empty boxes in the garage, she stormed through the kitchen and out the back door. Muttering between themselves, Monte and Derek followed her. Soon her movements resembled a small parade.

"Will you two stop it," she shouted, whirling around and confronting them. The tears had dried now and her face burned with the heat of anger and regret.

"We just want to know what happened," Monte interjected.

"Or is this going to be another one of your 'stay tuned' responses?" Derek asked.

"I'm moving out. I don't think I can make it any plainer than that."

"Why?"

"That's none of your business." She left them standing with mouths open as she trooped up the back stairs to her rooms.

Heedlessly she tossed her things into the two boxes, more intent on escaping than on taking care to ensure that nothing was broken. When she got to the vase that had held the roses Reed had sent her, Ellen picked it up and hugged it. She managed to forestall further tears by taking deep breaths and blinking rapidly. Setting the vase down, she decided not to bring it with her. As much as possible, she wanted to leave Reed in this house and not carry the memories of him around with her like a constant, throbbing ache. That would be hard enough without taking the vase along as a constant reminder of what she'd once felt.

The scene that met her at the foot of the stairs made her stop in her tracks. The three boys were involved in a shouting match, each blaming the others for Ellen's unexpected decision to move out.

"It's your fault," Derek accused Monte. "If you weren't so concerned about your stomach, she'd stay."

"My stomach? *You're* the one who's always asking her for favors. Like babysitting and cooking for you and your girlfriend and—"

"If you want my opinion…" Pat began.

"We don't," Monte and Derek shouted.

"Stop it! All of you," Ellen cried. "Now, if you're the least bit interested in helping me, you can take my things outside. Charlie will be here anytime."

"Charlie?" the three echoed in shock.

"Are you moving in with him?"

She didn't bother to respond. Once the suitcases, the

bags, two boxes and her clothes had been lugged onto the porch, Ellen sat on the top step and waited.

She could hear the boys pacing back and forth behind her, still bickering quietly. When the black sports car squealed around the corner, Ellen covered her face with both hands and groaned. The last person she wanted to see now was Reed. Her throat was already swollen with the effort of not giving way to tears.

He parked in front of the house and threw open the car door.

She straightened, determined to appear cool and calm.

Seconds later, Reed stood on the bottom step. "What's going on here?"

"Hello, Reed," she said with a breathlessness she couldn't control. "How was your day?"

He jerked his fingers through his hair as he stared back at her in utter confusion. "How am I supposed to know? I get a frantic phone call from Derek telling me to come home right away. As I'm running out the door, my assistant hands me a message. Some absurd thing about you saying goodbye. What is going on? I thought you'd hurt yourself!"

"Sorry to disappoint you."

"Ellen, I don't know what's happening in that over-worked mind of yours, but I want some answers and I want them now."

"I'm leaving." Her hands were clenched so tight that her fingers ached.

"I'm not blind," he shouted, quickly losing control of his obviously limited patience. "I can see that. I'm asking you *why*."

Pride demanded that she raise her chin and meet his

probing gaze. "I've decided I'm an unstable person," she told him, her voice low and quavering. "I broke my leg once and didn't shed a tear, but when I learn that you're going to a party tonight, I start to cry."

"Ellen." He said her name gently, then shook his head as if clearing his thoughts. "You're not making any sense."

"I know. That's the worst part."

"In the simplest terms possible, tell me why you're leaving."

"I'm trying to." Furious with herself, she wiped a tear from her cheek. How could she explain it to him when everything was still so muddled in her own mind? "I'm leaving because you're driving the Porsche."

"What!" he exploded.

"You tell me," she burst out. "Why did you drive the Porsche today?"

"Would you believe that my truck was low on fuel?"

"I may be confused," she said, "but I'm not stupid. You're going out with Danielle. Not that I care."

"I can tell." His mocking gaze lingered on her suitcases. "I hate to disillusion you, but Danielle won't be with me."

She didn't know whether to believe him or not. "It doesn't matter."

"None of this is making sense."

"I don't imagine it would. I apologize for acting so unreasonable, but that's exactly how I feel. So, I'm getting out of here with my pride intact."

"Is your pride worth so much?"

"It's the only thing I have left," she said. She'd already given him her heart.

"She's moving in with Charlie," Derek said in a worried voice. "You aren't going to let her, are you, Reed?"

"You can't," Monte added.

"He won't," Pat stated confidently.

For a moment, the three of them stared intently at Reed. Ellen noticed the way his green eyes hardened. "Yes, I can," he said at last. "If this is what you want, then so be it. Goodbye, Ellen." With that, he marched into the house.

Ten

"I'm swearing off men for good," Ellen vowed, taking another long swallow of wine.

"Me, too," Darlene, her new roommate, echoed. To toast the promise, Darlene bent forward to touch the rim of her wineglass against Ellen's and missed. A shocked moment passed before they broke into hysterical laughter.

"Here." Ellen replenished their half-full glasses as tears of mirth rolled down her face. The world seemed to spin off its axis for a moment as she straightened. "You know what? I think we're drunk."

"Maybe you are," Darlene declared, slurring her words, "but not me. I can hold my wine as well as any man."

"I thought we weren't going to talk about men anymore."

"Right, I forgot."

"Do you think they're talking about us?" Ellen asked, putting a hand to her head in an effort to keep the walls from going around and around.

"Nah, we're just a fading memory."

"Right." Ellen pointed her index finger toward the ceiling in emphatic agreement.

The doorbell chimed and both women stared accusingly at the door. "If it's a man, don't answer it," Darlene said.

"Right again." Ellen staggered across the beige carpet. The floor seemed to pitch under her feet and she placed a hand on the back of the sofa to steady herself. Facing the door, she turned around. "How do I know if it's a man or not?"

The doorbell sounded again.

Darlene motioned languidly with her hand to show that she no longer cared who was at the door. "Just open it."

Holding the knob in a death grip, Ellen pulled open the door and found herself glaring at solid male chest. "It's a man," she announced to Darlene.

"Who?"

Squinting, Ellen studied the blurred male figure until she recognized Monte. "Monte," she cried, instantly sobering. "What are you doing here?"

"I…I was in the neighborhood and thought I'd stop by and see how you're doing."

"Come in." She stepped aside to let him enter. "What brings you to this neck of the woods?" She hiccuped despite her frenzied effort to look and act sober. "It's a school night. You shouldn't be out this late."

"It's only ten-thirty. You've been drinking."

"Me?" She slammed her hand against her chest. "Have we been drinking, Darlene?"

Her roommate grabbed the wine bottle—their second—from the table and hid it behind her back. "Not us."

Monte cast them a look of disbelief. "How'd your exams go?" he asked Ellen politely.

"Fine," she answered and hiccuped again. Embarrassed, she covered her mouth with her hand. "I think."

"What about algebra?"

"I'm making it by the skin of my nose."

"Teeth," both Darlene and Monte corrected.

"Right."

Looking uncomfortable, Monte said, "Maybe I should come back another time."

"Okay." Ellen wasn't about to argue. If she was going to run into her former housemates, she'd prefer to do it when she looked and felt her best. Definitely not when she was feeling…tipsy and the walls kept spinning. But on second thought, she couldn't resist asking about the others. "How's…everyone?"

"Fine." But he lowered his gaze to the carpet. "Not really, if you want the truth."

A shaft of fear went through her, tempering the effects of several glasses of wine. "It's not Reed, is it? Is he ill?"

"No, Reed's fine. I guess. He hasn't been around much lately."

No doubt he was spending a lot of his time at parties and social events with Danielle. Or with any number of other women, all of them far more sophisticated than Ellen.

"Things haven't been the same since you left," Monte added sheepishly.

"Who's doing the cooking?"

He shrugged his shoulders. "We've been taking turns."

"That sounds fair." She hoped that in the months she'd

lived with them the three boys had at least learned their way around the kitchen.

"Derek started a fire yesterday."

Ellen couldn't conceal her dismay. "Was there any damage?" As much as she tried to persuade herself that she didn't need to feel guilty over leaving the boys, this news was her undoing. "Was anyone hurt?" she gasped out.

"Not really, and Reed said the insurance would take care of everything."

"What happened?" Ellen was almost afraid to ask.

"Nothing much. Derek forgot to turn off the burner and the fat caught fire. Then he tried to beat it out with a dish towel, but that burst into flames, too. The real mistake was throwing the burning towel into the sink because when he did, it set the curtains on fire."

"Oh, good grief." Ellen dropped her head into her hands.

"It's not too bad, though. Reed said he wanted new kitchen walls, anyway."

"The walls too?"

"Well, the curtains started burning the wallpaper."

Ellen wished she hadn't asked. "Was anyone hurt?"

Monte moved a bandaged hand from behind his back. "Just me, but only a little."

"Oh, Monte," she cried, fighting back her guilt. "What did you do—try and pound out the fire with your fist?" Leave it to Monte. He'd probably tried to rescue whatever it was Derek had been cooking.

"No, I grabbed a hot biscuit from the oven and blistered one finger."

"Then why did you wrap up your whole hand?" From

the size of the bandage, it looked as though he'd been lucky not to lose his arm.

"I thought you might feel sorry for me and come back."

"Oh, Monte." She reached up to brush the hair from his temple.

"I didn't realize what a good cook you were until you left. I kept thinking maybe it was something I'd done that caused you to leave."

"Of course not."

"Then you'll come back and make dinners again?"

Good ol' Monte never forgot about his stomach. "The four of you will do fine without me."

"You mean you won't come back?"

"I can't." She felt like crying, but she struggled to hold back the tears stinging her eyes. "I'm really sorry, but I can't."

Hanging his head, Monte nodded. "Well, have a merry Christmas anyway."

"Right. You, too."

"Bye, Ellen." He turned back to the door, his large hand gripping the knob. "You know about Pat making varsity, don't you?"

She'd read it in the *Daily*. "I'm really proud of him. You tell him for me. Okay?"

"Sure."

She closed the door after him and leaned against it while the regrets washed over her like a torrent of rain. Holding back her tears was difficult, but somehow she managed. She'd shed enough tears. It was time to put her grief behind her and to start facing life again.

"I take it Monte is one of the guys," Darlene remarked.

She set the wine back on the table, but neither seemed interested in another glass.

Ellen nodded. "The one with the stomach."

"He's so skinny!"

"I know. There's no justice in this world." But she wasn't talking about Monte's appetite in relation to his weight. She was talking about Reed. If she'd had any hope that he really did care for her, that had vanished in the past week. He hadn't even tried to get in touch with her. She knew he wouldn't have had any problem locating her. The obvious conclusion was that he didn't *want* to see her. At first she thought he might have believed the boys' ridiculous claim that she was moving in with Charlie. But if he'd loved her half as much as she loved him, even that shouldn't have stopped him from coming after her.

Apparently, presuming that Reed cared for her was a mistake on her part. She hadn't heard a word from him all week. Exam week, at that. Well, fine. She'd wipe him out of her memory—just as effectively as she'd forgotten every algebraic formula she'd ever learned. A giggle escaped and Darlene sent her a curious look. Ellen carried their wineglasses to the sink, ignoring her new roommate, as she considered her dilemma. The trouble was, she wanted to remember the algebra, which seemed to slip out of her mind as soon as it entered, and she wanted to forget Reed, who never left her thoughts for an instant.

"I think I'll go to bed," Darlene said, holding her hand to her stomach. "I'm not feeling so great."

"Me neither." But Ellen's churning stomach had little to do with the wine. "Night."

"See you in the morning."

Ellen nodded. She was fortunate to have found Darlene. The other woman, who had recently broken up with her fiancé after a two-year engagement, understood how Ellen felt. It seemed natural to drown their sorrows together. But...she missed the boys and—Reed.

One thing she'd learned from this experience was that men and school didn't mix. Darlene might not have been serious about swearing off men, but Ellen was. She was through with them for good—or at least until she obtained her degree. For now, she was determined to bury herself in her books, get her teaching credentials and then become the best first-grade teacher around.

Only she couldn't close her eyes without remembering Reed's touch or how he'd slip up behind her and hold her in his arms. Something as simple as a passing glance from him had been enough to thrill her. Well, that relationship was over. And just in the nick of time. She could have been hurt. Really hurt. She could be feeling terrible. Really terrible.

Just like she did right now.

Signs of Christmas were everywhere. Huge decorations adorned the streetlights down University Way. Store windows displayed a variety of Christmas themes, and the streets were jammed with holiday traffic. Ellen tried to absorb some of the good cheer that surrounded her, with little success.

She'd gone to the university library to return some books and was headed back to Darlene's place. Her place, too, even though it didn't feel that way.

She planned to leave for Yakima the next morning. But

instead of feeling the pull toward home and family, Ellen's thoughts drifted to Reed and the boys. They'd been her surrogate family since September and she couldn't erase them from her mind as easily as she'd hoped.

As she walked across campus, sharp gusts of wind tousled her hair. Her face felt numb with cold. All day she'd been debating what to do with the Christmas gifts she'd bought for the boys. Her first inclination had been to bring them over herself—when Reed wasn't home, of course. But just the idea of returning to the lovely old house had proved so painful that Ellen abandoned it. Instead, Darlene had promised to deliver them the next day, after Ellen had left for Yakima.

Hugging her purse, Ellen trudged toward the bus stop. According to her watch, she had about ten minutes to wait. Now her feet felt as numb as her face. She frowned at her pumps, cursing the decrees of fashion and her insane willingness to wear elegant shoes at this time of year. It wasn't as though a handsome prince was likely to come galloping by only to be overwhelmed by her attractive shoes. Even if one did swoop Ellen and her frozen toes onto his silver steed, she'd be highly suspicious of his character.

Smiling, she took a shortcut across the lawn in the Quad.

"Is something funny?"

A pair of men's leather loafers had joined her fashionable gray pumps, matching her stride. Stunned, Ellen glanced up. Reed.

"Well?" he asked again in an achingly gentle voice. "Something seems to amuse you."

"My...shoes. I was thinking about attracting a prince... a man." Oh heavens, why had she said that? "I mean," she mumbled on, trying to cover her embarrassment, "my feet are numb."

"You need to get out of the cold." His hands were thrust into his pockets and he was so compellingly handsome that Ellen forced her eyes away. She was afraid that if she stared at him long enough, she'd give him whatever he asked. She remembered the way his face had looked the last time she'd seen him, how cold and steely his eyes had been the day she'd announced she was moving out. One word from him and she would've stayed. But the "might-have-beens" didn't matter anymore. He hadn't asked her to stay, so she'd gone. Pure and simple. Or so it had seemed at the time.

Determination strengthened her trembling voice as she finally spoke. "The bus will be at the corner in seven minutes."

Her statement was met with silence. Together they reached the pavement and strolled toward the sheltered bus area.

Much as she wished to appear cool and composed, Ellen's gaze was riveted on the man at her side. She noticed how straight and dark Reed's brows were and how his chin jutted out with stubborn pride. Every line of his beloved face emanated strength and unflinching resolve.

Abruptly, she looked away. Pride was no stranger to her, either. Her methods might have been wrong, she told herself, but she'd been right to let Reed know he'd hurt her. She wasn't willing to be a victim of her love for him.

"Ellen," he said softly, "I was hoping we could talk."

She made a show of glancing at her watch. "Go ahead. You've got six and a half minutes."

"Here?"

"As you so recently said, I need to get out of the cold."

"I'll take you to lunch."

"I'm not hungry." To further her embarrassment, her stomach growled and she pressed a firm hand over it, commanding it to be quiet.

"When was the last time you ate a decent meal?"

"Yesterday. No," she corrected, "today."

"Come on, we're getting out of here."

"No way."

"I'm not arguing with you, Ellen. I've given you a week to come to your senses. I still haven't figured out what went wrong. And I'm not waiting any longer for the answers. Got that?"

She ignored him, looking instead in the direction of the traffic. She could see the bus approaching, though it was still several blocks away. "I believe everything that needed to be said—" she motioned dramatically with her hand "—was already said."

"And what's this I hear about you succumbing to the demon rum?"

"I was only a little drunk," she spat out, furious at Monte's loose tongue. "Darlene and I were celebrating. We've sworn off men for life." Or at least until Reed freely admitted he loved her and needed her. At the moment that didn't appear likely.

"I see." His eyes seemed to be looking all the way into her soul. "If that's how you want it, fine. Just answer a couple of questions and I'll leave you alone. Agreed?"

"All right."

"First, what were you talking about when you flew off the handle about me driving the Porsche?"

"Oh, that." Now it just seemed silly.

"Yes, that."

"Well, you only drove the Porsche when you were seeing Danielle."

"But I wasn't! It's been completely over between us since the night of the Christmas party."

"It has?" The words came out in a squeak.

Reed dragged his fingers through his hair. "I haven't seen Danielle in weeks."

Ellen stared at the sidewalk. "But the cleaners phoned about your suit. You were attending some fancy party."

"So? I wasn't taking another woman."

"It doesn't matter," she insisted. "You weren't taking me, either."

"Of course not!" he shouted, his raised voice attracting the attention of several passersby. "You were studying for your exams. I couldn't very well ask you to attend an extremely boring business dinner with me. Not when you were spending every available minute hitting the books." He lowered his voice to a calm, even pitch.

The least he could do was be more unreasonable, Ellen thought irritably. She simply wasn't in the mood for logic.

"Did you hear what I said?"

She nodded.

"There is only one woman in my life. You. To be honest, Ellen, I can't understand any of this. You may be many things, but I know you're not the jealous type. I wanted to talk about Danielle with you. Any other woman would've loved hearing all the details. But not you." His voice was slightly raised. "Then you make these ridiculous accusations about the truck and the Porsche, and I'm at a loss to understand."

Now she felt even more foolish. "Then why were you driving the Porsche?" Her arms tightened around her purse. "Forget I asked that."

"You really have a thing for that sports car, don't you?"

"It's not the car."

"I'm glad to hear that."

Squaring her shoulders, Ellen decided it was time to be forthright, time to face things squarely rather than skirt around them. "My feelings are that you would rather not be seen with me," she said bluntly.

"What?" he exploded.

"You kept taking me to these out-of-the-way restaurants."

"I did it for privacy."

"You didn't want to be seen with me," she countered.

"I can't believe this." He took three steps away from her, then turned around sharply.

"Don't you think the Des Moines Marina is a bit far to go for a meal?"

"I was afraid we'd run into one of the boys."

More logic, and she was in no mood for it. "You didn't introduce me to your friend the night we went to that French film."

His eyes narrowed. "You can bet I wasn't going to introduce you to Tom Dailey. He's a lecher. I was protecting you."

"What about the night of the Christmas party? You only introduced me to a handful of people."

"Of course. Every man in the place was looking for an excuse to take you away from me. If you'd wanted to flirt with them, you should've said something."

"I only wanted to be with you."

"Then why bring up that evening now?"

"I was offended."

"I apologize," he shouted.

"Fine. But I didn't even meet your assistant…."

"You left so fast, I didn't exactly have a chance to introduce you, did I?"

He was being logical again, and she couldn't really argue.

The bus arrived then, its doors parting with a swish. But Ellen didn't move. Reed's gaze commanded her to stay with him, and she was torn. Her strongest impulse, though, was not to board the bus. It didn't matter that she was cold and the wind was cutting through her thin coat or that she could barely feel her toes. Her heart was telling her one thing and her head another.

"You coming or not?" the driver called out to her.

"She won't be taking the bus," Reed answered, slipping his hand under her elbow. "She's coming with me."

"Whatever." The doors swished shut and the bus roared away, leaving a trail of black diesel smoke in its wake.

"You *are* coming with me, aren't you?" he coaxed.

"I suppose."

His hand was at the small of her back, directing her across the busy street to a coffee shop, festooned with tinsel and tired-looking decorations. "I wasn't kidding about lunch."

"When was the last time *you* had a decent meal?" she couldn't resist asking.

"About a week ago," he grumbled. "Derek's cooking is a poor substitute for real food."

They found a table at the back of the café. The waitress handed them each a menu and filled their water glasses.

"I heard about the fire."

Reed groaned. "That was a comedy of errors."

"Is there much damage?"

"Enough." The look he gave her was mildly accusing.

The guilt returned. Trying to disguise it, Ellen made a show of glancing through the menu. The last thing on her mind at the moment was food. When the waitress returned, Ellen ordered the daily special without knowing what it was. The day was destined to be full of surprises.

"Ellen," Reed began, then cleared his throat. "Come back."

Her heart melted at the hint of anguish in his low voice. Her gaze was magnetically drawn to his. She wanted to tell him how much she longed to be…home. She wanted to say that the house on Capitol Hill was the only real home she had now, that she longed to walk through its front door again. With him.

"Nothing's been the same since you left."

The knot in her stomach pushed its way up to her throat, choking her.

"The boys are miserable."

Resolutely she shook her head. If she went back, it had to be for Reed.

"Why not?"

Tears blurred her vision. "Because."

"That makes about as much sense as you being angry because I drove the Porsche."

Taking several deep, measured breaths, Ellen said, "If all you need is a cook, I can suggest several who—"

"I couldn't care less about the cooking."

The café went silent as every head turned curiously in their direction. "I wasn't talking about the cooking *here,*" Reed explained to the roomful of shocked faces.

The normal noise of the café resumed.

"Good grief, Ellen, you've got me so tied up in knots I'm about to get kicked out of here."

"Me, tie *you* in knots?" She was astonished that Reed felt she had so much power over him.

"If you won't come back for the boys, will you consider doing it for me?" The intense green eyes demanded a response.

"I want to know why you want me back. So I can cook your meals and—"

"I told you I don't care about that. I don't care if you never do another thing around the house. I want you there because I love you, damn it."

Her eyes widened. "You love me, damn it?"

"You're not making this any easier." He ripped the napkin from around the silverware and slammed it down on his lap. "You must have known. I didn't bother keeping it secret."

"You didn't bother keeping it secret…from anyone but me," she repeated hotly.

"Come on. Don't tell me you didn't know."

"I didn't know."

"Well, you do now," he yelled back.

The waitress cautiously approached their table, standing back until Reed glanced in her direction. Hurriedly the girl set their plates in front of them and promptly moved away.

"You frightened her," Ellen accused him.

"I'm the one in a panic here. Do you or do you not love me?"

Again, it seemed as though every customer there had fallen silent, awaiting her reply.

"You'd better answer him, miss," the elderly gentleman sitting at the table next to theirs suggested. "Fact is, we're all curious."

"Yes, I love him."

Reed cast her a look of utter disbelief. "You'll tell a stranger but not me?"

"I love you, Reed Morgan. There, are you happy?"

"Overjoyed."

"I can tell." Ellen had thought that when she admitted her feelings, Reed would jump up from the table and throw his arms around her. Instead, he looked as angry as she'd ever seen him.

"I think you'd better ask her to marry you while she's in a friendly mood," the older man suggested next.

"Well?" Reed looked at her. "What do you think?"

"You want to get married?"

"It's the time of year to be generous," the waitress said shyly. "He's handsome enough."

"He is, isn't he?" Ellen agreed, her sense of humor restored by this unexpected turn of events. "But he can be a little hard to understand."

"All men are, believe me," a woman across the room shouted. "But he looks like a decent guy. Go ahead and give him another chance."

The anger washed from Reed's dark eyes as he reached for Ellen's hand. "I love you. I want to marry you. Won't you put me out of my misery?"

Tears dampened her eyes as she nodded wildly.

"Let's go home." Standing, Reed took out his wallet and threw a couple of twenties on the table.

Ellen quickly buttoned her jacket and picked up her purse. "Goodbye, everyone," she called with a cheerful wave. "Thank you—and Merry Christmas!"

The amused customers broke into a round of applause as Reed took Ellen's hand and pulled her outside.

She was no sooner out the door when Reed hauled her into his arms. "Oh, Ellen, I've missed you."

Reveling in the warmth of his arms, she nuzzled closer. "I've missed you, too. I've even missed the boys."

"As far as I'm concerned, they're on their own. I want you back for myself. That house was full of people, yet it's never felt so empty." Suddenly he looked around, as though he'd only now realized that their private moment was taking place in the middle of a busy street. "Let's get out of here." He slipped an arm about her waist, steering her toward the campus car park. "But I think I'd better tell you something important."

"What?"

"I didn't bring the truck."

"Oh?" She swallowed her disappointment. She could try, but she doubted she'd ever be the Porsche type.

"I traded in the truck last week."

"For what?"

"Maybe it was presumptuous of me, but I was hoping you'd accept my marriage proposal."

"What's the truck got to do with whether I marry you or not?"

"*You're* asking me that? The woman who left me—"

"All right, all right, I get the picture."

"Okay, I don't have the truck *or* the Porsche. I gave it to Derek."

"I'm sure he's thrilled."

"He is. And…"

"And?"

"I traded the truck for an SUV. More of a family-friendly vehicle, wouldn't you say?"

"Oh, Reed." With a small cry of joy, she flung her arms around this man she knew she'd love for a lifetime. No matter what kind of car he drove.

* * * * *

Loved this book?

Let us know!

Find us on **Twitter @Mira_BooksUK**
where you can share your thoughts, stay up
to date on all the news about our upcoming
releases and even be in with the chance of
winning copies of our wonderful books!

Bringing you the best voices in fiction

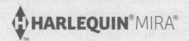

'The perfect Christmas read!' - Julia Williams

Jewellery designer Skylar loves living London, but when a surprise proposal goes wrong, she finds herself fleeing home to remote Puffin Island.

Burned by a terrible divorce, TV historian Alec is dazzled by Sky's beauty and so cynical that he assumes that's a bad thing! Luckily she's on the verge of getting engaged to someone else, so she won't be a constant source of temptation... but this Christmas, can Alec and Sky realise that they are what each other was looking for all along?

Order yours today at
www.millsandboon.co.uk